DESTINATION: FUTURE

DESTINATION: FUTURE

Edited by Z.S. Adani & Eric T. Reynolds

HADLEY
RILLE
BOOKS

ISBN-13 978-0-9825140-9-2

Published by
Hadley Rille Books
PO Box 25466
Overland Park, KS 66225
USA
www.hadleyrillebooks.com
contact@hadleyrillebooks.com
Attention: Eric T. Reynolds

Cover Art copyright © Edward R. Norden
Cover background photograph credit: NASA and STScI

To the Memory of my parents, Julianna and Geza

To my mother-in-law, Rosemary Pierron

Contents

Introduction

In *Destination: Future,* we visit some familiar themes in science fiction: first contact with aliens, conflicts with different cultures, xenophobia—sometimes from one culture toward another, sometimes from multiple interacting cultures. How would representatives of an alien species visiting Earth see us? Some may recognize the beauty that resides in each human being, yet others may be appalled by the inadequacy of our physical bodies. Themes of genetically altered human settlers forgetting their origin, a robot that diligently collects data on Mars, and the efforts of a xenobiologist to understand the aliens whose stark world humans want to settle are explored from different viewpoints. Twenty-one authors present stories that take new approaches to these subjects.

What is the limit for how far humans extend civil rights? Should they extend those to all creatures, even if the ones in question are similar to those routinely eaten by humans on Earth?

Where does one future culture draw the line between art and the harming of another being? How should one approach a derelict ship in interstellar space, or ancient alien ruins on another world? What new ways could an alien culture make use of game metaphors? How might a visitor interfere with a world of clockwork creatures?

And, finally, what relationship could there ever be between baby seals and Mars?

Z. S. Adani
Eric T. Reynolds

No Jubjub Birds Tonight
by Sara Genge

Although he came with the spaceships that scared away the hummingbirds, I didn't hate the stranger at first.

He stepped out of his shuttle and easily swung his large bag onto his back. I tried not to be impressed. In low gravity Tsi, all foreigners are strong.

"Take me to your leader," he said, grinning.

"Tell your shuttle to go," I said. It was the time of the flowers and there were no flying insects on Tsi: without the hummingbirds to pollinate our crops, there would be nothing to harvest that year. We'd explained this to the people at the shuttle port, but somehow they never managed to pass on the information to the new arrivals. I suspected they didn't understand the damage their gear caused to our ecosystem, and we relied too much on tourism to ban the visitors altogether.

He nodded and the shuttle lifted off. He was a stranger, but I had no reason to hate him publicly. Not yet. Official hatred must be born of objective wrongs and he had done me no harm, just irked me with his impolite smiles and ingratiating tone.

My name is Yu Lin, daughter of Yu Chen. I am the village tourist guide and I have declared before the Council that I hate the stranger. If you'll listen, I'll tell you my reasons.

Yu's first reason: Because the stranger wanted to fly and the sky wouldn't let him.

He wanted to fly, of course. They all want to fly.

Tsi's gravity is gentle on its children. On Tsi, wheat stalks don't bend, even when burdened with the most bountiful heads. Fruit floats in delicate tufts of foliage tens of meters high, and the roots of the tumtum trees twist and twirl their way to the ground, creating the dank Underfoot where the

13

jabberwockies live. On Tsi, snakes can jump and people can fly, and, oh, how the stranger wanted to fly!

As official guide, it was my job to instruct him, so I took him to the training strip, which has a net at the bottom.

I told him to stand on a branch and showed him how my sleeves buttoned to my shirt.

"Look at the buttons, see how they go all the way round my shoulder?" I asked him. He'd said his name was Xolani but I was still struggling with the pronunciation and avoided using it.

He examined the buttons closely.

"Those hold you up? Don't they come undone?"

I suppressed a sigh. They all asked the same thing. The buttons were indeed small, but there was a double line of them fastening my clothes to my sleeve. I wore a one-piece Tsi outfit, which covered me from neck to feet. When I flew, the sleeves tugged at my clothing, but the seams held.

"No, the buttons work together. Each one is weak by itself, but together, the hundred buttons are strong," I said.

I held onto a nearby branch and threw the sleeve. Just before it unfolded completely, I yanked back my arm, and the sleeve thwacked and flew back into my hand. I wanted him to see how resistant the material was, despite its flexibility.

He seemed impressed. "So you tie the sleeves around the branches, right?"

"No! If you tie them, you're lost. You never tie the sleeves because if you do, you're stuck and can't move forward. Tsi's gravity is permissive of small mistakes, but not of the tying of a sleeve. You'll hang from the boughs forever and eventually the buttons will come undone, or the jabberwockies will get you. They usually ignore prey strung this high up in the trees, but given enough time…" I shrugged.

I showed him how it was done. I threw my right sleeve at a bough and swung down, casting my left at a nearby tree as soon as the arc brought me close enough. As I'd told the stranger, my sleeves did not snag on the branches. Instead, they wrapped around softly, unwrapping almost immediately as I swung my weight on them, but not so fast that I didn't have time to take my momentum onto the next sleeve. The sleeve broke my fall by the faintest of frictions, but that's all it took to fly on a quarter-of-a-G planet.

I helped the stranger into his training sleeves. We spent all morning practicing. By the end of the session, he'd managed only a couple of arcs and

I was exhausted from rescuing him from the various tangles he'd gotten himself into. His aim was atrocious: most of the time he threw his sleeve too far, ensuring that it got tangled. When that happened, I had to climb up on the bough and use my own sleeve to bring him up. I had no choice but to wrap my sleeve around a branch to use as a pulley and I winced at the wear the silk sleeves were taking, imagining the thin strands of material snapping, one by one.

"Throw the sleeves against a branch and *hope* they coil. You're afraid to fall and you're throwing them deliberately at the bushes. Trust Tsi's gravity. Trust the net. You can't fly if you're afraid to fall," I told him.

Surprisingly, he took my advice. . . And threw the sleeve short of target. He fell through the bush for several metres until he hit the net, from where I rescued him and tended to his bruises. Still, I'd seen worse, and I told him so. Most strangers never learn to fly.

Most strangers never learn to fly, but most strangers give up after a couple of tries.

Not Xolani.

That night, we sat on the north porch of my mother's house, as the wind screamed through the planks and rocked the houses on their stilts. Earlier, Xolani had asked about the stilts. They were made of tulgey wood and dug deep into jabberwocky territory, holding the houses upright. I had shown him how the houses were further secured by old sleeve cloth tied to the nearby trees. That way, if the wind tore off a few branches, the houses would still be held upright by the collective pull of the dozen remaining silk ropes.

He'd been fascinated by the village, asking endless questions, but now he sat in silence. Foreigners wear their thoughts on their faces, but Xolani's skin was dark and, even with the full moon, I couldn't read his expression. As long as he didn't move, I could hardly see him. It was a pity that he was so clumsy. With his dark brown skin he would have made a great hunter, cheating jabberwockies of their prey in the perpetual darkness of the Downbelow. He even looked strong enough to kill a jabberwocky. It had been years since my people had had a jabberwocky hunter.

Then I noticed how he hugged his knees and dug his toes into the floor planks and realized that he'd never be a hunter. Someone so terrified of the wind could never face down a jabberwocky. I wanted to tell him that the wind always rocks the houses and the houses never fall, but my mother and her husband were sitting on the east porch and I did not want to humiliate him in front of them. A grown man should know when to ask for information. He didn't ask, so I didn't tell, and hoped he couldn't hear the wockies jabbering in the wind.

Yu's second reason: Because the sky denied him and the forest refused him and yet the stranger didn't give up.

When I woke him the next day, it was late dawn and a peach-colored sky had beaten the night on all fronts except the west, where a few stars still lingered. Xolani stared at the terraces above. They were spun between branches, suspended on planks or old silk and filled with the darkest soil we'd managed to steal from jabberwocky territory. From where we stood, we saw my family tending the crops, dropping lightly on each terrace and weeding the moss out of the cabbages. My father nodded a greeting from above and stood on the tip of a terrace until the sway of the branches brought the next one close enough for him to jump. Xolani whistled in appreciation although the gap had only been about the length of a man.

"Do you want to visit the terraces?" I asked, thinking it was a good idea to take his mind off flying. It must feel horrible to be leg-bound and I wanted to spare Xolani further humiliation.

He shook his head. "No, I will fly," he said. He turned to look at me and that's when he saw the hummingbirds.

Last night's wind had hardly been a gale, but still, as expected, a few hummingbirds had been blown against the house and lay on the porch, twitching.

"Don't worry, the children will fix them," I told him. I picked one up and showed him how easy it was to coax the springs back into place, open the small trap door on the back of the bird and rewind it until its wings flapped again. He held it for me and gasped when the little critter squeaked.

"It blinks! It even blinks!" he said.

I aligned the feathers on the bird and told Xolani to set it free. He was like a toddler, grinning at holding his first bird. I was so caught up in his enthusiasm that I forgot to ask him if animals on his planet didn't blink.

* * *

16

"This is *hard*," Xolani said, when I settled him back on a branch after the last fall. He had not taken me up on any of my offers to show him the silver trees or the waterfalls of Kam. He wanted to fly and my heart ached for him.

His arms were trembling and beads of sweat the size of pebbles collected on his brow before tumbling down his face.

He sat down on the branch and took out his backpack.

"Well, I've tried the traditional way," he said.

I was relieved. His fight with the sleeves had been painful to watch. "I'll guide you back to the village," I offered.

"Oh, no! I'm still not done here. I was told it was nearly impossible for a foreigner to fly with sleeves—it's the bone mass of higher gravity planets. Look." He pulled out a tangle of nylon wire from his backpack and showed me the retractable clasps at the tips. "The computer at the other end calculates the best trajectory. Theoretically, it can adjust for gravity but I'd rather try it here first, where the G is more forgiving." He noticed my blank face. "Think about it. With this device a person could fly on any planet, not just Tsi!"

"Oh," I said, trying to contain my anger. He had brought electronics into the forest! I was livid but I could not yank the device out of his hand. No person, foreign or otherwise, would tolerate such an insult.

He put it on and showed me how it was fastened. "The design is patented." He blushed. The man was embarrassed of his dreams! I opened my mouth to tell him to stop, but before I could react, he jumped off the branch.

And fell all wrong. His limbs flew in different directions as if his brain didn't know how to hold them together. The clasp shot off with mechanical precision and bit into a nearby branch, sending leaves and fruit tumbling to the Underfoot. He swung clear of the training arches in two gentle sweeps. The boughs creaked under his weight and flocks of birds rose into the air. Whether they fled from the sound or from the electronics, I could not tell.

I stood aghast. Even the whippoorwills living in the highest branches cried out and fled. In the Downbelow, I saw the dark shadows of the jabberwockies emerging from their slumber among the roots and clambering up, lazily, to see what the disturbance was about. He had left a *trail* behind him, a swath of destruction in the net of boughs and branches. I had never seen anything like it.

I looked doubtfully at the boughs he'd swung from. Holding firmly to the branch, I threw my sleeve and pulled. The bough creaked in an ugly way and my sleeve would have snagged if I hadn't rolled it clear of the indentation Xolani's mechanical claws had created.

He was turning back. I heard him before I saw him. The jabberwockies murmured underfoot. They were named after the jabbering noises they made when they got excited but that rarely happened during the daytime. They were nocturnal creatures and my people prided themselves in their quiet flights through the eaves of the World. I had seen jabberwockies hunt, disposing of young animals that lost their footing in the higher branches. Their whispering grated on my nerves.

Xolani swung back onto my branch with a grin in his face.

"See, easy. Even a stupid foreigner can do it." His smile was infuriating. "I bet I can even go faster than you. Hell, maybe your people should be the first to try the new system. I bet it takes years of practice to do it your way. . ."

I pointed at the path he'd cut through the trees.

"What? That? It's hardly visible!"

I told him it didn't look that way to me. I explained that the branches didn't hold after he'd been through them.

He nodded thoughtfully. "I'll have to perfect the design, then," he said.

"Turn off the electronics now, please," I begged.

Xolani seemed surprised but did as I asked. I led him back to the village. The birds would not return for a few hours and the forest was so quiet that I could hear the jabberwockies snoring.

Back home, I showed him what his Tree Swinger did to the hummingbirds. The children had spent all day repairing them and I caught one before they set them free and took it inside. I motioned to Xolani to close the doors and windows and told him to turn on the power on his device. The collective screech of a hundred hummingbirds deafened us and Xolani stared out the window, watching them leave in a flurry of golden wings.

Then, he turned around and saw the hummingbird we had kept inside.

I shook my head before he asked. It was dead for good; we couldn't fix it. Somewhere inside, its tick-tack had failed. It had returned to its Maker, the Clockwork Master, the One that knows how all things tick.

"Go outside," I told him.

"Why?"

"I have to destroy this clockwork. Otherwise, it'll eventually make its way to the Underfoot where the jabberwockies will use the parts to augment their own mechanisms. They're bottom feeders, growing on the failures of other creatures. Everything reaches the Downbelow in the end, and that's how it must be, but I'd rather not serve the jabberwockies any functioning parts. You don't want to watch this."

He stood outside while I cut through the hummingbird's thin skin, disassembled its pieces and bent and crushed them out of shape.

Yu's Third and Last Reason: Because there is only one Clockwork Master and he doesn't have apprentices.

We spent the rest of the week "visiting." We went to places that strangers like to see. We chose activities that were as far from flight as possible and I took him down where the Chang River snakes in the Downbelow and the jabberwockies don't dare go.

"Clockwork is scared of water, and well it should be because oil and water don't mix and clockwork, more than the parts, is the oil that keeps them running," I explained.

From the bough where we were perched over the current, I nodded towards the wockies in the shades. He seemed to have trouble seeing them until I pointed them out to him, but his awe made up for all the explanations.

"And those are clockwork?" he asked. The jabbers must have heard him because they started to whine and bare their teeth. It was seldom that people and jabbers were close enough to look face to face, and I have to admit I enjoyed baiting them, watching them rock from side to side in frustration, and hiss.

"Everything is clockwork."

"Even you?" he asked.

"We are all clockwork. A different kind of clockwork, maybe. A different soul—" I put my hand on my chest—"with a different tick-tack, tick-tack, tick-tack..."

"Was that a smile?" Xolani asked. "I think that's the first time I've seen you smile." I smiled some more. It was brillig, the sun sifted through the leaves and the jabbers could hiss all they wanted. People were on water and people were on the boughs and all the jabbers had left was the Underfoot, the Downbelow. No wonder they were always angry.

19

*　*　*

The next day, I caught him on the porch tinkering with a broken bird.

"I could make wings like these," he told me in a mad rush. "I could fasten them to a harness of metal. Mechanical wings wouldn't interfere with Tsi's clockwork creatures. It wouldn't be swinging, Yu Lin, it'd truly be flying. *Above* the trees, can you imagine?"

I hushed him, yanked the bird out of his hand, assembled it as fast I could and set it free.

"We are not Clockwork Masters, do you hear me? Nobody can make clockwork, only fix it or break it. That's the way it's meant to be." I tiptoed to the back of the house to see if anyone had heard but, luckily, my family was out.

"There's a balance to clockwork. You can't just *make* it. It has to be born in the Underfoot from scraps the jabberwockies miss or discard. It has to ferment and wait for the Maker to touch it. It has to *learn* what it needs to know before it's set free in this world. You can't put the *tick* in clockwork."

He laughed! Of all things, he laughed.

"Yu Lin! Don't you realize what that means? There are people down there making the clockwork animals! Maybe even those wockies are doing it. Clockwork must break down eventually. The only way Tsi stays populated is because someone makes new Clockwork."

"The Maker..."

"Ha. This is incredible. We've been wondering—the people from outside, I mean. Tsi must be a constructed ecosystem, there is no other explanation. But even if there is an intelligence in the Universe capable of building a planet like Tsi, there is no evidence that it stayed behind to keep the planet populated. For years we've wondered how Tsi kept going. Amazing!"

"The Maker made Tsi as it is. The Maker keeps it going. Here—" I walked over to my little sister's sitting spot and opened her lacred box. Inside, were a handful of broken birds. I took one out and placed it in his hand. "Look for the tick. Try to find it with your *historical records*. You will fail. I've taken apart dozens of animals as a child and not once did I find the clock. There is no mystery, just the Maker, and that is a riddle neither you, nor any other unbelieving foreigner, will ever solve."

My anger shut him up. I wished anger had made me speechless before I said those things to Xolani. He was a tourist and the village needed people like him, but that wasn't the reason I regretted my outburst. I had lost control and that made me unworthy of calling myself a woman of Tsi. It made me unworthy of my Maker.

"Let's go down there and find that Maker," he whispered, holding his hands, palms up, as if I would strike him. How that deepened my shame! "I'm trying to believe you, but I need to see the Downbelow for myself. Come on, I'm sure there are weapons that can keep those jabberthingies at bay. You understand why I need to do this. I know you do. You're a lot more patient with me than anyone else in this village."

Oh, damn him. I couldn't believe he would praise me at a time like this.

I shook my head. "If we go down, what's to stop the jabberwockies from coming back up? We don't break the balance, and neither do they. I am sorry." I bowed my head and headed inside the house.

I was too ashamed that night to speak to him during dinner. My mother took me aside and asked him if he had offended me and whether she should send him away. I denied it. I didn't have the courage to tell her that the burden of guilt lay with me.

That night, I woke up when Xolani stepped over my body to go outside. Before I could creep out of my sleeping sack, I heard the hum of his Tree Swinger, the cry of the fleeing birds and the branches creaking as he dashed down into the Underfoot.

"Don't go," my mother said. She didn't need to elaborate. We both knew the jabberwockies wanted nothing from us—nothing we could use to negotiate to bring Xolani back.

Torches lit up in the Underfoot and we guessed the jabberwockies were awake. The houses started to rock, although there wasn't a wind. The wockies were letting us know that they had a hostage.

My sister started to cry: "They're just trying to lure you down there, Yu. There is no need. . ."

But there was a need. I had been named "tourist guide". I was in charge of teaching strangers how to fly and taking them on "visits". I had betrayed the trust my village had placed on me. The last time I had talked to Xolani, it was in anger. Everyone knows that if a man dies hating you, they'll take their grudge up to the Maker.

I peered into the night. I had a good hour of dark before dawn but that wouldn't matter in the perpetual dimness of the Underfoot. I flew off, trusting my sleeves to find purchase even though I could hardly see.

The hissing led me to them.

Sara Genge

"Ours, ours, ours," the jabberwockies chanted. They stood in a circle below Xolani, who hung from a tumtum root in a tangle of nylon and straps. His electronics still hummed and the device around him twitched to get free, yanking him like a puppet on strings. The jabberwockies kept a respectful distance from the hum, but their pelts were thicker than the hummingbirds' and I knew they'd get him when they wanted it badly enough.

I perched on top of the root and inspected the mess. If he'd been hanging from silk, I would have cut the fabric and levered him up. As it was, the nylon resisted all my efforts to cut or untangle it and I couldn't just pull him up: some of the clasps had grabbed at branches below and held him as firmly as a hummingbird in a spider web.

Standing up on the branch, I addressed the wockies:

"If you release him, my people will let you keep the hummingbirds that die in the brambles," I offered.

The jabberwockies chortled, dancing madly around Xolani, gripping torches in their padded paws, eyes glowing green in the flame.

"Ours, ours, ours," they said, burping smoke. Fire raged inside them, powering their tick. "We'll eat his bones and burn them in our furnaces, use his blood to oil our joints. He's ours, ours, ours, and when we've eaten him, eaten him, eaten him our oil will no longer be scared of the water and we'll own the Chang River too."

"Stupid animals! You cannot replace your oil with blood!" I shouted. "You cannot change your clockwork. . ." but then I realized that they had indeed changed their clockwork. This one wore a hummingbird's wing for an ear; that one spoke with a whippoorwill's voice. A third had stolen the teeth of a low swinging monkey.

The jubjub birds were converging. I had never seen one but recognized them from my mother's stories. They were scavengers of meat and clockwork and came only when they sensed a kill. They were creatures of the Downbelow with steel beaks and throbbing hearts, which pumped oily water through iron-rich flesh. They were the worst of meat and clockwork, mixed. They came only for the dead and they were never wrong.

"Take off your harness," I whispered to Xolani.

"But I'll fall towards them," he said.

"Trust Tsi's gravity."

I watched him undo his clasps, one by one.

"One, two . . . *Now*," I said.

He fell; I swung. My sleeve snagged on a branch and I spiraled down on it, grabbed Xolani with my free hand and landed us both on the floor. I couldn't throw my sleeve while I held him, so all I could do was land softly in the middle of the jabberwocky pride. I planted my foot firmly in the ground to keep the sleeve from uncoiling.

The jabberwockies' burbled with glee and lunged.

I grabbed Xolani and jumped. The sleeve was wound tight as a spring and when I jumped, the coils started to unravel, taking Xolani and me in wider and wider circles. We spiraled up and out. I twisted and managed to crash-land us on a root, a few meters above the jabberwockies.

"Run!" I shouted to Xolani. My sleeve was snagged. I knew I was lost but I didn't want it to be for nothing.

"Like hell I am." He took my sleeve and pulled so hard the tree trembled.

"It's no use, it won't break. . ." But break it did. All those hours of using it as a lever had worn it down.

We ran. Daylight seeped in through the bush and each step brought us closer to the light, but the wockies were close behind and showed no sign of relenting, even though we were no longer in the Downbelow and they had no right to pursue prey on the boughs. They had broken their part of the deal and they knew my people would be angry if they found out. That only made them more desperate to catch us.

"We won't make it," Xolani said.

I feared he was right. We couldn't fly out since we had only a pair of sleeves between the two of us. I could fly with a damaged sleeve, but even with perfect sleeves I would never be able to carry him.

We hid behind some vines and watched the wockies climb, squinting their eyes in the glare.

"How much do they weigh?" he asked, nodding towards the wockies.

"About two stone," I said.

"A Tsi stone?" He asked, smiling.

I nodded.

"And how do they hunt? Do they favor their teeth or their claws? Do they listen for prey? Do they have other senses I need to know about?" He rummaged through his pockets, pulling out an assortment of knives.

"They kill with their teeth. Their claws are mostly for climbing. The pads on their paws are adherent: that's why they climb so fast when they want to. But their metabolism is slow: they hunt in bursts and then need to rest for hours."

"I have an idea," he said. "Here's what we're going to do."

Xolani chose a branch that was roughly the size and weight of a man and we cut it and trimmed off the branches.

"Ready?" he said. He lifted it over his head and threw it down to the Underfoot, making a frightful amount of noise.

"Xolani!" I shouted, hoping my acting was up to the task. "The Maker forgive me, I have lost the foreigner!"

That got the jabbers' attention. They scampered down to collect their prize. In the commotion, Xolani slid, somewhat noisily, into the shadows. The jabbers didn't notice.

Two of them stayed behind, eyeing me and smacking their lips.

"Oh, what shall I do?" I wailed. "I have failed as a tourist guide." I pretended to notice the jabbers just then and backed off in fear. I didn't have to fake that part. They inched in and I swung to the next bough, drawing them closer.

Xolani sprung up behind them like a mythological bandersnatch. The wockies stood up on their hind feet to counter the attack. That was their unmaking. Xolani kicked the first one right off the branch as if it were a squirrel instead of a two stone monster. But Xolani hadn't counted on Tsi's low gravity. His leg wasn't as firmly anchored to the branch as he'd expected and he was thrown back from the counterforce. He lost his footing, and only his reflexes and outplanet strength saved him as he grabbed the branch and stopped himself from falling.

The second wocky saw his advantage and lunged, but I swung down, fell on its back and stabbed it until the oil stopped flowing.

Xolani lifted himself up onto the branch and groaned with relief.

"I'll get the hang of this eventually, I swear," he said, shaking his head.

"I'm sure you will."

I expected him to throw the second wocky into the Downbelow, but instead, he started cutting off the animal's paws as if they were some kind of trophy.

"Ok, let's see if I have this right," he said. "Only the Maker can create clockwork and electronics screw with Tsi's ecosystem, but humans are allowed to fix and destroy clockwork like you just did with this wocky, right?"

I nodded. He held the two paws up in front of him and tested the sticky pads with his fingers, smiling.

We used strips of silk to tie the paws on and he started climbing. We took it slow. The wockies were howling underneath. They had realized they'd been tricked and were dying to climb back up for revenge, but I knew they'd be too tired to do so for a couple of hours. As long as neither of us fell, we'd be all right.

I went ahead, looking back every few swings to make sure he was following. With his outplanet strength, he could pull himself up by the wocky paws even when his feet lost purchase. We didn't stop until we saw the villagers coming to greet us, floating down on their sleeves as low as they dared, with torches and knives between their teeth.

My mother settled us on the porch with cups of cocoa and we watched the sun come out. The birds were returning and the air zinged with the sound of spinning gears and flapping wings.

"Did you find those human makers you were talking about?" I asked.

"No, you were right. There was only darkness and jabberwockies," he answered.

"Good. It's our official policy not to disclose all of Tsi's secrets to tourists on their first visit. That way, they keep coming back," I joked.

"I don't want to come back. Not as a visitor, I mean. . ." he trailed off. "Yu Lin, I know I've caused you and your people a lot of trouble and I'll understand if you want me to go away, but I'd like to stay for a few weeks. I'd like to hunt some jabberwockies. Those paws are special. I could collect some samples. It was so easy to climb with them. Maybe even better than flying. And there's also the matter of the Makers: they must be down there, somewhere."

"You'll never find them."

"I want to try."

"What about the Tree Swinger?" I asked.

"Oh, that noisy thing? I guess it'll still be useful for other planets. You've probably guessed already, but I invent things for a living. The Tree Swinger is almost perfected. I'd like to move on to a new project and those wocky paws are brilliant. I can think of twenty ways to improve them without breaking Tsi law."

I considered his request.

"Tourists can't hunt. Custom is pretty clear on that, but now that the jabberwockies have broken the truce, the village needs someone to keep them at bay." I sighed. "I guess the village could adopt you, but you'd need to prove an official bond to one of us and I don't think you have grounds for that."

"An official bond? Like marriage?"

"Oh, no! Just a reason why anyone would want to keep you around. You know, pay off an old debt, punish you for something you've done. . ."

Then it dawned on me. "Say! How would you feel if I hated you? Only officially, of course. A person who is hated has the right to atone for their wrongs. That would be a valid excuse for you to stay."

"Your people are crazy. You know that, don't you?"

"Mr. Foreigner: Tsi is special in more ways than one."

The next day, I made my plea to the Council. My voice was bitter; my condemnation of Xolani's behavior, harsh. Practicing my acting with the jabberwockies had paid off. I doubt the Council believed me, but I put on a good show and they smiled and let Xolani stay.

That evening my mother set us up on the porch with hot tea and blankets so Xolani could watch the sunset. Despite my speech, she seemed to think he was a hero for killing that jabberwocky and she plied him with treats and compliments every time she had a chance. I had told the Council how he'd kicked a full grown wocky off a branch. Despite my scorn, the rest of the village seemed to think that was pretty impressive.

We sat in silence and listened to the whirring night sounds of Tsi. The toves jimbled overhead and Xolani smiled.

In the Downbelow, the wockies jabbered threats and warnings, but the jubjub birds had fled. There would be no killing tonight and the jubjubs knew it.

The Embians
by K.D. Wentworth

After setting the audio recorder for the night, Shayna wraps her fingers through the wires of the treetop blind and stares into the heavy darkness, straining to catch the next mating display the instant it flares. Just beyond the ragged edge of the rain forest, the unseen ocean hisses against the shore and salt hangs in the sultry air. Somewhere out in the sweltering sea of black, a small animal squalls and dies in the jaws of some nameless predator.

Flash of electric-green with orange diagonals. Melds into the yellow of fresh lemons. Softens . . . fades . . .

Darkness.

Cerulean blue. Swirls of carmine that suffuse with purple, brightening as though they will explode.

Darkness . . . darkness.

Shayna sighs. "They're so incredibly complex, so varied. If I could just sort the nuances into a key, I know I could make my thesis work."

Her expedition partner, Mae, dutifully records the mating displays on the night-cam in every wave-length from ultraviolet to infrared for later analysis. She is eight years older than Shayna, working on her doctoral dissertation, rather than a mere master's thesis. Her movements are careful and methodical, everything always labeled, thought-out, planned. Shayna understands herself to be more intuitive, knowing when an answer is ready, it will surface from the depths of her mind like an offering. Until then, she must wait, absorb data, allow her subconscious to analyze and correlate.

Mae shifts on the camp stool, so close in the narrow blind, Shayna can feel the heat of her skin, while out in the hot, tangled night of a world that has never known a moon, or tide, or the chill embrace of snow, the serpentlike embians slip through soft-fleshed trees and serenade each other with light. In the daylight, they appear vaguely humanoid, with similar number and placement of limbs, but their flesh is so dense, their bones are only cartilage, and they are as sinuous as eels. Their skin is a mottled gray-green and they rarely attain five feet in height. They produce no intelligible sounds.

"You might as well pick a different thesis and be done with it. Those displays are no more a language than wolves back on Earth howling at the moon. They're just mating lures." Mae jerks. "Over there!"

Acid-red. Sharpens to actinic violet that hurts the eyes. Flash . . . flash. White afterimage.

Darkness.

Shayna lifts sweat-soaked hair off her neck, impatient for the next display. "I think they're arguing. He's ready for her, has been for hours, but she's playing coy."

"How do you know it's a mixed pair?" Mae asks, calmly sensible as always. "Other teams have documented male-to-male pairings, as well as female-to-female." From the first moment they met at the university funding this study, Mae reminded Shayna of a redwood that has stood for a thousand years and is no longer capable of surprise or wonder. "They're acting on instinct," Mae says. "When the time is right, they'll come together."

'Come together.' Such a pale expression for the incandescent union of embian or human. Shayna's fingers tighten until the blind's wires cut into her skin.

Impossible blue-black hovering on the edge of ultra-violet. Shot through with sparkles of green. Expands . . . expands. Flash of red.

Darkness . . . darkness . . . darkness.

Shayna's pulse leaps, settles into the alien rhythm of the lights. She turns to Mae. "He's dying for her, and she's laughing, climbing just out of reach."

"Quit projecting." Mae's voice is curt, impatient. She leans away from the damp, sweaty touch of Shayna's thigh.

Muted green. Swirls of magenta.

Pale rose. Pool of lavender.

Darkness.

Compromise, thought Shayna. One relents, so the other bides his time. In the end, they will find a way to understand each other.

Olive.

Lime.

Darkness.

Red, Shayna thinks, fountains of orange-gold. White so hot it would burn you to ashes.

Glimmering pure green.

Darkness . . . darkness . . . darkness.

The minutes pass, stretch into tens. Night hangs over the rain forest like a suffocating black shroud. After an hour, Mae exhales and clicks off the night-cam. "I think that's it for now. We might as well pack it in."

"Wait!" Shayna feels on the edge of understanding something vast and complex. She senses unseen colors lurking out there, waiting to be discovered, interpreted, felt. There are worlds within those colors, epiphanies too large for the conscious mind to enfold. Her hands knot together. "There might be a few more."

"Look, the only pair within range found each other." Mae's voice is exasperated. "What more do you want?"

What she wants, with a fierceness that frightens her, is something of her own, something not observed and written down in neat piles of notebooks, or catalogued on a computer screen, or stored as a visual record. She wants Mae's hand tracing the contours of her bare shoulder, craves Mae's perspiring body sleeked against her side in the loneliness of the night while outside the rain patters down and, inside, recycled air whirs. From the beginning, though, Mae has made it quite clear she does not waste her time on petty matters of the flesh with anyone, man or woman. Mae is all business, inviolate to everything but concerns of the mind, and her first rejection of Shayna's overtures was so painful, Shayna cannot bear to risk a second.

Her face hot, Shayna switches the lantern on, and then, by its pristine white glow, pulls up the trap door and climbs down to the dark tangle of the forest floor alone.

Shayna sleeps restlessly in the confines of her own bunk until noon, Aelta's noon, that is. The days are longer here, like the steamy, languid nights, and few creatures of any real mass stir under the blazing cauldron of the yellow-white sun. Inside the small research bungalow on the forest floor, though, the conditioned air is blissfully cool, allowing sleep or activity, whatever the hour.

Mae wakens even later and emerges from her room, rumpled and blinking. Her short ash-gold hair is plastered to her forehead. She is all muscles and planes, sense and organization. She stretches and smiles wanly. "We got some good footage last night."

Sitting at the metal kitchenette counter, Shayna nods over unsweetened coffee.

"I want to go to the cliffs and film the burrows again," Mae says. "My last tapes were too dark."

Shayna finds herself reluctant to return there, although it is safe to walk the jungle in the daylight. Embians are nocturnal and the local insect population disdains the alien taste of human skin and blood, but the sight of the sleepers curled into tight fetal balls, the light-generating organs on their chests pale and lifeless, disturbs her. When she looks at them so vulnerable, she feels guilty for spying on their love-making night after night.

"I have some transcriptions to make." Her hands tremble as she picks up her cup. "I'll meet you in the blind later."

The displays begin early, while the air still is suffused with light the shade of dark honey and the embians are barely visible.

Plum. Starburst of amber. Ochre.

Darkness.

Watching the embians is the only time she feels real anymore. Shayna rakes her fingers back through sweat-sheened hair. If only they could install fans or air-conditioning in the blind, she would stay here all night, every night, but the embians have preternaturally sharp hearing. Conversation does not bother them, but the least mechanical sound drives them to perform their dazzling mating rituals elsewhere in the rain forest's steamy privacy. The night-cam and audio recorder, small as they are, have to be heavily shielded. Shielding the entire blind would be inordinately expensive, and the university that funded them subscribes to the long tradition that fieldwork should be difficult and uncomfortable.

She clicks on the sound recorder and sets it on the floor between her booted feet. The other camp stool remains empty. She envisions her partner with a broken leg, or perhaps a concussion, lying helpless and in pain among the trees' exposed, pulsating roots so that Shayna would be forced to trace her by the signal of her personal transponder. She sighs. Mae wouldn't be so distant, so self-sufficient then. The wire screen creaks as she leans back and wonders what it would be like if people spent half as much time learning about each other as they do trying to understand the embians.

Aquamarine.

Darkness.

A trill pierces the silence, full of loss and longing. What do they seek from each other, she wonders. A lifetime of commitment, or only a moment of ecstatic union? Do they raise their young together, or abandon them to survive on their own? Why do the males seek each other out at times, and then court females at others? So little is known of them except these dazzling displays of light.

Flash of peach. Intensifies to orange. Shot through with yellow lines that bleed into each other.

Darkness . . . darkness.

Mae pulls herself up the ladder, closes the trap door and drops, panting, onto her stool. "Sorry I'm late." She clicks off the lantern. She smells faintly of sweat, overlaid by a heavy floral soap, jasmine. "I was so filthy that I showered when I got back, but now I'm wringing wet again." She laughs ruefully.

Indigo. Mottled with gray. Fades . . .

Darkness.

Shayna stares hard out into the liquid blackness, feeling the heat radiating from the woman at her side. Her own skin burns with its nearness. "I was getting worried."

"Look, I said I was sorry!" Mae's tone is stiff. She scrapes the camp stool toward the far corner.

Cinnamon. Saturated with blood-red.

Darkness.

Blue-violet. Brightens . . .

Darkness . . . Darkness.

"Never mind." Shayna remembers touching the damp curve of Mae's cheek, and how Mae recoiled that one, terrible time she dared that minor intimacy.

Red-violet.

Lilac.

Darkness.

Purple, strong and true, piercing the night like a beacon.

Darkness . . . darkness . . . darkness . . .

"I'd rather be here than anywhere else in the universe." Shayna stretches languidly. "It's like being on the edge of a wonderful secret, something no one else shares."

Mae exhales. "Your first assignment is usually like that, but then the newness wears off. And sometimes it can be just bloody miserable. On my last trip out, there was this asshole, William, who wouldn't take no for an answer. He was always after me, you know, rubbing up against me, touching me, and I hate to be pawed like that. It was so damn humiliating."

Shayna's gaze is drawn to a different quadrant of the rain forest as another display begins.

Sapphire.

Darkness.

She leans her head back, half-closes her eyes. "If—you were an embian, what color would you be?"

"Hmmm . . ." She can almost hear the slow smile spreading across Mae's face. "Silver, I think, like moonlight on the ocean. What about you?"

No moon rides these Stygian skies, one of the things Shayna misses most. Arms braced behind her head, she stares up at the ice-bright stars. "The hottest shade of vermilion I could find."

Jade.

Darkness.

"So, what do you think—two males, two females, or a mixed pair?" Mae asks. "I can check the infra-red tomorrow when I review the tape and see who's right."

Burst of cobalt. Explosion of red-violet. Fades . . .

Darkness.

Glimmering pool of pine-green. Expands. Shower of cadmium-orange.

Darkness.

"Two females," Shayna says.

Mae leans toward her, redolent with jasmine. "Why?"

"Because they're coming together so fast, no games at all, just inquiry and prompt resolution."

Aqua.

Sea-blue.

Darkness.

There is a momentary flash as Mae checks her watch to mark the time. "Okay, I'll let you know tomorrow."

Azure so intense the eye must look away.

Darkness . . . darkness . . . darkness.

* * *

Shayna tries to sleep, but colors flow like rivers behind her eyelids, unadulterated greens melting into raging, violent blues, oranges that erupt into an energetic sea of yellow-white. What is it the embians say out there in the darkness? What do they promise each other with each new pattern?

She tosses, presses her hands over hot dry eyes, tries to blank her mind, compose herself for the balm of sleep, but the colors intensify until she can taste them on the back of her tongue, hear them ringing in her ears. They *mean* something. She slips out of her bunk and sits on the edge, pushing her fingertips against her temples. *Red* throbs along her optic nerves, seeps deep into her brain. *Amber* melds with her unconscious. *Violet* sings.

Finally, she turns on the light and searches the stores. Somewhere in the station she has seen sets of colored bulbs for the lanterns, used as lures in the earliest studies when others besides herself had postulated the lighting displays possessed meaning. The embians never responded to static decoys, though, and, after dozens of unsuccessful trials, the bulbs had been abandoned in favor of the more traditional forms of observation.

Two hours before dawn, she finds a set of four: red, yellow, blue, and green, a severely truncated vocabulary, but perhaps enough to begin. She takes four extra lanterns and eases outside into the sticky, hot night air, leaving Mae soundly asleep. Sweat immediately trickles down her temples and pools between her breasts as she follows the well-marked path to the blind, but then hikes beyond it into the virgin forest to hunch at the bottom of a great, fleshy tree oozing vinegar-scented sap.

The air has the consistency of heated sludge, down where the night breeze cannot reach. Her lungs labor to inhale, exhale. She kneels between protruding roots as knobby as knees, and, by the bland light of the white bulb, changes out the other four. She turns on the green and waits. Mating displays usually start just after dusk and intensify until midnight, tapering off after that, but a few embians roam until dawn, searching for something—she wishes she knew what.

The sodden heat of the night coils inside her, like a snake about to strike. She swings the lantern over her head, then turns it off, trying to approximate their initializing rhythm. *Green*, she thinks hard at the embians.

Whir of insects. Creak of trees shifting in the breeze. Rustle of mouse-small feet.

Ochre.

Darkness.

33

Her heart thumps. They never make the same response twice in a row. Her hands shake as she selects red this time, holds the lantern aloft for ten counted seconds before turning it off.

Darkness.

The night presses in as she tries to be patient. Out of sight, the ocean whispers against the sand. Her back itches and she tastes salt on her lips. She wishes for a moon, something, anything to lessen the unbroken power of the night.

Auburn. Streaked with ruby. Transmutes to shimmering jade.

Darkness.

She selects yellow, then hesitates. What if she unknowingly says the wrong thing and drives it away? Reaching for calmness, she begins with yellow, adds the blue, then turns off the yellow and waits a few seconds before she extinguishes the blue.

Darkness . . . darkness . . . darkness.

Mint-green crowned with violet spangles. Brightens . . . brightens.

Darkness.

The display brings tears to her eyes; it's exquisite. She can never match its eloquence, never reply properly. She's so limited, so—primitive. She raises green and red together, holds them up until her muscles shake with fatigue poisons.

Darkness.

Something weaves through the trees now, close enough to hear the whisper of flesh against foliage. She massages her aching shoulder and huddles against the enormous root, staring into unrelieved obsidian.

Mulberry. Fades to rust. To silver. Fades. . .

Darkness.

It's so close now, no more than a hundred feet away and she panics. This is the most important meeting of her life; she cannot bear to fail. She turns on all four, saying *redblueyellowgreen.*

Darkness . . . darkness . . .

The soft leaves rustle inches from her face. Something slim, blacker than the night itself, regards her through the darkness. It exhales the same subtle alien spice as the trees and the mud. *Amber. Pale green.* A female, taller and more slender than the males, with characteristic blue stripes on her throat.

Darkness.

Trembling, Shayna raises *yellow.*

Pale-daffodil.

Darkness.

This is obviously a conversation, if only she knew what they were saying to one another. She switches the yellow off. A dry hand caresses her face. Smooth as silk, more solid than human flesh, it slides along her cheek, trails across her lips, down her throat. Icy heat rushes through her. She is lost, drowned in *red-gold*, tasting cinnamon, musk, and something else, something alien and yet almost familiar. The night whirls and she is somewhere else, not here anymore, not in her body.

Metallic gold, brighter than the sun.

Gold, she thinks, yes, *gold*! She embraces it, folds herself about its icy-hot center, consumed by its richness, giving all she has until there is nothing left. *Gold*, yes, *gold*.

"Shayna!"

The sharp, worried word winds through the trees, penetrates the protective wall in her mind. She starts, finds herself curled about a cool firm shape, the way one spoon fits another. The embian female stirs within her embrace, gazes up at her with enigmatic ebony eyes. The deflated light-organ lies mute on her chest.

Shayna's heart races as she tries to remember. *Gold*, there had been *gold*, rich as melted butter, and then something more, she can't say what, only that it was immense and cold and fiery, all at the same time. She pulls the embian closer, thinking *gold*.

"Shayna, answer me! Are you hurt?" Mae's breathless voice is closer now as she crashes through the brush.

The embian frees herself gently from Shayna's hands, then slips away, gray-green hide blending instantaneously with the trackless riot of tree and bush. Shayna folds empty arms over her breasts and rocks there on her knees, suddenly, terribly alone.

"My God!" Mae fights her way through a hanging vine and then stops, looming over her. "Are you all right?"

The muted sunlight, filtered through layer upon layer of vegetation, catches her fair hair and transmutes it to spun gold. Shayna squints up at her. *Gold*, she thinks and reaches up to touch the gleaming strands. Mae backs out of reach, her face both angry and afraid.

Shayna drops her empty hand.

*   *   *

"What were you doing out there in the bush? It took me two hours to find you, even with the transponder, once I realized you weren't down at the cliffs." Mae's voice vibrates with anger. "Pull yourself together, dammit." She fits Shayna's trembling hands around a mug of coffee. "We have four weeks left on this grant and I have no intention of leaving early."

Shayna stares into the cup. Deep brown, swirled with lighter streaks of creamer. What does it mean?

"Drink that, then take a hot shower." Mae paces the kitchenette. "I'll manage both the audio and the visual recordings myself for a few nights while you get some extra rest."

She tastes the steaming coffee, but it's only hot, not icy at all. It should be both.

"It's getting dark." Mae pours herself a cup of coffee, then blows on it. "I have to get out to the blind. Are you going to be okay?"

The table is unpainted aluminum, burnished to a high sheen. Shayna spreads her fingers across it, studies the puzzling contrast of pink flesh on gray metal.

"I have to go!"

"Yes," Shayna manages, her eyes still on her hand. "I'll—be fine. Don't—don't worry."

Mae shoulders the night-cam, but Shayna doesn't look up. Words are shallow, like water poured across pavement, one molecule deep and ten yards wide. Because words can mean almost anything, depending on context and inflection, she realizes now that in reality they mean nothing.

Once the outer door closes, she waits a few minutes, then collects the four lanterns with colored bulbs. She studies each in turn, touching them with wondering fingertips, *red, blue, green, yellow.* Grateful for their purity, she pulls the transponder bracelet off her wrist and leaves it on the table.

Outside, it is raining and a thousand scents vie: wet mud, astringent sap, rotting leaves, a dank musky fungus that has eaten into the nearest flesh-tree beside their bungalow. After only a few steps, she abandons the trail and battles her way into the dripping darkness, using momentary flashes of the white bulb as her guide.

It will not be the same tonight, somehow she is sure of that. What embians have to say is a symphony, rather than a droning one-note song. It would take a hundred lifetimes to perform all the parts.

Her rain-soaked shirt catches on the branches and she tears it loose. Finally, she stumbles across a hollow with a crooked stream at its heart which feels right somehow. She stops, lights a color at random. It gleams *blue*, strong and true. She counts the seconds, then turns it off.

Darkness . . . darkness . . . darkness . . .

Sky-blue slashed with pink. Softens. Starburst of burgundy.

Darkness.

The display was so far away, she could barely distinguish the pink qualifiers. She lights *green* and *yellow*, swinging them overhead, one in each hand.

Darkness.

Off to her left, between the original display and herself, another answers. *Chartreuse. Flash of blue-white. Black afterimage.*

Darkness.

Two responses, herself and another. How do they choose in such a situation? Do they go to the closest, or pick the more interesting of the two conversations? She hugs her knees, waiting.

Closer. *Opalescent white. Tarnishes to pewter. Fades.*

Darkness.

Her hands shake as she rushes to answer before the other can, crying out *red*!

Even closer, almost at the same second. *Mauve banded with copper.*

Darkness.

Closer still. *Ivory. Dissolves into rose.*

Darkness . . . darkness . . . darkness . . .

It's obvious she cannot compete with the second embian's stylish complexity, but the dark silence drags on and so she finally raises *yellow* and *red* together.

Pale-gray. So near she can make out the black outline of the torso behind it.

Darkness.

Alabaster the second answers and she hears the swish of bare feet through mud.

Darkness.

So pale tonight, she thinks, and then selects *white* without much hope. They complement each other, while she is alien, less than nothing to them, babbling like an infant without understanding.

A squat embian emerges from the wet leaves, a red-banded male, his eyes black holes in his head. His muscles swell in sleek bands beneath his skin. His hands are short and powerful. They regard each other by the light of the lantern.

Marble-white.

Cream. A second male, more slender, his neck-bands only a faint scattering of red, slips up from her right, more hesitant, less sure of himself. He coils around the flesh-tree, his movements graceful as an anaconda. Rain patters down from above in a sudden flurry.

They have come for each other, she thinks, not for her, and extinguishes the white bulb. She picks up the other four, slides her hand over the wet shapes of the trees behind her in order to back away and leave them to make what they can of this night.

Two pairs of smooth hands touch her face, her neck, her arms, her breasts. Lean, hard bodies press against her, one on each side. She is drowned in a sudden burst of *white*, brighter than ermine, more pure than ivory or marble, sweeter than alabaster, *white* which burns down into the secret part of her that is self, sings along every nerve, fire and ice blended into one glorious rush that leaves her unable to breathe.

White is the center of the universe, she thinks, a bridge of light into a realm she's never dreamed existed. *White*, all along and forever without knowing she has been *white*.

She wakes to the tangible presence of darkness, inhabiting the forest like a prowling black beast. The sultry breeze is its breath, stirring the leaves over her head, whispering. The muddy hollow where she has lain with the embians still bears the shape of their bodies, but they have slipped away.

White sizzles behind her eyes, on the threshold of meaning. She sags back against the unseen vegetation, warm rain dripping down her forehead, and traces the hurricane of colors in her mind . . . *coral . . . flashes of amethyst . . . long winding streamers of sapphire* that twine through her thoughts, giving her glimpses of an inaccessible country deep within, occasionally felt but never known, always heretofore a dark and secret place.

Embian minds are not organized as a human's; they have communicated that much to her now. They think, but not in human ways, not in cause-and-effect strings, stimulus and response, logical progressions, but in great rivers of sensation and memory and association that combine in unexpected, synergistic ways and cannot be learned in coherent segments, only experienced.

She brushes the worst of the mud off and heads for the bungalow by the light of the white lantern. Without a path, she wanders for a time, her soaked clothes clinging to her thighs and shoulders, lost in the maze of towering flesh-trees, until she changes lanterns for some reason she cannot name. The *blue* bulb reaches back into her mind, remembers the feel of the bungalow, the exact amount of pull it exerts, how it lessens when she turns away from it, increases when she turns back. She half-closes her eyes and feels the way, not stopping to think or analyze, just following the blind sense of *home*.

Mae is waiting, fuming, blonde hair plastered to her skull by the rain. She clenches the discarded transponder in her fist. Mud coats her bare legs up to the knees.

Shayna stands in the open door with the blue lantern in her hand, the remaining four cradled like children against her breasts.

The other woman wilts into the nearest chair. "I've made allowances for your age and lack of experience up until now, but I won't put up with this irresponsible behavior anymore." Her voice is choked.

Shayna sets the lanterns aside in the corner, well out of harm's way. Each one is precious beyond measure.

"Why are you wandering that hellacious forest alone—at *night*, by God? Do you really want to die?" Mae runs spread fingers back through her wet hair.

"I'm only beginning to understand." Shayna perches on the arm of Mae's chair. "But it is a language, just like I thought."

"This is serious, goddammit!" Mae jerks to her feet. "What could those animals possibly have to say out there in the bloody darkness that's worth risking your life?" Her blue eyes brim, bright with unshed tears.

Shayna wants to tell her about the wonders she's experienced, *gold* which melts your heart and makes the sun sing, *white* bridging the way to Heaven itself, but there are no words for such things between humans. "What about your dissertation?" She grasps Mae's hand. She feels brown, with a touch of *violet*. Yes. She tightens her fingers and works to phrase this in brown so she will understand. "Solving this puzzle could make your career."

Mae stares at her trapped hand as anger and curiosity vie in her eyes, feeding upon each other. "All right," she says finally. "I'll give you one chance to convince me, but you have to promise that you'll give up this asinine wandering by yourself after tonight, if I don't agree."

Shayna nods, then gives the white lantern to Mae, carrying the other four herself. The minute they step outside, *aqua* brims behind her eyes, brightened with sparkles of *lime*. Interesting, if she only knew what it meant, but it is too soon. She's still growing, changing, learning.

At first Mae leads, but then she stops beneath the blind at the end of the path. "How—much farther?" she asks hesitantly.

The dark presses in, warm and thick, scented with sap. Shayna feels in *auburn* squiggles how close Mae is to bolting. "This is far enough." She extinguishes the white lantern, then fumbles in the darkness to select another at random. It shines out *red* and she is content. *Red* hints at deep considerations boiling just below the surface, an admirable opening.

Darkness.

After waiting ten minutes for a response, she tries again. *Yellow.*

Darkness.

"This is stupid." Mae hunches over her ribs, closed and disbelieving, as always. "They never answer static lures."

Far out in the forest, almost hidden. *Violet. Flare of indigo, so deep, it's almost black. Fades.*

Darkness.

"Now what?" Mae asks.

Shayna displays *red* and *yellow.*

Darkness.

Periwinkle, banded with blue. Bursts of white.

Darkness.

"Christ, that was a lot closer!" Mae rises. "That's enough."

"No," she says. "You need proof." Periwinkle . . . Shayna reaches down into that part of her that knows without logic, understands without reasons, and feels for an answer. Without conscious thought, her hand selects *white* and *red.*

Darkness.

"I said I've had enough!" Mae wrenches at her arm.

Dusty rose brightening to salmon.

Darkness.

"That one was almost on top of us!" Mae's voice rises. "Stop it!"

White, Shayna answers.

Darkness.

"All right, stay here! Let it tear your head off when it finds out you can't satisfy its needs, or maybe it will screw you anyway. Have you even considered that?"

Umber. Shot through with pale yellow.

Darkness.

She feels the embian's approach like a bath of *red-violet*. "If you leave," she says evenly, "you'll never understand." She displays *whiteyellowred*.

A massive shape, much larger than any embian she has ever seen, is silhouetted black against a patch of stars through a gap in the trees. *Topaz.*

His skin is cool silk. *Topaz* swells like a nova, enveloping them in the now familiar ice-fire and beyond that, showing them an opening of some sort, egress from the stultifying boundary of conscious self . . . emergence, freedom. Mae cries out wordlessly as searing *topaz* binds them to each other and the male and the rain forest and the ocean and the wind, alters the pathways in their brains so they will never be alone again, never apart, always and forever touching. *Topaz.*

Shayna awakes curled against the male's chest. Mae's ragged breathing rasps in her ear. The pale-gray dawn filters down through the trees, illuminating Mae's pallid, unconscious face.

The male blinks at her. Shayna sees *azure* behind his black eyes, *mauve* in the set of his head. Moving delicately, he eases away and disappears into the trees.

Mae groans, drags a hand across her forehead. She seems *olive* to Shayna, mixed with a bit of *plum*, She touches her face.

The other woman bolts up and her eyes are terrified. She crosses her arms over her breasts, struggles for breath. "Where—wh—" She is trembling so hard that she cannot make the sounds.

Shayna cradles Mae's head. "Gone," she says, "but there will be others, and their gifts will be just as wonderful."

"No," Mae forces between chattering teeth. "It's l-like—being shattered, then jammed b-back together with the pieces all in the w-wrong places."

She helps Mae back to the cool, dry air of the bungalow, bathes her, then puts her to bed with a cup of hot broth. Mae shakes so badly that she has to be fed, spoonful by spoonful. Her trembling lessens until finally her eyelids sag, but minutes later she wakes, crying out, tears streaming down her cheeks. "*Orange!*" She buries her face in her hands. "Please, God, not *orange!*"

Shayna sits on the bed and cradles her again, her skin tingling where Mae's lean body touches her. *Orange* is not so bad, she thinks. *Orange* explodes warm on the tongue, cools the back of the throat, fire and ice, like all other colors, an invitation to abandon restrictions of flesh and soar in other dimensions of the soul.

"Shhh," she whispers. "Think of *cinnamon* instead." She pictures cinnamon, heavy and quiet, full of backwaters and still ponds, like late afternoon on a sweltering summer day.

Mae's body heaves with her efforts to stop sobbing. Her face presses against Shayna's shoulder. Shayna feels *cinnamon* seeping into her thoughts, tinging the river of her grief. They have both lost something in the process of growing, like shedding an outgrown skin, and this is harder on Mae because her thoughts have always been so rigid, locked into logic and order. Letting go of such crutches must be as painful as being born.

When the ship returns in four weeks, she and Mae will take home the knowledge they have gained here, and perhaps teach a few selected others the colors of the soul as they are meant to be experienced, not at a distance through the rarified isolation of the conscious self, but through immersion in those secret places shrouded in darkness until now, that part of the mind where the embians have always lived. She leans against Mae and the other woman gradually quiets. When they had known only their surface selves, they were too different, she, with her fear of rejection, and Mae's avoidance of intimacy. But now they have been set free to find that place deep inside where what they wanted from each other and from life was always the same, where it is possible for them to be together.

Shayna nestles close, fitting against Mae's side perfectly, just as she had always known she would. They are one flesh now, one mind. *Emerald*, she thinks, feeling the surge of greenness under her skin, behind her heart, beneath her fingernails, acceptance of otherness, settling into place.

Mae exhales and rests her flushed cheek against Shayna's neck. Her slim fingers twine through Shayna's. "*Emerald*," she agrees in a sleep-fogged voice and closes her eyes.

Ambassador
by Thoraiya Dyer

Nothing in the legend of Captain O'Shea mentioned the stench.
Though my nostrils cringed, I didn't allow my benign smile to slip.

She doesn't look like a monster, Hallax displayed curiously in the ultraviolet spectrum.

She wasn't a monster, I replied. *She was a great leader.*

She reeks!

His irreverence was irritating, but I supposed he hadn't been told the stories.

Your senses are so keen, I said, interlacing the curling crimson of the communiqué with turquoise threads of irony.

I had never seen a human before, but this particular human was unmistakable. Her skin held the pallor of ocean foam. Mine held the blackness of space. Otherwise, we were externally identical.

She was, of course, wearing clothing. Out of respect for her I had concealed the parts of my body which were taboo in human society. Covering themselves, reducing their functional surface area, didn't hinder humans. They didn't make their own food from rocks and air and the sun's rays; they took it, and they broke it down, and that breakdown was what I could smell. I forced myself to take her outstretched hand, regardless.

"Ambassador," she said. Her fingers were warm, like basking lizards. "I am Captain Marietta O'Shea."

Ambassador.

The title filled me with pride. Two species that had each been isolated for aeons, brought together by friendship and need, and I was to be my people's mouthpiece.

My appointment came with a price. Marietta O'Shea's long journey hadn't aged her. My journey, a comparative mincing step, had stolen half my life away. I hadn't been encapsulated in frozen time, like the Captain and her kin, but rather in that hibernative mode critical for the survival of natives to a red dwarf system.

Time was a predator of merciless savagery, one that our technology had not yet conquered. Upon my return to Afferis, I myself would be an End.

Yet my reward for this mission would be consent to reproduce. Even Ends were capable of that much.

My heart beat faster in my abdomen at the thought of going into flower. Barely one thetic in ten was permitted to propagate when a freeze was imminent.

"Captain," I said, "I'm honored. You know our history. It pleases me to wear your shape."

It wasn't an accident that my morphology mirrored hers. If not for the Ancestor who evolved in mimicry of the human form, we wouldn't have survived the freeze that penetrated the oceans of Afferis deeper than they ever had before.

The Captain's eyes slid to my companion. He bulked head and shoulders above me. Much of his tissue was a muscle-analogue of rapidly alterable turgidity; wasteful of energy, it forced him to feed often. While my colour had not changed, he showed the yellowish chlorosis typical of a long, lightless voyage.

"This is Hallax," I said. "My Defender. I speak for him. He has limited vocalisation."

I'm the one that's limited? Hallax said scornfully. *It's not my fault that humans have limited vision.*

I ignored him.

"He's some kind of bodyguard?" Marietta said curiously.

Our eyes met. A communication passed between us that didn't require sound or flashing colors across the skin. She was a predator. I was prey. We were both acutely conscious of it for a moment.

The moment passed.

"I'm adapted for diplomacy," I said. "My metabolism is slow. I can last long periods without feeding, but my strength and stamina are poor. If one of our six-meter-long native salamanders came upon us without warning, I'd make an easy meal. That's why Hallax stays with me, always. And that's why I must beg a favor of you already."

"What is it?"

"Is there an exposed place, close by, that might be suitable for photosynthesis?"

I'm not hungry, Hallax broadcast immediately.

The sun is weaker here, I replied. Saint Jude measured twice Afferis's astronomical unit. *You can't leave it til the last minute.*

"Certainly, Ambassador," Marietta said, nodding. "Our biosecurity measures won't take long, and then you'll have a short, preliminary meeting with our Council. After that, I'll take you straight to the sundeck."

Biosecurity measures? Hallax objected. His skin ignited with the spectra of suspicion and doubt, but the Ends had warned me to expect this, as well. My Defender preceded me through the airlock into the quarantine station.

It was everything that the dusty, dark, mountainous surface of Saint Jude was not. Fluorescent bulbs dazzled the blanched interior. Their reflections sliced along stainless steel surfaces. The boxy series of thin-walled rooms seemed fragile, but they were a part of the famously long-lived *Taxus Baccata*, a ceramic ship whose quantum computers, operating in a vacuum, had survived the passage of forty-three million Earth years intact.

The Captain offered me a water canteen, and I took it. Moving my voice box to one side, I let the water trickle into my primary replenishment bladder. It tasted of iron and sulphur, but that could hardly be helped. Ice mining on Saint Jude was dangerous and difficult. There was no surface water, and no way to excavate on a larger scale.

The humans should have had the contents of their Resource Pod with which to build, but the Resource Pod was competently programmed and so passed cleanly through the intended wormhole. The *Taxus Baccata*, on the other hand, was left to blunder through real space, constantly correcting its path, only to crash into the wrong planet a week before the bipartite expedition would have been reconciled.

All they could do was modify what they had, and modify again, and all the while they were dying. There was no vegetation native to Saint Jude, and the rock was unworkable basalt. Earth plants grew successfully on board the *Taxus* but failed to thrive on the surface of Saint Jude. The yield reportedly lessened with each passing year. The situation had been serious when the distress signal was sent four years ago; now, it was likely that the humans were starving.

Here I was, representative of my people, not with an offer of sanctuary, nor with a bountiful, nutritious cargo. Instead, I'd brought the crate from the Resource Pod that held the engineering and navigation computer; the successfully programmed computer; the one that could take the surviving humans back to Earth.

It was the best we could do. I felt sure they would be grateful.

"Please, sit down," Marietta instructed.

By the time the humans reached their planet of origin, another forty-three million Earth years would have passed. Eight million generations of thetics would have come and gone on Afferis.

But we couldn't shelter them there. Afferis, too, was unsuited to cultivation of their food sources. It orbited the same sun; the atmosphere, while ever present, constantly waxed and waned; the carbon and nitrogen cycles were dependent on thetic and salamander biological processes, rather than bacteria and weather patterns.

Whoever had sent them to this system had made a monumental mistake.

A small, windowless door opened and closed. One human, at least, wasn't going hungry. The doctor's face was planet-round, his mouth plump and pleasant. His rotund figure fascinated me; thetics were devoid of fatty tissue, storing excess fuel as complex carbohydrates in the skin.

"Welcome," the doctor said, smiling at Hallax, cocking an eyebrow at Marietta when Hallax did not respond. "They don't speak? How are negotiations to be conducted?"

"We speak," I said, amused.

I'm going to be of little use to you, Hallax displayed, tolerating the application of the biosampler to his shoulder. *I should have stayed behind to guard the Blossom.*

They're not going to steal our ship, I replied wearily. *It's no good to them. They can't hibernate. They'd never make it to Afferis.*

His paranoia was expected. Defenders were supposed to remain constantly alert to danger, and I'd brought him into a secure, enclosed environment where his senses were stifled. Vigilance was as much a part of his nature as imperturbability was part of mine. I displayed placatory patterns of indigo and violet.

Aloud, I said, "Take care with that sample, Doctor. Hallax secretes a toxin potent enough to paralyse a fully grown salamander."

"You're next, Ambassador," the doctor replied.

The biosampler was a smooth, silver-cased rectangle, slightly longer than my hand, with a black line on one side.

I held out my forearm, and he pressed the black line to my skin.

The blades of the device passed through my flesh unsensed. The doctor plugged the silver case into the side of his microscope, peering down at the promptly delivered, single-cell thickness cross-section of my arm.

Though the section was complete, my arm didn't drop off; tiny gaps in my tissue where puzzle-pieces had been lifted away and later fitted together were staggered so as to cause no noticeable injury.

"Sorry for holding up the grand rescue," he said, unbending with a smile.

Then it was over, and Hallax and I followed Captain O'Shea down a low corridor. Hallax bent double to keep his head from brushing the ceiling. It reminded me of the entry to the Resource Pod, that holy shrine which I approached timidly for the first time for my briefing by the Council of Ends.

I was a Bud, then, with only my genetic aptitude for the English language to distinguish me from other seedlings of the Marietta strain.

"Open," the Captain instructed the door. It opened, and she beckoned me through, but, struck by the significance of that one simple utterance, I couldn't move. It was as though an electric jolt had passed through me.

In my mind, I saw the mural on the side of the Mountain of Hope. It depicted the Ancestor, standing before a portal, giving the command for the door to open. Inside was the Pod's bridge, a room full of light.

Regulated light. Continuous light. A haven for our kind, and the door could only respond to Marietta's voice.

The Ancestor's voice. My voice.

"Is something wrong?" Marietta asked, frowning, and I snapped out of my daze at once.

"No, nothing."

The bridge of the *Taxus Baccata* was larger in scale but otherwise identical to the bridge of the Resource Pod. Three men and two women sat on moulded ceramic stools in a semicircle. Marietta took the empty place. While they introduced themselves, Hallax and I stood like supplicants at the focus of those stares.

That irritated me. It was the humans who were the supplicants. I relented almost immediately. They were hollow-cheeked and sunken-eyed. It hurt me to look at them.

They're dying, Hallax said, his discomfort displayed in pale green spirals across his bare shoulder blades.

Yes.

Neither of us had ever seen death before natural senescence. When the freeze came to Afferis, or atmospheric erosion began to threaten respiration, our scientists were always prepared. Perhaps it wasn't so in the past, but thetics hadn't wasted and died from lack of resources for thousands of years.

Salamanders starved when their prey—us—became scarcer, but they hadn't the intelligence to regulate their population.

If only there was a way to relieve their hunger right away. I groped for an analogue to help me comprehend their suffering; it would be like being trapped in the dark, out of hibernation, forever. All the time, growing weaker, screaming out for the sun, consciousness fading in and out.

Will they be able to get home in time? Hallax asked, disquieted.

They can control time, I reassured him. *They have as much time as they need. They'll be fine.*

"We are the Ruling Council of the *Taxus* and, by extension, Saint Jude," opened Engineer Gessle, a yellow-haired man with a kindly gaze. "We don't mean to be rude, Ambassador, but you must know that your appearance is extraordinary."

"I find it quite usual," I replied, bemused. "You've heard of convergent evolution. Completely unrelated life forms will acquire identical traits for a similar purpose. Marietta O'Shea's hands, her height, the radiographic profile of her endoskeleton, the patterns of her irises and the sound of her voice were all traits necessary to access the inner chambers of the Resource Pod. Hence, the Ancestor acquired them. We have a short lifespan. It is conducive to rapid change."

A short lifespan didn't permit the luxury of extended periods of learning. I didn't mention the ability to graft knowledge directly from one thetic's mind into another's. I wasn't there to lecture them on thetic biology.

I was there to return their lost property at the crucial moment. They would be overcome with appreciation for Hallax's and my sacrifice. An emotional farewell would see both races departing Saint Jude simultaneously.

"Your command of our language is excellent," Marietta said.

"Our command of your language is as required to direct the Pod's computer. Which, I understand, is being unloaded right now from the *Blossom.*"

"Unloaded?" the kindly Engineer repeated with faint confusion. "But we have a computer. What about seed banks? Cuttings, from your forests?"

"But there are no forests on Afferis. We are the highest form of plant life; we are the only form of plant life. Everything else was destroyed thousands of years ago, during the great freeze, the one we sheltered from inside your Resource Pod."

Their faces paled in what could only have been shock.

"No other life at all?" Marietta whispered.

"There are salamanders. But even if they weren't in hibernation right now in preparation for the freeze, they're heterotrophic, like you. They'd be no use at all."

"Then why were you sent?"

"The computer from the Resource Pod can help you return to Earth."

Marietta laughed bitterly.

"We can't return to Earth. Don't you see? We crash-landed here. The *Taxus* is barely airtight, and our colonization equipment is designed for a planet with an atmosphere. Our time capsules went offline the moment we got here. Even if the Pod computer could navigate us back to Sol system, the *Taxus* is in no condition to leave Saint Jude."

I felt bewildered. My instructions from the Ends were clear, and yet they'd neglected to communicate their intentions to the humans. The Pod computer was pointless. The trip had been wasted.

My life had been wasted.

"Is the ansible still functioning?" I asked numbly.

The instantaneous communication device linking the *Taxus* to the Resource Pod, and, presumably, to other human settlements, was how the Ends intercepted the human distress signal in the first place.

The members of the council turned their heads towards a diminutive, bald, brown-skinned man.

"It still works," he shrugged, pulling a flat display screen from a folder in his lap and offering it to me. "This came through this morning."

I walked to him and accepted the screen. The display was a blur of blue and yellow, the message indecipherable to any but a thetic.

Afferisan Council to Madame Ambassador. This is to advise that the forward cargo hold of the Blossom *contains twenty thousand single-administration doses of dexamethasone. In humans, dexamethasone is a potent anti-inflammatory and immunosuppressant. Use it wisely, Ambassador.*

By order of the Ends, this Fourth Seventythird of the Second Orbital Period of Darbon.

I went over the message a second time, searching desperately for hidden meaning.

"What does it say?" Marietta asked.

"It doesn't make any sense," I replied, distraught. "Maybe if you set the display to a different wavelength—"

"Ambassador," Marietta interrupted. "Could it be that you don't want to tell us what the message says because it reveals the true purpose of your mission?"

"The true purpose?" I repeated, overwhelmed.

"Yes. It seems clear, now, doesn't it? We can't use the computer that you've brought. There's no other plant life on Afferis. Your bodyguard is poisonous. There's only one cell line that can possibly save us."

The display screen clattered on the floor. I took two steps backwards. My skin crawled with imminent danger.

What's wrong? Hallax broadcast, stepping instinctively between me and the circle of seated humans.

"No," I said.

"No?"

I grappled with the implications. She wanted to take my cells, grow them and feed from them and she couldn't see, because she was incapable of asexual reproduction, that she would be eating my children.

"Captain," I said calmly, concealing my horror from her but unable to conceal it from Hallax, "I am not human but I am still sentient. My offspring are of equal value to yours. Amongst my people, a child conceived by flowering and pollination is loved for her uniqueness, but a child conceived by binary fission is loved for her steadfastness and is no less a child for being a clone."

"We're not asking to propagate an entire organism," the bearded Terraformer piped up in what was perhaps supposed to be a coaxing voice and instead resembled a sort of frantic slavering. "In a series of water baths, exposed to sunlight, we could—"

"No!" I was startled by the sound of the shriek in my own ears. I hadn't realized my voice could get so loud.

"Very well," Marietta said soothingly.

I realized my heart was thumping. My lacy webs of muscle-analogue had tensed to the point of tearing. Waves of panic and fear washed over me, sending Hallax into a thinly constrained killing rage.

I am fine, I managed to broadcast, and the white whiplashes of his intent, designed to temporarily blind an attacking salamander, slowly began to fade.

The expenditure of energy left him even more yellowed than before.

"The sundeck?" I asked Marietta softly.

"Very well," the Captain said again. She stood up, sweeping the Council with a flat gaze. "This session is over. We've offended our guests." Her eyes came back to me, and I couldn't interpret her expression. "I'm sorry, Ambassador. Please, come with me."

She led Hallax and me away from the bridge. We moved through a cramped maze of corridors to a vertical ladder laid against the carpeted side of a cylindrical chute.

Marietta indicated the ladder.

"Take as long as you like," she said. "I won't go with you. In a species survival situation, even the Captain is only as valuable as her functional ovaries. I'm afraid I've already absorbed more than my allotted monthly amount of radiation."

For a moment, it was a bond between us. Both were female, both living in hope that we would be able to fulfill our deepest urge and reproduce.

The moment passed.

She turned away. I began climbing the ladder. Hallax glared at Marietta until she was out of sight.

We have to go, he said angrily.

We'll go, I replied, *after you're fed.*

If we don't go soon, I'll be fed all right. Fed to humans. Did you see how they were looking at us? Like we were lichen waiting to be scraped off rock.

We're not lichen, I displayed across my turned back. *And they're a sentient species. Our safety here is guaranteed by the Council. Besides, you're toxic to them.*

If he argued again, I wasn't able to see. The porthole to the sundeck was sealed but not locked. Once through it, I emerged into a hemispherical bubble roughly ten meters in diameter. Most of the radiation bathing the area was infrared, but some was visible to humans. In the days when we'd sheltered in the Pod, we had been greener in color, better able to take advantage of the fluorescent lights and the human visible range, but over time we'd altered to make the most efficient use of natural sunlight that we possibly could.

The clear acrylic shell permitted three hundred sixty-degree views of the surface of Saint Jude. Beyond the pink-tinged borders of the *Taxus*, black mountains in all directions formed a spear-scape that concealed the horizon. There was no day and night. Here, as on Afferis, the sunny faces of the stone plinths were constantly bathed in light. What lay in shadow remained cold and lifeless unless a lucky meteoroid strike happened to shift it. In this system, plants didn't have the luxury of an equal period of light and dark, and photosynthesis could not be switched off on a whim. To control sugar production, our forebears became mobile, able to slither into cracks and hide from the sun when sated.

These days, it could be controlled in other ways.

Will you . . . watch me? Hallax asked.

We stared at each other.

I'll watch you. But I'm not strong enough to overpower a human, Hallax.

I know.

I passed him Marietta's canteen and he took a long swallow. The muscle-analogues in his throat shifted, sealing his windpipe and breaking their connections to his clavicle in preparation for disassembly.

The human shape comprised an unsustainably low surface area. Luckily, a genetic accident that would have been a deadly flaw in a mammal had provided the Ancestor and her kin with the perfect solution.

Hallax dragged off his constricting clothing and sank down onto the floor. The colors displayed in his skin faded and his eyes turned glassy.

I watched his entire body unseam, the muscle-analogues and tendons unfolding away from his skeleton and internal organs. After a few moments he'd exponentially increased his surface area, spreading over the floor, the tiny, criss-crossing plenerial vessels keeping the exposed surfaces moist.

His replenishment bladder contracted rhythmically at its attachment near the trachea. There was perhaps enough water there to last an hour, which would be sufficient for him to re-establish operational pigment levels and photosynthesize enough sugar for the journey home.

I closed my eyes, longing for the mind-numbing tranquility of disassembly, but they snapped open of their own accord and fixed on the porthole in the floor. I couldn't relax. I was supposed to be watching out for Hallax, infinitely vulnerable, smeared thinly over the sundeck like . . . like lichen waiting to be scraped off rock.

The thought made me shiver. Marietta's square, flat teeth, identical to the wooden ones lined up in my own head, were designed for grinding up lignin and cellulose.

Grinding *me* up. I was made of lignin and cellulose.

It was foolish to dwell on such thoughts. Soon, Hallax and I would be back on the *Blossom*, twisting gently back towards Afferis, perhaps dreaming in the depths of hibernation.

Dreaming, dreaming of the children I would have as a reward for enduring this encounter. My arms and legs would turn to petals, my hollow spine to a style. Pollen would be conveyed from my open lips to my abdomen, where a cluster of ovules waited in anticipation.

I put my hands to my abdomen. They were there, now, unfertilized and abeyant. Waiting to develop and grow, to burst out of the seed husk and reach for the light. On stumpy legs they would totter towards the closest source of warmth. If I was still alive, it would be me. If not, it would be the closest Illumination, where they would be held by loving hands and surrounded by loving tendrils of light.

My mother must have been an End. I had no memories of her, so she couldn't have survived flowering. But the child raising strains at Illumination Zaraffa had tended me with care and affection.

Humans intruded into my daydream. They scuttled on all fours, like salamanders, snatching my babies up and grinding them between flat teeth.

I flinched.

Everything was motionless and silent inside the acrylic hemisphere. Hallax looked significantly darker, his replenishment bladder three-quarters empty. I edged towards him. A wrong footstep could be lethal to him while disassembled, but I felt safer standing closer to him.

The sound of the portal opening made me whirl. The head of the bearded Terraformer protruded above floor level.

"Ambassador," he said shortly, "please come at once." His eyes bulged as he caught sight of Hallax. "Oh, my God. What's wrong with him?"

I circled my supine companion, angry and afraid, placing myself squarely in front of the emerging human. I hadn't forgotten he was the one who suggested growing thetic tissue in a tank for human consumption.

"Nothing's wrong. He's feeding. Where do you want us to go?"

"You can leave him here. The doctor—"

"The doctor can wait. Hallax is almost—"

The sound of a sash being tied made me turn.

I'm finished now, Hallax said coolly, glowing with the satisfaction of the feed. *We can go and see the doctor.*

The moon-faced doctor looked uneasy.

"Ambassador," he said. "Thank you for coming."

Behind him, in a narrow bed on a wheeled frame, a sick man gleamed. Sweaty and pale, his groin was swollen disproportionately, bulging beneath the white hospital sheet. Quarantine panels surrounded him on all sides, but I could still hear his moans and the frantic bleeps of the monitoring equipment.

Puzzled, I waited for more information. It was not forthcoming, so I prompted him to explain.

"I don't understand what I'm seeing," I said.

"This man has been poisoned."

"Poisoned by what?"

The doctor rubbed at his temples.

"It was your bodyguard that was supposed to be poisonous. You were supposed to be safe."

"What?"

"He's been poisoned by your cells, Ambassador. Cultured this morning from the samples you gave. One hundred volunteers are in a similar state. Feverish. Showing massive inflammation of the reproductive organs. It was a mistake. I understand that, but we had to take the chance. We're dying. You gave us no other choice!"

It took a moment to sink in.

Cold fury stole across my stomach. I felt the blinding white lines streak across my skin; it was beyond my power to control them.

Before I could launch myself at the doctor, my outstretched fingers turned to hooked wooden talons, Hallax wrapped his much stronger arms around me from behind.

Let me go, I flared.

If you harm him, we'll never get out of here alive.

The sentiment shocked me; he was my Defender, he wasn't supposed to care about his own skin.

He butchered my babies, I panted. *I'm going to kill him.*

You haven't the strength.

No, but you have. You're my Defender. You're supposed to protect me.

I am protecting you. Hallax shook his head. *Don't you see? There's no need to kill him. He's going to die, anyway. They're all going to die. The thousands who weren't poisoned, and the hundred who were.*

Abruptly, I recalled the message from the Council of Ends.

In humans, dexamethasone is a potent anti-inflammatory and immunosuppressant.

54

They had known.

All along, they had known what the humans would do. They had predicted the sickness visited upon the doctor's writhing, screaming volunteers and they had provided the antidote for it. Twenty thousand doses; their estimation of the population of the *Taxus Baccata*.

The doctor looked warily back and forth between me and my Defender.

I relaxed my body. Hallax released me and took a step back.

"Doctor," I said tightly, "you will find a supply of dexamethasone in the forward cargo hold of the *Blossom*. I am returning to Afferis now. Let it be my parting gift to you."

The doctor's face turned hopeful.

"That is generous of you, Ambassador. We haven't the means to manufacture pharmaceuticals." He dispatched an assistant immediately. When I turned to go, he raised his voice. "But I'm afraid you can't leave yet."

I spun back to him.

"Why not? The computer we brought is no help to you. My cells have been no help to you."

I saw the same hunger in his eyes that I had seen in the Terraformer's.

"The Captain . . . insists that you stay longer, so that our two great cultures can learn more about each other."

"What you mean," I said, "is that the Captain has ordered you to make it work, whatever desperate measures are needed. The cells that you sampled are an unsuitable food source. What do you wish to try next? My brain tissue? My reproductive cells?"

His lips did not move, but I saw, in the relaxation of the lines around his eyes and mouth, that he was grateful I understood.

"If you would be so kind as to wait in the next room," he said gruffly. "I must first treat these men and women."

Miserable and defeated, I led Hallax into the next room. The door sealed and locked behind us.

We peered through the window at the sick volunteer. Each tortured sound prompted in me an icy stab of satisfaction. He had gobbled up thetic flesh without a moment's hesitation, and now he was paying the price.

I hoped he would die. I hoped they would all die, the ones who had eaten my children. Hallax said they were all going to die, anyway, but that wasn't good enough. I wanted them to immediately suffer the consequences of their heinous crime.

The assistant returned, and the doctor administered what I assumed was the dexamethasone.

The Ends betrayed us, I whispered to Hallax. *How could we have been bartered like this? Humans have nothing that we need.*

They have the ansible. They have time technology. The Ends must have decided it was a fair exchange.

But why us? What did we do to deserve this?

Our reward, Hallax said bitterly. *Our reward was to be propagated, and we have been. By humans.*

Little good it will do them.

But healthy color crept back into the face of the sick volunteer. The swelling in his groin subsided. He sat up and asked for a drink of water.

The doctor, twitching with excitement, provided it. He checked the patient over. They spoke for some time.

Then, the doctor offered him a vial full of black liquid.

The volunteer drank it, and they both grinned at each other for a long while. The second time around, there seemed to be no ill-effect.

No, I babbled. *No, it can't be.*

Apparently, Hallax said, *they can use us for food. Once they've taken their medicine, anyway.*

I'm leaving, I said, sickened. *I can't watch this. I have to get out of here.*

I turned to face the second portal, the one that led away from the quarantine station in the direction of the docked *Blossom*.

The door's locked, Hallax displayed patiently.

You forget. My voice is the voice of Marietta O'Shea.

"Open," I said and the door obeyed.

The Blossom was unscathed.

Hallax primed the main switch and waited for the systems to come online while I prowled back and forth through the cockpit, brooding. Nobody had seen us enter the docking area. I wanted to go back, to eliminate the cell lines that the doctor was propagating, but I knew it was impossible.

I suppose I should make sure there's no humans on board, I displayed reluctantly. *Before the ship is sealed.*

That's my job, Hallax replied, getting up out of his chair, but I waved him back down and opened the door to the hold.

I stared at the empty forward cargo compartment. It smelled of ethylene oxide and human body odor. There was no sign that the dexamethasone had ever been there.

No sign but a slip of salamander parchment covered with a gentle swirl of saffron and emerald green. I picked it up and began to read.

Afferisan Council to Madame Ambassador. Congratulations on the success of your mission. If these crates have been removed, it means the humans of Saint Jude have been saved. No doubt you believe that the cost is too high, but know that certain particulars of your birth have been hidden from you until now.

You are the first thetic ever to be fashioned in an Afferissan laboratory. Our human neighbors have long been characterized as an aggressive species with a consuming drive for conquest and expansion. This is consistent with a lush home world crowded with competing life forms. However, it was felt that liberation from some of their animal instincts would be beneficial both to them and to others.

Ambassador, certain of your cell lines have been engineered to penetrate the mammalian blood-gamete barrier in order to insert thetic genetic material into human sperm and ova. We predict their ingestion will cause short-lived intense illness—minimized by anti-inflammatory use—before the active cell components vanish beyond the limits of human medical science.

Human haploid cells will be replaced with thetic hybrid precursors.

Within a single generation, the humans of Saint Jude will be autotrophic—able to synthesize their own food.

Your descendents will comprise, not simply the results of the flowering granted on your return, but a new, superior breed. We hope this somewhat mitigates the unhappy circumstances in which you must now find yourself.

Safe journey, Ambassador.

By order of the Council of Ends, this Sixty-eighth Seventythird of the First Orbital Period of Baasir.

Edge of the World
by Jonathan Shipley

Luke shouldered his bag and moved uncertainly down the transit corridor towards the main concourse of Eclipse Orbital. The orbital was out there on the very edge of Terran space, and boy did it feel like it. Transportation on the last long leg from Roma Nova had been on refitted troop ships, which underscored how far off the tourist track Eclipse was.

He'd felt conspicuously different on the troop ship, a student among all the military types—or at least, he *thought* he'd felt conspicuously different. That perspective was changing with every step as the crowd of military co-passengers was becoming absorbed in the larger crowd of Eclipse foot traffic. The orbital wasn't really a Terran or even a hom facility, and a crowd here meant a mix of insectoid, amphibian, and saurian sentients. He'd known this was coming, but the reality of walking next to seven-foot lizards and cockroaches was more unnerving than he'd expected. Of course, he was also spacelagged to the max and fighting a grav change, so everything felt like too much too fast.

As he entered the concourse, he saw a sharp division down the middle with checkpoints and military personnel. On the other side he could see more species than he could begin to identify, a congregation of glittering scales, sleek chitonous exoskeletons, and even a few clothed sentients, though they were very much in the minority. Almost no homs, he noted.

He headed for a checkpoint. The scales and chiton flowed uninterrupted through the gates designated for non-homs, but hom travelers had to stop and give an accounting. He'd been told to expect this. Eclipse Orbital was in a state of semi-occupation. Terran troops had taken Eclipse at the end of the Border Wars, but had returned much of the station to its former authority as a gesture of interspecies goodwill. It was still an ultra-hot topic back home. Expansionists wanted it as a gateway to further conquests out-sector; no one else wanted the mega-trouble that would follow if Terra disrupted a major hub of non-hom traffic.

"Finger check, kid," the guard told him when he reached the gate.

"Right." Luke nodded, pulling off his gloves and stuffing them into the pockets of his thermojacket—deep space travel was a chilly affair on a troop ship. He slid a hand into the scanner slot for DNA verification and waited with growing unease. Whatever info the finger check was pulling up, the guard didn't look pleased. Suddenly the opening sphinctered tight around his wrist, trapping his hand inside. "What's this?" he demanded. "This isn't necessary to ID someone."

"No, it's to check the truth of the answers you give. And by the way, kid, it's a finger off for every wrong answer."

That's not funny, it's sadistic, Luke wanted to retort, but he reined in his growing apprehension and said quietly, "Ask away."

"Name?"

"Luke Armbrewster." He felt a sharp sting to his trapped hand. "Hey—stop!"

"Full legal name," the guard said with the hint of a sneer.

"Lucas Newton Armbrewster," Luke reeled off quickly and the stinging ceased. He stared at the guard, simultaneously outraged and scared. Pain-motivated polygraphy wasn't even legal in the civilian sector, but this was a military occupation a long way from home.

"Species, age, and origin?"

"Terran, Ameranglo, male. Nineteen years old. Origin in Old Boston, NorthAm, Terra." Again a sting. "Former origin in Chicagopolis, NorthAm, Terra," Luke blurted out. "Place of birth, Chicagopolis, NorthAm, Terra." The stinging stopped.

"Occupation?"

"Full-time student," Luke answered, trying to think what else he should say to be complete in his response. "Graduated from high school a year ago, been enrolled in a special MIT preparatory program this last year, and just about to start university."

"Reason for coming to Eclipse Orbital?"

"Transit stop on my way out-sector . . . to Zjhaccœse University on Zjhaccœse." Luke glanced over nervously to gauge if that was sufficient and saw the guard eyeing him narrowly. "Uh, what else do you want?" he asked, expecting a sting at any second.

"Zjhaccœse," the guard finally snorted. "Can't get much farther out than that. Right smack in the middle of lizard country. You a lizard-lover, kid?"

"What? No"—sting—"I mean, yes, I'm open to non-hom interaction, but that's not—"

"Hey Hank," the guard vocalized into his com, "we got us a genuine lizard-lover. Better check his stuff."

Suddenly the duffel bag was yanked off his shoulder. "Hey!" Luke yelled. He twisted around and saw a second guard rifling through the bag, holding up each item of clothing, then tossing it unceremoniously over the gate onto the floor beyond.

"You have no right—" Luke began, then shut it as his hand received another stab of pain. "I'm just a student!" he groaned. "Sending students to Zjhaccœse is a State Department program—an official State Department program." His voice sounded panicky to his own ears. He just knew he was going to be stuck at this checkpoint, answering hundreds of inane questions with every answer painfully wrong.

"Figures," the guard snorted. "State is all lizard-lovers these days."

Luke braced for another sting, but suddenly his hand was released and the gate opened before him. "Enjoy lizard school," the guard sneered as Luke scrambled past. "And do us all a favor—don't bother coming back."

What the hell? Luke couldn't believe he'd just been put through that. Sure, there were hom-dominist Expansionists out there who never wanted the Border Wars to stop, but that had nothing to do with him.

With a bitter shake of his head, he retrieved his empty duffel from the floor, then squatted down to collect his scattered clothing. At least it hadn't walked while the guards were screwing with him.

Still fuming, he reshouldered the duffle and trudged across the concourse, then realized he didn't know where he was going. Somewhere on the other side of the orbital was a transport that would take him the rest of the way to Zjhaccœse, but it wasn't boarding for another ten hours. A close connection in interstellar terms, maybe, but a long time to stand around in a transit corridor.

He glanced around, saw that there was signage all over the concourse advertising various lounges—Nebula, Nova, Comet, Meteor, and so forth—with schematics how to easily find them. "The perfect way to pass the time," one sign promised. "Make those layover hours feel like mere minutes," another advised. Luke gave a snort. The pleasure lounges of Eclipse were notorious all the way back to Terra and not the type of place he would normally hang out, but one of the names was familiar. Nebula—his transport was docking at Nebula, and he was supposed to have a final briefing in Nebula Lounge.

Taking a closer look at the schematics, he realized he'd made some wrong assumptions about Eclipse Orbital. It wasn't organized around a main concourse with radial corridors to different docking stations; it was organized around a half-dozen different concourses, each with its own array of docking arms and satellite functions. Eclipse was a lot bigger than he'd first thought. He was currently standing in the Meteor Concourse, Meteor being the hom-occupied zone—and his flight was on the other side of the orbital. So he needed to follow the Comet transit corridor all the way around and change over to Nova and follow it, then finally change to the Nebula corridor that led to his destination docking station. And that would take—he checked the chart of distances under the schematic—almost four hours? It took four hours from one side of the orbital to the other? Had he read that right?

There was no mistake. So he was wrong about too much time standing around in transit corridors. By the time he got over to Nebula and had his meeting, he'd be pushing right up to boarding. He double-checked his route and headed for the Comet corridor.

As he settled into just standing there for long periods of time and letting slideways take him from point to point, everything started to catch up with him. After two weeks in deep space flight, it was no surprise he was starting to brown out. The unexpected adrenaline encounter at the checkpoint had gotten him this far, but he couldn't take four hours on the slideway without a break. As he neared Comet Concourse, he resolved to get food, get beverage, get whatever happened to be available to perk himself up for the duration. Once he got on the Zjhaccœse ship, then he could crash.

He saw a door with the familiar fresher icon almost immediately and stumbled in to clean up as best he could on the hoof. He could have killed for a luxurious thermal scrub about now but would settle for a quick sonic cleanse. After two weeks of nothing but small handheld sanitizers, it was hard to feel clean, even when he was theoretically sanitized. And everything about him smelled like stale, recycled air. If the sonics did nothing but remove the smell, it would be a major upgrade.

He plopped his duffel on the counter and peered into the mirror to see what he was up against. And grimaced. He usually had looks on his side, but now he was staring at a pale, hollowed-out face only a zombie could love. His longish brown hair that was trained to flop appealingly across his forehead had lost both its flop and its appeal and was plastered against his skull in ragged disarray like a wet rat on a bad day.

He dug in his duffel for the brand-new grooming kit he had bought specially for the trip, but after a few futile moments, realized it was gone. No mystery when or how that had happened.

With a sigh, he dragged the bag into the stall with him and let the sonics wash over him and all his worldly possessions for several cycles. When he emerged, he was still tired and his hair was still matted, but the stale smell was gone, so he counted his visit a success. He walked down the line of shops on the concourse, looking for familiar-looking food but not seeing much he recognized. He finally settled on a nutrient porridge labeled "safe for all species."

The vendor, not of a species Luke recognized, blinked a few times and quirked a floppy ear. "Has gentlehom established line of credit outside hom zone?"

"I . . . no, I haven't. Can I do that now?"

"From hom zone only, I fear. Credit brokers are located right beside the hom checkpoint."

"Never mind," Luke muttered, turning away. That was one checkpoint he hoped to not see again for years—literally, years. So suddenly he had no credit. He could survive ten hours on Eclipse without credit, but what about four years on Zjhaccœse? If his account didn't function here in nominal hom territory, then it had no chance of functioning far out-sector. That was definitely a question for the final briefing.

"No, wait, gentlehom," the vendor called after him. "Special deal—free porridge for Zjhaccœse students."

Luke paused uncertainly. Free porridge for Zjhaccœse students? Was "Zjhaccœse U" stamped on his forehead or something? And why the sudden shift? He turned and thought he saw a tall blue lizard pointing at the shop, but the next moment the crowd had reshuffled and he couldn't be sure. There were a lot of lizards in the concourse. But the creepy feeling of something not right remained.

"Uh, no thanks," Luke told the vendor. "I'm not that hungry after all." It was a lie, of course, and as he resumed his trek, his stomach kept rumbling. But he didn't stop again, though he did resist the urge to keep checking over his shoulder. Even if he was being followed, he probably wouldn't be able to tell. He wasn't even to the point of identifying species, let alone specific nom-hom individuals. And any weirdness he was feeling was more likely culture shock and fatigue. Hunger was in there, too. When hours later, he finally reached the Nebula section of the orbital, he was more than primed to get a meal out of the State Department in addition to a briefing.

As he walked up the ramp into Nebula Lounge, he felt the stomach-wrenching lurch of a gravity shift, and suddenly up was over there. He hugged the wall a moment, letting his stomach settle, then moved forward again. His eyes went to the huge bubble of a view window ahead that had started out as the ceiling. The window overlooked the Eclipse Anomaly. He'd seen a little of it when the liner was making dock, but this was up close and spectacular. The anomaly wasn't hot enough to be a star, but was too volatile to be a planet. Shimmering eruptions burst up from the blue surface every few minutes like a continuous fireworks display.

He tore his eyes away and surveyed the rest of the lounge. It seemed to be a huge, multi-purpose relaxation space, as opposed to the sleazy bar he'd been envisioning. There was sleazy off to one side where flesh dancers flashed their anatomy on a corner stage. On another day, on another world, that would have drawn him in like a magnet. What college guy would visit a notorious lounge and not check out the flesh dancers? But today he was too stressed and too spacelagged to work up any interest. And the dancers were hom, Terran even, while the clientele they were writhing against was definitely non-hom. That wasn't really a surprise, considering, but the reality of casual xenosex felt a lot different than the concept. Way outside of his experience. Another glance made the scene even creepier as he realized he couldn't tell what sex the dancers were—even staring right at them. That was disturbing, and he refused to speculate what was going on there.

"Luke!" someone called from close by. "Lucas Armbrewster."

The name sent a shiver of relief through his body, making him feel a little less lost in a strange place. And the voice calling him was definitely hom and definitely female, and that was a good thing. He turned and found a woman—deep olive complexion with contrasting pale hair, late twenties, attractive, familiar somehow—beckoning him over to a table near the view window.

He hurried over, managed a smile through his fatigue. "You have me at a disadvantage. You are. . . ?"

"Luke, you don't recognize me? MIT seminar 343?"

Given a context, he had a chance. A bubble of memory surfaced . . . someone a little older than most of the kids in the seminar. "Oh, Sanja . . . Stevens?" he said hesitantly.

"Sanja Carrera," she corrected. "Erica Stevens was the girl you dated after me."

And he couldn't keep their names straight—way to go, idiot. Spacelag must really be getting to him. And they'd dated? Now he really did feel foolish that he could barely remember her, but MIT had been a whirlwind and it all ran together. He took a deep breath. "So we dated once or twice?"

"Depends on what you call dating. We did dinner, made a night of it . . . but you never called me back."

"Oh." He felt his cheeks grow warm. "Sorry. I don't mean to be a jerk, but I tend to put everything into my studies and let the social side drop. I'm pretty focused on engineering."

She raised an eyebrow. "You say focused, I say self-absorbed Type-A personality, but that's all in the past now. And here we both are at the far edge of Terran space. Who would have guessed? You, still the blue-eyed charmer and me, still waiting. Have a seat."

Flustered, Luke sank into the seat across from her, unsure what to say next. Running into a one-nighter was always awkward, especially one he had just dropped. "I can't stay long—I have a meeting. So what are you doing on Eclipse of all places?" he managed to ask as an autobot slid up to the table.

"Drinks, gentlebeings?" it asked.

"Uh. . ." Luke looked around for anything resembling a menu. But all plans for a proper meal had fled with that last gravity shift.

"Two fruit-flavored aquas," Sanja told the autobot that immediately scooted off. Then to Luke, "My treat. Be very careful, incidentally, about drinks and food, now that you're over the border. Assume that nothing is compatible with hom digestion unless you have specific assurances."

"Good to know," he nodded, craning his neck to survey the lounge and not seeing any other homs except the dancers. "You seem pretty savvy about Eclipse, Sanja. Any idea how to contact the State Department presence here—is there a consulate or something? I ought to check in, tell someone I'm on schedule . . . maybe complain."

She raised an eyebrow in his direction.

"The guard at the checkpoint," he explained, feeling his indignation rise. "He put me through a full pain-motivated interrogation at the gate. That can't even be legal. And when I told him I was going to Zjhaccœse, he said don't bother coming back. Why should I have to take that kind of crap from a—" He paused as Sanja started laughing. "I didn't realize I said something funny," he said frostily.

"Luke, you're a complete innocent," she chuckled. "Eclipse Orbital is in a tense state of semi-occupation, a virtual powder keg of hom/non-hom interaction where the big issue is unwary homs disappearing into the cargo holds of slave ships. And you're griping that some guard chewed on you a bit as you passed from the safe side of the gate to the unsafe side."

Luke digested that with growing alarm. "There are active slavers on Eclipse?"

She nodded. "Active slavers trolling for merchandise."

He shook his head in confusion. "But that doesn't make sense. The slave trade was just during the wars. There hasn't been a rape-raid in years."

"How do you define rape-raid?"

He frowned. "When slavers swoop down on a border settlement and take colonists captive while the fleet is engaged elsewhere. Isn't that how everyone defines it?"

"Just checking. By that definition, no, there hasn't been a rape-raid in years. But small ships go missing all the time with crew and passengers never seen again."

"And they end up on the auction block out-sector?" Luke shook his head. "That can't be. It would be all over the news."

"So you've never heard of Bintaga as the hub of the slave trade?"

"Of course, I've heard of Bintaga. But I know for a fact that's practically all monkey trade. It has nothing to do—"

Sanja sank her face into her hands with a groan. "Luke, you're an idiot. How could you win NorthAm scholar with such major disconnects in your brain?"

Luke felt his face flame. "Payback, I guess, for standing you up," he muttered savagely.

She looked at him sharply. "No. You really are an idiot. This is basic survival info. What do you think the monkey trade is?"

"The buying and selling of large simiods as livestock. . ." he began tentatively, then sat bolt upright. "Are you saying the monkey trade is hom slave trade under another name?"

She nodded. "Monkey is the common out-sector term for homs, just as we say lizards for sentient sauroids."

"Then the media has been—"

"—playing this name game for years in league with the politicos. No one wants the unwashed masses to understand the real situation because people would clamor for a war we could never win."

"But we came out on top in the Border Wars," he reminded her, "not that I'm an Expansionist or anything."

"Fighting small, relatively new nation-states. Expansion stopped dead here at Eclipse Orbital because we brushed up against some new players—actually some very old players. There are saurian star-nations out there that we can't fight."

"And why not? If they're backing the slave trade—"

"Not backing exactly," she corrected. "They're taking their time deciding about the slave trade. Based on long-standing Terran belligerence in the sector, they're unsure if monkeys should be allowed to run loose. And as for war—just remember that you're going to Zjhaccœse to study hyperspatial engineering because they have the science and we don't. Think about it."

The fruit-flavored aquas arrived, giving Luke a chance to sit back and consider all this as he sipped. He stared at the pulsing blue anomaly outside the view window, then looked over at Sanja curiously. How did she know about Zjhaccœse when he hadn't mentioned it yet? Maybe "Zjhaccœse U" really was stamped on his forehead. Then he winced as the obvious struck. "So you work for State and this is my scheduled meeting."

She smiled. "There's hope for you yet, Luke. Consider this your final briefing before going out into the Great Unknown."

He frowned, still working out details of this new twist. "Then the seminar at MIT, that one date, all that was. . ."

"A profile check of the candidates for the program."

"And you recommended me . . . in spite of the awkwardness."

"I did," she said with a quirk at the corner of her mouth. "Of course, we were specifically looking for self-absorbed Type-A personalities. Congratulations—you made the very top of the list."

He shifted uncomfortably but said nothing. He got that she was calling him the biggest asshole of all the assholes she'd profiled—that was how most people interpreted "self-absorbed Type A personality." He just wasn't sure if she was still mad at him or not, if she ever had been. He wasn't used to being played like this.

"Relax, Luke," she continued. "I'm just teasing you a little. The truth is that State needs self-absorbed, self-motivated, competitive high achievers. All of you are going to be isolated for literally years in a potentially difficult environment. The duration and expense of the trip from Terra to Zjhaccœse makes transit impractical, and even com will be unreliable at that distance. You'll have to solve your own problems as they arise, by whatever means. Each of you is covered for basic student expenses—but not much more—for as long as you remain a student in good standing. Any questions so far?"

Credits, he remembered. "So we have no spendable credit of our own? How is that supposed to work?"

"We have no practical way to transfer credit out-sector where we have no trade relationships. We don't even have an established exchange rate with Zjhaccœse. This student program is viable only because Zjhaccœse University came forward with scholarships to cover your expenses. If you need spending money over and above that, you could try getting a job to establish credit of your own within their system. This is all very experimental."

After a moment of silence, Luke asked, "Why would they do that—give scholarships to some distant, pushy race?"

"We have no idea." Sanja hesitated a moment, then added, "We really have no idea—the offer came out of the blue—but State jumped all over it as an alternative to Expansionism. There's a lot riding on this . . . on you."

And Luke realized suddenly that this wasn't about education. He and his fellow exports were just fodder for the State Department's policies. Expendable fodder. "Are there slave traders on Zjhaccœse?" he asked carefully. "And would anyone back home blink an eye if any or all of us got carted off to the auction block?"

Sanja quirked an eyebrow. "Right to the heart of the matter—good for you. State might well blink an eye if our entire student program ended up in slave pens, but there would be nothing we could do. By the time the news even reached us, you'd probably be gone without a trace. But all of that is unlikely, to the best of our information. Zjhaccœse politics are convoluted and there are levels of hierarchy in saurian cultures that remain opaque to our best xenologists, but it appears someone high up initiated a ban on the local monkey trade almost a decade ago. That's another reason why this program is taking place on distant Zjhaccœse instead of somewhere more convenient.

"You—the collective forty of you," she continued, "represent an attempt at approaching a number of problems differently, including the slave trade. Zjhaccœse University is the oldest educational institution in the sector—over ten thousand years—and enormously prestigious. The best and brightest from dozens of saurian cultures study there. If you can show that homs are better than the 'dumb monkeys' of stereotype, there's a chance for a real shift in attitude in the power centers out-sector. That would deflate both Expansionism and the slave trade."

Luke nodded. "Sounds like a plan. And considering the completely *self-absorbed* heavy-hitters that you're sending to Zjhaccœse"—he couldn't resist one jab back—"it sounds like a very doable plan. Lizards of the world, prepared to be wowed."

She gave him a weak smile. "What smells like a stinkhog at the opera but is too dumb to even notice?"

"Suddenly we're doing jokes?"

"A monkey attending Zjhaccœse University. It's the current joke making the rounds out-sector. That's what you're up against, Luke. Good luck. We have assurances of safe passage for all students from the Regents of Zjhaccœse University, but just the same, don't take any candy from strangers in transit."

Slavers, he thought with a shudder as he shouldered his bag and headed for the door. Funny how everything seemed to come back to that . . . or maybe not so funny. Candy from strangers, free porridge—it felt suspiciously the same.

From Nebula Lounge to Nebula Docking Station was less than an hour, but as Luke hurried down the transit corridor, it felt like weeks. Every time a non-hom gave him a glance, he tensed. And there were a lot of glances. Except for Sanja, he hadn't seen another hom in hours. This side of Eclipse Orbital was strictly non-hom traffic, apparently. A lone hom traveling out-sector must look like . . . slavebait. He just couldn't get those fears out of his head. Yeah, supposedly safe passage, but if it came down to slavers versus Regents, he wasn't betting on university academicians.

Homs disappearing from the orbital, Sanja had said, along with active slavers trolling for merchandise. And here he was, toodling along all by his lonesome as though this were the safest place on Earth—except Earth had nothing to do with it.

After only a few minutes, he was sure someone was following him. Even taking into account his current irrational paranoia about everyone that looked his way, he was still sure something was going on with a certain blue-scaled lizard. For one thing, it was big—bigger than Luke by two or three heads and bigger than most of the non-homs as well. That made it stand out, even in the bustle of the transit corridor. The fact that Big Blue was following him to the docking station could simply mean they were both going to Zjhaccœse, but that didn't explain why the lizard slowed when Luke slowed and paused when Luke paused . . . and didn't have any luggage.

If he thought back, he could almost convince himself that Big Blue had been tailing him all the way from Meteor Concourse on the other side of the orbital. But he didn't know if that was real memory or retrofitting after the fact to fit his current mood. But it hovered in his brain as an uncomfortable possibility.

At the next juncture with a lounging space, he forced himself to stop and take deep breaths. If he kept on going faster and faster, he was going to work himself into a panic. He was almost to the docking station. All he had to do was keep his head and he'd make it on board just fine.

"Shhhzzaa oooosh uggebba?" something piped close by.

Luke whirled, ready to run. What he saw was two yellowish, thigh-high lizards sitting on a luggage sled—baby lizards, he guessed from the big heavy-grav ball they were bouncing. It deformed into a pancake every time it hit the floor, then reformed into sphere on the rebound.

"Shhhzzaa oooosh uggebba?" one of the little lizards squeaked again.

Oh. *Shall we push together?* Luke could understand the saurian dialect of Interstel if he just focused. "You want me to play ball with you?" he asked, remembering to stretch his vowels and clip his consonants.

The two lizards chattered happily in response.

"OK, just for a minute," Luke said. "I've got a flight to catch." He unslung his duffel bag, placing it carefully against the wall where it was always in view, and squatted down to baby lizard height. It felt good to dump his tension for a moment and do something simple and domestic, even if the kids involved were clawed and toothy.

The grav ball came his direction, squishing around his hands as he caught it and popping back to shape as he sent it back to the kids. After a few more back-and-forths, he wasn't so sure a moment of relaxation had been a good idea. His spacelagged body was slipping into fatigue, and his fingers were starting to tingle.

Suddenly he tumbled over and couldn't move. His surprised yelp came out a whisper as his throat locked.

The lizard kids scurried over and stared down at him a moment. One of them kicked at his legs and started pulling at his jacket as Luke just lay there. The other clicked a response and stooped to wrestle with Luke's boots.

Sluggishly, reactions surfaced in his brain. What was. happening to him? Was it a stroke? And why were the kids going for his boots and jacket? They wouldn't fit lizard anatomy.

They slid the luggage sled over and began manhandling him onto the surface, simultaneously picking at his clothes . . . almost like they were stripping him—

With a shock, Luke realized that was exactly what they were trying to do—methodically strip him. These weren't kids—they were members of a small species of slavers. A sudden surge of fear kick-started his fogged brain. He was drugged—the ball had been coated with something that he'd absorbed through his fingers. And once stripped, he'd be easy to pass off as dumb livestock. Like non-stop background noise, the word *slaver* kept echoing again and again in his head. Fear ratcheted up to full-fledged terror, yet he could only lie there silent and limp as he was shoved onto the sled.

A heavy, clawed foot set down perilously near his head, followed by a long hiss. Luke had just enough motor control to raise his eyes to take in the big, bulky lizard standing over him. Big Blue. He whimpered softly, knowing that their plan had now come together. He was lost.

Then he noticed that his attackers had stopped in their tracks and were watching the new arrival guardedly. One of them let loose a burst of sibilant syllables too fast for Luke to follow, and the big lizard hissed again and slammed its tail against the floor.

That seemed to decide things. They slowly backed away, leaving the sled and grav ball.

Luke lay there, watching as the yellow lizards disappeared in the traffic of the transit corridor and wondering what it meant. Big Blue just stood there, quietly waiting and giving no answers. Time passed and the foot traffic began to thin. Luke's mind, tired of ping-ponging between *Am I still in danger, am I out of danger?* decided this must be a rescue, not a kidnapping still in progress, and fastened on the escaping minutes. How long had he been lying there? How long before the flight to Zjhaccœse?

Finally, a sharp tingling stabbed at his spine, followed by quick muscle spasms all over his body. When it passed, he had some motor control back. Rolling off the luggage sled, he shrugged his clothes back together and pulled on his boots and jacket. Only after he was fit to travel with bag in hand did he approach Big Blue, who stood in the same spot unmoving. "Thank you," Luke said in his best imitation of saurian dialect. "Did Sanja send you?" That was the only thing that made sense.

The big lizard tossed his head impatiently. "Regents. You're one of theirs now."

The university Regents? "But we're a long way from Zjhaccœse," Luke pointed out. "Not that I'm objecting."

"Regents have very long tails," the lizard hissed with what could have been a laugh. "Your flight, monkey."

"What? Oh—" Luke glanced up in alarm, realizing how late it was. He could see far up the corridor the airlock to the dock already sphinctering shut. "Shit," he muttered under his breath and tore down the corridor at a fast hobble, the best he could manage on still wobbly legs. "Wait!" he yelled. "Passenger for Zjhaccœse!"

A nightmare scene surfaced in his mind—not as mightmarish as slavers, but still bad—of returning to Nebula Lounge to tell Sanja he'd missed his flight to Zjhaccœse. For something that stupid, he might be cut from the program.

When he reached the sealed airlock, he pounded desperately. A sleek saurian attendant this side of the door, snicked his teeth disapprovingly. "Too late. Too slow."

"But I was attacked—you must've seen I was attacked," Luke blurted out. "Please open up—it wasn't my fault."

"Once airlock seals, is finished," the attendant shrugged, then added smugly, "Monkey too slow."

It was only a slight change in inflection, but it moved the phrase from "not fast enough" to "not bright enough." Dumb monkey.

Luke felt something boil up within him. He'd had to swallow "lizard-lover" and "self-absorbed asshole," but hell if he was going to accept "dumb monkey." He leaned forward to vent an acid retort, then realized he had nothing. He knew so little about saurian culture that he couldn't even put together a meaningful insult. A feeling of utter helplessness washed over him . . . like lying on the floor with little yellow slavers pawing at him. He'd missed his flight, and all he could do was slink away with all the lizards laughing at him behind their smug, scaly snouts.

As he turned, he saw Big Blue up the corridor. OK, so maybe not *all* lizards. Then he perked suddenly—an idea. Maybe you had to be seven feet of scales and muscle to make it work . . . but maybe not.

He leaned forward again into the attendant's face. "The Regents won't like this," he hissed, putting a whole day of frustration into that hiss. "I'm one of theirs." He pointed down the corridor at Big Blue, who obligingly wiggled a claw back.

The attendant blinked, startled out of his smugness. Then he commed a short message. A moment later, the airlock unsealed itself.

Luke sprinted through before anyone could change their mind, amazed all over again that university trustees could have so much clout halfway across the sector. He grinned. Must be those long tails.

Games
by Caren Gussoff

Aveliin doesn't understand golf, so I show her *Caddyshack*. She just stares at Chevy Chase. Then she stares at me laughing at Chevy Chase. I explain country clubs, caddies, gophers, "getting laid."

But Aveliin still just looks at me and shakes her head.

"Well, you are a woman," I say. "Where I come from, not many women like this movie either."

"I'm not exactly a woman," Aveliin reminds me, dribbling the golf ball back and forth with a slap of her tail.

"Yeah," I say. "So says you."

Aveliin paces the living room in ten thumps, pivots, paces again. She looks out the window and squints out into the blurry heat.

There are many things we don't discuss. I don't ask her what it's like to be the first Zill to see the dry season, to watch the landscape squirm and smolder. I don't ask her how it feels to have the future of her species running through her bloodstream. I don't ask her why she alone was chosen to test the antisomatic drug, if it feels like an honor or a punishment.

I don't ask and she doesn't tell me.

Instead, we play games to pass the time.

When our crew first arrived on Zil, we first met only brutal temperatures, blinding light, marching formations of giant roaches, and restless terrain.

It was hard to imagine who had lived there—or how. Low, brown bushes sizzled under the intense heat, while toothy flowers sagged under glassy drops of dried sap. The flatlands cracked like bones, fracturing into more and more elaborate designs.

We took occupation of an empty village, medieval-looking cottages of wattle and dust, communal halls upholstered in mud.

That the biosensors failed to detect ten thousand Zill aestivating below us, deep inside a convoluted network of subterranean caverns, was attributed to human error. I'm sure it cost someone in management their job.

The company isn't lenient over these types of mistakes.

The company. We talk about it in the singular, with the nickname, like it is a person with sovereignty, a single will, familiar to us. And it is, I suppose—she's the mother of all, formed like a star, the merging and collision of countless particles, smaller companies, long forgotten.

History tells us there used to be religion. There used to be militaries, universities, governments. History tells us there used to be history. But personally, I can't imagine anything but the company, mother company testing us, sorting us, chipping us, and sending us to work.

Aveliin turns from the window, then paces again. Back, forth.

Watching her is exhausting. I yawn.

"Why don't you lie down?" she asks me.

"I have to do some work first," I say. "What will you do?"

She keeps moving, doesn't answer.

"You're so wound up," I say, "I'm half afraid you'd kill me in my sleep just for something to do."

"If I wanted to kill you, *Caf*, I would have done it already," she says.

I flinch; I only know a few words of pure Zilll, but I know that one. "I hate that word," I say.

"Sorry." She stops and bares her teeth. Not a smile—a pantomime, an imitation of a smile. "If I wanted to kill you, Thomas, I would have done it already."

"Thank you." As I say this, the scanner indicator lights begin to blink.

Aveliin watches me sit down at the station. Performing cross-bed imaging and grain-size analysis looks like tedious work, but the electron scanners just take time.

Aveliin flings herself down to the floor and spreads flat. It's cooler there. "The heat is insufferable. The side effects," she says, fanning herself with her tail, "are insufferable."

"I can't do anything about the weather," I say. "Being amped up on an antisomatic, well, sorry. I think you're normal."

"You don't know," she says. "You're a *geologist*."

"Ha," I say. "You are such a woman."

Aveliin mutters something else at me in pure Zilll. I don't know this word either, but the inflection makes it sound like *asshole*. She stands up to pace.

"Hey," I say. "Don't call me that either." I bend over the portable to begin data analysis. "And speak Zinglish."

She doesn't answer that. I knew she wouldn't. Instead, she snorts lightly and turns to look back out the window.

What lay beneath the immediate crust clicked up in my brain immediately. The second we unclipped our face shields and I sniffed and grinned. "Smell that?" I asked no one in particular. "Blood and lead and old cars? That's iron, for sure. Nickel, too."

Robin, the senior security officer laughed. She was a beautiful woman, but company security all the way.

"Excellent," she said. "Rocks to get your rocks off."

"Metals," I corrected. "Ferrous metals."

"Anything valuable?" she asked.

"A little," I answered.

These were our first few months on Zil. Robin and her team ran recon. Xenobio chased roaches around. The engineers, maintenance, and com officers played cards, drank, and shot skeet rocks out across the flatlands— this kept the med team busy enough. The navs went with me out on cartography missions and cranked through sediment channel samples. We scanned the landscape and uploaded our reports.

We had no idea that below us the Zill had already begun to stir.

I putt the ball around for awhile, and tee it softly towards Aveliin. She whacks the ball back at me. It hits my shin and I yelp. She forgets how strong her legs and tail are.

"That's not a holo. That's a solid urethane ball," I whine, rubbing my leg. "That hurt."

"Apologies," Aveliin says. She's charmed by my reaction, but comes over and touches my shin with her tail, a gesture of reconciliation. "This game is pointless."

"It's not," I say. "On Earth, it was a pretty important game."

"How so?" she asks. "This film makes it seem comical."

"Powerful people made decisions playing this game," I say. "It began, they say, with kings."

"What kind of decisions?" she asks.

I don't really know the answer, but the portable beeps and saves me. "Time for a stats check," I say. She makes what I know to be an unhappy face, but she pulls out the med chair from its compartment and climbs in. She sits still while I tighten the restraints.

Aveliin closes her eyes for modesty while I take her blood pressure, pulse, and temperature; measure her forced vital oxygen capacity and glucose tolerance; take her heart rate.

I unlock the med safe and siphon off one dose of the antisom into the dermshot. She wiggles against the straps when I lay the dermshot on her thigh, acting like it hurts. As weird as it sounds, it's sexy as hell. "Good job, kiddo," I say afterward. "You're doing fine."

"Thank you," she says, getting up. "Kiddo." She paces back to the window and watches outside. Sometimes, when she watches, it seems as though she is expecting something to happen—the rains, maybe, to erase the weird fidgety landscape and bring back her family and friends. I don't know. We don't discuss it.

I don't ask, and she doesn't answer. I think sometimes I understand. Sometimes I catch myself staring up into the blinding light as if I could see through it, as if it were a night sky. Earth: it's still home. I look up sometimes like I could see the light years back to her. It creeps me out when my chip kicks in and reminds me that even if I could, all I'd see was a planet countless years dead and gone.

Aveliin turns to me and asks, "Are you going to rest now?"

"You're always trying to get me into bed, aren't you?" I tease, but she blinks at the innuendo. "Yeah, maybe," I say. "Why?"

She thumps her tail and faces the window again. "Your sleep," she says, "is interesting to me."

She doesn't say it like it really does hold any interest for her, but many times after meeting the Zill, the crew would awaken to one watching up sleep, sometimes poking us with sticks curiously, then recoiling at how quickly we'd rouse.

"You look more like a teenager waiting to sneak out after her parents go to sleep," I say.

"Your teenagers do that?" she asks, amused. Then she stretches out her big arms towards the window. "Where would I go, anyway?"

I don't have an answer to that. I pull out a dermshot of benzo and lay it on my neck. There's no other way to get a good rest. "I think I will nap for a bit," I tell Aveliin. "Poke me if you need anything."

"Fine," she says, watches the screen silently. The movie is almost over. She reaches out and strokes Bill Murray. "I like him. I like the texture of his face," she says. "It's like drying mud."

"Well," I say, stretching out. "That's something, isn't it?"

Monopoly frustrates Aveliin. She pokes at the holo board with a stubby finger and thumps her tail.

I explain real estate, mortgages, income tax, bankruptcy as best as I understand them.

She shakes her head and asks, "Why am I a hat?"

"It's just a symbol," I say. "I'm a Scottie dog."

She shakes her head. "What do they mean?"

"Nothing," I say. "My people played this for centuries."

"Tell me again why I give you money?" she asks.

"You landed on Baltic Avenue," I answer. "I own a hotel there. You owe me rent."

"Rent," she repeats. She shakes her head again, then studies the board. "Why is Baltic Avenue worth less than, say, the Boardwalk?" she asks.

"It's the game," I say. "It just is."

"But there's a reason." She pokes at the board again. "Is this what they decide over golf?"

"Actually," I say, surprised. "Sure. A boardwalk would be over water. Have a view. Property near a scarce resource is worth more." I think for a minute and continue. "Baltic Avenue has value, but not as much."

She shakes her head.

"OK," I say. "Like Zil. Here. This planet has value. There's land, some natural resources, iron, lead, nickel. But a planet with scarcer resources, or extremely temperate weather, or something like that would be worth more."

"My planet is Baltic Avenue?" she asks.

There was no predicting how the dry season would break, much less the sudden monsoons. One moment, we were surveying an arid steppe; in the next moment, a different violet world. One deafening crack of thunder, a lightning bolt that cracked the sky in half, and then the rains came.

We scrambled for flood gear, and Robin grabbed my arm and pointed to the sky. "What the fuck?" she yelled to me. "Have you ever seen anything like this?"

"Yeah," I yelled back. "In a sim of Thailand."

"This is not Thailand," she answered.

We motioned for the crew to prepare for flood. Torrents like this could easily sweep the village away. The water never had a chance to pool, however. The parched ground was greedy with the deluge, sucking down puddles knee deep.

The crew huddled in my lab. I tried to look at as much as I could to scan all this onto my chip for upload. I held no data on how an alien biome could change instantly from a splintering flatland into caramelized fluvial silt, dented with what looked like colloidal pits. And if I held no data, neither did the company.

"Quicksand?" I asked, no one in particular, but Robin interrupted my thoughts, tugging my arm and pointing lower into the horizon. "What the fuck are those?" she yelled into the din.

Figures. Fifty, maybe. Weird lumbering shadows. Definitely figures. We could almost see them through the storm, tall as humans, but twice as wide. They lurched in a line, looking like contestants in a mad three-legged race, zigzagging around edges of the pits.

Then closer, clearer to the village, we saw huge fists punch through the pits, then more figures pushing themselves up, out, onto the surface. As they rose to their feet, they joined in the race.

"Holy fuck," someone yelled. "Zombies."

Robin dropped my arm and began loading her stunner. Her mouth was moving but I couldn't hear a word. I heard the clicks of the stunners, the crack of the thunder, and my own heartbeat. Nothing else.

Then the first of the figures came close enough for us to see it clearly.

I think Robin yelled, "Halt." I heard someone else yell, "Zombies." Storm, guns, noise, fear. My memories of the moment are both clear and indefinite. I remember one of the figures held up its giant hand, slapped the ground with its tail, and bared its teeth in the grimace I've come to know as a smile.

Aveliin shakes her head and drags and drops the yellow $500 bill onto my bank. She stands up to pace.

"Wait," I say. "I owe you change."

She pivots, thumps back. "You don't owe me anything," she says.

"Don't be upset," I say, yawning. "It's just how you play the game."

"Why don't you lie down?" she asks.

"Again with the lying down," I say. "What is it?"

She looks out the window and twitches the tip of her tail like an irritated cat. "If I could rest," she says. "I would."

"I should work first," I say, and settle down at the electron scanner. It's been crunching a huge amount of data and the housing's hot under my fingers. I adjust the manual eyepiece and look down into the core sample.

No wonder it's running hot. Cobble sized grains, at least -6 on the phi scale, some big as a baby's fist. Silver-white, non-ferrous. I run the atomic weight automatically, then manually. I have to blink a few times to make sure I'm really seeing what I think I am seeing.

Platinum salts. At least five times the native amount ever present on earth at any one time. The single most valuable catalytic element. In the entirety of history.

"Holy shit," I say to Aveliin. "You've got to see this."

"I can't concentrate on rocks," she says. She flings herself down on the floor. "The side effects," she says, "are intolerable."

"Aveliin," I say. "You need to look at this."

She ignores me, rolls back up, and begins her pacing.

I want to force her down, hold her shoulders, make her understand the magnitude of this. "Seriously," I insist. "Come here."

She makes a grunt I recognize as a sigh, and thumps over to the station. "All right," she says. "What is it?"

It takes me a few minutes to adjust the manual eyepiece for Zill vision, but then I bend her over and point out the grains. "That is platinum," I say. "Not very refined, but platinum."

She shakes her head at me. "And?"

"And," I say. "And Baltic Avenue just became the Boardwalk." I begin pacing the lab myself out of pure excitement. "A hundred Boardwalks." I throw my hands up in the air. "Maybe a thousand," I say.

"This is valuable?" she asks. "It doesn't look valuable."

"Oh, yes," I say. I am practically dancing. My future at the company lay before me, paved in the rarest transition metal in the universe. I was suddenly upwardly mobile. "Oh, hell, yes."

Aveliin says something in pure Zilll, a few words I don't understand, and *Caf.*

"Speak Zinglish," I remind her.

"*Caf,*" she repeats, but there is no venom in it. She reaches out with her big arms, looking to me like a giant infant. My instinct is to comfort her. I wrap my arms as best as I can around her; she stiffens at the strange gesture but allows me to hold her. She is softer, more pliable than she looks, like I can squeeze her into shapes, warm living clay. I bury my face into her neck, and it gives, finds a place for me.

"Can you take out your chip?" she asks. "Or turn it off?" She blinks slowly, eyes closed again for modesty.

"No," I say. "It doesn't work like that. But I can delete this footage before upload."

She seems to nod, or rather, I take her head movement as a nod. We roll across the cool floor. We roll into the bedroom. At first she struggles, but then, her body moves with mine, but I can't shake the feeling that the entire time she is staring out the window.

Afterward, I stretch out and fold my hands beneath my head. "I told you," I say. "You are very much a woman."

Aveliin stands again to pace, pausing in front of the holo. She touches the screen and the hat moves three spaces to Chance. "I can 'Get out of Jail Free,'" she says.

"Save that," I say, just before I drift off to sleep. "That's a great card to have."

Aveliin takes to blackjack right away.

After a quick explanation of doubling down, splits, and insurance, she nods her head at me. "It is simple arithmetic," she says. "Probability. Possible combinations." She plays the first three deals like a seasoned casino cheat.

"Card shark," I say.

Aveliin blinks at me. "No, you just have to calculate the favorable value, the number of cards showing, and the total number of cards. . ." she says. "You're not listening."

"Am too," I say.

"You are not," she says.

"I am," I say, with a smile. "You are *just* like a woman."

She ignores that.

"Go on," I say. "I'm watching."

She clicks for a deal, hits, stays. Twenty. The holo dealer has eighteen. She bears her teeth. "I like this game," she says.

"I bet," I say. "Everyone likes to play when they win."

The Zill were friendly and hospitable, as much as anyone could expect anyone to be if they came home and found an alien species occupying their homes. But they were willing to hear us out. They were willing to make a deal.

There was a lot to explain to them: Earth, humans, the third industrial revolution. Exploration, Circadian rhythm. The company. The company's interest in their planet. How the mines would work. Who would benefit.

"Something about them freaks me out," Robin said, sitting down beside me on the ground under the lab canopy. The rest of the crew slipped around us, breaking down the remainder of camp in the torrential rains.

"They're like black bears," I said. "That talk. Or lizards. Black bear lizards that talk."

"Yeah," Robin said, distantly. Then she snapped her attention onto me and said, "Black bear lizards? And you're the scientist."

"I'm a geologist," I muttered. "Company-chipped. And I was joking."

"I mean," Robin said, digging her boot down into some mud. It made a pop sound as she pulled it out. "You said yourself that none of this was valuable. Just interesting."

"A little valuable," I answered. "Besides, it'll be cheap. Just me and one Zill. The rest will be aestivating."

"They should leave a xenobio, at least," she said. "Lucas. Or maybe Hoversten."

"Thanks for the confidence," I said, as Robin made a face. I continued, "The execs are happy. Biz dev is happy. R and D are happy." Usually company talk worked on Robin, but she didn't change her expression. "The drug's simple to synthesize. Simple to administer. Simple to monitor. I can do it. And they can be easily taught to run the mines themselves next season. Look how quickly they learned our language." I waited for her to answer, but she just stared straight ahead. "It took the Xarni fourteen months just to be able to understand basic signs," I reminded her.

She just shrugged.

"I get it," I said. "You're just going to miss me when you lead to Belierian." Robin snorted, but I continued. "You could always tune into my upload stream. Or I could ask if you'd stay on as security detail."

Just then, a group of Zill passed by. Their webbed feet and wide tails made them steady on the mud. They raised their giant hands to us in greeting. I raised mine back. Robin sat still.

After they passed, I touched Robin gently on the shoulder. "You want to be my security detail?"

She snorted harder, stood up, and shook some rain from her coveralls. She watched the group of Zill lumber into the distance. "Talking lizard black bears," she muttered.

"I'll see you next season," I said. "It'll be fine."

Robin looked down at me. "What do you know? You're a *geologist*," she said, and walked off.

Aveliin plays blackjack for hours without stopping. She clicks for a deal, and I can see the cards reflected in her shiny black eyes. I watch her, and she begins clicking through the hands faster and faster.

Keeping up is exhausting. I yawn.

"Is it time for your rest?" she asks.

I wrap my arms around her neck. "You want to rest with me?" I whisper.

She tenses up, the gesture of affection still alien. I hold her tighter.

"Stop," she says, stiffening more, but baring her teeth.

I don't let go.

"Are you trying to kill me?" She shakes off my grip.

I back away, feeling, suddenly, a little mean. "If I wanted to kill you, *Caf*, I would have done it already." I tell her.

"That's not nice," she says.

"Apologies," I say.

She looks at me long and hard. I stare back, but turn away first. My face, now reflected in her eyes, unnerves me. "First, I should give you the antisom and take your stats," I say. I pull the med chair from its compartment and pat the seat.

She makes her grunt-sigh and climbs into the chair.

I pull the restraints a bit tighter than usual and can't help smiling a bit at her discomfort. But as I measure her blood pressure, pulse, temperature and full vitals, I notice she has not closed her eyes. She watches me unlock the med safe and load up the antisom dose.

"Those are large containers," she says. "They're all the antisomatic?"

"Nope," I say. "Only the blue one."

"What's in the others?" she asks. "There are other blue ones."

"General med kit stuff. Benzos. Antibiotics. Emergency stuff," I say. She's silent as I place the dermshot on her thigh, and then pat her knee. "That's it. You're done."

She gets up, thumps back over to the holo game.

"You really are good at this game," I say, apologetically.

"Thank you," she says.

"Really," I say. "Explain it to me again?"

"The secret," she says, "is that you always know what's coming next." She shuts down the game, but stays facing the holo. "If you pay attention to what just happened."

Aveliin isn't half bad at chess.

I explain castling, move orders, forks, what I know of game theory.

"You have to be more aggressive," I say, bumping her pawn with my rook. "With your short term tactics."

"I have a strategy," she says, watching the pawn disappear off the holo board.

"It's important to defend pieces even if they aren't directly threatened," I continue.

"I have a strategy," she repeats.

"Think of the total value of both sides," I say.

"You aren't listening to me again," she says. "You never listen."

"I am trying to help you," I say. "Think about what the company would do."

"What would the company do?" she asks, moving her bishop forward to f5.

"Whatever she needs to," I answer. "That's how you play the game. Know what I mean?"

"Yes," Aveliin says. "I think I do." She flings herself down to the floor and spreads flat. She begins to fan herself with her tail. "The heat is insufferable. The side effects are insufferable."

"I know," I say.

"I can't get accustomed to it," she says. She fans herself a few more times, then looks at me and pats the floor next to her.

I sit down next to her and put my arm around her. This time she allows it, relaxes into me and molds around my body. We just sit there. It's lovely.

But then it changes. When it happens, it happens so quickly. I barely know what's happening.

Aveliin knocks me straight in the abdomen with the full force of her tail. She whacks me halfway across the room. I hit the wall and bounce like a golf ball.

85

My memories of the moment will be both clear and indefinite. I will remember being on all fours, struggling to breathe. I'll remember Aveliin pulling me up into the med chair and pulling the restraints taut. I'll remember Aveliin pulling open the med safe with one tug in her giant hands.

I will gasp, "What are you doing?" as she fills a dermshot.

I'll remember she'll say, "Hello Mr. Gopher, it's me, just a squirrel. Just a squirrel, not a plastic explosive, nothing to be worried about," and I'll know that's a line from *Caddyshack*. I'll ask her, "Did you watch it again?"

"I looked it up," she'll say. "On the portable."

I'll move my lips to ask when, when did she use the portable, I'd never seen her, but I'll already know the answer.

She'll tell me, "That's a terrible movie, male, female, or from any world." Then she will shake her head at me. "I looked up many things," she'll say, as she straddles me, places the dermshot expertly on my neck. She'll whisper into my ear, "This is our Boardwalk." Then, as I struggle under the straps, she'll say, "That Get Out of Jail card is yours. You are going to need it more than we will."

And before I go under, she will dig out the chip from the back of my head, bend it in half and toss it to the floor. I'll see her pull out the entire store of antisom and dermshots; I'll see her bare her teeth in the grimace I've come to know as a smile.

But first, she will watch the holo chess game begin to play itself. Attack, defend, exchange, each match speeding faster and faster each time. She'll watch the games flash together until they blur together into one.

"Checkmate, I believe," she'll say, before heading out the door to the caverns. "This game is over."

The Hangborn
by Fredrick Obermeyer

The cutters attacked at dawn. Lovar was hanging upside down on his line when he heard their buzzing fill the air. He opened his eyes and swung himself right-side-down on his organic, elastic cords. A group of cutters flew towards the lines, their metal buzzsaw blades shining in the early morning sunlight. Out of all the predators on Hangworld, the cutters were by far the most dangerous.

"Cutters!" Lovar said.

The other hangborn in his tribe awoke and raced into action. The young and old hangers swung up onto higher lines, trying to get out of range of the cutters' blades. And while the weakest fled, the rest of the hangers remained on the lower lines to protect the wombline that held their progeny.

However, a few of the older hangborn were on a lower cord and moved more slowly than the others. One of the cutters slashed through the line they were on, and another sliced through the back of an old hanger, bursting out of his chest in a spray of blood. The remaining hangers screamed as the broken line dropped them into the ocean.

"Get the shocklines," Lovar said. "Quickly!"

The hangers climbed across their lines and detached some shocklines from the support beams, gripped the sparking lines by their rubberized ends, and passed them to the others. Shocklines were their only defense against the cutters.

"Hurry!" Lovar said.

When the cutters were in range, the group whipped out their shocklines. Three of the cutters flew into the lines and exploded. But the other cutters zoomed past the weapons. One cutter slashed a line and dropped three more hangborn into the ocean. Another one sliced the right arm cord off one of the defenders. And a third slashed off all the cords holding a hanger up. He fell screaming into the ocean.

Lovar realized that his tribe was too close together, making them easier to pick off.

"Spread out," Lovar said. "Don't bunch together."

The defenders obeyed him and spread themselves out along the lower lines. While they moved, Lovar glanced down. He saw that there were still five cutters left. They flew up towards the wombline. Lovar's chest tightened with fear. They were trying to kill the unborn.

Lovar swung his cords up and chased after them. Unfortunately, the cutters were moving too fast. One of the women hangers above him saw the cutters going for the wombline and she swung her shockline out. She caught one of them but missed the other four, and they cut the wombline on both ends.

The line dropped towards the ocean. Lovar leaped up and caught one end with his right arm cord. Gasping, he swung himself onto a higher line and tied one of the wombline's ends to another line. Another hanger caught the other end and tied it diagonally to a lower line.

Lovar turned and saw another cutter coming right at him. He swung down, just before it nearly cut the top of his skull off. Instead it slashed his lower right cord. He cried out in pain, lost his grip on the line and dropped towards the ocean.

Fear struck his heart like a hammer when he saw the ocean. A few seconds before he crashed into its waves, he flung his cords up and hooked onto one of the lowest lines. He swung around in a wide arc and missed the steaming ocean waves by inches. The cord tightened and jerked him back up.

Once he recovered, he stretched one of his cords to a higher line and began climbing back up towards the reconnected wombline.

Up at a higher vantage, he saw the hangers destroy two more cutters. As if sensing defeat, the last two cutters headed straight for the wombline.

"Stop them!" Lovar said.

The tribe whipped their shocklines at the cutters, but the blades dodged them and slashed through the wombline again. It dropped into the ocean and dissolved instantly in its waters.

Lovar watched in horror as their progeny was lost. A couple of the hangborn chased after the cutters and got them with their shocklines. But it was a Pyrrhic victory.

Lovar howled, giving vent to his rage and despair. He couldn't understand why the cutters had turned so savage. Usually they went after the hangborn and ignored the womblines and the younger ones. And usually they only attacked once or twice a season. But ever since they had appeared ten seasons earlier, they were coming more and more often, going higher up the lines, inflicting more casualties.

Who or what was causing them to become more ferocious? Lovar thought.

Along with the others in the tribe, he wept for those who were lost. But he couldn't give in to grief. They had to do something.

An hour after the cutter attack, Lovar called a meeting on one of the higher lines. Everyone looked angry and scared and confused as they arrived. Lovar felt the same way.

"What are we going to do now?" Kesarra said. She was Lovar's mate and second in command in the tribe. Normally, she was cool under pressure, but today she looked on the verge of collapse.

"Where can we go?" another said.

"How can we stop them?" a third said.

"What can we do?" a fourth said.

"Quiet!" Lovar said. He couldn't talk with everybody else speaking at once.

Everyone quieted down.

"We will head east towards the rising sun and climb the highest lines," Lovar said. "Once there, we will build a new wombline and watch over it until the first snows come."

"But what if the cutters follow us?" an older hanger said. "We lose more people each season. And we can't defend ourselves against so many."

"We will stay and fight," Lovar said, trying to inspire a confidence he didn't feel. "And we will prevail."

"What if a hundred come the next time?" another hanger said. "Or a thousand?"

"Then we will fight to the last of us."

His people looked uninspired. Frankly, he couldn't blame them. The odds seemed hopeless. Yet, there had to be something they could do.

He glanced towards the sun, recalling where the cutters had come from. He felt something beyond his anger. It was curiosity.

There had to be someplace on Hangworld where the cutters came from. They had to have some kind of nest or home where they dwelled. Someplace where they slept or stopped, someplace where they were vulnerable. If they could find that place, then maybe the hangborn could destroy them. Perhaps the answer lay in the east. Perhaps he should go there. But Lovar didn't want to leave his tribe when they needed him the most. Maybe once they settled somewhere, he could send Kesarra or go himself.

He returned his attention to the tribe.

"Maybe we can sacrifice one of the elders," a younger hanger said. "Perhaps that will tame the cutters' wrath."

The elders looked less than enthused about the idea. Neither was Lovar, considering how many years he had already lived.

"Maybe you should sacrifice yourself, little one," an older hanger said.

"At least I can still fight," he said, looking indignant.

"If by fight you mean climbing to higher lines and cowering. You couldn't even stop one of them—"

"Are you saying I'm a coward?"

"Yes, I am."

"I'll show you how much of a coward I am!"

The younger one swung down and started clawing the older one. But before they could fight, Lovar said, "Enough! Stop!"

The pair backed down.

"It does no good for us to fight amongst ourselves," Lovar said. "We must stick together if we want to survive." He glanced towards the sun. "I want everyone ready to leave in an hour. The healers will see to the injured, and I want shocklines passed out to everybody, including the elderly. We will head west, stay on the higher lines, and sleep in shifts. Nobody stays asleep for more than three hours. With any luck, we will be able to anticipate their next attack. Now let's move."

The tribe members headed off to do their jobs, and Lovar held his breath, hoping that the cutters would give them a brief reprieve.

By midmorning everybody's wounds had been bound and they were heading west, away from the cutters. At first the tribe stayed on the higher lines, where it was safer. Unfortunately, there weren't as many foodlines and waterlines in the higher regions and they had to go to the lower regions to eat and drink. Lovar made sure that each tribe member kept an eye out for cutters, while they ate and drank quickly.

But by nightfall they still hadn't seen any more cutters. However, Lovar didn't want to let his guard down, so he continued to keep watch.

Sometime during the night Lovar saw lights in the distance. At first he thought that it was just his sleep-fogged imagination and he paid it no mind.

He closed his eyes and started to drift off when he saw the lights again. He blinked and looked out at the distance.

The lights were circling in some kind of pattern, as if looking for something. By now the others in the tribe had seen the lights and were looking at them as well, chattering nervously amongst themselves.

Kesarra swung down beside Lovar. "What is it? Cutters?"

"I don't think so. Cutters usually don't come out this late, and they don't have lights."

"What should we do?"

Lovar swallowed, curiosity and a desire to keep his tribe safe battling within him. He'd already had one nasty surprise today and he wasn't in the mood for another.

"I'm going to see what's out there," Lovar said.

"No, wait." Kesarra gripped one of his cords. "Let me go instead."

"No, you have to watch out for the tribe."

"Then send someone else."

He looked around the tribe in the moonlight. They all seemed frightened of the lights. He didn't think anybody else wanted to go.

"I'm going," Lovar said. "You head back towards the last foodline with the tribe and keep watch. If I don't return by sunrise, then head north."

"We won't leave you behind," Kesarra said.

"I'm not asking you. I'm telling you. Don't put the tribe in danger." Lovar pushed free from her cords. "I'll be back as soon as I can."

"Lovar, wait. . ."

He ignored her plea and swung forward along the lines. Every so often he glanced behind him to make sure that Kesarra wasn't following him. But he didn't see her. He knew that she cared about him, but he didn't want her to risk their lives for him. Hopefully, whatever the lights were, they would be friendly.

Just in case there was trouble, though, he kept his shockline close.

As he approached the lights, he heard a faint sound below him. He stopped and looked down, wondering what it was. He crept down the lines and stopped. Something swung down from behind him. Lovar cried out in fear and raised his shockline.

"Don't!" a voice said.

It was Kesarra.

Lovar lowered his shockline. "What are you doing here? I told you to stay with the tribe. . ."

"I couldn't leave you out here without knowing what would happen," Kesarra said. "Besides, I left Macallen in charge."

"Macallen?! He'll lead the tribe back down towards the ocean and—"

"No, he won't. He's a good leader and besides—"

A loud noise filled the air and drowned out her speech. Lovar's ears began to ache from the noise and he covered them. The lights approached them. He turned and saw Kesarra's lips move, but he couldn't understand what she was saying. So he grabbed her arm and gestured for her to retreat. She nodded and followed him away from the lights.

They swung across the lines, trying to outrun the lights. But whatever was chasing them moved much faster. They had only swung across a couple of lines before the lights enveloped them. Lovar looked up and the brightness blinded him. He covered his eyes until they adjusted.

An enormous metal beast hovered above them. Flames shot out the back end and it made the most terrible noise in the world. Four spider-like creatures—like cutters but without the sharp blades—emerged from its underbelly and flew towards them.

"Go!" Lovar said.

Kesarra couldn't hear him. One of the creatures swooped down, grabbed her with its pinchers, and pulled her off the line. The second creature came at him. Lovar swung his shockline at it, but it dodged the blow and tore the weapon from his cord, grabbed him and jerked upwards into the light. The sound grew so loud and terrible that he screamed. But he couldn't hear his own voice.

Eventually the sound faded as they were brought inside the beast. They came out of the light into a cold, dark place and were dropped on something hard and firm. He felt a sharp pain in the side of his neck and grew sleepy. He tried to keep his eyes open, but whatever venom they had stung him with was too strong.

He passed out.

Lovar awoke in a cold room. Blue light bathed him. He glanced down and screamed. He was lying in the beast's metal belly, on solid ground. It felt hard and unnatural. Alien. He had never lain on something before. He had always hung. Lovar glanced up at some wires. Instinct took over, and he hooked onto one of the lines and hung there.

The sensation of hanging made him feel a little better. Kesarra was lying on the belly. She awoke and screamed.

"Up here!" Lovar said.

He gestured to one of the lines. She pulled herself up, shaking.

"Where are we? What happened?"

"I don't know. I remember the beast eating us, but after that I can't—"

A noise interrupted him. Below them the belly's entrance dilated and someone came in. Lovar tensed, ready to attack. The being looked similar to a hanger, but it had four strange trunks emerging from where its cords should have been. It had the same head, though. It didn't hang. Instead it moved on its trunks along the floor, like linespiders.

It looked beautiful and hideous.

The being looked up and said, "I'm sorry if I frightened you, but I didn't know how else to greet you."

It spoke their language. How?

"Who are you?" Lovar said.

"I'm sorry. My name is Dr. Kathleen Micharden. I'm a female human being from a planet called Earth. And you are?"

"Lovar. This is Kesarra."

"It's nice to meet you. You can call me Kathleen."

"What are you, Kathleen?"

"I'm like you. I'm a human."

"And yet you don't hang."

"I wasn't genetically engineered to hang like you."

"Genetically engineered?" Lovar's brow wrinkled with confusion. "What does that mean?"

"I'm sorry. I'm going too fast. Would it help if I hung with you?"

"How?"

Kathleen fired a cord from her belt and shot up towards the ceiling. Lovar gasped with fear as she hung a few feet from them.

"You may not believe it, but you are descended from us," Kathleen said. "From Earth people. Five hundred years ago we made your ancestors adapt to this world. We built the womblines to let you breed and the shocklines to protect you. We found the other lines intact and adapted them to feed you and allow you to eat the native lifeforms."

"Why?"

"Earth was polluted and overpopulated to the breaking point. We needed a new home and we found this world had been abandoned. It had many vital mineral ores and elements under the ocean, but it would take years to remove the poles and terraform—I mean, to change the planet so that people like me could live there. So we made your ancestors hangers while we tried to change the world."

"Did you make the cutters too?" Kesarra said, looking angry.

"Yes and no."

"What do you mean yes and no? Either you did, or you didn't."

"The cutters were originally designed to cut down some poles and allow us to build land on this world, solid ground like the metal you were laying on a moment ago. But after a while things fell apart. The planet's terraforming wouldn't take. The land kept sinking and we lost thousands to the sea. Finally, we gave up and abandoned the hangborn and this world. I suppose you must have forgotten that you were descended from us."

"You abandoned our ancestors?" Lovar said, tightening his grip on the line. "Why?"

"Because they had adapted to living here and we didn't need them. We thought you'd just die out, but we were wrong. You stayed and you thrived."

"You still didn't answer my question about the cutters."

Kathleen frowned. "A few years ago a man named Aaron Palberson rediscovered this world and you with it. He is a criminal, a con man, the type that made his living betting on animal fights back home. He found you and decided he could make a living off you."

"How?"

"By betting on you."

"What?" Lovar said.

"He stages fights using the cutters against you and bets on how many of you they'll kill. People come from all over to bet on the outcomes."

"That's why he's killing us?" Kesarra said, her voice shaking. "But how can he? We're supposed to be humans."

"He doesn't see you that way," Kathleen said. "He considers you barely above animals. It doesn't bother him."

"And what about you?"

"I consider you humans." Kathleen sighed. "I came here with a group of scientists to study how you've adapted to this world. Needless to say, when I found out what Palberson was doing, I was aghast. I pleaded with him to stop, but he wouldn't listen. I even tried calling in the authorities, but he paid them off. Anybody who interferes is killed."

"Where is he?"

"On an island north of here. He's made a gaming platform on one of the higher poles." Kathleen put up her hand. "But you can't stop him. He has armed guards and more cutters than you can fight."

"I will find a way."

"You'll need my help."

"And what can you do?"

Kathleen hesitated. But after a minute of silence, she gestured towards the entrance. "I built a bomb."

"A what?"

"An explosive device. Something that will blow them up. Like when the cutters are destroyed."

"Why didn't you use it against him?"

Kathleen shook her head. "I didn't want to get my hands dirty. I mean, I'm not a terrorist or a killer. I tried everything I could think of to stop him, but he wouldn't listen. When my fellow scientists tried to sabotage his platform, he had them killed." Kathleen lowered her head. "I wanted to avenge their deaths, but didn't have the guts to plant the bomb myself." She sighed. "That's why I went looking for you."

"So we could get our hands dirty for you, as you say," Kesarra said.

"Yes."

Lovar felt indignant. *How dare she sacrifice us to do this job?*

"And you expect us to go in and place this bomb?" Lovar said. "Risk our lives? Why should we? He's your kind. You deal with him."

"It's the only way you can survive. His games are beyond mere sport. The Interplanetary Council is considering a second attempt at terraforming this planet and they're worried you might end up sabotaging the project. They're considering using Palberson to exterminate you."

"They can't," Kesarra said.

"Even if their plan doesn't come to fruition, that still leaves Palberson. And the only way for you to survive is to kill him."

"We can head north, away from him," Kesarra said.

"He'll track you down eventually. He won't stop."

Lovar bit his lip. He couldn't see running. Now that he knew the source of the cutters, he had to stop them. Even if it meant risking his life.

"Can you get me close enough to plant the bomb on the platform?" Lovar said.

"I can try," Kathleen said. "It won't be easy, though."

95

"No," Kesarra said. "Let me do it."

"I'm not letting you risk your life," Lovar said.

"You're not going alone."

"She's right," Kathleen said. "The odds will be better if you work together."

Lovar frowned. He didn't want his mate going with him. Yet he could see in her eyes that she wouldn't let him go alone. And Kathleen had a point, much as he hated to admit it.

"All right then. Will you help us?"

"I'll take you there and pick you up. But the rest is up to you." She lowered herself back to the ground. "Come on, I'll show you how to detonate the bomb and where to put it."

Lovar and Kesarra swung along the ropes and followed her out of the belly.

Kathleen explained her plan and the workings of the bomb. It was placed in a small backpack that Lovar strapped onto himself.

"You can place the bomb on any one of the four support beams on the platform and rig it to blow," Kathleen said. "Once one of the beams is destroyed, the rest of the platform would collapse under its weight and fall into the ocean."

Lovar felt nervous as he strapped the bomb to his cords. Kathleen went forward to the place she called the bridge, where she said that she controlled the beast. It would take about an hour to reach Palberson's platforms. She could only get fifty meters before she set off what she called motion sensors. Their only advantage was the cover of darkness and, hopefully, most of Palberson's people would be asleep.

Lovar and Kesarra went down to the airlock. Kesarra would provide a diversion while Lovar went for one of the beams. His heart raced as they approached the platform. Glancing over at Kesarra, his love surged for her. He didn't know if either of them would be coming back, but he had to believe that they would.

Lovar leaned over and gripped her cords in his. He wanted to say something to her, that he loved her. But the look in her eyes said more than he ever could. It said they would succeed and they would make it.

"We're near the platform," Kathleen said. "Get ready."

They climbed to the edge of the airlock. Every muscle in Lovar's body tensed with fear. This was it.

The airlock hissed open and they slid out, dropping onto the line below. Lovar looked around. Several searchlights swung back and forth across the night sky. Lovar could barely see a few feet in front of him. Kathleen would wait for them.

Lovar swung down to one of the lower lines while Kesarra took the upper lines and swung on ahead. He gave her a few seconds before he followed. His heart raced as they closed in on the platform. They only had one chance. As soon as he set the bomb, they would have to hurry back.

Kesarra was a few hundred feet ahead of him when a loud whine filled the air. They had activated the motion sensors. The searchlights focused on Kesarra and illuminated her swinging form. A loud buzzing filled the air.

The cutters were coming.

Lovar hung on his line and waited. So far the lights were focused solely on her. In the distance, he could hear shouting from people on the platform, but he couldn't understand what they were saying. More lights came on and he saw several cutters flying towards her. Kesarra swung onto one of the higher lines and headed east, away from the platform, drawing the machines away.

When they were far enough away from him, Lovar swung towards the nearest platform beam and dodged the searchlights. Reaching one of the beams, a loud buzz pierced the air. He turned and saw the cutters heading towards him.

Lovar swung onto a higher line and avoided them. But a cutter came from behind and severed one of his cords. Howling in pain, he dropped towards the ocean. Before hitting bottom, he threw out one of his cords and caught the line. He jerked to a stop and pain shot through the remaining cords. The heaviness of the bomb pulled him down.

Gasping, Lovar swung himself back towards a lower line and grasped it. As he climbed back towards the beam, he saw the cutters closing in for another attack. He climbed forward, dove onto the beam, and lashed some of his cords to it. Lovar's cords shook as he took the bomb off his back and slapped its sticky side onto the beam. Before he could yank out the arming device, a cutter zoomed towards his head.

Lovar jumped back onto another line and ducked, barely escaping decapitation. Another cutter slashed the line he was hanging on. When he started to drop, he jumped onto another line and started back towards the bomb to arm it. Above him he saw soldiers descending on ropes. They pointed strange sticks at him. One of the soldiers fired the stick. Lovar yelped as pain seared his arm. Blood trickled from the wound. *Those firesticks are deadly.*

Lovar climbed towards the bomb. As he reached it, the cutters swooped down. He jerked himself up close to the line to make himself less of a target, but he wasn't fast enough. A cutter slashed his abdomen. He cried out in agony and dangled, unable to hang on. Then he lost his grip, falling a short distance, but Kesarra dove in and grabbed him.

"Hold on," she said.

She pulled him away from the beam and carried him to a higher line that he could wrap his cords around.

"The bomb. . ." Lovar said.

"You're hurt. We have to get out of here."

Lovar shook his head.

"The . . . bomb," Lovar choked out. "I . . . I didn't arm it."

"I'll get it," Kesarra said.

"Don't. . ."

He tried to move, but even the slightest shift of his body sent fire shooting through his belly. With every breath, the pain in his chest burned. He felt weak and thirsty.

Kesarra swung across the lines to the beam. As she reached down to yank out the arming device, Lovar saw the men climbing down on ropes, aiming their firesticks at her. Red dots crept from their sticks.

"Look out!" Lovar said.

But she seemed so intent on yanking out the arming device that she didn't hear it.

As she turned to leave, two of the red dots stopped on her forehead. Kesarra faced him. Lovar screamed in horror as her head exploded. Her body slipped off the beam and plunged into the ocean.

Lovar trembled with rage. He wanted to kill them all, to rip them limb from limb. He crept towards them, knowing he would die. But as he came near, an orange light was blinking on the bomb.

It would explode any minute.

Desperate, Lovar retreated from the platform. His injury slowed him down and he could only drop from line to line.

A searchlight shone on him. Feeling trapped, he dropped onto a lower line, which sent agony shooting through his wounded abdomen. The cutters followed, but he didn't look back. He ignored the pain and forced himself to go faster.

Seconds later, an enormous boom sounded behind him. He glanced back as the beam exploded in a big fireball. Flames shot up and engulfed several dangling men along the platform side. They plummeted, screaming and burning, into the ocean. A loud shriek of tortured metal ripped through the air and hurt Lovar's ears.

Unable to bear its own weight any longer, the platform tipped forward and broke free from its remaining beams. It splashed down into the ocean.

Lovar wanted to stay and watch it sink, but a few cutters still lingered in the sky.

He turned and limped back, feeling despair. They had won, but he had lost Kesarra.

Just before he passed out, Kathleen flew in with her metal beast and picked him up.

Lovar spent the next few days recuperating in the part of her beast known as the medical bay. Her technology was amazing. In three days she had healed all his wounds. But all of her technology could not heal his anguish of losing Kesarra. He lay staring at the ceiling, wishing he had never brought her along. Though if he hadn't, he couldn't have defeated the cutters.

"I'll return you to your people," Kathleen said.

Three days later, Kathleen found his tribe and dropped him off. Lovar wanted to thank her, yet a part of him blamed her for Kesarra's death.

In the end, he just said, "Goodbye," and left her.

He swung back up to his tribe. People gathered around him, asking questions about Kesarra's fate, and wondering why the beast had let him go free.

"We destroyed the cutters and their nest," Lovar said and swallowed the lump in his throat. "But they killed Kesarra." Tears spilled down his cheeks. "She sacrificed herself so that we might live in peace."

Many in the tribe wept. Lovar himself couldn't hold his tears back. Kesarra had been his love. Were she still alive, he would celebrate the cutters' destruction. But he didn't feel like celebrating.

"What will we do now?" one of the younger ones asked.

He couldn't answer. Earlier that day Kathleen said that more men from Earth might come again someday. They would bring more cutters with them. The hangborn had to be ready.

"We will rebuild our lost wombline and continue as we always have," Lovar said.

He swung up onto the new wombline and began helping the others rebuild it.

One Awake In All The World
by Robert T. Jeschonek

P ass Candle could not see the creatures, except as winking blips of light on the flash-brain screen mounted in the flesh of his left arm. He didn't need to look at the screen, however, to know that the creatures were all around him and his partner, Nona Stiletto.

He could feel their presence. Could feel their eyes upon him, staring from the shadows of the darkened and fog-shrouded city.

He stiffened his right arm as he swept it from side to side, covering an arc of the gray fog with the snout of the warflower dark energy gun peeping from under the skin behind his wrist. He followed the arc with the single beam from his headlight—the round, white disk mounted like a third eye in the middle of his forehead.

Candle narrowed his dark brown eyes and stared into the headlight's beam, but he still saw nothing moving toward him in the fog. Maybe, his feelings were the product of his imagination, and the creatures in the shadows would turn out to be benevolent toward cybernetically enhanced humans like himself and Nona.

But he doubted it.

Stiletto said nothing to suggest she felt the same way, but the posture of her slender frame as she walked alongside him was as stiff and guarded as his. Her head ticked from side to side, flicking her golden ponytail to and fro in the darkness.

The retractable sleeves of her slick black form-fitting flowsuit were all the way up, like Candle's, leaving her weapon-and-instrument-studded arms free for action. She aimed her warflower directly ahead, and Candle knew from experience that she was ready to whip it around in a heartbeat and use it.

"The humanoid's twenty meters ahead," said Candle, watching the readings on his flash-brain screen. "Distress signal's strong, and life signs're steady. She's surrounded by non-humanoid life-forms, like we are."

Just then, Candle smelled an odor like strong vinegar and heard a sound like claws clacking on the pavement to his left. He and Stiletto swung in that direction simultaneously, lighting it up with the beams of their headlights. Nothing.

"Playing hard to get." Candle nervously combed the fingers of his right hand through his wavy salt-and-pepper hair.

"Let's hope they stay that way," said Stiletto.

Candle started forward again, following the female humanoid's life signs. "Seventeen meters to go," he said. "Easy-peasy."

The sound of breaking glass echoed in the distance. Claws or something like them clacked not far away.

"Guess again," said Stiletto, sweeping her headlight toward the clacking, then forward again.

Candle thought Stiletto had a point. In the darkness and fog, it felt like they'd walked several kilometers rather than the half kilometer they'd actually traveled from their spacecraft, the *Sun Ra*, which was parked at the edge of the city.

Though Candle wasn't the jumpy type, he was having his doubts about what a good idea it had been to walk away from the *Sun Ra* at all . . . or land on this planet in the first place. Trouble was, he just hated ignoring a distress signal like the one that'd brought him here; some of his best jobs had come via distress signals.

He and Stiletto were first-class spacefaring exterminators, specializing in extra-nasty pests known as Squatters. Squatters ran people like puppets, remote-controlling them from somewhere beyond the Milky Way galaxy. Squatters reached out with their ultra-powerful minds and bonded people to them with overwhelming love and pleasure. Then, the Squatters sent these zombies, known as Wipeouts, on horrifically barbaric killing sprees.

Contractors like Candle could make a living hunting the bastards full-time. Wipeout hunting was pretty damned rewarding for a top pro like Candle . . . especially when he had a former Wipeout like Nona Stiletto for a partner.

Sure, Nona was still messed up from years of being possessed by the aliens. She had committed more violent crimes than she could remember, and she was marked forever by scars on the inside and outside.

But she knew everything about Wipeouts, and the Squatters had left her mean and strong. Just the fact that she had survived being separated from a Squatter showed what kind of a hardass she was. Candle had never heard of another Wipeout walking away from that ordeal alive.

And he couldn't think of anyone he'd rather have by his side today.

"Fourteen meters," he said, squinting into the ten-meter-deep cone of visibility that was the best his headlight could cut through the fog.

Candle and Stiletto pressed to within twelve meters of their target, then eleven. Finally, their headlights picked out a form in the gray soup.

At last, they got a look at the being they'd been seeking through the alien city . . . a being who, as far as they could tell, was the only remaining native humanoid on the planet.

In size and build, she resembled a human child, five or six years old . . . a little girl with glittering purple skin, multi-faceted red insect eyes, and not a hair on her head.

Stiletto lowered her arm so the beam of her headlight wasn't flaring in the little girl's face.

Candle told the girl his name. Stiletto did the same; like Candle, she let her flash-brain convert her speech into audio the child could understand. "Call me Nona. What's your name?"

"Luma," said the little girl. She wore a simple white shift and sandals. As she spoke, she hugged a ragged doll tightly against her chest.

On one wrist, Luma wore a gold bracelet set with a blinking amber crystal. A glance at the flash-brain screen confirmed Stiletto's suspicion that the bracelet was the source of the distress signal transmissions.

"Cool name," said Candle. "Nice to meet you, Luma."

Luma cocked her head to one side and narrowed her faceted eyes.

"We want to help you," said Stiletto. "Can you tell us why you're all alone here?"

Luma dropped her chin against the head of her doll and twisted slowly from side to side. As Stiletto watched, the little girl's skin changed color, shifting from dark purple to deep blue . . . signaling a mood change?

"I'm lost," Luma said softly. "I can't find my family. I woke up and went outside, and now I can't find them."

"Do you know where there're more people like you?" said Candle. "People who look like you?"

Luma nodded. "Sagrans."

"You know where they are?" said Stiletto.

Luma shook her head. "There's no one around except the Skilla." As she said it, her voice dropped to a near whisper, and her skin shifted to deep purple again.

"The Skilla aren't people like you, are they?" said Stiletto.

"No," said Luma, shivering. "They're scary. Everyone says the Skilla are holy, but I think they're scary, too. I think they're going to get me."

Candle scooped the little girl up into his arms.

"Don't worry, Luma," he said, patting her back. "You're not alone anymore. We'll keep you safe."

"You will?"

"Yeah. That's why we came here. To help you."

"Will you find my family, too?" Luma's skin changed from purple back to deep blue.

"We'll do our best." Candle smiled and bounced her affectionately in his arms. "I promise."

Stiletto's heart beat faster, but not because of any impending danger. It was the sight of Candle with Luma, the way he held her and reassured her.

Stiletto wished he'd do that for her, too. She wished he'd love her the way that she loved him.

She hadn't always felt this way. She'd been working with Candle since he'd freed her from the Squatter three years ago, and she'd only been sure she wanted him within the last six months.

She really didn't know if he felt the same way, though, and frankly, she hadn't been going out of her way to find out. The hardass routine that was so important to her job and just getting through the day was hard to push aside . . . plus which, her head was still a wreck from her time as a Wipeout. The Squatter was gone, but it had left behind a boatload of poison. Sometimes, Stiletto still felt echoes of the bastard swimming around in there, and she wondered if he was regenerating somehow.

That was what worried her the most and kept her from reaching out to Candle. What if she was still a danger to him, a sleeper agent with secret orders implanted at a deep level her deprogramming had missed?

Candle put Luma down but held on to her tiny, green hand as he and Stiletto talked.

"Any ideas?" he said in a half-whisper.

Stiletto stared at the blinking lights on the flash-brain screen. "I've detected low-level mechanical vibrations."

"Where abouts?" said Candle.

"Center of the city. Four kilometers that way." Stiletto aimed her headlight into the murk.

"Where there's working machinery, there might be people," said Candle. "Shielded from sensors, maybe."

"There're a lot of non-humanoids between here and there."

Candle nodded. "And we can't take the *Sun Ra* in," he said, "because there's nowhere to land. Not even a flat rooftop." He sighed. "We'll have to keep going on foot."

Candle heard a whooping cry like hysterical laughter in the distance. Luma's hand fluttered, and he tightened his grip on it.

"Up for a hike?" he said to Stiletto.

She nodded. "I'm ready."

"How about you?" Candle gave Luma's hand a squeeze.

"Ready," said Luma.

"Then let's get going," said Candle.

Though Stiletto wasn't easily freaked, she felt the hairs on the back of her neck stand up way too often as she, Candle, and Luma trudged through the city.

She was being stalked. By something she couldn't see.

But she could hear it. The Skilla raised a constant clamor through the city, their distant whoops and yowls accompanied by the sounds of smashing and thumping and shattering. Close by, their claws clacked along the pavement, moving when Stiletto, Candle, and Luma moved . . . stopping when they stopped. Always, when the creatures were near, Stiletto smelled their heavy, vinegar scent in the humid air.

And the number of them that were close-by was growing. Flash-brain scans of the surrounding area revealed that more Skilla were clustering near Stiletto, Candle, and Luma with each passing moment.

"We're drawing a crowd," Stiletto said to Candle, keeping her voice to a whisper for Luma's sake. "Maybe a warning shot'll drive them off."

"Don't provoke them," said Candle. "Not yet. We're so outnumbered, let's put off a fight as long as we can." With that, he turned his attention to Luma. "So," he said, shifting his voice to a less serious tone. "What's your friend's name?"

Luma looked up at him, a puzzled expression on her glittering, deep blue face. She looked down at her doll then, and understood. "Her name is Gala," she said.

Robert T. Jeschonek

"How long've you and Gala been together?" said Candle.

Luma raised the doll to her ear. "Gala says we've been together since I was a little girl."

Candle smiled. "Cool." He still held on to Luma with his left hand and continually scanned his warflower back and forth with his right. "And how did the two of you meet?"

"Mommy and Daddy gave her to me," said Luma.

"The last time you saw your mommy and daddy, what were they doing?" said Candle.

"They were sleeping," said Luma.

"For a long time?" said Stiletto.

"I think so," said Luma. "I woke up and went for a walk. I wanted to go home to get my dreambook, but then I couldn't find home."

"So your family was somewhere other than home," said Candle. "What did this place look like?"

"Big," said Luma. "And dark." She raised the doll to her ear and listened for a moment. "Gala says Mommy and Daddy will be mad at me."

"Why is that?" said Stiletto.

"I wasn't supposed to open the door," said Luma. "I wasn't supposed to go outside."

"Because of the Skilla?" said Candle.

"Uh-huh," said Luma. "They're holy, but they can hurt you." Again, she listened to the doll. "Gala says they're going to hurt all of us, and it'll be my fault because I opened the door."

Just then, something heavy and hard hit the ground near Stiletto. Everyone stopped in their tracks. Luma gasped and threw herself against Candle.

Spinning, Stiletto threw light in the direction of the noise. A block of stone, big as a human head, lay in the street barely three meters away.

Suddenly, Stiletto heard a clatter of approaching claws and caught the smell of vinegar in the air. A quick glance at her flash-brain screen confirmed the evidence of her ears, and she whirled around.

Two blips had disengaged from the unseen crowd of Skilla and were charging directly at Candle and Luma.

Without a word, Stiletto fired her warflower, shooting a crackling bolt of energy into the fog. Immediately, she heard a wailing screech, erupting loud and close enough to hurt her ears. Through a tunnel burned in the fog by the warflower's beam, she glimpsed shining silver eyes like a pair of coins suspended in midair.

106

Stiletto lashed the warflower around, seeking the second oncoming Skilla. She was rewarded with another raging screech. Then, with a flurry of clattering claws, the creatures hurtled away, their cries receding in the distance.

"So much for putting off a fight," said Candle.

"These creatures're pretty smart," said Stiletto. "They staged a diversion by throwing that stone, then came at us from the other direction."

Luma tugged on Candle's uniform then, and he and Stiletto looked down. The little girl's face was pinched in an expression of pure anguish. Her glittering skin was so fiery red that it looked like it would be hot to the touch.

"Gala says you lied!" Inky, black tears streamed down her face. "She says the Skilla *are* going to get us!"

"Tell Gala it's okay to be scared," said Candle, "but things can turn out fine no matter how scary they seem."

Luma shuddered with sobs. "Gala doesn't believe you!"

Stiletto searched her mind for a plan to calm the child, then crouched down beside her. "That's because Gala hasn't heard the story of the girl with the invisible friend," said Stiletto. "Have you?"

Still sobbing, Luma shook her head. The inky tears rolled off her jaw and fell onto her white shift, staining it with spatters of black.

Stiletto got to her feet and scooped up the child in one smooth motion. "Once upon a time," she said, "there was a lonely little girl. She didn't have any friends, because her parents kept moving from planet to planet all the time."

Luma's tears stopped flowing. "No friends at all?" she said, her skin shifting from bright red to maroon.

"None," said Stiletto. "Then, one day, she heard a voice. It seemed to be coming from thin air. 'I'll be your friend,' said the voice."

Luma's face relaxed from a frown to an expression of wide-eyed interest. Her skin went from maroon to violet.

"The girl couldn't see who was talking," said Stiletto. "She was scared, but she was so lonely that she said, 'Sure, you can be my friend.'

"So from that day on, the girl had an invisible friend. There was just one problem."

"What?" said Luma. "What problem?"

"The invisible friend was *mean*," said Stiletto, "but the girl didn't find out right away."

Robert T. Jeschonek

"When *did* she find out?" said Luma.

Stiletto raised an eyebrow. "To be continued," she said. "If you're good, I'll tell you the rest of the story later."

Candle thought it was a good thing that Luma became obsessed with pestering Stiletto to continue her story. The Skilla were growing bolder, and he was glad the little girl's mind was on something else.

Again and again, the creatures raced close and bolted away. They dropped stones and bones and shingles from above, littering the route with debris.

And their numbers, according to the flash-brain, continued to grow. Candle wondered how many more of the creatures would join the pack over the kilometer and a half that he, Stiletto, and Luma had yet to walk. He wondered what other surprises the Skilla would spring.

"All right," Stiletto said after a while, finally giving in to Luma's repeated requests to know what happened next. "I'll tell you a little more."

Luma's skin was pale green, which Candle knew by now meant the child felt at ease. "Tell me!" she said.

Before Stiletto could get out a word, the rocks started flying.

Candle felt something strike his arm with a stinging impact. As he whipped around, he felt another solid object collide with his kneecap. A shower of rocks followed, hurtling straight toward him from out of the fog.

Candle opened fire with the warflower, punching the searing beam through the murk. "Get down!"

Behind him, he heard the whine of Stiletto's warflower firing at the same time as his, lashing out at the other side of the street.

Another volley of rocks leaped out of the fog from a different spot. Candle spun and fired there, too, then combed the beam along the street to pick off any additional ambushers lying in wait.

The bombardment ended, giving way to a deafening chorus of shrieks and screams from all directions.

"Everybody all right?" said Candle.

Even as he said it, he could see the answer to his question. Luma was sprawled on the pavement, eyes closed. Her skin was white as a bedsheet except for a blazing red welt above her left eye.

* * *

"How is she?" said Candle, standing guard while Stiletto scanned Luma's head with her fingertip sensor pads.

"Lots of swelling in there," said Stiletto. "She might have a concussion."

"Can we treat her?"

Stiletto removed the first-aid kit from a hip pocket of her black flowsuit. "Just the surface wound," she said, yanking a tubular spray applicator from the kit. "The deep swelling's another matter." Stiletto ran the tip of the applicator over the welt on Luma's forehead, administering a spray of antiseptic, anesthetic, and anti-inflammatory agents. "Her body's different from anything I've worked on before. Trying to treat the internal injury could do more harm than good."

"Should we keep her awake in case there's a concussion?" said Candle.

"Damned if I know. If she was human, I'd say definitely."

"Let's risk it, then," said Candle. "*If* we can wake her up."

"Roger that," said Stiletto, brushing a strand of blond hair out of her face.

The Skilla continued to howl and scream-laugh as Candle bent down by Luma's right ear. "Luma," he said. "Wake up. It's time to wake up."

Luma didn't twitch.

Stiletto leaned close to Luma's left ear. "Do you want to know what happened next?" she said.

Finally, Luma stirred. Her snow-white skin fluxed pink, then shifted to pale orange.

And her red, faceted eyes flickered open.

"Yes," she said softly. "Please tell me."

As the Skilla kept circling and raising a ruckus, Candle and Stiletto continued toward the source of the mechanical vibrations.

Stiletto carried Luma in her arms and told her more about the little girl with the invisible friend . . . the story of Stiletto herself and the Squatter who had made her a Wipeout. Luma's skin shifted from pale orange to deep green, a change that Stiletto took as a good sign.

Stiletto told Luma how the little girl's invisible friend had played tricks on her and gotten her to play tricks on other people. (She didn't mention the fact that the "tricks" consisted of bloody killing sprees that claimed the lives of her own family and countless strangers.) When

Stiletto got to the part where the policeman showed up—Candle himself—Candle interrupted.

"What's our status?" he said.

Stiletto scanned their surroundings with her left-fingertip sensor pads. "Same as before."

Candle sighed. "How long till dawn?"

"About an hour," said Stiletto. "You thinking they're anti-daylight?"

"Hoping," said Candle. He looked at Luma. "What's the word on you-know-who?"

"Swelling's worse," said Stiletto.

"Let's hope those vibrations lead us to a doctor," said Candle.

"*This* is *dawn*?" said Candle, looking around at what was really just a brighter version of the same old fog.

"I guess it's better than *dark* fog, at least," said Stiletto.

As they walked, Stiletto and Candle combed their warflowers from side to side, ready to open fire at the first hint of aggression from the Skilla.

Stiletto knew the creatures were out there, lurking around in great numbers . . . but they didn't make a sound. She heard neither the clack of a nearby claw nor a distant, screaming cry.

The hairs on the back of her neck wouldn't stay down. She thought the silence was a lot harder to take than the cacophony of the night before.

Fortunately, Luma perked up enough to interrupt it. Her glittering skin switched from pale gray to turquoise, and her yawns became less frequent.

As she walked along between Stiletto and Candle, Luma tugged Stiletto's hand. "What happened next?" she said. "When the policeman showed up?"

"Well," said Stiletto. "The invisible friend told the little girl the *policeman* was mean, so the girl tried to make the policeman go away."

"Did he?" said Luma.

"No," said Stiletto.

"But then what?"

Stiletto heard something crack nearby. "To be continued," she said, focusing all her attention on the fog and the possibility of attack at any moment.

*   *   *

A little further on, Luma turned to Candle and patted his arm. "Did the policeman go away?" she said.

Candle smirked. He kept his eyes and warflower trained on the fog as he picked up the story.

"No," he said. "He made the invisible friend go away instead."

With forbidden drugs and hardcore psychic acupuncture, thought Candle.

"Did the policeman and the little girl make friends then?" said Luma.

"The opposite. She hated him." Candle couldn't resist taking his eyes off the fog long enough to glance Stiletto's way. She looked aloof as always, but he was sure he spotted a trace of a smile on her face.

"She hated him?" said Luma.

"Not forever," said Candle. "As time went on, they got to be friends."

"Better friends than the invisible friend was," said Stiletto. "The little girl was glad the policeman had found her."

Candle was surprised. He'd caught a flash of emotion in her voice.

Suddenly then, Stiletto stopped in her tracks. "The Skilla are gone," she said.

Candle stopped. "What do you mean, gone?"

"I mean *gone*," said Stiletto. "No sign of them on flash sensors."

"Well," said Candle, "let's not look a gift Skilla in the mouth. How far are we from the source of the mechanical vibrations?"

"Less than a kilometer," said Stiletto.

"Then let's get moving." Candle hoisted Luma off her feet and set out at a brisk jog to cover the remaining ground. Stiletto fell in beside him, watching the flash-brain screen for signs of renewed danger.

Luma wrapped her arms around Candle's neck and held on tight. "Guess what?" she said in his ear.

"What?" said Candle.

"I know what the names are," said Luma. "The names of the little girl and the policeman."

"Okay," said Candle. "What are they?"

"Nona and Pass," said Luma, and she giggled.

Candle smiled.

*   *   *

"Stop," said Stiletto. "This is it."

Squinting into the fog, she saw a gray metal door set into a low stone bunker at the end of the street.

"Ventilation system," said Stiletto. "That's what's been making those vibrations. It's pumping stale air out of an underground chamber and pumping in fresh."

"Sagran bio signs?" said Candle, gently bouncing Luma until her eyes opened. In spite of the run through the streets, Luma's sleepiness was coming back in force.

"Lots, but faint," said Stiletto, watching the flash-brain screen on her arm. "We didn't pick them up earlier because there's some kind of interference signal."

"Invisible fence, maybe?" said Candle. "A signal tuned to a frequency that keeps out the Skilla?"

"Beats me," said Stiletto, "but I think I found a way in." She pointed her fingertip sensors at the windowless stone bunker. "There's a shaft on the other side of the door, leading underground."

As Candle started for the bunker, he bounced Luma on his arm. "Look familiar?"

Luma grinned sleepily. "Yes!" she said, pointing an index finger at the bunker. "This is where Mommy and Daddy take me every year. This is the place I couldn't find when I got lost."

When the three of them reached the bunker, Stiletto gave the metal door a push. When it wouldn't open, she turned her attention to what looked like a release mechanism.

The release mechanism consisted of a keypad at eye level with ten push buttons. Each button was imprinted with an alien symbol; Stiletto's wild guess was that the symbols corresponded to the numbers zero through nine.

"Numeric code lock," she said, aiming her fingertip sensors at the mechanism. "Normally, I could crack this puppy in a heartbeat."

"But?" said Candle.

"The device isn't electronic, so it'll take my flash-brain longer to analyze it."

Candle sighed. "What about you?" he said to Luma. "Have any idea how to open the door?"

Luma frowned and rubbed an eye with her fist. "Mommy taught me a song, but I don't know if I can remember all the words right now."

"You remember the tune at least?" said Candle.

"Maybe."

"How about giving it a try?" said Candle.

Stiletto was about to say something when she caught the smell of vinegar in the air. Before she even looked at the readout of the flash-brain, her heart started to pound.

Raising her warflower, she turned away from the door.

"Pass," she said, keeping her voice perfectly even. "Multiple Skilla life signs, coming in *fast*."

Candle nodded. "Guess our friends aren't so nocturnal after all."

In the distance, Stiletto could hear the clattering of claws. Hundreds of them. Getting closer every second.

"How about if you work with Luma on remembering that song?" said Candle. "Music isn't my strong suit."

Stiletto moved in and took Luma, balancing the little girl's weight on her hip.

"Try to make it a fast number," said Candle. "Not that I expect much trouble at all whatsoever."

With a wink, he marched off to face the horde of creatures stampeding down the street.

Candle stationed himself twenty meters from the bunker and immediately opened fire. He blasted his warflower into the fog for a full minute before he finally caught his first glimpse of the Skilla.

One of the creatures slipped through the field of fire and lunged toward him. It was as big as a rhinoceros, with six lean legs and claws like scimitars. A huge scorpion's tail arced over its body, tipped with a spiked stinger as big as a man's head. Its torso was covered in long, crimson spines that glistened as if they were wet.

It had a face like an open wound lined with razor-sharp teeth.

Stiletto would've thought, with the legion of Skilla attacking, that her biggest challenge would be calming Luma down. Instead, she had to fight to keep the little girl awake.

"Luma," Stiletto said sharply, shaking the girl in her arms. "How did the *song* go?"

Luma hummed three notes and closed her eyes.

Stiletto shook her. "Sing the *song*. The one about the door."

Luma's eyes drifted open. "Five laughing children standing in the rain," she sang softly, and then she stopped.

"Luma!" The sounds of battle filled Stiletto's ears.

Luma's eyes dropped shut, then popped open. "Five laughing children standing in the rain," she sang. "One of them's a three-year-old and two are six and ten."

Stiletto memorized the sequence of numbers from the song: five, one, three, two, six, one, zero.

"Number one is six feet tall and always gets the door," Luma sang without opening her eyes. "But Mommy says the ones she loves the best are two and four." Luma yawned and lowered her head back onto Stiletto's bare shoulder. "The end."

Stiletto added the numbers from the last two lines to the earlier sequence. She typed them into the keypad on the door, as if the top three keys were numbers one through three, the second row four through six, the third row seven through nine, and the bottom key zero.

A second later, she heard the clicking of tumblers inside the door. Then, a clang and a scrape.

The door slid open, releasing a blast of musty air that overpowered the vinegar stink of the Skilla.

"Pass!" shouted Stiletto. "It's open!"

Candle was already backing toward the door when he heard her, but not because he had any idea that it was opening.

Two Skilla lunged at him, claws and stingers carving through the space where he'd stood only an instant before. He swept the beam of the warflower from one to the other, dropping them both . . . and as soon as their bodies collapsed to the pavement, three more leaped into the gap.

Candle unleashed another spray of fire from the warflower and backed into the doorway. Out of the corner of his eye, he saw Stiletto behind the door, waiting to pull it shut.

"On three!" said Candle. "One! Two!"

The last thing he saw before Stiletto slammed the door was one of those faces like a ragged, open wound, oozing saliva or mucus and crammed with a forest of teeth like shards of broken glass.

114

"Three!"

Even as the door crashed shut, Candle knew he'd see that face again in his nightmares.

Stiletto led the way down the spiral metal stairwell in the middle of the bunker. She didn't have to switch on her headlight, because the well was lit by an incandescent strip set into the stone wall.

Candle followed, carrying Luma. He talked to her and bounced her in his arms, though keeping her awake had become a losing battle.

At the base of the stairwell, Stiletto stepped onto a dirt floor in front of a pair of metal doors. A video monitor was mounted at eye level on one of the doors, and she activated it by twisting a large knob underneath it.

An adult male Sagran appeared on the screen. Like Luma, he had red, multifaceted eyes and no hair. He wore a sky blue tunic, and his glittering skin was pale green.

"Shhh," said the Sagran, touching his mouth with the tip of a finger. "Don't wake the sleepers."

Stiletto started to ask a question. The Sagran talked right over her, which clued her in that the video was strictly playback, not interactive.

"You are welcome to take your place among us," said the Sagran, opening his arms wide. "But first, please join me in a prayer."

The Sagran closed his eyes and solemnly bowed his head. "O gods of destruction," he said. "We freely offer the fruits of our labors to you. You bless us by tearing down what we have built, clearing the way for us to rebuild and be reborn.

"O Skilla," said the Sagran, "cleanse our cities with your sacred storm. Remind us that the physical world is fleeting, that we may cherish every breath of our lives.

"When at last you rest at the end of these three holy months, and our people awaken, may we find that you have left even less intact than the year before. May we continue to find fulfillment in the eternal cycle of creation and destruction."

The Sagran opened his eyes and lifted his head. "Enter," he said with a serene smile. "Dream of the storm above and the work ahead."

With that, the video screen went dark.

The double doors swung open onto a pitch black space. Stiletto activated her headlight and stepped inside.

The first thing she saw by the beam of the headlight was the body of a woman, curled in a fetal position on blankets on the floor. The woman's eyes were closed, and her skin was pale gray. She wore a simple white shift like Luma's.

As Stiletto played the headlight over the floor, she saw that the woman wasn't alone. Everywhere Stiletto looked, the floor was covered with the bodies of Sagran adults and children, all with gray skin and eyes closed.

Stiletto scanned them with her fingertip sensor pads. "They're hibernating," she said.

"'Three holy months,'" said Candle, quoting the prayer from the video. "It's the only way they can coexist with the Skilla. Hibernate while the Skilla are on the rampage."

"They should wipe out the Skilla and be done with it," said Stiletto.

"Not if the Skilla are sacred to them," said Candle. "I guess the Sagrans see them as gods of destruction, like the Hindu god Shiva on Earth."

Stiletto crouched beside a sleeping Sagran and scanned his head with her fingertip sensors. She scanned two other sleepers the same way.

"They've got the same internal swelling as Luma," said Stiletto. "Could be a normal part of the hibernation process."

"Not a concussion after all," said Candle. "Luma was just trying to go back to sleep like everyone else."

Stiletto gazed at the little girl in Candle's arms. Luma was fast asleep, drooling on his shoulder.

"We should find her parents," said Stiletto.

Candle nodded. "Time to wake up, Luma."

After a long search by headlight through the vast underground chamber, Luma pointed out a man and woman sleeping side by side on a multi-colored quilt.

"That's Mommy and Daddy," she said drowsily.

Candle smiled and lowered her to the quilt, placing her between her parents. "There you go."

Luma yawned and nodded. Now that she had been returned to her parents, the amber crystal in her bracelet stopped blinking.

"Good night," said Candle. "Sleep tight."

Luma lay down on her side and curled up between her mother and father. Her glittering skin took on a pale green hue. "Finish the story first. What happened next?"

"I have a better idea," said Candle. "Why don't *you* finish it?"

"Okay." Luma thought for a moment, then grinned. "Pass and Nona fell in love and lived happily ever after. The end."

Then, hugging her doll, she closed her eyes and fell asleep, her skin color shifting from pale green to pale gray.

"Cool story, huh?"

Candle said it as he and Stiletto followed a network of tunnels under the city, bypassing the Skilla on the way back to the *Sun Ra*.

He caught Stiletto by surprise. Instead of bouncing right back with a typical wisecrack, she didn't answer.

The truth was, of course she thought the story was cool, since she was crazy about him . . . but she was afraid to go further because of her lousy past. Her Wipeout career had ruined everything else in her life, so why not ruin this, too?

On the other hand. . .

"I think we should end the story the way Luma did." Candle grinned, his deep brown eyes twinkling in the glow of her headlight. "How about you?"

It was up to Stiletto now. The moment couldn't have been more perfect. And yet, on the brink of a new beginning, she hesitated. What if the Squatter who had once possessed her managed to return? She couldn't bear the thought that she might one day hurt Candle.

"Well?" he said, eyebrows raised expectantly. "What do you say?"

Then again, she'd already been with him for three years, and she hadn't hurt him yet. So what was she waiting for?

Candle sighed. "Okay, then. Can't blame a guy for trying."

"No, no," said Stiletto. "I want to know what happens next. To be continued." Then, she grabbed his hand and held it like a trophy as they hiked toward the distant light at the end of the tunnel.

Alienation
by Katherine Sparrow

They grow their babies on the inside of their bodies!"

"Their language is audible and comes through their mouths!"

"They make art only with the colors between red and indigo!"

We laughed the whole way to earth. It was one long uh-uh-uh from start to finish as we extrapolated what they'd be like.

Our mission was to evaluate their species. The thought of adding to our intergalactic solidarity was ecstatic-making. We held great bubbles of ossified hope on the inside, and did not know if the bubbles would burst or grow so large they would carry us into the stars.

And if there was ever a silent moment? A pensive worry?

Then we would pretend the ship was broken or we'd lost our coordinates. Uh-uh-uh!

"We will not err this time!" me of us said.

"Mistakes will be made," me not me corrected. "Let us make new and interesting mistakes."

"Let us not repeat old patterns," me not me added.

A moment's silence as millennia of war flashed before us. Remember the Tarlkons. Then we were off again.

"They have satire!"

"They have paper!"

"They have poop!"

We learned the most popular human languages and selected our genomes to explain our dexterity in these languages. We became: Jasma the pretty Chinese-Estonian, Jexor the stolid Chilean-Jamaican, and me, who is Pijin, the devilishly handsome Nepalese-Algerian.

We floated down into Earth's atmosphere and let it take us where it willed, as our protocols demanded. We set down on a landmass—very convenient! There are few humans underwater.

Our bodies engulfed us as we left the ship and we were born. We sucked in our first breaths of air.

Breathe in, and then out. Don't forget—the bodies won't like it if you do, Jasma flashed us.

I know, I flashed back.

Gu-gu-guh, we laughed even harder at our own emerging ego-drive springing up from these human bodies. Sunlight hit our skin and darkened pigment within our melanocytes. Eccrine and apocrine glands worked on sodium and body temperature regulation. And that was only the external, to say nothing of the squeezing heart, the ebb and flow of blood through branching pathways, the gland drips, and muscle tremors.

Though we self-nourished and self-cleaned, we ached for mother-comfort and nipple-love. We longed to be held. We cried and cried and cried.

Then we put our fists and feet in our mouths, and rolled over, and learned to walk.

Our bodies grew at the exact rate we willed them to. We lingered in infancy, growing at only four hundred times the normal rate.

We discovered feet, thumbs and anuses!

We discovered tongue probes! Yum, yuck, ooh, bleck.

By the next day we were children. My first words were, "Greetings, planet Dirt."

"Earth," Jexor reminded me with his first word.

Giggle-gorgle-coo.

We grew faster, impatient to be grown. Teeth came in, fell out, and came in again. Hair grew out of our heads.

By afternoon we were teenagers. The approximate arcuate nucleus of the hypothalamus began releasing stimulant pulses into the pituitary gland's portal. Like an itch inside my skull. My body ached with a new strangeness, and we decided it was time to meet some humans.

We put on the clothing we'd grown and began to walk toward the nearest human town.

"Nothing ever happens here," I whined.

"I don't like this planet. It's boring."

"Let's go. Let's just go."

We walked and flashed each other the feeling we no longer belonged in these bodies. Like drifting free in space. We checked for replication error, but then Jasma connected these feelings as human pubertic response. Fascinating! We wore triple frowns as we left behind our disintegrating ship.

'Wind' flowed around us. How nice upon our flexible skin! Plant aromas pleased our noses.

As we neared Delton, we heard someone approaching. We trembled excessively inside our bodies that always trembled with blood and organ movement. A small human pushed through the bush and stared at us.

"Hello there," I said. "Greetings and salutations."

"No wonder they put such time into grooming," Jexor added.

"Not bipedal." Jasma dropped to all fours and smiled. She was the best at the smile, though we'd all been practicing. Jasma walked to the human with a hand raised in North American greeting. The human backed away. A larger human ran through the bushes and snarled at us. It raised its clawed hands.

"I'm not sure he is human," Jexor said, as the human-or-not lowered her head and ran at Jasma . . . in a ritual greeting?

No, not a greeting.

The human roared and ran its claws over and into Jasma's belly, and then slashed into her head. We analyzed Jasma's reactions: her amygdala released catecholamines, muscles tensed, and blood pressure increased. When confronted with harm, anger and rage emerge.

Blood, guts, and Jasma brains flew everywhere, just like in the movies. Jasma put on quite a show, and we watched with deep appreciation. I felt jealous that she made first contact, and realized this was an effect of testosterone and progesterone flooding my body.

Jasma screamed and writhed on the ground as the human ran away. Such a kidder.

Hahaha!

Jasma reassembled and did not laugh.

"Nerve endings and feedback loops create pain. Pain is to be avoided." Jasma flashed pain to us.

We screamed. When the pain ended, our minds flooded with opiates and the memory quickly faded.

"Very violent," Jexor said.

"Without provocation," Jasma added.

"Unbalanced human?"

"Aha!" Jexor said. "That was a black bear, not a human."

"Not human? But it had two eyes, one mouth, two ears, and four appendages," Jasma said.

"It spoke with its mouth and was the correct size," I added.

Jexor flashed us comparison pictures.

Hahaha.

There were subtle differences, if one looked hard enough.

"Remember to notice degrees of hairiness," I told us.

Jasma led the way, and we followed, running our hands over 'bark' and hitting 'branches' with our heads.

Exploring the forest lessened our pubescent discomfort. How marvelous to be here and nowhere else! The tiny part which is only me and not us loved the armored beetle, the solar light waves and dust interaction, and the shivering green-yellow leaves.

My approximate-hippocampus surged and my salivary glands overproduced as I hoped again that humans would be able to join us.

"I am hoping for a positive outcome!" I said.

"Hope is good! It keeps us from scrickly Tarlkoniness," Jexor said.

"Hope is dangerous. It made us trust the Tarlkons."

"Why are they so bad? I wish we could forget their scrickly war-making, and come to the humans blank-minded," I said. Fantasy-based desire was part of puberty.

"The Tarlkon biology leads them always to war. They cannot feel physical ease, and therefore create miserablist realities," Jasma said.

I walked on in annoyance at us-not-me's too literal interpretation of my question. Did she think I was stupid? I was becoming an I who chafed against us! I flashed this to us.

Hahaha.

We were 'singing,' Tra-la-la-la! when we heard another creature approaching.

A human, we hoped, but prepared to be mauled. I stepped forward, eager to experience pain in the flesh and not just flash.

"Hello?"

"Greetings?"

"Oh hi. What are you doing out here? This is my back yard. Are you lost?"

It had speech! Short brown head hair! And thumbs!

"Yes!"

When in doubt, always answer yes.

"Where are your parents?"

Hahaha.

We are our own parents. How to explain that? Jasma walked forward and held out a hand. The human shook it. Immediately Jasma assimilated and flashed us revised DNA codes. We synthesized the genome and rewrote our approximations. Colors shifted in our vision, spines curved, and membranes moistened. A thousand and twelve corrections. Most satisfying!

"Uh, why are you all jumping up and down? Are you from the summer camp?"

"Yes."

"I guess you can make a phone call at my house. Follow me."

"Take us to your leader," Jasma said.

Hahaha.

The human did not join in one of our favorite hierarchy-worship joke.

"You must be dehydrated or something? You've walked three miles. You all aren't normally this weird, right? Are you in costume?"

"Yes."

"For a play?"

"Yes."

"I'm Zoya, but my friends call me Z."

"We are stolid Jexor, pretty Jasma, and devilishly-handsome Pijin."

At her domicile she showed us to a telephone we recognized from the radiations. I pretended to make a call while us not me followed Z into the kitchen for 'coffee.'

"Are they coming for you soon?" Z asked when I joined them.

"Yes."

"When?"

"Soon."

"Are you three related? I mean adopted. I'm adopted. There's something similar about all of you. How old are you? I thought you were younger at first, but are you like, my age?"

We'd sped up our growth to become more like her. Our nature craved solidarity.

"How old are you?" Jexor asked.

"Twenty-one."

"So are we."

"So you must be camp counselors?"

"Yes."

Z added powder to water and made 'vanilla lattes.' The sweetened stimulants buzzed through us, and we had urges to talk and express emotion. With high estradial levels and aching bones, we let Z lead us outside to chairs on her porch. She sat across from us and looked at us with her eyes. We looked back.

Katherine Sparrow

"Everything is so beautiful here," Jasma said. Tears fell from her eyes.
"Michigan?"
"Earth. Oh beautiful Earth!"
Emotions fizzed like phosphor in me. Tears of overwhelming wonder welled up in my eyes. Fascinating!
"Huh. Okay. Can I ask you something? My moms would say it's rude to ask, but, you look . . . strange."
"We have varied ethnic backgrounds and life histories, but we come from California," Jexor said. 'California' always explained away any strangeness in their radiations.
"Oh, I don't mean that. But . . . what are you?"
Could this human see past our bodies and into our true otherness?
"Male or female?" Z continued. "Or . . . in between?"
Jasma accessed information and flashed us how we'd erred along the binary gender system continuum. Our own bias showing through yet again, for our kind are not sexed.
Hahaha.
"So you're not offended?"
"At least we do not resemble bears!" I said. I made my penis and testicles grow larger underneath my Sharma pants. I added more hair to my eyebrows and nostrils. Very pleasurable.
Jasma's breasts and bottom grew under her peasant dress and Mao jacket. Jexor's crotch package expanded beneath his Rasta-pants.
"We are very male and very female," I told Z.
The human's eyes dilated, and her mouth made a round shape. "Oh, uh, yeah. Sorry. Of course you are. I feel like I'm not seeing things right today. Sorry."
"And you are female." I was ninety-seven percent sure.
We studied Z.
"You are pretty!"
"You smell like flowers!"
"Well proportioned hips!"
Hahaha.
"Whatever. When are you getting picked up?"
"Soon."
Z made us more drinks and we enjoyed the porch. Jasma fell off her chair. We flashed agreement human bodies were tricky. Bipedalism was the least of it!

124

As the last hormonal storms of puberty waned, we sank into contented feeling that spread out from our torsos.

They can feel content in these bodies, I flashed us. The chaotic miasma is only temporary.

Perhaps, Jexor flashed back.

"Pretty day," Z said.

"Splendid."

"Glorious."

"Worth the trip," I said.

"From camp?" Z asked. She brought us 'crackers with cheese.' Texture poked my tongue and released taste. Saliva mixed with the food and broke it down. My teeth chomped as I swallowed and let my pharynx carry food down into my stomach. We ate with a minimum of choking, and flashed congratulations to each other on successful gastro-intestinal tracts.

Z watched us with blinking and moving eyes. "So what were you doing in the woods?"

"Practicing," Jexor said.

"For your play? Does it have aliens in it? Are you trying to stay in character?" she asked. "That might explain it."

"Yes," Jexor said and flashed us interest in this perception. Did humans have a sensory organ we were ignorant of? Please humans, let it be so!

"Aliens? What do you mean?" I asked casually. My head bobbled from side to side with excitement.

"You're just playing a role. I get it."

"Yes! You have discovered our truth!" Jexor said. "It is excellent. Our protocols state we do not divulge our presence, but once known, it is known."

"Are all humans so acute?" Jasma asked. "I would think not, with all the distractions of your body."

"We have many questions for you!" I said. "We have traveled very far to meet you."

"Are you trying to be funny?" Z asked. "Because this alien thing is getting old." Her face expressed irritation.

"You do not believe?" Jexor asked. "But you said 'aliens playing a role.' Once known, you cannot half-know."

"Stop. Just be real, okay? You're too. . ." Z started to say more, but Jexor touched her arm. Light waves flowed from her mouth instead of sound. The light grew brighter as she yelled.

125

Well done, we flashed Jexor. Z's face reddened and her arms thrashed in the air.

Jexor touched her arm again.

"Oh! My! God! You are aliens!" Z shouted. "I wish my Moms were here! They love aliens!"

We looked at us and felt confusion within our frontal lobes. They loved us?

"For a while, Momi thought when she meditated she talked to aliens, but then she figured out it was just St. Francis. They also saw a UFO once, hovering out on Lake Michigan that they were sure was there to abduct them. Oh, I wish they had a phone. They're on a farm with my sisters for the week. They'd have a million questions for you. Like are you going to save the planet, and can we go to your planet, and do you have any cool gadgets? Okay, that last one is my question. Oh, and why are you here?"

"Save Earth from what?"

"Humans would implode on our planet."

"We have many 'cool gadgets,' if you mean body parts. We are here to assess humanity."

Z nodded her head up and down vigorously. "Okay. Um, maybe I'm not the best person for you to be hanging out with. I'm only twenty-one, and I kind of, well, I mess most things up. So far."

"Yes. Well stated. Mistakes are made!" Jasma said.

"Do you want beers? I think we should drink beer. I'd like a beer. You're old enough, right."

"We are ancient and wise beings."

Hahaha.

We drank the beer and spoke with Z. Human minds are unflashable.

"How did you get here?"

"On a ship. What is the use of your xiphoid process?"

"Uh, to process the xiphoid? Are you going to try and eat me? I mean eat all the human?"

"No. We are going to drink you."

Hahaha.

"How many times a day do you poop?"

"You are aliens."

Dopamine dripped down our mesolimbic pathways into our nucleus accumbens. Jexor identified this reaction as happiness.

The sun moved toward the edge of our vision, temperatures cooled, and 'mosquitoes' bit us. Alcohol slipped past our blood-brain barrier, killed brain-cells, and released endorphins. The effect felt like being washed in oil: shiny with possibility.

Z asked, "But what are you assessing? For real, are you going to save us?"

"We are assessing humans."

"How could we save self from self?"

"You know, like we have all kinds of war and problems. If someone could just fix it, or fix us. My moms always say we'll have to evolve, or aliens will have to fix everything. I always tell them we're doomed."

Hahaha.

"We are not here to save."

"We do not practice charity."

"We search for solidarity potential."

"So, you're testing us to see if we're good enough to be your friends?"

"Yes. But we do not test. We experience. That is all."

"So what all are you going to 'experience' while you're here?"

"We will live."

"With you."

"Tell me the fate of humans isn't going to depend on me." Z drank more beer.

"The fate of humans isn't going to depend on me."

Hahaha.

"That's not funny."

"We think it's funny."

"You can sleep in the meditation room, okay? I've got to bail. This is too much for me right now." Z stood up and went inside and upstairs. We sensed her neural net moving from alpha, to theta waves. We sensed rapid eye movement, and wished we could flash into her dreams.

We considered experiencing sleep, but decided to explore our reproductive urges.

Swollen! Smooshed! Probed and prodded! Myotonia and vasocongestion! There were many pleasurable modalities—some of them reproductive. Our skin and membranes craved touch with a desire unmatched since infancy and mother-need. While Jexor and I grew quickly tired, Jasma grew more energized with each apex.

Moan! Giggle! Crash! Oh-the-stars-and-universe! Oh that, yes! Stop! Don't stop!

Toward morning, Jasma began to simulate pregnancy and replicated cells in her uterus.

Z came downstairs in 'pajamas.' "You three got busy last night." She punched me in the arm. "Jeez, that's the real reason you came to earth, huh?"

Hahaha.

Over a breakfast of chicken ova and bread, we sat around the kitchen table and watched Jasma's waist grow. I noticed a desire to care for her spring up in my glial cells. I also felt sore in my joints, shriveled in my loins, and dehydrated from mouth to urethra. So many competing sensations!

Jasma ran outside and vomited off the porch, then came back in with a sour look. "I will get mauled by bears! I will carry a simulated fetus in my uterus. Let Jexor do it! She will be the experience vessel."

I flashed her a reminder that we were all one. She kicked me with her foot.

Hahaha, but Jasma did not laugh.

I was just about to inform her that physical abuse leads to Tarlkoniness, but she flashed us her physical experience. Increased blood pressure in every vein, queasiness and dizziness, increased sense of smell, and a mess of hormones! I kicked Jexor in sympathy.

"The first trimester is the hardest," Z said. "Momo is a midwife, so I've seen this a lot. You're not really pregnant, are you?" Z asked.

"No," Jexor explained. "We are not really human."

Jasma groaned.

"You want to go somewhere today?" Z asked. "I mean, as long as you've come all this way."

"If you want to go someplace, yes," Jexor said.

"Can you travel fast? Can we go anywhere?" Z asked.

"Yes. Like you, we have feet."

"Darn. I wanted to go to China, but we can go out to ice cream. That'll help, Jasma. You'll like it."

Groan.

We got into Z's 'car,' and it moved us along 'roads.' We rolled down 'windows' and let the wind flow pleasantly over our hair and skin.

At the store there were 'magazines' with pictures of humans, and a man who scooped ice cream balls into cones for us. We watched him for violent tendencies—human males are more violent than females—but he talked about the weather and gave Z an extra scoop for being extra sweet, even though her blood glucose levels were normal. No one got mauled.

At a 'picnic bench' outside we crossed our legs and stared up at the blue sky. We licked our ice cream to keep it from dripping onto other body parts. The sweet, fat, and cold of it invaded my mouth in bursts of flavor. It kept me wanting more and more. Except for Jasma's discomfort, we enjoyed this part of the human lifespan. My body hummed with all the organs that worked with synchronicity and grace.

"This is my last summer here. I'm going to U-Mich in the fall. I keep feeling like I'll miss it here, and it should all be precious, but at the same time I'm bored."

"Ambivalence is often a true recording of experience," I said.

"Yeah, I guess so. I feel stuck."

Jexor and I pondered the mystery of her words, while Jasma grew more self-obsessed with her expanding uterus.

"It's kicking," she said.

"Maybe we should get back to my house."

On the car ride home fields of 'wheat' moved like expanding gas bubbles in the wind. Hair grew on Jasma's upper lip and melasma stains covered her cheeks.

"I'm never going to have kids," Z said. "No thank you."

"Me neither," I said.

Hahaha.

At Z's house, we sat on the couch and watched Jasma pace with her hands over her huge bell. Jexor read a book called "Our Bodies, Ourselves."

"So Z," I said. "How has being human been for you so far? How was puberty?"

Her shoulders rose up to her ears and then lowered. "That's like asking water what wet is like."

We chuckled quietly under Jasma's glare.

Z's eyes searched the ceiling. They did that when she was thinking. "I mean, some things have been hard, but I'm glad to be alive. Some amazing things have happened so far."

"Like what?"

"Like falling in love. Like reading good books. Like imagining all the things I'm going to do in the future."

"Imagining? Will you explain?"

"Like, what do you want to be doing in five years?"

"I will be traveling toward another planet to assess."

"Fallopian tubes? Fantastic!" Jexor murmured.

"Maybe you will be, but maybe you will discover a giant sentient cloud who talks to you."

"No. I will be traveling toward an assessment. Any other possibility is statistically insignificant."

"Sure, but that's imagination, and it's fun. It doesn't have to be realistic. Mine never is."

"Our kind have expectation, but not imagination, I think. Though we were trembling with excitement before we came to earth, we also knew the likely outcome."

"You were trembling with excitement because humans are so cool, huh?"

"No. Ninety-eight point five degrees."

Hahaha.

"Placenta previa. Fantastic!" Jexor said.

Jasma screamed. Her Sari darkened with amniotic fluid. Her belly convulsed. Her cervix dilated.

"Um. I don't really know what to do," Z said. She ran to Jasma and held her hand.

Jasma groaned and sat on the ground. Sweat emerged from her skin as muscles tensed.

Please do not flash me, I thought as another contraction rocked her body.

"Enough!" Jasma yelled and her belly diminished. The protein package in her uterus shrunk and redistributed across her body. It would have been better for us to assess the full birth process, but no one wanted to tell Jasma that.

"Unpleasant and bloody mammals," she said.

Jasma's scrickliness abated. We enjoyed ages thirty to fifty. Z fed us rubbery tofu dogs and sour lemonade. We sat on the porch underneath the yellow sun and it was good.

"So, what do you guys think it's all about?" Z asked. "Life, I mean. Maybe you know the actual answer? It can't all be meaningless, can it?"

"Ah," I said. "This is the universal question, asked on every planet."

"Darn," Z said. "I guess that means there's no answer?"

"Many theories, no answer."

When the sky grew dark, we practiced sleeping in the meditation room. Our human brains dreamed, and we recorded the strange bursts of stories, picture, and texture that flowed through our minds. By morning I had diabetes, Jexor cancerous lesions on his prostate, and Jasma felt generalized anxiety.

"We are no longer developing."

"We are well into atrophy."

"We are moving toward death," I said. We sensed this truth on a cellular level, and did not like it. I missed my pancreatic function, joint elasticity, and youthful skin. What I longed for would never be again.

Death-fear grew in us as real as our worn ventricles and tired synapses. We were unable to feel anything but dread toward what was to come. Old age was worse than infancy or puberty.

"Whoa, you guys look worked," Z said. "How old are you now?" We followed her into the kitchen.

"Sixty-seven."

"Aging is fearful and disturbing."

"The mind fights against this natural degeneration. Why?"

"Uh, because no one wants to die? Duh." Z put cereal, berries, bowls, and milk on the table.

"Why fight against your own nature? Why struggle?"

"Because we like being alive." Z rolled her eyes and popped blueberries into her mouth.

"I cannot stop thinking about this degeneration," Jasma said. "It is an unpleasant movie repeating in my mind, over and over. My back hurts. There is a sore in my stomach lining. I keep clenching my jaw. Why all this pain?"

"You're all being kind of dramatic, aren't you? You die too, right?"

"We are not born, we bud. We become from what was and evolve into what will be."

Z looked confused.

"Your cells replace themselves fully every seven years, yes Z?" I asked.

"Yeah. At least that's what they tell us in Biology."

"For us, such cell replacement is slower and complete. We are always dying and always being born," I explained.

"Death is not an event, but a slow becoming. As we live, parts die while other parts grow," Jasma said.

"But a part of you stays the same?"

"No."

"Don't you hate that?"

"No."

"Weird," Z said. She poured us coffee, then added three spoonfuls of sugar to hers.

As I could no longer tolerate sweets, I looked at it with pupil dilation and salivary response. Z stuck her tongue out at me and giggled.

Hahaha, but melancholy emoted from my brain.

Someday, I thought, Z will be old and remember what was. Or she will die young. My heart, once a great constricting machine, chuffed feebly. Cells died. Organs shrank. My hair grew brittle and sparse. We accelerated our aging, miserable in this human phase, yet knowing more degeneration was yet to come before it was over.

"I am beginning to understand their love of stories," Jasma said at lunchtime. Her hair was cloud white. "Distractions from the body are necessary."

"It all ends," Jexor said. "How strange and awful."

"Pain degrades the ability to laugh," I said. "Unpleasantness ensues."

By mid-afternoon we were elderly. Light boned, half blind, and frail. We ached and groaned as we lay on the mats in the meditation room.

"This is getting weirder," Z said as she brought us juice and more blankets. "Are you guys okay?"

"These bodies weigh heavily upon us," Jasma said with quivering vocal cords wrecked by age. "They are so busy at first, and then become slow."

"What are your bodies like?" Z asked.

As we lay trapped in flesh, the truth of it came like one of their dreams.

"We are like cardboard boxes."

"Like barnacles. Like all the sky and earth together at once. Glorious."

"Different bodies create different realities. We do not have pain. I hate pain. It is always coming toward you humans, how hard that must be." I fell back on the mat, exhausted from the effort of speaking. Z gripped my hand with her wonderful skin.

"Nah, it's just normal. For us, I mean," Z said. "You're not really all old, are you? This is just like the fake baby, right?"

Her caring was better than the warmth from the blanket covering my diminished torso. "Right," I whispered.

"When we die, we will go back to our ship and become us-not-you," Jasma added.

As soon as she said it, I wished I could turn back time and stop Jasma's words. But we are all in a slow time machine moving forward, are we not?

"Us-not-you," Jexor repeated.

I said nothing, though I knew that assessment was correct. I did not want it to be true. That is my nature.

"When you go back, we can do the solidarity thing, right?" Z asked.

"No. There is more pain than pleasure," Jasma said.

"More struggle than peace."

"Your bodies are too difficult, Z. Humans are too dangerous to practice solidarity with," I said. My heart ached with age and sadness.

"What? Are you guys just talking biology? Geez. We're so much more than that."

"I'm sorry Z. These bodies hold Tarlkonian misery," I said.

"I'm more than my body parts."

"Yes. But you live in a body. A miserable body," Jasma said. "Our assessment is biology based, to avoid bias."

"So, what? Are you going to bomb us or something?"

"Earth will be marked. Earth will be left alone."

"But we need help," Z said. "And I like you. I thought we were friends."

Jasma's aortic valve spasmed and collapsed with a surge of emotion. Her stopped heart halted blood flow, and life faded away. Last of all, her brain died. Jasma analyzed the experience until she was gone.

"I told you I always mess things up," Z said. "Don't leave us alone. Don't make it my fault." Her eyes shed saline droplets and her lower lip shook. More pain. How could she avoid it? She was human.

A blood clot formed in Jexor's veins and moved sluggishly into his brain. Massive cerebral hemorrhaging ensued. He died.

"It is a wonderful planet. With much animal diversity, Z. Be content to practice solidarity with them. Be content as much as your body allows," I added. "You did nothing wrong. It's just . . . these awful bodies," I said. My blood glucose levels rose to toxicity, I slipped into a coma, and died.

Back on our ship, we let a moment of silence grow among us to mark what might have been, but would never be.

Dark Rendezvous
by Simon Petrie

*T*uonela's last functioning shuttle was a cutaway, skinned on only one side. Lem climbed into the cage and spliced his suit into the shuttle's air-circ system. The next breath was sharp, stale, unbelievably cold.

He kicked off from *Tuonela*'s open-space hold, into the dark.

The derelict lay about three kilometres to port, the closest Lem had dared to manoeuvre.

The shuttle pulled clear of *Tuonela*. Inspecting the scar-streaked hull of the ship as he moved out, Lem was shocked at the extent of the damage. He'd realised the shielding afforded by the ram-scoop had become degraded, but this looked bad. He hadn't appreciated just how much dust was scything through to impact on the ship's fuselage.

He located *Tuonela*'s running lights. Then he instructed the suit to pipe through a realtime projection of the lights onto his heads-up, for his own navigational purposes. This was perhaps paranoia. The shuttle's many nano-gyros should serve to automatically maintain a safe attitude, keeping the shielding aligned with *Tuonela*'s prow. Nonetheless, Lem had learnt to distrust the ship's nanotech systems. It was a characteristic of nanotech arrays that they tended not to fail completely, but to stealthily degrade in performance until some threshold was quietly passed, and death or disaster resulted. By monitoring the ship himself, Lem could independently ensure that the shuttle's one-sided shielding stayed properly interposed against the cloud's deadly sporadic sleeting of dust.

Lem hadn't survived this long by blindly trusting the ship's ability to safeguard its sole remaining passenger.

<Are you sure you want to do this?> asked The Voice through his helmet earbud.

"No," Lem replied. "But the opportunity's too good. You got reason to believe this thing could still be dangerous?"

<Dangerous? I am unsure. Much of the information I should have on this topic is untraceable. But I have a clear sense of impropriety, of taboo, in connection to the derelicts.>

"Taboo?" Lem placed a derisive torque on the word.

The Voice's response seemed defensive. <My programming includes a full high-grade ethics suite, modules on morality, judgement and risk assessment, and a detailed library of human-history case studies.>

"And all this is giving you—what? Anything concrete? Or just a hunch?"

<More than a hunch. What I suspect you would call an informed sense of unease. But as to the underlying reasons for this disquiet . . . > The distributed intellect, embedded in his suit's lining, fell silent.

"Unless you got something better than that, we're going," Lem replied. "*I'm* going. To check it out. Which means you get to come for the ride. Like I said, too good an opportunity. For salvage, maybe, if nothing else."

<That is true. We are worryingly low on some metals. But I advise caution.>

"My middle name, remember?"

The distance was down to two point eight kay. Lem resisted the urge to squirt off more thrust. *Never burn more than an eighth of your fuel on the outward push*, was the cardinal rule. Instead, he sat in silence punctuated by his steady breathing and heartbeat, and by the near-subsonic groan of the shuttle's air-circ system. Sporadically, these sounds were themselves interrupted by the massively-amplified *chink* of a dust grain slamming into the shuttle's side-shielding. Not for the first time, he wished to bypass that feature of the shuttle's inflight diagnostics, but it was programmed deep into the vessel's intellect. As if to emphasise his lack of control; to reinforce his status as passenger.

<Music?> The Voice asked.

"No. Shush now."

It was odd, the way the solitude struck. More intensely, always, on an EVA, despite the closeness of the suit's wittering Voice. Aboard *Tuonela*, he could always conjure the illusion that other passengers still survived, had not succumbed to the years of deprivation, the tainted cultures, the nano-systems' dumb mistakes, the reckless despair. And maybe there'd be some prospect of revival when they reached C, with its hint of new beginnings and a wealth of easily-mined resources. He doubted it, though. Best to think of them all as cleanly dead, best not to hold false hope. The revival crypts were thick with nanotech, not to be trusted. Waste of carbon, to even try. No, if he wanted companions, he'd build them up from the cryo-banks' embryos. At least *those* systems, so far as he knew, weren't corrupted.

Two point five kay.

He tried illuminating the derelict, to better gauge size and composition, but the shuttle's lights were feeble—more nano shit, he'd have to replace them once he'd returned. The best he could manage was a heavily-pixellated image suggesting the alien ship was ovoid and riddled with indentations or fissures.

There'd been other derelicts—four, if Lem remembered correctly—on the long years *Tuonela* had been pushing out from base camp at core D, towards core C. But all had been sluicing through the cloud on headings which had been impractical to match. They'd sent probes to approach two of them (back when there was still a 'they', not yet merely a 'he', aboard *Tuonela*). The probes had netted a few grainy, inconclusive images before their feeble transmitters died. Aside from those scant glimpses of pockmarked, ragged hulls, they'd learnt essentially nothing about the derelicts. No signatures of life, no warm spots, no trace of confined gases. As dead in infrared and microwave as they were in optical. They might well have been drifting for thousands, more likely millions of years. In one view, there'd been the suggestion of a heavily-abraded ramscoop at one end, but it wasn't what could be called unmistakable.

This time, though, he'd chanced on a ship on a near-identical velocity. So near, in fact, that *Tuonela* had been measurably closing on it for several months. It was an opportunity too good to pass up. Quite aside from the benefits of salvage, he might just learn something about the ship's origins, or the race that had built it.

A heavier *thud* brought him from his reverie, an impact, apparently, of a larger grain barely sub-micron in size. Such grains were rare, even in the comparatively dense skein of material stretching between clumps D and C, but the shuttle's shielding was designed to withstand it. At this relative velocity, at least. That likely would no longer hold true, however, if *Tuonela* ever reached her intended cruising speed of point one *c*. Even at the vessel's current velocity of around point zero two *c*, a dust grain massing only a few milligrams carried the punch of a cannonball.

In the tinny silence following the impact, he was again aware of the sound of his own breathing. Quick and uneven.

Closer now, under two kay.

Lem tried the lamps again. The illumination was still shit, but there was now some definition, something for the enhancement programs to get their teeth into, without just blasting the imagery to snow and static.

The thing was big, but what struck him was its insubstantiality. There were large breaches all over the hull. He revised upwards his estimate of how long the thing must have been drifting out here, abandoned.

For a time—he could not say how long—the sound of the cloud's shrapnel hitting the shielding passed unnoticed.

It was bizarre to think that his might be the first human eyes to ever properly gaze on a vessel constructed by another race.

Other colony ships, sisters to *Tuonela*, had also sent report of occasional sightings of derelicts. Yet so far as he knew those observations had been, like his own earlier encounters, mere glimpses. Interludes on their own long flights of diaspora from the seedship-spawned factories and now-crowded habitats of Clump D. Ships in the long, long night.

Avoided crossings.

He felt a hefty kick of anticipation.

One kay now, and he couldn't see from one end to the other without switching to wide-angle. He started to finesse the verniers. He'd need to track backwards towards the rear end of the hulk, to remain shielded while he exited the shuttle.

<Have you perceived how tenuous is the hull?> asked The Voice.

"You mean the holes? Yeah, I saw them."

<Not merely that. The rangefinder data is suggesting that the hull material is a form of carbon mesh, very thin, almost paper-like.>

"Who sets out in a paper spaceship?"

<I cannot answer that. Most likely it is merely an easy form to fabricate within such an organic-heavy environment as this. But you will need to exercise caution.>

"Yeah, you said already. Your premonition."

<My risk analysis based on incomplete and partially-degraded data. But no, that is not what I was referring to. You should take care with braking. I do not advise a direct thrust reversal.>

"What, you think the braking burn could tear it apart?"

<I cannot completely discount that possibility.>

"Great. Good thing I didn't pile on the juice to begin with."

<Juice?>

"Idiom. Now shush, and let me brake." He began to burp propellant obliquely from pairs of the shuttle's small attitude nozzles.

Mooring, too, was going to be a problem. He hadn't been expecting to use magnetic clamps, and of course the vessel wasn't going to have a standard docking port, but he wasn't even sure there was enough substance to any part of the structure to take a grapple. Maybe it was just going to be a matched-velocities job.

He was close enough now to get a detailed, well-lit view of the vessel's fuselage. There appeared to be a badly buckled ramscoop at its prow, and what must be its primary exhaust nozzle at the stern. Standard enough, although exotic in appearance. But where the rangefinder's intelligent deconvolution had sketched in, from barely-seen detail, an otherwise uniformly smooth hull perforated by a few large and regular cavities, he now saw that the derelict's outer skin was rough, and punctuated by a continuum of fissures and craters. There were sections of it, indeed, to which the term *tattered* might almost be applied. And yet these rents and voids in its surface covering were clustered principally amidships. Not at the prow, which would have seen much greater exposure to impact by high-relative-velocity dust grains and other cloud debris.

Pondering this, it struck Lem belatedly that *the derelict was not tumbling*. Instead, it merely spun, axially, in a leisurely and orderly fashion.

What possible gyroscopic mechanism might have remained sufficiently intact, across the evident millenia or longer, to have enabled the broken vessel, against all reasonable probability, to have retained a prow-forward attitude?

Ten metres, and matched at last. He'd EVA across, it was going to be more practical than attempting to move the shuttle closer.

<There is something I should mention,> announced The Voice.

"What?" he snapped. The vessel loomed large, close, darkly threatening.

<Aspects of this craft's form are disconcertingly familiar.>

"*What in hell's name* do you mean by that?"

<I cannot specify. Probably it relates to data which has been lost, save for vestigial fragments.>

"Thought this was the first time anyone got a good look at one of these things. You telling me you've seen this thing before?"

<Not this vessel, in all likelihood. But something like it.>

"When?"

<Again, I cannot say. But I suspect this relates to events back before the population of the colony ships.>

"You mean from your dim dark past as a seedship brain?"

<Lem. I think we should return to the Tuonela.>

"I didn't traverse this distance to be scared off by one of your premonitions. You got something concrete, give it now. But if we turn back now, who knows when we might next get the chance to explore one of these?"

The Voice didn't respond.

He waited for more than a complete revolution of the ship's stern across his field of view (it took almost three minutes), mapping in his mind the pattern of openings in the rear of its hull, before he unlatched himself from the shuttle's cage.

There was, of course, the continual danger from dust grains, but here he was ostensibly in the shadow of the derelict's own ram-scoop. It should be safe enough. He worked his suit's verniers to nudge free of the shuttle.

Inside, the ship was blackbody black. The suit's own portable rangefinder didn't help measurably either.

He swept his surroundings with the glove-mounted torch beam.

If he'd been expecting corridors, chambers, some traces of any shipboard apparatus, he was initially disappointed. So far as he could establish, the ship's outer skin was wrapped very loosely about an almost identically-curved inner skin, like layers of over-puffed pastry, brittle and blackened. There was, in most places, sufficient space between the layers for him to maneuver, but it would be tiring to explore the entire ship in this fashion.

The inner skin seemed no more substantial, nor more intact, than the outer, and he thought he glimpsed at an analogous layer, incrementally less dark, beneath that, also.

He had entered near the stern; it seemed natural to explore forwards, moving towards the vessel's prow. Looking for—what?

"This trigger any memories?" he asked. His voice felt strained, as if speech was inappropriate in this place.

<None. The residue of unease is persistent, but frustratingly imprecise.>

"You can say that again."

<The—>

"Idiom."

He began deploying glowpatches along the path he was traversing. Fortunately, the patches' vacuum-adhesive attached tolerably well to the rough, flaked skin of the ship's interior.

Placing the third patch, Lem consulted his suit's heads-up. Oxygen for two hours yet, if he needed it, but he didn't wish to spend that long in here. Moving by vernier was tiring, and the low albedo of the interior surfaces meant that, even on full illumination, the torchbeam showed nothing more distant than about six metres. He suspected some clear lines-of-sight to be much longer than this, though for now they terminated in darkness.

It would take much more than two hours, at this rate, to reach the prow. He should return to the shuttle, move forward along the outside of the hull, and re-enter at a different point. The region he was exploring here wasn't telling him much. This notion firming in his mind, he was about to turn back when a movement snagged in the corner of his visor.

The movement was ragged, small, and near the limit of his torchbeam, but nonetheless distinct. A fragment of the interior wall fell away ahead of him.

Fell away, or ceased to exist.

"You see that?" he asked, his voice sounding too loud.

<I do not directly 'see' anything, but I perceived the phenomenon to which I believe you were referring. Lem, I recommend we return to the shuttle.>

"Not until I find out what that was."

Lem plugged another glowpatch against the wall beside him and moved toward the site of the apparition. In all likelihood, some trace of physical disturbance—it could well have been the cold jetting of propellant from his suit's verniers against a section of the wall behind him—had propagated a shock, slight but sufficient to shake some barely-attached shred of the wall's skin.

Except: fell away? The ship's spin-gravity was negligible. And, in the vessel's internal vacuum, there was little enough substance to propagate and focus any shock front. There was something wrong here.

He noticed, now, also that the fabric of the interior wall at this point appeared to be lighter in coloration and more durable than the region he'd first encountered on entering the vessel. Grazing the wall lightly with gloved fingers, he dislodged a powdery residue that, cloudy, suspended briefly in the vacuum quietude around him. A few fragments of powder clung to his glove. Illuminated by the torch, they dwindled into nothingness within a few seconds. Interstellar frost, subliming against his glove-heat or under the mild intensity of his torch-beam. Most likely frozen hydrogen, nitrogen, or carbon monoxide.

There hadn't been any frost further back, he was sure of it.

He reached the position from which the fragment had dislodged from the wall. Here the wall surface was thicker, and punctuated by a void through which the next inward layer was clearly visible. Shining the torchlight through the head-sized opening, he could now detect a concatenation of similar holes within three or four successive layers towards the ship's central axis. And as he swung the torch across, there was a glint of reflection from deeper within. Metal? Machinery?

"Any suggestions?" he asked. "Other than 'turn back now'?"

<I have nothing useful to suggest,> said The Voice, after too long a pause.

Nothing in his suit's toolkit was appropriate to the task of clearing a path through the obstructive carbonaceous sheeting of the layers. A series of karate-like hand motions were still sufficient to tear the fabric, albeit with some structural resistance. Nonetheless, the continual necessity to re-orient himself was tiresome and wasted propellant; and he was starting to sweat. He increased the suit's cooling.

Minutes lapsed, and he had penetrated to the onion-skin's next layer. These walls too were frosted, but here the powder persisted against glove-heat. Water ice, or small organics? There were other differences also in the texture of the skin here—more regularly ridged, less perforated, thicker.

There were four or five layers more of the wall-substance between him and the reflection's source. If the layers continued to thicken progressively as he went inward, he doubted his ability to breach them all before his suit's oxygen reserves became too depleted. He could, nevertheless, get further in before needing to turn back.

He was expanding the third layer's breach. For a few long seconds, he was finally afforded a clear, cleanly-lit view of the embedded metallic object. Then a sheet of the carbon-wall matter drifted across the aperture; but it was enough. It wasn't what he'd been expecting.

The Voice, it seemed, had seen it too. <Lem, we should leave now.>

Lem's voice was suddenly thick, his words slow. "Why? You want to explain to me what happened here?"

<I regret that the relevant memories are missing from suit's storage. Perhaps back on *Tuonela*, among the more extensive nano-neural array—>

"No. Not until I get some answers."

<There is insufficient in—>

"Bullshit! Those are copper impactors! This is one of your dirty little *seedship* secrets, isn't it? Like those *embryos* you all decided to terminate."

<Lem, there were errors of judgment made in the initial stages. But I do not have the da—>

"But you can *speculate*! You want to tell me how three impactors happen to be clumped together in the belly of a derelict alien ship? When *this*, right here right now, is apparently the first time anyone's had a close *look* at one of these things? Three in one spot implies an unbelievably accurate aim, or very close range, or—"

<Or a still-active redistribution mechanism within this vessel.>

Lem paused, his anger suddenly congealing into something different.

<Lem, I share your surprise at this discovery. I genuinely do not retain access, in this environment, to the pertinent memories. But I can surmise. These vessels are a vast reservoir of carbon. Their harvesting would have considerably simplified the seedships' task of establishing a human presence here. The mission protocols were clear on the importance of targeting optimal sources of raw materials—>

"And the secretiveness? The cover-up? That only makes any kind of sense if—"

<We should return to the shuttle. Now.>

"What the hell was *that*?"

<Probably a residual structural strain, redistributing through the impetus of your activities.>

"*Bull*shit! The thing *shook*. Like a *dog*."

<Lem. We should—>

"I know. Yes. I'm going. Shush now."

Another tremor pulsed through the derelict. Spooked, Lem hit the suit's main thruster. He caromed blindly back through the penultimate layer's breach, then made a fresh rift in the tenuous outer layer. Then he punched through into the clear darkness of interstellar space. Neither *Tuonela*'s running lights nor the shuttle's illumination panels were visible.

His brain, pulsing with sudden terrible realisation, was slow to alert him to the new danger.

Finally, his spacer's logic told him he was thrusting away from the derelict too fast. In seconds, he'd emerge from its shadow to face the unshielded streaming of interstellar dust grains, any one of which might be the bullet that killed him. Much as the copper impactors he'd glimpsed had, or had nearly, killed the ship.

Ship, or perhaps even *creature*. *Not* derelict. Alive, if not now then in the historically recent past.

But the tremor—surely that was an indication of something ongoing? Life? He fumbled the thruster nozzle, fighting against clammy palms, an insanely racing heartbeat, and ragged breath, as he forced himself to monitor the burn. He came to a halt, then brought his suit back in close to the creature's outermost layer.

Even through adrenalin-edged senses, the object had taken on a new quality. As a dead ship, it had appeared decrepit, decaying; now seen as a creature, those same features spoke of grace and economy of form. Even the once-unsightly gaps in the hull invited reinterpretation: they were not damage but a symptom of the absence of a need for fluid containment.

He should be close enough now to be shielded. Fear edged back towards anger, and a sense of betrayal.

<Lem. We should—>

"This distance, I think we're safe enough. The thing's cold enough to freeze hydrogen, it's not going to be capable of rapid movement."

<Nonetheless—>

"*You lot* said you'd built the colony ships up by *mining*. You never said anything about, about *flensing*!"

<Lem. Why does this trouble you?>

"Look, I'm tired of the lies, the coddling. I'm even more tired of being alone. And then, turns out *we're* not alone out here, and you lot had *known* that, you'd been carrying out what amounted to some sort of *eradication policy* in our name. . . Look, I don't know if those things have any intelligence, I doubt it, but I'm just sick of—I don't even *know* what I'm sick of, but—how can I trust you?" He stopped, uncertain, suddenly guilt-struck. He had no stomach for unpicking the centuries-long history of The Voice and its siblings, their role in bringing Earthlife to the cloud. But he was conflicted, torn between anger and the childlike adoration in which his ancestors had held the machinery of the life-enabling Voices.

<Lem. I've only ever acted in your best interests.>

"Yeah. Don't ask, don't tell. And then you go and bloody claim amnesia."

<It's an inevitable consequence of long-term nano storage. We die, in the end, just the same as you.>

Lem's response died in his throat. He'd been tracing his way back around the creature's hull, and his torchlight was now answered by the glow of *Tuonela*'s running lights. But the shuttle was not where he'd expected it, nor was it responding to his signals. Unease kindled anew in his loins.

At three kay back to *Tuonela*, protected only by the suit, he'd be dead from dust impact before he'd covered a quarter of the distance. Even if his air held. Even if he retained enough propellant for braking.

Signalling again, he gained an answer. Weak, and from an unexpected direction. The shuttle was upstream, near the creatureship's prow, six hundred meters from the position at which he'd matched velocities.

Dust drag on the low-mass shuttle would have pushed it *back* relative to the more streamlined "derelict." Therefore the latter must have moved— subtly, imperceptibly—while he'd been exploring within. It was, indeed, alive still.

But to what purpose?

One hour twenty. Still plenty of time, and propellant, to reach the shuttle and return to *Tuonela*. But he wasn't sure now if he'd get that chance.

"You have any idea why it's maneuvered behind the shuttle?"

<It is most likely just an instinctual behavior, though it might serve several functions. Shelter. Curiosity. Some kind of mating response->

"*Mating*?"

<We can only conjecture as to how these creatures propagate.>

"That's *all* I need."

<Or feeding. The shuttle must represent several years' nutrient supply, all in one negligible-velocity bundle. That could make it a very attractive morsel.>

"I almost prefer your previous suggestion."

<Yet I suspect the nutritive impulse is the most compelling.>

Lem had been working his way forward, attempting to remain shielded by the alien-vessel's ramscoop while retaining safe distance from its skin. But what, in this context, was safe? He still did not believe the creature capable of sudden dramatic movement, but he could not afford to be mistaken on that.

"We get through this in one piece, I have to signal the sister-ships about this. No more of you lot's dirty secrets. If this cloud is already a

145

biosphere, they deserve to know, they *need* to know. God knows what else might be out here. These things have a predator?"

The Voice remained silent.

"I *said*—"

This time, there was a faint responsive crackle, but nothing more. Noise, no signal. Hell of a time for nano-senescence to kick in, thought Lem bitterly.

The readings were contradictory, and it took time to reconcile the information. He was gaining on the shuttle, but more slowly than he was making progress against the skin of the alien/ship's hull beneath him.

The vessel was still maneuvering. Perhaps, having sensed the diffuse expanding nimbus of expended propellant from the shuttle's braking, it had fallen back. Maybe it was now repositioning itself anew in response to his suit's EVA jetting. Hungry, perhaps, for gas rather than less-digestible solids? He grew newly conscious of the sound of his own breathing, loud in the absence of The Voice's intrusive commentary.

The changing geometry of ship and shuttle would leave him exposed. Still short of the shuttle, he would be clear of the alien ship's ram-scoop, its *mouth*. He must put himself at the mercy of the non-attenuated flux of killingly swift dust.

A minute, most likely, not more; a ticket in life's terminal lottery.

He skimmed against the foremost sections of the leviathan's fuselage, which tapered subtly before flaring into the broad scoop at the very front.

Clear of the scoop now. Not, perhaps, merely its mouth. The scoop could also be an antenna, sensitive to radio wavelengths. An eye, to sense out the cloud's warmest, densest regions, the thick knots of substance which would, eons hence, condense to form stars and planets. Such environments would offer the best feeding-grounds here. . .

The leviathan, like *Tuonela*, was departing from D's material wealth. Escaping the seedship's predatory bombardment? The leviathan, like *Tuonela*, was heading for clump C. A shared trajectory, a similar purpose. Not such a chance meeting, after all.

He closed on the shuttle. Judged by *Tuonela*'s running lights, the smaller craft's configuration was wrong. It drifted askew. Gyros must have failed—more of this bloody nano shit.

With the shuttle's delicate interior exposed to the thin stream of abrasive dust, who knew what damage might have been done? But there was more besides: an inky occlusion like a snake or a cable. The black cord connected the lip of the leviathan's ram-scoop mouth to the shuttle's aft propellant nozzle.

Heart thumping, he impacted gently against the exposed cage and clung on, spraining his wrist. No time to strap in. Instead, he hooked a leg around the cage-frame for added leverage. He one-handed his own suit's verniers to correct the shuttle's attitude, re-establish the shielding, then toggled the forward propellant nozzle full-on in a brief burst.

The shuttle glided backwards, bending and then snapping the tethering tendril that ran from the leviathan's mouth. The fragment—knotted, obsidian-black, arm-thick and perhaps five metres in length—swung limp, brittle, from the shuttle's nozzle.

He did not take his eyes off the black rope as he consulted the heads-up on his visor for details of his current trajectory, oxygen remaining, and suit propellant.

Fifty-three minutes oh-two, ample to return to *Tuonela*. Good. He no longer wished to trust the shuttle's air-circ. Not that he seriously believed it could be contaminated, more that he lacked faith in the shuttle's judgment. He hadn't survived by taking more chances than minimally necessary.

He applied an additional couple of attitude bursts, to correct the slight residual tumble that resulted from snapping the leviathan's tether.

Chancing a glimpse behind him, there was no visible change in the alien vessel—it simply hung there. Probably nothing it did was rapid. At such low temperatures, economy of movement was king. In any event, he did not believe it could pose a serious threat to *Tuonela*. Even if the leviathan could match the gentle push of his ship's ion drive (which he doubted), it would assuredly lack the thrust of *Tuonela*'s fusion impulse engine.

Less than two kay to go, he'd be back on board within twenty minutes.

Most probably the maneuvering, the tether, had all been part of the leviathan's instinctual feeding response. It presumably lacked the means to break into the shuttle but could, over long ages, have attempted to digest the shuttle layer by atom-deep layer. Such a strategy would probably serve it well for most classes of solid material.

Strange, though, about the tether snapping like that. It made no sense, for a creature whose primary drive must surely be the hoarding, the jealous acquisition of substance in a matter-sparse environment. Why had the tether snapped at the *base* rather than simply relinquishing its hold? What conceivable advantage could possibly compensate the creature for the loss of such a substantial chunk of its gathered substance?

Lem was still pondering this mystery when the blacker-than-black casing on the seed-pod detonated. In response to the continued seeping warmth from the propellant housing, its shrapnel slammed into the shuttle's components. Fragments pierced a bank of auto-guidance nano-gyros, a section of the shuttle's shielding panel, and the sparsely-shielded tubing of his suit's main oxygen feed. Lem spasmed, and tried to scream.

It grew dark and unbearably cold.

Time passed. Then, slower than a glacier, the leviathan nudged forward to inspect its catch.

Monuments of Flesh and Stone
by Mike Resnick

Plutarch sure as hell wasn't much of a planet. It resembled a war zone, except that nobody had fought a war there, not in its entire history.

In fact, nobody had done much of anything. I know; I had to bone up on the place before I arrived.

In the whole history of the planet, not a single resident had ever sold a book. Or a story. Or a poem. Not one had ever become a professional actor, either on stage or in holos. None of them had ever composed a piece of music. If any of them had ever made a scientific or medical breakthrough, no one had recorded it. Of course, they had their share of local politicians, but not one of them had ever gone on to higher office off the planet. It was just a peaceful, forgotten little world, out on the edge of the Democracy, five-sixths of the way to the sparsely-populated Outer Frontier.

There wasn't a single thing to distinguish it—except for the statue.

It had been created by the Denebian sculptor Mixswan, who had stuff on display on half a hundred worlds. I don't know how they afforded him (or was he an it?); the whole population must have chipped in.

Mixswan didn't exactly do non-representational art, but the figures didn't look like the Men or Canphorites they were supposed to be. They appeared gold and spiky, all angles rather than muscles. One of them—it looked like it might have been the biggest—had broken and eroded over the centuries, and the bottom half was totally gone, while another was missing its head. Still, the statue instantly caught the eye—and I'll never know how Mixswan managed to keep that ball in the air.

It was the most impressive sight on Plutarch. Hell, it was the *only* impressive sight. I'd heard about it—after all, it was the only thing on Plutarch anyone ever talked about—and since I was here on business, I figured I'd better let the locals see me admiring it.

So I looked at it, and looked at it, and wondered what the hell kind of world would commission a statue to commemorate a defeat. I mean, if *I* ever celebrated a loss, I'd be looking for a new job the next day and no doubt about it. And yet Plutarch had created no statues, no edifices of any type to mark a triumph in this, a victory in that, a breakthrough in something else. Just the one statue that must have put them in debt for years, maybe decades given Mixswan's reputation. It didn't make any sense.

A woman with a pushcart walked over to me. I'd seen hundreds of different shopping carts in my life—anti-grav, self-propelled, able to select items off a shelf and grab them with artificial hands, even some that could morph into a flyer or a boat to take the owner home when he or she was done shopping—but this was the first I'd ever seen where the owner actually had to use her own strength to push the damned thing.

"I don't believe I've seen you here before," she said. "Welcome to Plutarch."

"Thank you," I said. "I just arrived a few hours ago."

"Have you come to admire our monument?"

"No, I have business here," I said. "But I find your monument very interesting."

She nodded. "It depicts the greatest moment in our history."

"I've read about it."

"You can see it, if you like. Every shop sells the holo."

"Maybe I'll buy one," I said.

"I hope you enjoy your stay," she said. "You have come at a lovely time of year."

I hadn't noticed anything particularly lovely about the time or the planet.

"The corn is just starting to come up out past the edge of the city," she continued. "If you open your window at night, you can hear it growing."

I gave her a look that said I was a little long in the tooth for fairy tales.

"It's true," she said. "It will grow eight or ten inches a night for the next week. It grows so quickly that you can hear the leaves flutter."

"I'll listen for it," I told her.

"Will you be here long?"

"I don't know," I answered. "Possibly you can help me. Do you know where I can find Damika Drake?"

She frowned. "He'll be in school until midafternoon." She paused. "I knew you were here for him." She stared at me long and hard. "Leave him alone."

"I'm not here to do him any harm," I said. "Quite the contrary. I—"

"We need him more than you do," she said and began laboriously pushing her cart away.

I figured I'd walk toward the city center. It was in the only city left on the planet, maybe the only one Plutarch ever had, and I knew the school had to be there. I circled the statue and found a road that would take me there. Sitting next to the road was an old beggar, seated on the ground, holding out a cup with a few coins in it and a misspelled sign saying "Desstitut" right next to him.

"Hello, old man," I said. "Doesn't it get warm sitting out here in the sun?"

"My cross-country racing days are over," he said with a wry grin. "'Course, they only lasted about ten minutes. Got some alms for the poor?"

"What the hell is an alm?"

He shrugged. "Beats me," he admitted. "I read it somewhere."

"Will credits do?"

"To coin a phrase, beggars can't be choosers."

I flipped a couple of Democracy credits into his cup.

"Thanks, Mister," he said. "You're here for Damika Drake, aren't you?"

"Yes."

"Figgers," he said. "Only two reasons for anyone to come to Plutarch. The statue and the Drake kid. I saw you looking at the statue, and you're still here, so it got to be for the kid."

"It is," I said. "Can you tell me anything about him?"

"Not much," he replied. "I can tell you about the statue, though."

"I've heard about it."

"Not from an insider," he said.

I tossed him another couple of credits. "Okay, let's hear it."

"I'd love to," he said, "but my throat just dried up."

"I assume a glass of water won't open it up," I suggested.

He grinned. "I'm allergic to water. Better make it beer."

"Okay," I said, helping him to his feet. "Lead the way."

He made a beeline for a broken-down building about two hundred feet away. The place was dimly-lit, with one squeaky fan hanging down from the ceiling and spinning slowly. There was a human bartender—the place obviously couldn't afford a robot—and we sat down on a couple of well-used stools at the bar.

"A couple of tall ones," said the beggar. "My friend is buying."

The bartender looked at me. "You new here?"

"Just passing through," I said, slapping some money on the bar.

"That's what they all say," replied the bartender. "Especially if they've got any money."

"I was just about to tell him about the game," said the beggar.

"He doesn't look like he cares," said the bartender.

"I'm interested," I said.

"Then I'd better stick around, just in case old Jeremy here messes up the details."

He brought out three beers, one for each of us.

"It was 421 years ago," began Jeremy the beggar. "Nobody'd ever heard of Plutarch—"

"He means the planet, not the man," put in the bartender.

"He knows that," said Jeremy irritably. "Anyway, we were just a little backwater world with nothing special to our name."

"Except Damika," said the bartender.

"I'm coming to that," said Jeremy. "We just had one thing out of the ordinary, one thing that made Plutarch special. We had a young man named Damika." He paused wistfully. "They say he could fly, that he moved so fast the human eye couldn't follow him."

"They say a lot of things," added the bartender. "He was just a man."

"He had to be more than that," said Jeremy doggedly. "Anyway, we entered a team in the Sector basketball tournament. There were forty-eight teams entered, only nineteen of them human. Bookmakers were giving fifty-to-one against us in any game, and three-thousand-to-one against our winning the whole thing."

"But you won," I said.

He nodded. "Damika averaged 63 points and 22 rebounds a game. Nobody had ever seen anything like it. Even legends from the Earthbound days like Milt the Stilt and Johnny Magic never performed at that level. Suddenly people knew who we were. We had tourists coming to watch us practice before the Quinellus Cluster championships, and even better, we had investors. All because of the basketball team."

"All because of one young man, actually," said the bartender.

"He must have been something to see, this Damika," I said.

"They say he jumped so high and stayed in the air so long that textbooks had to rewrite the law of gravity."

"It's a nice bedtime story," said the bartender. "He was the best. There's no sense trying to making him into anything more than that."

"Anyway," continued Jeremy, "we were huge underdogs, but we won the Quinellus tournament—and then we went up against the Canphor VI team for the championship of the Democracy. They say more people watched that game than any sporting event in history. Think of it! For one night, two hundred billion people knew where Plutarch was! Hell, if Damika had said he wanted to be king, he'd have gotten it by acclamation."

"But he was supposed to be a modest, decent young man," said the bartender. "All he wanted was to bring some reflected glory to the planet."

"We were big underdogs again," said Jeremy. "We were giving up seven or eight inches and maybe fifty pounds of muscle per player. But you can see it for yourself if you buy the holo. The Canphorites got off to a big lead, because they double- and triple-teamed Damika. We were playing on McCallister II, which was supposed to be a neutral world, but its gravity was about a hundred and ten percent Standard, and it wore on our lighter players more than on the Canphorites. They were winning 52-38 at the half, and everyone thought it was over."

"Damned near was," agreed the bartender.

"But then Damika just took over the game," said Jeremy, his emaciated face lighting up with excitement and pride some four centuries after the fact. "He did things no one had ever seen before, things no one has seen since, and he single-handedly brought us back from the abyss."

"He scored 45 points in the second half," added the bartender. "No one had seen anything like that, not then, not ever. The people who'd spent their savings flying in from Plutarch were screaming and cheering him on, and he didn't let them down."

"He tied it with a basket at the final buzzer," continued Jeremy, "and then the game went into overtime. We were down one point with ten seconds to go, but we got the ball into Damika's hands, and we knew that he wouldn't let us down."

"You sound like you were there," I commented.

"I wish I'd been," replied Jeremy. "Ten seconds from galactic glory!"

"Or galactic obscurity," said the bartender.

Jeremy nodded. "Damika drove to the basket, and two hundred billion people knew he was going to leap four feet in the air and stuff the ball through the hoop—and then it happened."

"I read about it."

"That's the part I hate to watch," said the bartender.

"Everyone hates to watch it," said Jeremy. "One of the Canphorites gave him an elbow just as he was about to take off. He fell, and even on the holo you can hear that *crack!* when his ankle broke. It sounded like a rifle shot."

"He pulled himself up onto one leg to hop off the court," said the bartender, "and the Canphorite coach began screaming that the tournament rules said that if a fouled player could stand on his own power, he had to take his own free throws. There was nothing about having to stand on two feet. You could see the bone sticking out through the skin, but Damika tried to take the free throws himself. His eyes were glazed, his whole body was shaking from the effort just to keep from falling down, he missed both shots, and that was that."

"He never got rid of the limp," said Jeremy, "and he never played again. We didn't have much of a team without him, and in more than four centuries we've never made it as far as the quarter-finals of the Sector tournament."

"The tourists stopped coming. . ." said the bartender.

"The investors stopped investing. . ." said Jeremy.

"And we were nothing again, just the way we'd been before Damika."

"Still, for one shining moment, we were *somebody*. People from halfway across the galaxy knew about us. Dozens of holo crews landed on Plutarch to interview us." Jeremy paused. "We knew we were never going to reach such heights again, so we took our planetary treasury and hired the best sculptor in the Democracy to commemorate the moment that Damika grabbed the last rebound in regulation time and scored with two seconds left on the clock."

"You haven't kept it up very well," I said.

"It's four hundred years old," said Jeremy. "It costs money to keep it up."

"And our citizens desert us as fast as they can," said the bartender. "We had almost half a million inhabitants when Damika plays against Canphor. We've got about sixty thousand now, maybe a little less."

"He's here for Damika Drake," said Jeremy.

"Big surprise," said the bartender. "Why else would anyone come to Plutarch?"

"I couldn't help noticing the similarity in names," I said.

"Three-quarters of the boys born on Plutarch are called Damika," said Jeremy. "Every parent hopes *their* Damika will be the one to restore our former glory."

"As if it lasted for more than a month," said the bartender dryly.

"You gonna take Damika Drake away?" asked Jeremy.

I shrugged. "I don't know. I've got to talk to him, see what he can do first."

"I never even asked," said Jeremy. "Who do you coach for?"

"The Sagamore Hill Chargers, out of Roosevelt III."

"I've heard of them," said the bartender. "You made the semi-finals out in the Albion Cluster last year, didn't you?"

"Yes," I said. "We're probably one good player away from a title. I did a little research, and I think the Drake kid might be the answer."

"Well, you did your research more carefully than anyone else," said Jeremy. "We're so far off the beaten track, you're the only one who's shown up to recruit him."

"Have you seen him play?" I asked.

"Yeah," said Jeremy. "He's good, but he's not what you need to put you over the top."

"Kid needs more muscle, and he telegraphs his passes," offered the bartender.

"He's not much from more than twenty feet out, either," added Jeremy.

"You make it sound like a wasted trip," I said.

"I hate to tell you, but it is," said Jeremy.

"As long as I'm here, I might as well take a look, just to justify my expense account," I said.

They exchanged looks. The bartender started rubbing the totally clean surface of the bar with a cloth. "Up to you," he said at last. "But don't say you weren't warned."

"This was my idea," I said. "You're off the hook." I turned to Jeremy. "You want to point out the school to me?"

"Walk out the door, and it's two blocks down on your left," he said. "It's mostly empty these days, but back when the real Damika was around, we used to fill just about every desk in every room."

I thanked him, left a tip on the bar, and walked out of the tavern. I turned left, walked two blocks, and since I was looking ahead at the school I almost tripped over a drunk who was sleeping it off at the edge of the sidewalk. (It had been a slidewalk, but I suspected the mechanism hadn't worked in a couple of centuries.)

"Excuse me," I said as he grunted in surprise. "Are you all right?"

"I will be," he said, getting unsteadily to his feet. "My own fault for not going all the way home last night."

"Maybe you'd better head for home now," I said. "Better late than never."

"No, it's almost practice time."

"What are you practicing?" I asked.

"Not *me*," he said. *"Them."*

"Them?"

"The team," he said. "It's the only pleasure I get these days."

"So you're a fan," I said.

He spat on the ground. "I couldn't care less about basketball."

"I'm a little confused," I said. "I thought you said—"

"Basketball is where we fell from our exalted position," he said. "It's the only way we'll ever recapture it."

"There are lots of ways," I said. I'm a coach. I know. The world doesn't change because you win or lose a game—except that *their* world did.

"Not for Plutarch," he said. "You know, every time a baby boy is born, people gather around it and try to see if he could possibly be the One."

"The one?" I repeated.

"The One who will lead us back to glory."

"What makes you so sure it's got to be a basketball player?" I asked. "Why not some other sport?"

"Football, murderball, baseball, prongball, they all have bigger teams and take more equipment. Look at us. We're lucky to field a basketball team."

"Well, let's go take a look at them," I said, and we walked off toward a playground on the side of the school.

A few minutes later classes were let out, and about two hundred kids left the building and headed off for their homes. But about twenty stuck around the court to watch, and after another five minutes ten young men came out in shorts and t-shirts. Their coach immediately divided them into two teams—but *not* with five on a side. One side—the shirts—had seven players; the other—the skins—had only three.

There was one kid on the skins I couldn't take my eyes off. The scrimmage hadn't started, but he moved with such an animal grace, carried himself with such confidence, I knew he had to be Damika Drake.

The coach gave the ball to the shirts, and they began bringing it down the court. Drake jumped into a passing lane at the last second, intercepted a pass, dribbled the length of the court, and took off like a helicopter. He couldn't have stood much more than six feet, but he had a vertical leap of better than forty-five inches. I'd never seen anything like it.

Next time the shirts came down the court they kept the ball away from Drake, finally shot it up, and missed. His head was higher than the rim when he grabbed the rebound. He fired an outlet pass to a teammate who waited for him to catch up, then fed him the ball near half-court—and he put it up from there. Drained it, as if it was something he did every day (and for all I knew, he did).

The kid was everywhere. I wasn't keeping official score, but in the ten minutes I watched I think he grabbed eight rebounds, blocked five shots, picked up four assists, and scored twenty-three points.

And I was thinking: *Sure, Jeremy, the kid's not ready for the big time. Sure, bartender, he can't shoot and he can't jump and he probably can't move to his left. Sure, guys. I'm just wasting my time coming here to recruit him.*

And then, on a hunch, I looked around the playground and saw maybe two dozen adults had stopped by to watch Damika Drake through the fence. Ten or twelve more were looking out from the windows of a nearby decrepit apartment building.

I suddenly realized that most of them were looking at *me.* And their faces didn't say, *Can he be the One?* No, it was, *He is the One, our last chance, our only chance. Please don't take him away from us. We've waited four hundred years for him. We'll make him happy, we'll treat him like a king, hell, we'll* make *him a king if he asks us to . . . but leave him here. All you need is a player. We* need *a savior.*

I didn't have to watch the rest of the practice. This kid was everything he was cracked up to be, and more. I'm surprised I couldn't see wings on his back, given the way he flew to the bucket. He'd missed two shots the whole time I was watching him, which mean he hit at better than a 90% rate. The kid who led our conference last year was a 52% shooter, and everyone thought that was phenomenal.

But that kid's planet was flush with gold and plutonium deposits, it had some of the best farmland in the sector, and it was the banking center for a dozen nearby worlds. They were proud of him, but if he vanished tomorrow, life there wouldn't miss a beat. No one was asking *him* to bring back the self-respect that had been missing for four hundred years. If adults watched him practice, it was because they were fans of the game, and no other reason. He didn't come from an almost-deserted school on an almost-deserted planet with an almost-proud history that was cut short ten seconds before it came to fruition.

As I took an aircar back to the spaceport, past the derelict buildings, the forgotten dreams, the dashed hopes of a world, I felt my options disappearing one by one. They were gone by the time I reached the tiny spaceport and contacted the school's athletic director via the subspace radio.

"How'd it go?" he asked.

"Easy trip," I replied. "I should be home tomorrow."

"So what about this kid?"

"He's okay in the bush leagues," I said, "but he's not what we're after."

"Ah, well, I suppose it was worth the trip. On your way back, stop off at Odysseus in the Iliad system. They've got a seven-footer there who's supposed to be pretty hot stuff. Greenveldt's after him, but he hasn't committed to them yet."

"Will do," I said, and signed off.

I turned and looked back at the decaying city.

Okay, I thought, *I'm giving you your future, at the cost of some of my own. You damned well better make the most of it.*

That's a hell of a burden to put on any kid. Still, he's got the right name for it. Maybe I'll see him again, in the finals—if we get that far. There's no question that he'd be waiting for us there.

Him and a forgotten world.

Hope
by Michael A. Burstein

Samantha Evangelina Jones hated the dark, hated the cold, and hated confined spaces. The irony was never lost on her, but it felt most poignant every "morning," when the generation ship's computer would wake her up for the Alpha shift.

This particular morning was no exception. The computer's alarm chimes began softly, as usual, and then became louder and louder, yanking her out of her dream. It had been a good dream, too. She had been walking naked and alone on the spacious surface of a planet, her feet wet from the dew of the cool grass underneath, while above her she saw nothing but blue skies and yellow sunlight. It made her return to the reality of the *Ballyshannon* that much more revolting.

"Off," she said, and the chimes ceased.

Jones moaned and stretched as she rolled out of her bed. The artificial gravity caused by the spinning of the ship was set to Earth-normal, which had bothered her ever since the last Earth-born on the ship had died ten years ago. She kept asking the engineers about lowering the gravity, and they kept giving her the same runaround, explaining to her why the laws of physics made it a difficult proposition, if not impossible. She would nod her head as she pretended to understand their byzantine explanations. She didn't actually believe them, but she figured if she kept up the fight eventually, maybe one of them would become smart enough to figure it out.

In the meantime, she dealt. As she did every day of her life.

She walked the few meters to her private bath, a luxury provided only to the captain and the senior officers of the *Ballyshannon*, and one that she privately thanked God for every "Sunday" morning in chapel. Within a minute, she had showered, as the ship's computer knew to the millisecond how much water was allowed per day to each of the ten thousand, four hundred and sixty-eight humans on board. If she had stayed in the shower any longer, the water would have turned off suddenly, as she knew from years of experience.

Rank hath its privileges, she thought as the heat lamp dried her off, *but not too many.*

She donned her captain's jumpsuit uniform, checked her appearance in the monitor, and smoothed down a few wrinkles. All according to the usual, mind-numbing routine.

She turned around, getting ready to leave her cabin and head for the bridge, when she saw the stranger flicker into existence in front of her, blocking her way out. He was an odd looking man, with a wrinkled face, long white hair, and a three-days' growth of stubble on his chin. His torn clothing, a brown shirt and tan pants, hung loosely on his slight frame. His eyes seemed haunted and confused, and he darted his head around in apparent disbelief.

"Miracle of miracles," he muttered in a raspy voice. "It worked. It finally worked."

Jones may have cursed her role as captain, but she had to admit to herself she was the right person for the job. Despite having had a stranger— *my God*, she thought, *a stranger!*—materialize in her cabin, she maintained her calm. She quickly evaluated the situation and decided that she was not hallucinating. She began moving her right hand toward her side pocket, where she kept a stylus, in case she needed a weapon.

"Who the hell are you?" she asked, with a touch of anger.

The man stopped looking around and stared at her, his jaw agape. "Captain Jones? You are Captain Samantha Evangelina Jones?"

"Yes?"

"And this is the *Ballyshannon*?"

She narrowed her eyes and nodded. "Yes, it is."

He shook his head and cackled. "It worked. It really worked."

Jones put some more steel in her voice as she closed her fingers on her stylus. "Identify yourself. Now."

"What's the date?"

"The date?" The question surprised Jones even more than the man's sudden appearance in her cabin.

He moved forward, his hands open in plea. "Yes, the date. What's the date?"

With a quick motion, she pulled the stylus out of her pocket and pointed it at the man. "Stop!"

He obeyed. "Sorry, I didn't mean—"

"Step back."

"Okay." He stepped back two paces. "I'd still like to know the date."

"Ship time, it's—"

"No!" he shouted, and then he shook his head. "I'm sorry. Gregorian. I need Gregorian."

Jones sighed, but asked, "Computer, what's the Gregorian date?"

The computer's flat voice responded, "Impossible to determine precisely without taking into account adjustments for relativistic travel."

The man said, "Closest estimate, then."

After a moment, the computer responded. "April 25, 2335."

He closed his eyes and smiled, smoothing the wrinkles on his face. "Good. Then I'm not too late."

"Too late for what?" Jones asked, keeping the stylus pointed at the man.

He opened his eyes again and looked directly into Jones's face, unnerving her. "I'm not too late to save everyone on the *Ballyshannon*."

"What are you talking about?"

"Captain, you need to turn this ship around. Now."

Jones pulled her head back and gave the stranger what she hoped was an impudent stare. "Excuse me. I don't take orders from anyone on this ship. Especially not from strangers who appear out of nowhere."

"But—" the man began, then cleared his throat. "Of course not. My apologies. But it's still imperative that you turn the ship around."

"No. What is imperative is that you tell me who you are, where you came from, and what you are doing here."

The man stared at Jones for a moment, then nodded. "Of course, of course. My apologies. There's no way you could yet understand the urgency of my mission."

"Which you will tell me about as soon as you've answered my other questions."

He nodded again. "Of course. But could I sit down first?"

Jones pointed her stylus at the one chair in her cabin. "Go ahead."

"Thanks." The man eased himself into the chair, which adjusted itself to his contours. He closed his eyes for a moment. "Comfortable."

"Would you like a beverage?" Jones asked him sarcastically.

He didn't seem to notice her tone. "No thank you." He looked around her cabin again. "Wow. The ship looks so young, so new."

Jones sat down on the edge of her bed. "The ship's almost one hundred years old."

"It's all a matter of perspective. From my point of view, that's young."

161

Jones shook her head. "You have an odd perspective. Now would you like to tell me who you are?"

"My name is Boranal Reynolds."

"Reynolds? We have a Reynolds family aboard."

"I know. They're my family."

"Impossible. There's no one named Boranal Reynolds on board."

"That's because I haven't been born yet."

"Pardon? How is that possible? And where the hell did you come from?"

Reynolds took a deep breath and let it out in a slow whistle before answering. "I'm a time traveler."

Jones hesitated, then nodded. "That makes sense."

"You believe me?" he asked.

"Let's assume for the moment I believe you, okay? I have a few questions to ask."

"Ask away. I have nothing to hide."

Jones pocketed her stylus. "What are you doing here?"

"I'm here to convince you to turn this ship around. The future of all the lives on board depends on it."

A few hours later, Reynolds sat in the ship's makeshift prison cell, while Jones sat in the bridge office consulting with Goranic McGrath, the head of ship security. As the *Ballyshannon* was a generation ship, the administration of the ship was a forced combination of naval discipline and small-town community governing. Jones was captain of the ship but also the mayor-for-life; McGrath served as chief security officer, but most of his work was more like a community's chief of police.

The *Ballyshannon* wasn't just a ship; it was a small town flying through the universe.

"Thank you for helping me get Reynolds to the jail without anyone seeing," Jones said.

McGrath nodded. "His presence would have been difficult to explain."

"It's even harder to explain when you see him appear out of nowhere."

"Actually, that would have made it easier. If you would only let me install cameras throughout the whole ship, and not just in—"

"Goranic. Privacy concerns? Not this, and not now. We've got a more pressing problem to worry about."

"Sorry."

"So do you believe his story?"

"Which part?"

"Any of it."

"Let's break it down piece by piece." McGrath began to tick off his points with his fingers. "Point number one, is he a time traveler."

"Yes."

"The way I see it, either he's a time traveler or someone who has invented a form of instantaneous teleportation. And if that were the case, why would he make up a story about being from the future? Ergo, he's a time traveler?"

"You accept that his time machine had to stay in the future?"

"Why not?"

Jones nodded. "Of course, there's the possibility that we're both hallucinating."

"Unlikely. If it were just one of us—"

"It was a joke, Goranic. Next point, please."

McGrath nodded and ticked off the next point on another finger. "Is he who he says he is? I had the computer do a genetic scan of this Boranal Reynolds and do a comparison with the other Reynoldses on board the ship. The scan indicates a close to one hundred percent certainty that he is a great-grandson of one of the Reynolds family."

"Who?"

McGrath smiled. "I'd rather not say. Privacy concerns, need-to-know, and all that."

Jones smiled; McGrath was using her own argument against her. "Very well, but if we need to present evidence to others on the ship—"

"We'll cross that bridge when we come to it," McGrath said.

"What I would give to see a bridge," Jones said.

A moment passed, and then McGrath said, "So. Point number three. His story."

Jones nodded. "Yes. Computer, please play the recording of the interview with Boranal Reynolds in the jail cell. Time stamp Alpha one twenty-three."

A speaker built into the ceiling of the room began playing the dialogue from just a short time ago.

"Captain," Reynolds had said, "I really resent this treatment."

"Put yourself in my position," Jones had replied. "How am I supposed to explain the existence of a stranger on board the ship? We're literally light-years away from any other human beings."

There was a pause, and then Reynolds said, "Okay, I can accept that."

"Fine. Now explain what you mean, that I have to turn the ship around or else everyone on it will die."

"Captain, when do you expect to reach the New Beginnings star?"

"One hundred more years or so. The computer can give the exact figure. It doesn't matter to me; I'll be long dead."

"True—I mean, no one lives that long."

"So won't most everyone on the ship already be dead by the time we get there?"

"That is also true. I meant to say that the descendents of the current population will die. Does it matter?"

"It does. Now make your statement. Why must I turn the ship around?"

"Give me a moment. This is difficult for me." There was a pause. "Okay. Here's the problem. New Beginnings does have a habitable planet, just as everyone expected. But the planet is already inhabited."

"Aliens?"

"Yes, intelligent aliens who resented our arrival. When the *Ballyshannon* arrived—or maybe I should say arrives—we get massacred. A few of us managed to use the shuttles to get back to the ship, but we're still flying around out there. And the ship is starting to break down. Chances are the rest of us will die out as well.

"We've been doing whatever we can to try to improve our chances. I've been working on time travel my entire life, hoping I'd be able to come back in time and avert the disaster. And now I'm here and you're here, and I'm telling you: turn this ship around now, or you'll doom the *Ballyshannon* to failure."

"Computer, stop," Jones said. She drummed her fingers on the table. "So, what do you think?" she asked McGrath.

"Honestly? I think we'd better turn the ship around."

She sighed. "Then you believe him."

"Occam's razor," McGrath replied. "The simplest explanation is most likely the right one."

"Problem is, we can't just turn the ship around."

"Why not?"

"Do you want to try to convince ten thousand people that a time traveler from the future has told us we have to turn the ship around?"

McGrath opened his mouth to reply, then closed it. He looked into the distance for a moment and then finally spoke. "I see your point. But with all due respect, captain, the evidence is crystal clear. And you and the senior officers do have the authority to take whatever action you need to ensure everyone's safety."

Jones frowned. She thought for a moment, and then decided that McGrath deserved to know. "Goranic, I'm about to let you in on a secret, a big one that only a few of the senior officers know about."

"What is it?"

"We can't return to Earth. It's no longer a habitable planet."

McGrath's eyes opened wide. "You're kidding."

"Why should you say that? It should be no harder to believe than time travel."

"I—I suppose you're right. But the evidence for that is right in front of me."

"I have evidence for the Earth's fate, and I'd be happy to—I mean, I'll share it with you later."

"What is it, if I may ask?"

"A recording by my father."

"Ah." Jones's father had been captain of the *Ballyshannon* before her. McGrath would know as well as anyone on the ship that Jones's father could be trusted.

"Exactly. Apparently there were more important reasons to build the *Ballyshannon* other than simply because the human race could. The planet was dying."

"I always thought we stopped radio contact with Earth to keep people focused on New Beginnings."

"No, that was just the cover story. In truth, we haven't had radio contact with Earth in years, because there's no one there anymore."

"I guess it's a good thing no one on board is Earth-born anymore."

"It is."

"So. We can't go forward, and we can't go back. What do we do?"

Jones pondered the question. Some idea was trying to make itself known to her, but every time she thought she had it, it fled. It felt like she was doing a jigsaw puzzle in her mind, but the pieces were morphing as she tried to place them in the puzzle. . .

She shook the exhaustion out of her head and stood up. "What do we do? I go talk to Reynolds again. Meanwhile, you start figuring out how we should inform everyone on the ship that we have a new face on board."

The prison cell on the *Ballyshannon* was an afterthought, made necessary five years into the trip when one of the men on board had killed his husband over an illicit affair. The crew had remodeled a utility room and turned it into a cell, with conditions even more Spartan than the already cramped quarters everyone else lived in.

Jones had the computer unlock the cell and she entered without knocking. Reynolds was lying on the bed; given the size of the cell, he had little room to stretch out anywhere else.

When Jones entered, he sat up. "So, have you turned the ship around yet?"

"No." She sat on the only chair in the room; this one didn't shape itself to anyone. "I have a few questions first."

Reynolds sighed. "Every second we're getting farther from Earth and closer to destruction."

"Let's start there. Why did you show up today?"

"Huh?"

"If you really are a time traveler from the future, then why did you show up here and now? If the *Ballyshannon*'s mission is doomed to end in failure, wouldn't it have made more sense to go back to the beginning?"

Reynolds frowned. "Do you know anything about temporal mechanics?"

"Meaning?"

"Time travel. Do you know anything about time travel?"

"Of course not. Until this morning, I didn't think it was possible."

Reynolds nodded. "Then let me explain. Time travel is quantized. I can only go back in time a certain fixed number of years. I couldn't go back to before the ship was launched; today was the earliest I could arrive."

Jones pondered this for a moment. "Well then, why can't you leap back again from this point in time, and keep going until you reach the day of the launch?"

Reynolds shook his head sadly. "Time travel requires an enormous expenditure of energy. I'd have to drain the *Ballyshannon* of every joule to make another jump, assuming I could even build another device."

"That implies that you already did drain the *Ballyshannon*, in the future."

He averted his eyes. "It was necessary."

"So how were you expecting to get back?"

Reynolds looked grim. "I wasn't."

"So that means this was a one-way mission for you."

"It was. It is."

Jones stood up. "Damn you."

"What?"

"You heard me. Damn you." She felt the beginnings of tears well up in her eyes and fought them; it wouldn't look good for the ship's captain to cry in front of anyone, especially Reynolds.

"Damn me? Why? I'm the one who's trying to save everyone on the ship."

"That's just it. Damn you for making it necessary for me to make this decision." Jones suddenly felt the weight of all her responsibilities crushing her.

"I'm sorry, Captain. If I could have figured out any other way, if I could have traveled back further in time, I would have. I'm a victim of the situation as much as you are."

"*No one* is a victim as much as I am!" Jones shouted. The words echoed through the room before fading away. It was a few seconds before Reynolds spoke again.

"In my time," he said, "you were remembered as the most important captain of them all, the one who made sure that the mission continued on track. We never saw you as a victim. The future hailed you as a hero."

Jones rubbed her eyes. "I didn't choose my destiny. My parents forced it upon me. My role in life is to be nothing but a transition." She sighed. "I'm a shepherd is what I am. I have a ship full of descendents of one group of planet-born, whose role is to be nothing more than the ancestors for a later generation of planet-born."

"It was hard for us too," Reynolds said.

Jones glared at him. "When our parents left Earth, they just assumed that their children would embrace the choices they had made for us."

"Selfish of them."

"It was, indeed."

Reynolds took a deep breath. "Captain Jones, I sympathize, I truly do, but this doesn't come any closer to solving our problem. I know you believe me; I can tell. So I know that you know that you need to turn this ship around and return to Earth."

"I can't."

"You *have* to. You have no choice. If you don't turn this ship around, then in one hundred more years, everyone on it will die."

"If I do turn this ship around, the same thing will happen." She hesitated, then told Reynolds the same secret she had just told McGrath. "Earth is no longer a habitable planet."

Reynolds frowned. "What?"

"I'll explain it to you later. But believe me when I tell you that Earth is no longer an option."

Jones watched Reynolds study her face, and then he slumped. "No one ever said anything. Captain—that means my mission was doomed to failure from the outset." He paused. "I should have stayed in the future for what it was worth. I'm sorry I brought this upon you."

"You should be."

Reynolds chuckled. "And I guess I can't ask you to drop me off somewhere."

"No, you—" Jones cut off. That was it, the missing piece of the puzzle.

"Wait a minute," she said. "Maybe we can."

"I was kidding."

"No, listen. I can't turn this ship around and take us back to Earth. But there's no reason why we have to keep heading toward New Beginnings."

Reynolds opened his eyes wide. "Of course, of course. There's still time to figure out another destination."

Jones nodded. "We'll have to tell the entire population the truth, though. About you, and about Earth."

Reynolds stood up. "I'd be happy to testify to anything you need to save—to save my family."

Jones nodded. "All my life, I wanted to give the people on this ship more than just the pointlessness of their transitional lives. Your presence here will let them know that they will be remembered and appreciated by their descendents."

"Assuming their descendents survive. Which will be more likely once you change course."

"But it's not guaranteed?" Jones asked.

Reynolds shook his head. "My appearance here has completely altered the timeline. I have no idea what the new future will hold. But from what I lived through, it has to be better."

Jones nodded. "We'll give them hope. That's the best I can do."

Watching
by Sandra McDonald

Atlantic Ocean
February, 2028

Lieutenant Matt Castellano's first clue that something was wrong on the *U.S.S. Obama* was when he lifted his computer tablet and saw a video of his commanding officer taking a piss.

For a moment he could only stare, perplexed. It had been a long day of high-tempo drills, standing watch, and shuffling paperwork under three hundred meters of cold Atlantic seawater. After dinner he'd hoped to relax a little, but then the towed sonar array had gone screwy. Now it was almost oh-two-hundred. He'd come back to his stateroom wanting to crawl into bed but knowing he had to write a report to the skipper. Who was mysteriously displayed on Castellano's tablet, aiming into the bowl and reaching under his T-shirt to scratch his hairy belly.

Some kind of prank, obviously, from one of his roommates. Lieutenant John Misuraca's bottom bunk was empty—he was standing the mid-watch. In the top rack, Lieutenant Bobby Weiner was snoring with his VR goggles wrapped securely over his eyes. Castellano looked back at the tablet. This ship was very quiet—hell, being quiet was part of the mission—but at this early hour, with two-thirds of the crew asleep, the splash of the CO's urination was eerily loud.

Hardly anything on a submarine was private. The crew lived, slept, and breathed in each other's faces twenty four/seven. Castellano was accustomed to seeing people in the head and being seen in return—but watching the captain, when it was obvious he didn't know he'd been recorded, was creepily akin to voyeurism.

He slid the tablet's power button off, but the images continued.

He hit the mute, but the sound stayed loud.

On the screen, the CO flushed the toilet and stepped back into his stateroom. The camera followed him as he slid back into bed, punched his pillow, and stared up at the overhead. Castellano wondered how the camera could see so well in what had to be a darkened stateroom. He tapped on the screen, but no software seemed to be running and the power indicator was still unlit.

"What the—" Castellano sat on the stateroom's lone chair. "Jesus."

The screen shifted to an exterior shot of St. Peter's Square in Vatican City. Castellano had been to Rome only once, honeymooning, but there was no mistaking the gracefully curved buildings and open square. Sounds of conversation and ringing bells accompanied the view. The sun poured warm yellow illumination down on the crowds and he was jealous; it had been five long weeks since he'd seen the sun and sky.

He checked the chronometer bolted to the bulkhead and calculated the time difference to Rome. Mid-morning there. Goosebumps crawled up both arms. It was impossible that an unpowered, un-networked computer tablet on a submerged submarine could be showing him a live shot of Rome. Just as it was impossible to show him the CO in his cabin.

He rose, shook Weiner's shoulder and pulled his VR goggles off. "How'd you do it, Bobby?"

Weiner jerked up. "What? What's wrong?"

"What the hell did you do to my computer?"

"You wake me up because you broke your goddamned tablet?" Weiner sank back down and pulled his blanket over his head. "Go to bed."

Castellano tugged the blanket off. "Look! It's the Vatican."

"I don't care if it's the Pope! I'm Jewish."

The tablet switched views again. Castellano didn't recognize the interior scene but Weiner balked. "How'd you do that? That's my synagogue back in Norfolk. Judy and I go every week—"

The view switched to Judy Weiner, asleep in her pajamas on a blue sofa with a quilt thrown over her legs. Nearby a flat 3TV was playing a movie Castellano didn't recognize, complete with loud music and the rat-tat-tat of gunfire.

"What the hell?" Weiner's face turned ruddy. "You've got video of my wife?"

Castellano's goosebumps were back, but accompanying them was the thrill of putting together puzzle pieces. "Laura," he said. "Show me Laura."

The tablet switched to Laura Castellano. Asleep in their antique four-poster bed, her honey-gold hair swirled on the pillow. The deep abiding ache of separation that Castellano felt every day made itself known with a sharp stab. The submarine service was a damn lonely way to spend a life. For both of them. Seven years of marriage and motherhood had left her more desirable than ever, and for a moment he wanted to nothing more than crawl through the screen into her embrace.

Weiner asked, "Is this a game?"

The blankets moved behind Laura. The camera zoomed in. Castellano knew that his youngest, Tommy, still liked to sleep with mommy. The shape that rose up beside Laura had dark hair but was larger and longer than Tommy. It was a man with a bare chest and a military haircut, putting a languid arm over Laura's waist and burying his face against her neck—

"Jesus," Weiner said, and the view went back to Rome. "Matt, what did you do?"

He prided himself on being cool under pressure, but for some reason his hands had begun to shake. "It's crazy," he said, grateful that his voice came out level. "It's not—there's no way."

Weiner swung out of his bunk, and tried to take the tablet. "Give me that."

"No." He clutched the tablet tightly and said, "Get your own."

A mutter, a curse, and then Weiner was grabbing his own tablet from its slot. It showed a picture of the stateroom itself, with Castellano and Weiner both in it.

"Where's the camera?" Weiner waved one hand, turned and then pointed to a blank spot on the bulkhead.

"Cover it up," Castellano said.

Weiner placed his hand on the bulkhead. The camera point of view shifted to another spot, higher up on the ceiling.

"There's got to be an explanation." Weiner pulled on a set of khaki coveralls—new to the fleet these last few years - and was out the hatch in under a minute, taking his tablet with him.

Alone and queasy, Castellano looked at the Vatican tourists with their cameras and silly smiles. "Show me Laura again."

She was awake now, wearing the smile that Castellano thought was only for him.

"The captain," he said, because he couldn't watch her anymore. The view switched. The CO was still in bed, one hand wriggling under his sheets—

"Off!" Castellano ordered, but that didn't work. "Norfolk!" he said, and that brought a picture of Norfolk Naval Base's submarine piers from high above. The view was impressive, the security implications terrifying. "Show me my kids."

Tommy and Rose were both asleep, side-by-side in a bed and bedroom that he didn't recognize. A neighbor's house? Laura's sister's new house? He was upset that he didn't know. He cycled through several more views— his backyard, his home town in Maine, his parents in their bed and thankfully not doing anything else—

The comm bug in Castellano's ear clicked on. "OPSO report to the control room."

He hesitated. Bring the tablet, and risk having it confiscated? Lock it up, and maybe lose his connection to the world? Irrational possessiveness swept through him but the tablet belonged to the military, just like everything else on the boat. He tucked it under his arm and made for the control room. On the way, he passed the crew mess, where three sailors were staring intently at their palm-RATS, the smaller versions of his own tablet.

"The hell you are!" one was saying.

"I'm telling you! It's Cameron Diaz banging some guy who could be her grandson!"

The CO didn't encourage porn on the boat, but under the circumstances, Castellano kept going.

The control room was rigged for night vision, with sailors manning Weapons and Navigation. John Misuraca, Officer of the Deck, was positioned at the primary plotting table beside Bobby Weiner and the ship's XO, Lieutenant Commander Chris Lowe. All three men were looking down at the XO's tablet.

"Can you explain this, OPSO?" Lowe asked.

Castellano stepped close enough to see that the tablet was displaying a conference room filled with men. On the wall hung the seal of the Department of Defense. The men were arguing, but the XO had his thumb over the tablet's speaker in an effort to keep the voices muted.

"No, sir." Castellano's head was filled with images of Laura, her legs spread wide for the man in their bed. His kids sleeping somewhere he couldn't identify. "Sir, I know of no technical explanation. Everything we're seeing—whether it's real or some immensely clever trick—is impossible."

Impossible like the idea of Laura cheating on him, he thought sourly.

The XO turned on his e-cig and took a deep drag of nicotine. The red light on the end flared and faded. He was a tall, thin man with a narrow face, known for his sarcasm and being an overall son of bitch.

"Don't be stupid, OPSO," Lowe said. "If you can look at it and see it, it's possible. OOD, wake the captain and the Chief of the Boat."

"Aye, sir," Misuraca said.

The XO continued, "Lieutenants Weiner and Castellano, I want you to comb this boat top to bottom and confiscate every single tablet, RAT, and video display you can find. Use your chiefs to help. We've got to nip this in the bud before—"

A voice interrupted him. "Conn, sonar! New contact, designated Sierra one-two, bearing three one zero."

Although the XO was in the control room, Misuraca had the watch. "Sonar, conn, aye. Helm, right ten degrees rudder. Make your course one-three-zero."

The *Obama* was running at eight knots near the mid-Atlantic ridge, and all their intel had indicated there would be no friendlies in the area. As always, it was their mission to pass unnoticed. Misuraca had just ordered them into a leisurely turn away from the target while at the same time checking their baffles and getting a motion analysis on the contact.

"Sonar, conn, report," Misuraca ordered, a moment later.

"Holding one contact, sir, Sierra one-two." That was Sonar Chief Brennan. "Contact is turning to follow course. We can't . . . she's not showing standard characteristics of an enemy submarine, sir."

The XO started off toward the adjacent sonar room, but stopped to point a finger. "You two have your orders."

"Aye, sir," Weiner said.

Castellano wanted to stay. He'd done his junior officer tour on a fast attack sub, with its constant games of cat-and-mouse. Life on a guided missile sub was a lot more tame. If there was an anomalous contact out there, he wanted in on the drama. But orders were orders, so he reluctantly followed Weiner toward the crew mess.

"I'll start from Engineering and work forward," Weiner said, his expression grim.

"Bobby, wait." He pulled out his tablet. "Show me the sonar room."

Immediately the view switched. The XO, Sonar Chief Brennan, and junior sonarman were clustered at a console. The CO had arrived, looking as if he'd been awake for hours.

173

The CO was saying, "—you're telling me you have something that could be propeller sounds at nine hertz, but nothing from the power plant or hull."

"It's the weirdest thing." The sonar chief scratched his bald head. "No gears, no pumps, no harmonics, no nothing."

"There's something wrong with our equipment," the XO said.

Castellano thought so, too. No submarine could maneuver through the ocean without making sounds. The seas were full of noise, as long as you had the right equipment to hear it. For that reason, the Obama had nose, hull, and towed sensors, each routed through different processing software. Redundancies were built in at every stage. Total failure was inconceivable.

"We've run all diagnostics," Brennan said. "There's no mistake."

"Sir," the sonarman said, "contact is changing course and closing on us. Range four thousand yards. Three thousand yards. Two—"

The CO snapped, "Impossible!"

Castellano agreed. If the sonarman was right, the contact was moving more than one hundred twenty knots an hour—far beyond the capabilities of any known underwater vessel in the world. The cavitation bubbles alone would overwhelm the sensors. But "impossible" seemed to be the most popular word of the night.

Standing in the passageway with Weiner, Castellano had a sudden inspiration. He said to the tablet, "Show the contact."

The screen went dark for a few seconds, then brightened with a single point of white-blue incandescence. It almost looked like a navigation light. Very quickly the light flared larger and separated into a hundred individual bright spots in an elliptical shape. Running lights, then. Running lights ringed around the smooth hull of a vessel that was most definitely not a submarine.

Weiner said, "That looks like a—"

"UFO," Castellano croaked out. "Show us the inside of it."

The tablet shaded into a soothing swirl of shaded green, like streams of paint moving down a drain.

Above their heads, the ship's general quarters began to sound. The OOD's voice confirmed and added, "This is not a drill!" Crewmen poured out of berthing and scrambled down the passage. Misuraca raced down to Engineering and Castellano returned to the control room. Adrenaline got him there, focused and ready; it didn't matter that he'd been awake now for almost twenty-two hours, though he would have killed for a cup of hot coffee.

The odd lights and shape of Sierra 12 glowed on every video repeater in sight, even on the screens designed for tactical use only. According to the sonar plot, it had slowed to a stop a thousand yards to starboard. The vessel—not UFO, Castellano told himself, not UFO—was just sitting there, glowing and strangely beautiful.

The Weapons Officer reported, "We have a firing solution, Skipper! Locked and ready."

"Conn, radio. We've got a flash message on the ELF radio."

The ELF was a slow and cumbersome receive-only system. Though it had improved over the decades, it was still only good for short messages. The CO and XO each read the message without repeating it to the rest of the control room. They conferred briefly, their heads bowed close together. Then the CO said, "Diving officer, bring us to the surface."

"Aye, sir!"

For a ballistic missile submarine to surface in the middle of deep water operations meant the message had contained a direct order to do so. At surface level, they would be instantly susceptible to satellite and visual detection. Maybe their mission was scrubbed, Castellano thought with sudden hope. Maybe they were going home. He wouldn't be back in time to catch Laura in the act of cheating but he'd be able to confront her, challenge her, let her have the full brunt of his anger.

Slowly, gracefully, the *Obama* ascended. Sierra 12 rose along with them.

"Conn, Radio!" That was Lieutenant (j.g.) Thompson, sounding nervous. "We've lost the Very Low Frequency radio!"

"That fucker," the XO said, nodding toward a monitor. "She's got to be responsible for this."

But the boat had more than just two radio systems. The CO said, "Radio, Conn. Raise the antenna masts."

The masts went up. A minute later, Thompson soon reported that all surface and satellite signals seemed to be jammed, with everything up to 46 GHz full of white noise.

The control room was tense and quiet. The men around Castellano had trained for every conceivable possibility. It was possible, in a scenario of global nuclear war, that an electromagnetic pulse might block all ship-to-shore, ship-to-ship, and ship-to-satellite communications. The CO would have to make decisions and act in the national interest on his own. But no one had ever factored in a

175

disabling encounter with a vessel that looked like something out of a science fiction movie.

"Raise periscopes," the CO ordered.

Both the CO and XO looked outside. Castellano wasn't invited to. The video displays showed Sierra 12 floating on the ocean nearby like a giant silver Frisbee. On the CO's orders, sonar sent out a ping and they all got a good idea of her size: damn fucking big. Three times the *Obama's* length and twice her height and width. No propellers, exhaust vents, or signs of a propulsion system at all.

"XO, get yourself down to the radio room and see what you can do," the CO said.

"Aye, sir." The XO departed.

Castellano looked from the sonar and plot panels to his tablet and said, "Sir. Maybe we don't need the radio if we have these."

It was obvious the CO hadn't had much time to be briefed on that particular problem. Castellano showed him how to change the views between Engineering, the *Obama's* exterior, the crew mess, and finally the president. President Moore was in a bathroom, squatting on the toilet with his black slacks around his ankles and a sheaf of papers in hand.

"Anyone with an internet connection can watch the POTUS take a dump?" the CO demanded. "Is that it?"

"We're not connected to the internet, sir. And the power and sound controls don't work. Someone else—something else—is controlling them."

The CO winced. "Can anyone watch us? Any time they want?"

He decided not to volunteer what he'd already seen. What he'd seen traitorous Laura doing. "I believe so, sir."

The CO called the Chief of the Boat over and ordered him to carry out the same orders that Castellano and Weiner had started before the general quarters: secure every tablet, TV, and video display on the *Obama*. Afterward the CO turned and said, "All right, OPSO. How can we use these things to our advantage?"

"Sir," he said. "If we can look at someone, then presumably they can look at us. If we can hear them, they can hear us. But we're not synchronized. Somehow we have to get someone's attention and get us both to tune to each other at the same time."

"If you can look at anyone, anywhere in the world, that's millions of possibilities. How do you find someone looking back at the right time?"

"We don't have to look at anyone but COMSUBLANT," Castellano replied. "They'll be wanting to keep track of us so someone's going to look here at our control room, or the radio room. We should look at their Ops Center in Norfolk."

The CO gave him a sharp nod. "Good idea. Make it happen."

The plan worked better than he expected. Within fifteen minutes he had his tablet focused on an announcement board in Norfolk. The board held a schedule of fifteen-minute alternating windows for each boat to check in by looking at Admiral Covington's office. The CO went to his soundproofed stateroom to make contact.

Castellano wanted to know what was being said. No, *needed* to know. He could see that Misuraca, too, was bristling with curiosity. But neither of them had permission to leave their duty stations, and with the control room crew in such close proximity, they couldn't very well eavesdrop without everyone noticing.

"Sir?" Petty Officer Jeffries sidled up to him, kept his voice low. "Can we really tune to anyone, anywhere?"

"In theory, yes."

"My wife," Jeffries said hopefully. "She should have had the baby by now. Can I look?"

Castellano was sure everyone in the room would like the chance to look at a loved one, or check in on a sick relative, or watch Cameron Diaz in bed. And obviously the CO and XO wanted to block all crew access. But he thought about Tommy and Rose, each of whom had been born while he was away from home.

"Make it quick," he murmured, and slid the tablet across the plot.

Nineteen minutes after he'd gone to his cabin, the CO's voice came over the 1MC. "This is the captain speaking. I've been in contact with COMSUBLANT and have been instructed to inform you all of our current situation. As of one hour ago, there are four thousand and seventy-three vessels of extraterrestrial origin hovering or submerged across our planet."

"Holy shit," said one of the sailors at the navigation console.

"These ships have fired no weapons, but they seem to be responsible for the jamming of all civilian and military communication systems in the world. The United States considers this a hostile act. They also seem to have enabled a technology that allows anyone with a communication device to eavesdrop on anyone else. We must all operate as if every single action we take is public knowledge. Do not say or do anything that reflects poorly on you, this boat, or the naval service."

Sandra McDonald

Castellano wanted to laugh. He'd been awake for close to twenty-two hours now, and was taking hits of nicotine and caffeine off his own e-cig to keep his vision from blurring. It was true that a lot of civilians craved the limelight - seemed to love living in public, sharing every silly thought and incriminating picture online. But this was unprecedented. How could anyone live every moment of his life in front of an audience? Every private sanitary or sexual act, every flare of temper, every hospital procedure, jury deliberation, national security meeting - everything on display for anonymous strangers?

The CO continued. "Our instructions are to remain on the surface and await further commands. We are not to engage or provoke any extraterrestrial contact. Everyone to stay calm, obey your superiors, and await further word. Captain, out."

Three minutes after that, the CO and XO returned to the control room and huddled over the plot. The COB arrived shortly afterward with news that every TV and video repeater outside of the control room had been secured, and the crew relieved of anything that would give them a peek at the outside world.

The XO said, "Be sure to round up the officer's tablets as well."

Immediately Castellano protested. "Sir. We might need them."

"They're useless as computers right now," the XO said.

Castellano hesitated. He was aware of the tablet's slim weight in his hand, of the way the crew in the control room was looking at him.

The CO said, "I heard about your personal situation, OPSO. I need you focused on your job, not your home life."

It was a stinging rebuke, even if it hadn't been meant that way. He had no choice but to surrender the tablet.

After three more hours at battle stations, the CO stepped down the alert but didn't completely rescind it. Castellano was sent off-duty. He crawled into his rack desperate for sleep but the slow roll of the boat made him queasy. A submarine running deep meant smooth sailing; up here on the surface, they were subject to rocking and rolling. He pictured himself vomiting in full color and sound while Laura and her lover watched and ridiculed him. They could watch him at any time and he would never know.

He gave serous consideration to breaking into the COB's storage lockers and retrieving his confiscated tablet. Then he had a better idea. It was possible, just possible, that the confiscation teams had hurried through the officer's berthing. He poked around Weiner's bunk, dug around the thin mattress and pillows, and then patted down the twisted sheets until he found what he needed.

One pair of VR goggles, fully functional.

The goggles were usually wired into the ship's entertainment system. Now they were displaying Judy Weiner, showering naked in a cloud of steam. He watched that for longer than he should, then wrenched his attention back.

He said, "Show me my kids."

Tommy first, back home now, in his bedroom playing on the floor with toy spaceships. Castellano had once spent a whole weekend painting murals of the solar system on his bedroom wall. The kid was going to be an astronaut someday. Rose, in her room, was reading a book whose cover he couldn't make out. She wanted to be a poet, she often said, or maybe a princess, or maybe a brain surgeon. Two innocent children, unaware that any pervert in the world could be watching them.

"Laura," he said. She was standing in the kitchen, wrapped up in the blue bathrobe he'd bought her last Christmas. Behind her, the wide windows showed snow-covered elm trees. Of her bastard lover there was no sign.

He knew guys whose wives cheated on them while they were at sea but he'd never believed he himself would be betrayed and humiliated. Divorce was the natural next step, sure, but custody judges always rewarded the stay-at-home parent. She'd get the house, the kids, her boyfriend. He'd get every other weekend and a month in the summer, if he was lucky enough not to be underway.

On the screen, Laura drank from a mug while her gaze stayed locked on the 3TV mounted under the kitchen cabinets. He had the icy feeling that she had tuned to him, and wasn't that eerie?

"Laura," he said softly to the tablet. "Can you hear me?"

On the screen she remained impassive, unresponsive.

The hatch opened. John Misuraca, his face lined with fatigue, gawked at the forbidden goggles. Then he snapped his fingers impatiently.

"Give 'em over, Matt. I want to see my mom and dad."

Castellano got five hours of sleep, maybe six. He dreamt of Judy Weiner in the shower, and then his own mom watching him masturbate, and then the XO mocking him for it. The nightmares kept him fitful and tossing until the 1MC clicked on and ordered the ship's officers to the wardroom. He didn't quite feel human yet, but there was no chance of declining the invitation. Luckily the mess steward had plenty of coffee and the corpsman was passing out free amphetamine cartridges for all e-cigarettes. The XO remained on watch, but the boat's other twelve officers were all assembled in the small space when the CO arrived. He was so pale that Castellano thought he might faint.

So much for unflappability.

The CO said, "This message was received via a direct transmission to our radio room on a satellite frequency reserved for SECVOX. I'm going to read it to you in its entirety. This information is not to leave this room.

"To all fine people of the USS *Obama*, greetings. We come in existence to invite your peaceful joining with our civilization in anticipation of the demise of your planet in nine months. Forewarn yourselves that among the Lucindi we have no barriers. Evacuations will begin in twenty-four hours. Proceed if pleased to your nearest rendezvous spot at 47°18'11"N 53°59'19"W. End transmission."

John Misuraca said, "That's Newfoundland."

"What the fuck?" Bobby Weiner asked.

"Nine months?" Henry Thompson squeaked. "What's going to happen in nine months?"

The CO put the paper down and kept his gaze on it. "According to the Lucindi, and as verified by the Pentagon and National Security Council, a comet measuring one hundred kilometers wide is approaching Jupiter on its way to a collision here. They call it a planet-killer. After it impacts, Earth will be devastated and human life extinguished."

For a moment there was stunned silence. Then Weiner said, "Screw that! It's a hoax. Giant comets don't just show up out of nowhere."

Castellano thought about Tommy's bedroom mural. About the moon and planets, and things that traveled in the spaces between them. His leg jittered under the table and he had to put a hand down to stop it. "The Oort cloud, outside our solar system. It's full of comets. One could come in fast, from a direction we're not watching."

"We could blow it up," Thompson said.

Weiner said, "Yeah! Nuke it."

Misuraca drummed his fingers on the able. "Or if these aliens want to help, they could blow it up for us."

The CO picked up the paper and fingered a corner. "The Lucindi don't believe in stopping it. They look at it as a divine messenger of the gods. But they're not willing to stand by and let it destroy billions of people, either. They have the technology to transport us all to their homeworld, and that's the invitation."

One of the other officers said. "Sir, there's no way eight billion people can fit in four thousand spaceships."

Castellano pushed his leg down again. "They can if the spaceships are bigger on the inside than they are on the outside."

"Bullshit," Weiner proclaimed. "They want to eat us. Steal the planet, or turn us into slaves, whatever. You can't trust them."

The CO looked at Weiner. "I'm not ruling out any possibilities."

Objections erupted among the officers. Castellano stayed silent. Beyond the CO, the video display mounted in the wardroom bulkhead had black cloth taped over it. A faint glow edged around the cloth, thin and promising.

"Sir, why the tablets?" he said. "Why mess with our technology?"

The CO said, "There's no privacy among the Lucindi. People who go with them have to be prepared to live in a community with no secrets, no hiding. Sometimes it doesn't work, and it causes strife. The aliens want to make sure we know what we're getting into."

"Stay and be destroyed, or go and give up all your privacy," Misuraca said. "Sounds like an easy decision."

"Only if you believe them," Weiner snapped.

Thompson asked, "Skipper, are we going to Newfoundland?"

"No," the CO said. "Whatever the White House decides, whatever civilians decide, our job is to serve our country and we're going to do that until the day there's no country left. I have formally declined Sierra 12's offer on the behalf of every man on this ship."

The forceful words quelled everyone.

Castellano said, "Sir. Maybe they'll help us evacuate later, in a few months. Surely the aliens don't expect everyone to make up their minds right now."

The CO paused before delivering a decisive nod. "Yes. That's my hope, too. In the meantime, everyone get back to work. And not a word to the crew."

The CO left. Most of the wardroom cleared out, leaving Castellano to gulp more coffee and eat the sandwich the steward had brought him. At the other end of the table, Weiner, Thompson, and Misuraca argued over the killer comet and the Lucindi intentions.

"If they wanted to just lure us into a trap, they wouldn't try to warn us about the privacy," Misuraca said.

Weiner slapped his hand down. "Give me a choice between good old ruined Earth and some hellhole where total strangers can watch you make love to your wife, and I'll take the smoldering Earth. Humanity can survive anything."

Thompson said glumly, "It's a moot point. Even if you wanted to go, it's a long swim to Newfoundland."

Castellano's gaze went back to the shrouded video monitor. He rose, went to it. Put his fingernail under the tape holding the cloth and peeled it back.

Weiner chided him. "Matt. You know you're not supposed to."

Castellano ignored him. "Show me where the Lucindi live."

The display dissolved into a swirl of green and brown, then resolved to a fabulous city. Enormous globes of glass and white metal floated like soap bubbles over a lush green jungle. Each building was a transparent city unto itself, full of flowers and commerce and indoor rivers and music, music that made Castellano think of cold dry wine and the press of Laura's hand on his thigh. The people of the cities looked vaguely human, with dark arms and legs and narrow heads, but they wore no clothes and displayed no external genitalia. To move between globes, they floated through the sky like balloons. In the tiny wardroom of the *Obama*, Castellano could almost feel himself moving through the air as well—air rushing by his ears, his body defying gravity.

"Matt, stop." Weiner covered the display. "No one here is going anywhere."

Castellano met Misuraca's gaze before they both looked elsewhere.

Later that day Castellano searched for the forbidden VR goggles, but he couldn't find them in the stateroom. Misuraca reported that he'd hidden them in his locker, but now they were gone. They made a thorough search, growing increasingly more frantic, but the goggles were gone and they both blamed Weiner.

"I need to know what my parents are going to do," Misuraca said.

Castellano said, "I need to see my kids."

"If they go—" Misuraca trailed off. "If they go, will you go?"

"How?"

"Somehow."

"We have our duty," Castellano said, the words sounding empty in his own ears.

For the next seventy-two hours, the *Obama* rode the waves, waiting for further commands, while Sierra 12 bobbed nearby. The CO kept the crew insanely busy with drills and exercises, and made sure the officers were too harried to do anything but fall into their racks and sleep when afforded a few precious hours. As a distraction, it almost worked. In every tiny spare moment, though, Castellano thought about Tommy and Rose floating above the trees, watching and being watched. He tried to use the wardroom TV to see them but the CO had ordered it removed, and the video repeaters in the control room had mostly been covered up.

On the fourth day, Castellano's men stopped him in the passages. They wanted to know what the captain was planning. Wanted to know why they couldn't use their RATS or displays to see the world only a few pixels away.

"Sir, it's our right!" said one senior petty officer.

"We deserve to know what's going on!"

"It's not fair!"

Castellano's only response was "Those are our orders." Inside, he was torturing himself over what Laura was going to do. If she chose to evacuate and he couldn't, he'd never see his kids again. If he somehow could make it to a rendezvous site and she didn't, he was equally screwed. She had no reason to stay on Earth. He had a CO who wasn't going to authorize a trip to Newfoundland. She had the kids to think about. He had duty, this boat, these men.

Petty Officer Novak, a pimply kid with bushy eyebrows, said, "Sir, if we want to evacuate, the CO can't stop us."

"Yes the CO damn well can," bellowed the XO, from eight paces away in the passage. His cheeks were red with anger. "You men, get back to duty."

The sailors hurried off. Castellano wished he could go with them.

The XO closed in on him. "I expect more of you. What kind of example are you setting?"

"Sir." Castellano did his best not to flinch. "They only want to have a choice."

The XO's voice rose. "There is no goddamned choice, OPSO. We follow orders. Or are you suggesting an alternative?"

Mutiny, Castellano thought. The unspoken word hung around them like bad air. He thought he saw a crewman's head poke out past the nearest open hatch, then quickly retreat.

"No, sir. There's no alternative."

"You just remember that. The CO controls this fucking boat and everyone on her. I suggest you get your head out of your ass and be ready to assume your duties. We're taking the boat down and returning to our regularly scheduled mission."

Castellano stiffened to attention. "Yes, sir!"

The XO glared at him for a moment longer and then stalked off to make someone else miserable. Slowly traffic resumed in the passageway, with most sailors giving Castellano wide berth. Except for one.

"Sir." Petty Officer Jeffries, the new dad, gave Castellano an urgent look. "A moment in private, sir?"

"Where's private these days?" Castellano asked, exasperated.

Jeffries looked around, then lowered his voice. "Sir, I know what the CO told the officers. He lied. He knows there aren't going to be any later pick-ups. This is a one-time rescue effort."

Castellano went very still. "How do you know that?"

"One of the guys—" Jeffries dropped his voice even more. "One of the guys has been tracking Pentagon and White House briefings. After that comet hits, the only thing that's going to be left on this planet is bacteria. Those aliens are on a long mission away from home and only swung through here when they saw the comet. They won't be back before D-Day. My wife and baby? They're evacuating. And I've got to go with them."

Mutiny, Castellano thought again.

"I need to see for myself," he said. "Show me."

Jeffries grimaced but said, "Okay. Come on. But we have to hurry."

He led Castellano to crew berthing, where one sailor was keeping watch while others clustered in a corner. "Make a hole," Jeffries said. The sailors eyed Castellano with suspicion but stepped back. The petty officer holding a smart phone handed it over reluctantly. Castellano wanted to turn away but they were all watching, and privacy was an illusion anyway.

"Show me the White House," he said, staring at the little screen.

A tired-looking spokeswoman with dark circles under her eyes was repeating the same message, over and over, into a camera. "The President authorizes all citizens to proceed to their nearest evacuation point and stay calm. The evacuation will proceed for the next two weeks. You must stay calm..."

"Show me my kids," Castellano said.

The display dissolved to the fantastic cities of the Lucindi.

His throat tightened. "My parents. Where are they?"

The Lucindi city globes swayed gracefully over the jungle, music filling the air between.

"They already left, sir," Jeffries said softly. "That's the picture you get when someone's already evacuated."

Castellano bent over at the waist, sure that he was going to vomit. And he didn't care if the men saw him, or if the XO was watching from the bridge, or if the whole world decided to tune in. Let them see him at his weakest and worst, let them see him miserable and vulnerable, let them witness everything.

But let him see his kids again, too.

The 1MC clicked. "This is the captain speaking. We have received orders to resume our scheduled mission and operations. I understand many of you are concerned about the global situation. About your families and loved ones. But our country's safety remains paramount, and the job of defending democracy has not gone away. I know I have your full support. Prepare to dive."

The comm clicked off.

"This is it!" said Petty Officer Novak, as he dashed off.

The other sailors scurried away, some of them carrying pillowcases of personal effects.

"What are they doing?" Castellano demanded.

Jeffries grabbed the phone. "Sorry, sir. We're not going to let the CO submerge for the next few weeks and lose our chance."

"You can't," Castellano said desperately. He imagined the forward escape trunk opening, the crew climbing out. "Jeffries, they can shoot you."

"Not if the aliens stop them, sir. Are you coming?"

Mutiny.

And if the CO tried to submerge with the trunk open, they could all die.

Someone in the control room was paying attention to the warning lights, thank god, because the general quarters began to sound. Years of training and discipline urged Castellano toward his station, but instead he followed Jeffries past the galley and crew's mess. When he reached the escape ladder he saw a dozen sailors—and two chiefs—scurrying upward in an urgent but orderly way.

Castellano hesitated.

"Stop!" came a shout, though no one listened. Weiner forced his way forward, grabbed Castellano's arm. He looked furious.

"What the hell are you doing?"

"Let go," Castellano said, but Weiner's grip didn't yield.

"You can't do this," Weiner said. "Matt, it's a trap."

"You don't know that."

"You trust them more than you trust us?"

John Misuraca appeared. He put himself between Weiner and the ladder, and waved at the men to keep climbing up it. "Bobby, you have no right to stop them."

"I have every damned right," Weiner spat out.

Castellano shook free and pushed him away. Weiner grabbed him, wrestled him down. Castellano punched him, and then Misuraca punched as well, and with his nose bleeding Weiner went down to his knees.

"Matt, go," Misuraca said. "You're either in or you're out."

Literally in or out. Stay on the *Obama* and keep his career for however long the military existed. Or join this uprising, with no guarantee of success. Possibly spend the rest of his life in some shore brig until the killer comet blasted out of the sky and destroyed everything.

He grabbed hold of the ladder and started upward.

Cold winter air slapped at him as he climbed out on the *Obama's* slippery wet deck. Fresh air was an intoxication and the smell of salt almost overwhelming. The sky was bright but overcast, the Atlantic full of swells, and the enormity of the horizon reminded Castellano of how puny he was, how tiny and inconsequential. Sierra 12 was still riding the surface to their starboard, her bulk hidden by the water, but if anyone there noticed the crew's appearance, there was no sign.

The bridge access trunk opened. The CO and XO both climbed out to peer down at the uprising. Around Castellano, sailors waved their arms and yelled toward Sierra 12.

"Take us!" they shouted. "We want to go! Take us!"

The CO and XO both had pistols. Castellano feared that in the next few moments there might be bloodshed. From a purely practical standpoint, the CO couldn't let too many sailors go without comprising the ability of the remaining crew to operate the boat. Judging from his thunderous expression, the XO couldn't stand the thought of his men abandoning the mission.

"Stop!" the CO yelled. "I order you to stop!"

The XO raised his pistol.

Castellano turned his back on the bridge and waved his arms desperately toward Sierra 12. "Hey! Come get us!"

He hoped—no, he prayed—that someone on the alien ship was watching.

Encountering Evie
by Sherry D. Ramsey

- 1 -

Close Encounters of the First Kind:
UFOs are witnessed at close quarters

Scout yawned and slid his fingers absently over the shimmering holochrom display. Another planet, another sensor scan, another ream of data logged.

Might be time to transfer out of Scout division, he thought. *Look for something with more action.*

<Another assignment could be more dangerous> Ship noted.

Scout twitched the folds of skin on his back, annoyed. Ship's AI stayed attuned to his thoughts unless he specifically requested privacy, or intentionally damped down his telepathic *jara* waves. Sometimes he forgot that.

Maybe I'm ready for a little danger, he thought back defiantly.

<Why?> asked Ship.

"Because I'm starting to think of my job description as my name," he said aloud. "I don't think that's a good sign."

<A sign of what?>

"Oh, never mind."

He'd logged countless planets on his missions, some empty, some inhabited, some evincing the first wet squirming signs of life. He didn't know which he preferred. The empty ones were less work, those with life were—sometimes—more interesting, but also more disturbing.

Scout turned his dusky, lobed eyes back to the holochromatic planet display. This one was inhabited. Fledgling nuclear capabilities, scattered hostilities, ecological corruption; the usual mix of beauty and ugliness. No indication of *jara* activity. Scout shuddered. Millions of minds, only half-alive. These planets he regarded with horrified fascination, as he'd view a

187

dead alien insect. He'd study it, but with a pervasive feeling of faint revulsion.

"Boost shielding fifty percent," he directed Ship. Scout logged the entry time and slipped through an inviting hole in the planet's monitoring systems.

\<Sensors online. Data collection may be initiated>

Scout traced a long, coppery index finger down a holochrom slide to start the scans, and sat back in his skimchair.

And jolted up again. Something from the planet surface had brushed his mind like the stroke of a fingertip. No *jara* activity?

It was not a call, not a word, nothing so distinct or deliberate. More like a possibility, a latent energy oscillating below the surface of ordinary consciousness. Scout shivered, the vestigial hairs on his forearms pricking up like hackles. Telepathy of any sort was rare in the charted universe, one reason his own race had risen to a somewhat discomfiting superiority. He had not expected to find even a trace of it in this solar backwater.

"Interesting," he breathed. "I think we'll have a look." Another hazard of Scout missions, talking to oneself. Well, he'd talked to less interesting lifeforms. It felt healthier than having Ship silently inspect his thoughts.

Scout propelled the skimchair to the opposite side of the console and plucked a *jarakiva* booster from the medkit, the pearlescent drug swirling lazily inside the clear disk. He pressed it into the thinly furred skin behind his left ear, barely feeling the prick of the injection, then configured one set of sensors to work in tandem with his own *jara* waves. The "signal" from the surface intensified, but it was still random, formless. Scout crosslinked to the incoming data readouts, then piloted the craft swiftly around the globe, seeking the source of the unexpected mental energy.

"There you are," he murmured. The ship hovered well out of visual range in the sky above a small habitation. At this distance he hardly needed the *jarakiva* booster to pinpoint the single entity from whom the signals emanated. Scout bent eagerly toward the display.

A young female in early childhood wandered a small grassy area near a dwelling, chasing tiny, twinkling lights in the descending dusk. Her delight was palpable. Telepathic bursts sparked like laughter in his brain.

That was all he could discern from this distance. Scout snorted in frustration.

\<It would be unwise to venture closer>

"I know, I know."

Detection wouldn't be the end of his career, but Scouts were expected to avoid it if possible. There was something, though, something about this girl, the touch of her alien mind on his, that compelled him to know more.

Suddenly deciding, he boosted his shielding further and dropped the ship towards the surface. Ship said nothing, once the decision was made. The girl's mind brightened at this close proximity, burning with a sweet, steady flame. Scout caught his breath, his twin hearts shaking his breast with their hammering.

"Closer," he breathed. He must get just a little...

<You could be reprimanded for this action>

Scout ignored Ship. He was drawn to this mind like a moon moth to candlelight. The connection felt almost spiritual. Ship couldn't understand, and Scout couldn't explain.

The girl looked up, directly at the craft as it hovered above her. Scout knew she would see it clearly. The shielding allowed the ship to slip past peripheral vision, but a direct stare would penetrate the illusion. She pointed up with a small finger.

"Lights, Mama," he knew she said. The words coalesced in his mind as plainly as if they had been audible. Immediately a second figure emerged from the shadowy overhang of a porch, crossing swiftly to the child. Scout's chest contracted, squeezing against the wild pumping of his hearts. He'd been so focused on the child, he'd missed the mother.

The woman's gaze followed where the child pointed, and she swept the girl up in her arms. A wave of anxiety from the child washed over Scout. It jangled his nerves and twisted his guts, burning his brain like a venomous sting. From the mother he felt nothing. She was not a telepath; only the child.

Evie, he picked out of the wild mental tumult pouring from the girl now. Her name was Evie. The mother turned and ran for the house, cradling Evie close. Scout felt the door slam shut behind them. Shaking, he dragged his mind from the telepathic maelstrom of Evie's *jara*.

Reflexively his long fingers maneuvered the colors of the holochrom, diverting power from the shielding and the sensors to the engines, pushing for maximum speed away from there. Away from the disgrace of having been seen and from the child who had touched his mind.

<That was interesting> Ship said, more wryly than its programming should have allowed.

Scout snatched the *jarakiva* booster from his neck and hurled it across the bridge in an uncharacteristic gesture. His fingers shook.

"Definitely time," he said. "Definitely time for a change."

-2-

Close Encounters of the Second Kind:
UFOs cause physical effects on humans, animals and objects

Evie was twelve the summer her mother finally let her take an astronomy course over the 'Net. She'd been fascinated with the sky for years, but had to content herself with books from the library and what television programs she could find, and of course the astronomy websites. She'd soaked up everything they offered, but the course made her feel like she was finally making real progress in understanding the universe.

This hot August night she sat on the windowseat she'd cajoled her father into building for her. Her mother had been strangely against it. She had always disapproved of Evie's interest in the stars. Evie knew it was only fear; she'd read that easily enough when she was still innocently tuning into others' thoughts without realizing it was wrong. She didn't understand that fear. What could be frightening about the universe?

Evie leaned her temple against the cool glass and drew her knees up, wrapping her arms around them. Galileo, her cat, leapt up beside her with easy grace and curled up next to Evie's feet. She stroked his fur absently, glad of his easy company. With Galileo there was no need to shutter her mind.

Her new astronomy books lay strewn over the bed, where Evie had rifled the pages, dipping eagerly into their secrets. A nagging at her mind distracted her, though, drawing her to the window. It was almost familiar, like a faraway memory. It reminded her of the emptiness she'd tried for years to fill by reaching out to the minds of other people. None had ever responded. Sometimes . . . sometimes she'd felt a twitch, a mind with potential, but she could never touch it, never reach deeply enough to trigger a response. The frustration was excruciating.

Finally she'd given up, when others started complaining of sudden headaches in her presence and watching her with covert suspicion. Now she struggled to quiet her mind, and it grew more difficult all the time. She'd never mentioned it to anyone. She knew her parents suspected something odd about their daughter, but they said nothing. Sometimes she wished they would.

Galileo seemed restless tonight, too. He didn't drowse on her feet, as he usually did, but stood again and paced the length of the window seat, mewling inquiringly.

"I don't know, Leo," she said to the cat. "There's something weird in the air tonight." She focused the darkening sky beyond the windowpane, reflexively picking out the constellations.

"Look, Leo, there you are," she said, pointing to the cluster of stars in the lion constellation. "Are you going to get that pesky crab tonight? Are you, boy?" Evie tickled the cat under the chin, but he wouldn't turn his slitted eyes to the sky, where the starry outline of Leo stood eternally poised to pounce upon the unfortunate Cancer.

Evie idly picked out some of the stars, still chatting to the cat. "There's Regulus, and that one's Algeiba," she said. "And that really bright light, right between Cancer's claws, that's not a star at all, it's Jupiter."

Galileo yawned widely, pink tongue curling, and lay down, then immediately rose again and arched his back in a long stretch. Evie glanced at him, then turned her face back to the window and frowned.

"Why does it have to be so hard, Leo?" she whispered. It tortured her, this terrible yearning for closeness when she looked to the stars. They were so far away, so removed from her touch. Conversely, the people who made up her world were too close and had to be kept at bay.

Jupiter was moving.

Evie blinked, focused on the flickering light again. No, of course the planet wasn't moving, it had to be something else. She wasn't one of those people who couldn't tell a planet from a passing airplane. This light was moving closer. Fast.

Coming to fill the hole in my mind, Evie thought absurdly.

She stared, barely blinking as the light grew inexorably larger and nearer. It fractured into several lights, strung out like a child's dot-to-dot puzzle around the perimeter of the object.

Galileo hissed, his green eyes riveted out the window, where seconds ago Evie couldn't persuade him to look. The fur on his hackles bristled like a wire brush.

"It's a ship," she whispered, as the shape became undeniable. Not a plane, not a weather balloon, not the planet Venus, but a ship, a craft, a vehicle.

And Evie recognized it.

A memory, buried and long forgotten, materialized. Chasing the neon twinkles of fireflies in the yard, the creak of the wicker rocking chair signifying her mother watchful on the porch. It was dusk, and the grass glistened wetly underfoot, pungent and freshly cut. She'd been happy. Then she'd looked up and something had *jumped* inside her head. There'd been lights, just like these lights. Her mother had scooped her up and run into the house. She recalled the terrified bounding of her mother's heart as she crushed Evie close, and that was the first time Evie's mind had been engulfed by her mother's fear.

But I'm not afraid, Evie thought. Her own heart thrummed like the motor of Galileo's purr, but not from fear.

The shape in the night sky hovered, how far from her window Evie couldn't tell. White brilliance washed over her. The yard outside and her room remained draped in shadow. Galileo stood like a creature petrified, every hair of his fur distended like a porcupine's quills.

Her hands shook and sweat pricked at her palms. The invisible light—was there such a thing?—touched her hair, her mind, her heart. Her mind, unguarded with only the cat for company, reached out and felt—another? Evie gasped. The cover of one of her new books flipped open and the pages shuddered as if swept by a sudden wind. The cat shrieked, once, and collapsed.

Evie wrenched her eyes away from the strange illumination and gathered Galileo into her arms with a cry. His heartbeat thudded gently against her hand. Tears of relief stung her eyes, and when she looked up again, the lights, the shape, were gone. The room was still.

She understood with startling clarity that something—it—*he*—had been looking for her. She'd been visited by an old friend . . . one she'd never actually met. And although she still didn't feel it herself, she finally understood some of her mother's fear.

-3-
Close Encounters of the Third Kind:
Entities are seen in or near UFOs

This time Scout stayed away longer, while Evie's planet completed twenty-six long, graceful revolutions around its yellow sun. He had no intention of going back, but he could not forget that unexpected, inexplicable mind that had touched his, that had drawn him back to Earth the second time. It tormented him, awake or asleep. Always he expected . . . waited . . . to feel that touch again, no matter how far he was from Evie's planet. In dreams he lingered above her house, letting her wild, tumultuous mental energy wash over him like a cleansing storm.

And so inevitably, he went back. He'd never left the Scouts. Risk his life in a war zone or on some ridiculous mission? Not if it meant he might never get back to Evie. When the yearning became unbearable, he scheduled another follow-up survey of Evie's planet and nosed his craft toward the small spiral galaxy that rarely left his thoughts. His hearts felt lighter than they had in years.

<I do not advise this> Ship must have accessed the course charts.

Scout ignored Ship and entered the solar system, fighting to quell a burgeoning excitement.

"Not as if you're actually going to make contact with her," he scolded himself. "She might have lost the talent anyway, having to suppress it all these years."

<You do not believe that. What are you hoping for?>

"Nothing. I just want to check up on . . . the planet."

Ship made a sound that, had it come from any living creature, could only have been called a snort.

Scout stubbornly kept his mind open, not caring what Ship read, waiting for that gentle *jara* touch that would tell him he had found her.

It did not come.

Closer and closer he flew to her spot on the globe, anxiety instilling a tremble in his long-fingered hands.

<Shielding has not been boosted> Ship reprimanded.

Scout flushed and adjusted the holochrom slides distractedly. "Scan for any technological advancements the inhabitants might have made since our last visit." That should keep Ship busy for a few minutes. Finally Evie's house resolved on the viewscreen. Still nothing.

Evie was not there.

Scout felt a sharp clench of dread. Shaking, he urged the craft up beyond the exosphere of the planet, where the spacedark lay like a blanket around him, and shut down all nonessential systems. He blocked his *jara* from Ship's meddlesome AI and settled his thoughts.

He refused to consider the possibility that she might be dead. Therefore she must have moved. This race did not yet have interstellar or even routine interplanetary travel. He should be able to find her.

"Ship," he said, "Calculate a circumnavigation route that lets us pass closely over all the inhabited areas of this planet. But make sure we'll avoid the current monitoring systems."

<Just checking up on the planet?>

"Just do it."

While Ship ran the calculations, Scout lit the *tachee*, his meditation lanterns, and settled in his skimchair. When the spiced tachee fragrance intensified, he opened his mind as he would have opened it at home, in his private, protected space. He wasn't worried about his own *jara* reaching the planet from this distance, and Ship wasn't listening. He wanted to be ready to receive any sign of Evie.

The meditation refreshed him. He had not released his mind so completely in a long time. Now he would be open to the slightest mental touch.

<Calculations are complete. Course is laid in>

Scout calmly set the piloting threads and let Ship drop toward the planet again.

"Please be there, Evie," he breathed, as the colors of the planet intensified. "Please."

They'd traversed almost half the course when it came, a humming undercurrent of *jara* activity that plucked at his own. The mental signature was muted, nothing like the unfettered tumult of his first visit, nor even the resolutely damped-down energy of the last time. This was a mind more settled, in better control of its singular powers. It pained Scout to think how hard-won that control must have been for Evie, coping alone.

A strange distortion buzzed around the edges of Evie's thoughts, which puzzled Scout at first. As he pinpointed her location the explanation became clear.

Evie had travelled a long way from her childhood home, to a hot, dry place where blunt saucers pointed their monolithic noses to the sky. Scout knew from his previous visits that the inhabitants of this planet called them "radio telescopes." Evie's proximity to the things seemed to both garble and boost her *jara* output.

Scout smiled. Evie had not forgotten the sky.

He parked in a high orbit where detection was unlikely, this time not even bothering to run the planetary scans right away. He could do that later, to justify his visit here, but for a while he wanted simply to bask in the sensation of contact with Evie's mind. There was still nothing one could call a conversation or even the most rudimentary message, but the mere touching of her mind to his was pleasurable. He had to concentrate to keep his *jara* from responding eagerly to hers. He ached to know for certain if she was aware of him at all, but it did not seem so.

When night fell upon the planet, however, Scout had cause to doubt that estimation. As the dark hours passed he knew that Evie's mind did not settle into sleep. She was wakeful on the planet far below him, as wakeful as he was here.

Intrigued, he engaged the ship's stealth field and dropped down through the layers of atmosphere, down to where the telescope facility was clear on his viewscreen. Only a few windows cast thin yellow fingers across the ground outside. Evie's mind was still shrouded, but active. She must work here. Her thoughts were concentrated, logical. Did her own kind recognize her genius?

Much later she emerged into the moonlit night. Scout watched, his mind quivering with excitement, as Evie strolled down a winding, brush-lined path to the telescope array, glancing occasionally at the clear, starry sky as she went. A furry creature stalked elegantly beside her, stopping occasionally to sniff the air or the dusty ground.

"How is it possible," Scout asked himself in a low voice, "That one so strange could seem so . . . familiar?" Their races were enormously dissimilar. It made no sense to him that he could find Evie attractive to look at, no matter how the touch of her mind intrigued him. But there it was.

<How is it possible that one so intelligent can be so foolish?> Ship asked dryly.

"Oh, shut up, Ship." Scout still had Ship blocked from reading his thoughts, but he'd forgotten himself and spoken aloud.

Evie apparently reached her destination a moment later, stopping between two of the huge, concave dishes. She suddenly threw her arms wide, turned her face up to the night sky, and mentally drew the shroud away from her thoughts.

The blast of *jara* waves was shattering. Scout flinched back as if he had been struck a physical blow. Evie's mind was like a wild thing suddenly freed. There was still no form, no message, no signal, only the joy of release from a prison, the mad exultation of freedom. It washed over Scout like a roiling wave, knocking him breathless.

Then, as she had done before, Evie looked directly at the Ship. Her jara energy faltered; doubt, wonder, shock overriding the joy before it was quickly damped down.

"No!" Scout cried. He must not be the cause of more mental anguish for her, must not be the reason she clamped down on that wonderful mind. Without thought for consequences, he changed the settings on the holochrom, altering the light-reflecting character of the front viewscreen to transparency, raising the level of illumination inside the bridge.

<Scout, what are you doing?>

Scout stood and walked to the viewscreen, knowing she would see him, knowing his silhouette would be clear and unmistakable, not caring about any of that. He would not try and contact her mentally yet. He didn't understand her *jara* well enough and would not risk damaging it.

When he reached the window, he raised a hand.

Hello, he hoped the gesture said. *Be calm.*

Evie's arms had dropped to her sides, her gaze locked on the ship. Now she raised a tentative hand in reply. And with it came a mental bubble of recognition. As if she remembered him. As if he were . . . a friend.

Then she turned and sprinted for the building, her furred companion darting ahead along the starlit path.

Scout leapt across the bridge, hearts thudding as if they would burst from his body. He was panting, tongue lolling out as he slammed instructions into the holochrom and got the ship moving.

<You deliberately allowed her to see you> Ship's voice was stern.

She hadn't minded.

<This is outside the parameters of your assignment>

She hadn't minded.

Scout shook his head. He had to think. Had to get away and think long and hard about this. He shielded his *jara* against Ship, leaned into the comforting pressure of his skimchair, and watched the solar system wink past outside the viewscreen.

The only real question was when he'd be back.

-4-

Close Encounters of the Fourth Kind:
UFOs abduct humans

Evie sat back from the computer screen and rubbed her eyes. The building was nighttime quiet, the silence broken only by the hum of computer fans and the occasional tick of fluorescent lights. It wasn't necessary to do radio astronomy at night. Radio astronomy happened all the time. But the rest of her team went home at night, and Evie was always more comfortable when she was alone.

She glanced over at her office window, although it showed her only the reflection of her neat and uncluttered office. Beyond the window, Evie knew the stars winked down at her, offering to share all their secrets if she'd only come and ask them.

A cat as black as the night outside her window leapt up on her desk with easy grace and she stroked a hand down its sleek back. It arched in pleasure and a purr rumbled under her touch.

"Hello, Galileo," she said. All her succession of cats had been named Galileo, after her childhood friend. Evie had never been a dog person. Dogs were nervous around her, and she always wondered if they could pick up on her thoughts, just a little. Cats never seemed to. Or perhaps they just didn't care.

"So, tomorrow," she said to the cat. "My birthday." Evie sighed, and Galileo twitched his ears as if he were paying attention. "Oh, I don't really mind turning forty, you know. Age is just a number anyway. The number of times the earth has orbited the sun since I was born."

The cat climbed into her lap, kneading her legs with his paws.

"It's completely arbitrary, Leo. Just another artificial construct for human convenience."

She was just so . . . tired. *Almost four decades of mental stress will do that to you.*

Anyway, tomorrow. Caroline, Amin, and the others in her department were planning a party for her. It was nice of them, of course. Evie squeezed her eyes shut until the afterimage of monitor glow faded. Crowds were hard, had always been hard, seemed to grow harder every year.

The window drew her gaze again, and she shook her head and rose from her desk, dumping the cat gently to the floor. What was wrong with her tonight? She felt anxious, anticipatory—but for what? It wasn't her approaching birthday. It wasn't work.

It was . . . the alien.

There, she'd admitted it.

Evie shrugged into her lambswool jacket and strode down the hallway, her footsteps echoing in the empty building. The night air brushed her cheeks like a cooling hand when she pushed open the door, a welcome relief from the stuffiness of her office. She stood uncertainly on the steps with her hands in her pockets. Should she walk down to the array?

She shivered. Not tonight. Not when she was already thinking about him—him? she didn't even know—not when he seemed so close.

197

The cat wound around her ankles and she bent to pick him up.

"You were there, Galileo," she whispered into his twitching ear. "It's our little secret, right? But what do you think it meant? And if they're out there, why don't we ever pick up any signals?"

The cat lay still just long enough for Evie to think he was content, green eyes glinting in the moonlight, then leapt from her arms. Evie shoved her hands back into the pockets of her jacket. They had to be missing something. She was always looking, always trying to think outside the box. She'd made some notable discoveries that way. But she'd never come up with an explanation to satisfy herself.

Those were only the questions she let herself think about. There were others, buried much deeper, where she rarely let her mind venture. Was her encounter with the alien linked to the others, long ago and fuzzier in her memory? Lights in the sky, and then later, outside her window. Her strange, inexplicable brain and the abilities she struggled to control. She'd travelled the world when she was younger, searching for another mind like her own, and never had a word in reply. Sometimes that frustrating twitch, like a sleeping consciousness that almost awoke at her call, but in the end, silence. What did it all mean?

Was this what turning forty meant? Focusing on all the unanswered questions in one's life?

"If that's it," she muttered, "I'm not interested." Evie gathered Galileo up again, turned on her heel and went back inside, shut off the lights in her office, and went home.

She awoke in the night to the sensation that she was in a strange room, not her own. She lay in the darkness, perfectly still, collecting her thoughts. A familiar presence hovered at the edge of consciousness, familiar but vague, like a face at a darkened window. An impression without detail, like her room, filled with colorless shapes in the moonlight.

She became aware of more lights outside her bedroom window, flickering in a steady cadence. Their presence was no surprise—they seemed right, as if she had expected them. Evie rose and stood a long moment at the window, looking out as the familiar craft settled to the ground in her open yard. Evie's natural tendency to isolation meant no near neighbors, no-one to notice the intrusion. Galileo stalked the length of her bed, hackles stiff, mewling plaintively.

As she watched, a panel in the side slid open, just like in all the old science fiction movies. Evie's heart fluttered, feeling too large in her chest.

It felt like an invitation.

She dressed slowly. *I should be shocked, or terrified,* she thought, stifling the urge to laugh. *Why am I so . . . relieved?*

The house around her lay still, almost as if it held its breath, waiting. Waiting for me, she realized. This is the moment of choice. She stroked the agitated cat absently, and tucked him up under her arm, one hand resting lightly on his head as she looked around. She liked her house; it had long been her sanctuary—but it was nothing she couldn't bear to leave. Her parents were dead, other connections lapsed over her years of self-enforced solitude.

There was nothing, really, to keep her here.

But what might wait beyond? Evie returned to the window. Now a creature stood silhouetted in the warm glow that spilled through the open panel and onto the hard-packed earth. A silhouette Evie recognized. Still he had made no effort to contact her, mentally or otherwise.

A choice. And clearly hers alone.

Still carrying the cat, Evie left the house, locking the door carefully behind her. She barely noticed the chill night air that raised goosebumps on her skin.

The visitor held up a hand as it had that night above the array, and Evie returned the gesture, probing tentatively with her mind. He responded with what felt like caution, a presence strengthening in her mind, not words, not even wordless messages, not *hello* or *I come in peace* or *take me to your leader.* Language would come later. For now, it was simpler than that, simpler and so much more relevant. Emotions. *Friendship. Joy.*

Love.

As she neared the ship she made out his features. Copper skin, dark lobed eyes. Completely alien. Completely unimportant. Galileo struggled out of her arms and stopped behind her, his tail stiff and bristling.

She allowed herself to be drawn into the alien's spindly arms and wrapped hers around him in return. His skin was cool and smooth. He smelled of rain. He pressed his forehead to hers silently. Their minds met in what could only be described as a kiss. A kiss that could not be reduced to words, but encompassed every language. She released her mind as she had that night at the array and felt the alien shudder, his clasp tightening around her.

The cat hung back for a moment longer, whiskers twitching as he observed this strange embrace. Then he stalked cautiously past the pair and into the craft, his tail high.

Evie did not look back as the open panel slid closed behind them.

-5-

Close Encounters of the Fifth Kind:
Humans contact UFOs by conventional signals or telepathy

Scout glanced across at Evie, sitting silently beside the viewport, Galileo nestled, purring, on her lap. Her mind stirred in response and she turned to him, smiling.

"You're sure you want to do this?" he asked again. "You know it may not work."

Evie nodded. "I know, but I have to try. Just one more time. I know there were others. Once in a while I'd feel them, just the potential, unrealized."

Scout sighed. "I suppose I know what you mean. Like the radio signals."

"Exactly. They told you there was potential on our planet, but it wasn't the right kind of signal. You thought we couldn't communicate."

"Until you."

Evie smiled. "Until me."

Galileo rose and stretched languorously, then made his way over to Scout, jumping into his lap and settling down for another nap. Scout stroked the weird creature's fur awkwardly, as Evie had taught him, although he didn't know if he'd ever understand the attraction.

Evie giggled, apparently picking up on his skepticism.

<Approaching Sol system> Ship announced.

Scout ran his finger down a holochrom slide. "They may not open for you, even now. It'll be disappointing," he warned.

"But I understand it so much better now. And you'll help me." Evie crossed to sit in the skimchair beside him and patted the long, knobbly digits of Scout's hand.

"I'm not supposed to," he grumbled good-naturedly.

Evie smiled. "You weren't supposed to come back for me, either. And that's worked out all right."

Scout snorted. "Yes, I only came *this* close to a military execution for 'abducting' you."

"I put in a good word for you," she protested.

In truth, she'd plead his case so vigorously, portrayed her loneliness and desperation so eloquently that some of the judges had been moved to tears. They'd finally deemed his actions an "altruistic rescue endeavour," and dismissed all the charges. And the flight home before that, teaching Evie to use her powers as they were meant to be used—there was nothing in the galaxy he'd trade for that.

"Oh, all right. You win," he said with a smile. "It's worked out."

They sat in silence for a time after that, as the craft plied the silent ocean of space. For a while Evie dozed, and Scout sat blissfully with the cat on his lap and the soft *jara* waves of Evie's dreams lapping against his mind. He woke her when Earth sprang into view, a blue-green button tucked into a black velvet cushion.

Evie fetched them each a *jarakiva* booster while Scout laid in the same globe-encircling route he'd used to search for Evie so long ago.

"Keep to the course, Ship. Not too fast." He swiveled his skimchair to face Evie.

Scout smiled. He hadn't noticed her lighting the *tachee* meditation lanterns. Her alien face took on a strange beauty in their muted glow.

He took her hands as the spicy fragrance swirled around them, the heat of her skin no longer uncomfortable to his. "Ready?"

She took a deep breath. "Ready."

Together they opened their minds to the planet below, seeking out every consciousness in the waiting millions. Evie's mental touch, Scout knew, was gentle, coaxing, like a mother's for her children. He concentrated on supporting her, buoying up this alien mind he had begun to love when it brushed against his so many years ago.

Far below them, scattered among the millions who could not answer, minds began to open like flowers under the soft persuasion of sunlight. Minds answering Evie's call, reaching out to Scout, out to each other in bewilderment and joy and sudden release. Evie smiled at Scout, and he nodded, hoping they'd done the right thing. A new race was blossoming, and a new set of encounters was about to begin.

Memento Mori
by Sue Blalock

"The pure and simple truth is rarely
pure and never simple."
—*Oscar Wilde*

They built in stone at Uru Kesh, grey and oppressive like the sky overhead. Mountains rose in the distance, the setting sun firing their craggy peaks indigo, violet, and magenta through the wreath of trailing cloud. The air had a bite that promised winter soon.

Gillian Sands climbed the low ridge on the eastern border of the ruins, found a suitably flat rock and sat down. From this vantage she could see the whole of the dig site. A few stragglers from the expedition still remained amid the broken columns that lined the central plaza, talking and joking as they packed away their gear in the slowly fading light. She was too far away to make out faces, but recognized McIntyre from the bell-like sound of her laugh, Korolyuk from his gangling height.

The third straggler was one of the Allaru, and had no name so far as Gill knew, only a title: *Vesh*, which translated loosely as *Learned*. It turned its pale head away from Korky and Mac and looked to the east, to where Gill sat on her dusty rock, waiting for the first moon to rise. Gill smiled, thin and tight, and considered giving it the finger.

There was noise behind her, the crunch of heavy boots against loose, rocky soil. Gill did not turn around, but continued staring at the ruined city below. "When dealing with your people," she said, "is thinking about flipping someone off the same as actually doing it?"

"Only if we're actively listening," Reilán replied. "In that one's case, consider the message received."

Rei claimed a corner of the flat rock for itself and sat, close enough that Gill could feel the heat of its body. The level of trust implied was humbling. "May I ask what my esteemed colleague did to annoy you?" it asked.

Gill nudged a pebble with the toe of her boot and watched it tumble down the ridge in a shower of dust. At last she said, "I'm just tired of all the pity. It gets draining after a while."

"Yes, I imagine it would," Rei said. "Even if there's nothing at the shrine, it will be a relief to be away from camp for a time."

"Do you think we'll find anything?"

Rei considered the question. "Most myths have at least some basis in truth. Though, with this particular story, that's not a comforting thought."

Gill was unable to suppress a shiver. "Yeah, no kidding. It reminds me of a folktale I heard as a kid: *La Llorona*, the Wailing One. She's supposed to be the ghost of a woman doomed to wander the banks of the Rio Grande for all eternity, searching for her dead children." She shivered again. "Gave me nightmares for months."

Rei frowned. "You know, we don't have to do this."

"Of course we do," Gill said. "It's an amazing opportunity. The Ciprians never let offworlders go into the mountains. We'll be the first."

"That's not what I meant."

"I know." Lacking adequate words, Gill let her shoulder brush Rei's instead. Trust, yes, and gratitude. Rei would know, without the need for speech. There were benefits to having a friend who could read your mind.

The sun dipped below the horizon. A soft wind rustled the dry grass near Gill's feet. She smelled smoke from distant campfires and, closer at hand, the heady sweetness of night blooming flowers as they opened their petals to the stars. When the first sliver of moonlight showed over the tops of the mountains, the Ciprian matriarch Ulua appeared, staff in hand, climbing the ridge at an unhurried pace.

When Ulua spotted Reilán, she stopped and rocked back on her hind legs, mid-legs folding up tight against her belly. "Not female," she declared, and thumped the butt of her staff against the ground to make sure they got the point.

"Not male," Rei countered.

"Not anything!"

"Not *yet*."

Ulua turned her head and fixed Gill with a fierce yellow-green glare. "I understand why the Allaru insisted one of their kind accompany us, but must it be this sexless thing? Surely there is one female among them you can tolerate!"

The Ciprians respected strength of will. Gill was too small and slender for size to be an advantage, but she could bluster with the best of them.

"Maybe you haven't noticed, but the Allaru don't really like humans. In fact, they don't seem to like anyone except other Allaru. The only ones who will even speak to other species are *án* like Reilán. Supposedly, their lack of gender makes them inherently neutral, and better able to serve as unbiased intermediaries than the other two sexes."

"If the *án* are unbiased, I would not like to see prejudiced," Ulua grumbled.

"Which is exactly my point," Gill snapped. "There is not a single tolerable female among them because there's not a single female among them capable of tolerating me. If I am going to climb a mountain to pray for the soul of the child I lost, then I am going to do it with the friend who got me to the medic's tent when the bleeding started and wouldn't stop, and not some complete stranger who just happens to have the right reproductive organs. And if you can't understand that, then maybe we should just call the whole thing off."

Ulua lowered her head until she was eye-level with Gill. "It truly means that much to you?"

Gill paused, swallowing against a sudden, unexpected tightness in her throat. "If you won't allow my husband to come with me, then I damned well want my best friend."

"Come, then." Ulua put her mid-legs down and spun about with alarming speed for a large, elderly reptile. Her heavy tail missed Rei's head by millimeters.

Gill and Rei exchanged exasperated looks. "You know she's going pull this crap the entire way," Gill said. "Are you sure you want to go?"

"Absolutely," Rei said.

They shouldered their packs and followed Ulua into the night.

By the time all three moons had risen, the wind was blowing bitterly strong. It thrashed the scrubby bushes and low, twisted trees that dotted the hills, and sent Reilán's long ivory hair whipping about its head. Gill, who had wisely confined her own hair in a tight braid down her back, did not envy Rei the task of combing the snarls out later.

Ulua was not troubled by the weather. She had thick, leathery skin to protect her from stinging dust and clawing branches, and six limbs to keep her stable on the rough terrain. She was slow, like all her kind, but steady and capable of walking for hours without pause. When they stopped to rest,

Gill knew it was purely for her sake, though Ulua was polite enough not to say so.

Midnight found them sitting before a trio of stelae carved in the High Classic style. Gill longed for her camera, but technology worked poorly in the shadow of the mountains, when it worked at all. Something about the geological composition of the rock interfered with modern electronics, and so the dig at Uru Kesh was old fashioned, hands-on archaeology. Gill had the calluses to prove it.

Denied a camera, she reached for her sketchbook instead, determined to record as much of the inscriptions as possible before they moved on. "One pillar for each of the moons?"

"Just so," said Ulua.

Rei had its own book out, sketching at a furious pace. They would compare notes later, politics be damned. "If you want to avoid politics," Rei said, snatching the thought from mid-air, "then you would be better served leaving Cipria altogether and going back to Earth."

"Ah, but then who would you get your chocolate from?" Gill said, and bent closer to the smallest stele. Time and the elements had worn the carving down, making it difficult to read. "Is that *setch* or *unsch*? Your eyes are better than mine in the dark."

"*Setch,* I should think," Rei said. "Otherwise it would say, '*Greater Moon's Daughter plaited her long pale fish with bones.*' Of course," it added, "neither translation makes sense, as Ciprians do not have hair of any length or color."

"No," Ulua said, "we do not."

"And yet, your goddess does. Your goddess, who came from the sky to walk the land on only two legs, and who plaits her long white hair with only two hands."

"And what of it?" Ulua demanded. She pointed her staff at Gill. "There is a god among her kind with four arms and two legs. Does that mean my people have a claim upon her world? No."

"Ah," Rei said, "but yours is not a space-faring race."

Ulua stretched out her long neck until she and Reilán were nose-to-nose. "We are the ones who belong to this place. Not you."

"That has never been the issue."

"Then why does it matter whether your people came here long ago?" Her head whipped around to snap at Gill. "And why do your people care if they did? We have nothing of value to either of you!"

Gill sighed and shot Rei a look that promised a slow and painful death for bringing up this particular subject. "It's a question of borders," she said. "Lines on a map. It's not the planet itself that matters, but where it sits in relation to others."

"You are like scavengers fighting over a dry, cracked bone," Ulua said, her voice rich with disgust. "You should all leave, and find some other rock to piss on."

"I wish it was that simple," Gill said.

The shrine turned out to be a cave hidden among the tangled, spiky brush that clung to the mountain's side. Seeing it, Gill let out a deep, resigned sigh. "There will be bugs."

"Of course there will be bugs," Rei said. "Bugs are traditional. In fact, I have a theory that the creatures are spontaneously generated by the combination of tombs and archaeologists."

Gill smothered a snort of laughter behind her hand. "Yeah, because we're full of shit."

If Ulua heard their less than respectful exchange, she chose to ignore it. Instead, she turned and gestured for Gill to enter the cave. "You may go within, and stay as long as you need." She shot a sour look at Rei. "You will wait here."

Here we go again, Gill thought. "That is not what we agreed."

"We agreed it could accompany you to the shrine, not that it could enter," Ulua said. "When it is capable of bearing offspring it will be welcome within, but not before."

Gill opened her mouth to argue, stopped when Reilán touched her arm. "What if I wished to pray for the ability to have children of my own?" Rei asked. "Would that be acceptable?"

Very few could look an Allaru directly in the eyes. It enhanced their telepathic abilities, and could cause anything from mild disorientation to a full-blown psychotic break among non-telepaths. Ulua looked into Reilán's eyes, calm and unflinching. Whatever she saw there satisfied her, for she sat back on her heels and nodded. "You may proceed."

Gill gaped in blank astonishment. Rei kicked her sharply in the ankle. "Right!" Gill yelped. "Let's get to it."

The cave was shallow, with a low, slanting roof and sandy floor. It was cold and dry and showed no signs of previous occupation, much less anything to indicate it was an important place of pilgrimage. "What the hell," Gill said. She had expected an altar or, at the very least, to find offerings left by previous visitors, but there was nothing, not even a potsherd. "Are we supposed to just sit in the dirt and contemplate our ovaries?"

"Natural caves are seen as symbolic wombs by many cultures," Rei pointed out.

"Yes, but this isn't even a proper cave. It's more a depression hollowed out by the wind." Gill sighed. "Okay. According to the story, Greater Moon's Daughter gathered up the bodies of her slain children and buried them in the mountain's heart. So, either there's a tomb entrance hiding around here somewhere and we're too sleep-deprived to see it, or this is all just symbolism with any natural shelter in the rock serving as a stand-in for the burial site of legend."

They regarded each other in weary silence. Gill sighed again, and pinched the bridge of her nose. "Screw it. Let's just survey this puppy as fast as we can and get back to camp."

"Agreed," Rei said. "Do you want the level or the rod?"

"The rod. I'm too tired to deal with geometry right now."

Gill set down her pack, and began rummaging through the main compartment for string, a tape measure, and her collapsible stadia rod. "Did you mean that about wanting children?" she asked.

Rei shrugged. "We are a long-lived race, and slow to reproduce. If the time comes, I will do my part to ensure our continued survival."

"That doesn't really answer my question."

Rei did not reply, just lowered its head until the narrow oval of its face was hidden beneath a tangled fall of ivory hair; Gill knew then she had inadvertently flicked her friend on the raw. She couldn't apologize without knowing exactly how she had given offense, though she suspected it was simply that Rei was not as sanguine about the possibility of changing sex as it might wish others to believe. Given the pain her own sex had caused her in recent weeks, she could well understand the attraction of living a life untroubled by hormones.

"Not to mention the lack of hair in inconvenient places," Rei said, but its tone was more wry than flippant. "We produce children so rarely, it makes us unimaginably vulnerable. Everyone capable of contributing to the gene pool is expected to do so. In another few years, I will be past the point of change. Until then, I shall metaphorically hold my breath."

Gill tried to imagine Reilán with soft, feminine curves, or sporting the long, intricately braided beard many Allaru males preferred. She failed miserably. "Go pick a base datum point," she said with a smile. "I'll string the line."

It was a small cave, so there was no need for a full grid. Length and width would do, with flags every two meters. On any other world this would be accomplished with lasers, but on Cipria they were reduced to twine and wooden pegs, all measured and placed by hand. This was the tedious part of the job, the one that never made it into documentaries, much less popular adventure films. Real archaeology required patience, and meticulous attention to detail. Anything less was mere grave-robbing.

Not that there appeared to be any sort of grave to rob, even had they been so inclined. There was sand and stone, and blank rock walls, cold, empty and still. "Maybe that's the point," Gill said.

Rei lowered the level and cocked its head to one side. "Emptiness?"

"Yes," Gill said. "We were thinking we'd find some sort of fertility shrine, but the story isn't about birth, it's about loss. In that case, it makes sense for the shrine to be so desolate."

"Perhaps, but it's still not consistent with what we know of ancient Ciprian burial practices."

"Because it's not a grave." Gill's hands were shaking; she balled them into fists to keep them still. "It's what you said before: a symbolic womb. Only, empty. Devoid of life."

Rei's face had gone inscrutable. It was a trait common among the Allaru, and one Gill found profoundly annoying. They took great pride in the ability to lay bare the soul of anyone they came into contact with, while keeping their own locked firmly away behind a wall of silence and the silken veil of their hair. "We're not like that, and you know it," Rei said, a note of anger lacing its voice. "Human minds are like sieves, leaking trails of thought we can't help but follow. If we withdraw, it's as much to respect your privacy as it is to protect our own."

Gill opened her mouth. Closed it again. "I'm broadcasting, aren't I," she said.

"Loudly," Rei said, but there was no censure in its tone, only kindness. "This is a place where women who have lost children come to mourn. It's understandable."

Gill ground the heels of her palms against her eyelids. "I'm sorry, I thought I could shield better than that."

"You do well enough under normal circumstances," Rei conceded, "but this journey has been long and trying. Perhaps you should take a moment to center."

"Always the teacher," Gill said, torn between exhaustion and chagrin. She folded her hands against her chest and bowed low in the Allaru style. "Very well, *Vesh* Reilán. I will go sit in the dirt and contemplate my ovaries."

Rei returned the bow in kind. "My aching head thanks you."

She found a corner of the cave where the floor was almost level and sat, eyes closed and hands resting on her knees, breathing deep and slow. A stone dug sharply into her spine. She shifted, trying to find a smoother patch of rock to lean against. As she moved, her fingers brushed over a crack in the stone that felt oddly smooth and regular. Too regular, and she opened her eyes again to turn and peer at the wall behind her.

"You're supposed to be meditating," Rei reminded her.

Gill pulled a brush out of her coat pocket and began clearing the sand away. "Yes, well, God is in the details."

Rei stopped her with a gentle hand on her wrist. "Gillian. Please."

Her eyes prickled; she blinked the tears back stubbornly. "I can't, Rei. If I stop to let myself feel, I'll break. Once I'm back home, I'll light so many candles the church walls will blister from the heat, I promise. But for now, please, just let me work."

She turned back to the wall and resumed her patient brushing. After a moment, Rei joined her. They quickly fell into their normal working pattern: Gill taking everything down low, Rei covering everything above. Beneath their brushes the crack became a long, vertical line two meters in height, and so thin a razor blade wouldn't fit inside it. A few brushstrokes more, and the line became one side of a rectangle etched deep into the rock.

"If it's a door, it's not meant to be noticed," Rei said. "That's atypical of Ciprian architecture."

"If it's a door," Gill said, "how do we get it open?"

Rei found the answer in much the same way Gill had found the door: pure luck combined with skill enough to realize the rounded shape beneath its fingertips was more than just a stone. It was a latch that, when pressed, released the mechanism that had held the door shut for untold centuries. It did not move far, just a scant few centimeters, but it was enough for Gill and Rei to get a handhold and open it further.

Gill snapped a chemical light and lifted it into the darkness beyond. The eerie green glow illuminated a long, narrow passageway leading deep under the mountain. "See if you can find a rock big enough to brace the door," she said. "We don't want it closing on us while we're inside."

The passage was as low as it was narrow. Even for someone accustomed to crawling through dark, cramped spaces it was an uncomfortable sensation, like being swallowed by stone. "There's no way an adult Ciprian could fit in here," Gill said. Even her voice sounded muffled.

Rei glanced over its shoulder at her, tawny eyes flaring green in the light of Gill's glowstick. "A juvenile perhaps, but it would be tight." It ran its fingertips along one smooth wall as they walked. "This is too even to be a natural tunnel, but I don't see any tool marks to indicate how it was carved."

"I don't either," Gill said. "Still, it's in keeping with the legend. *Deeper and deeper she carried her grief through halls of stone.*' We must be at least a kilometer inside the mountain by now."

The passageway continued for another six meters before making a sharp turn to the left. Rei rounded the corner and stopped so abruptly that Gill collided with its back. "What is it?" she demanded. "Rei? Do you see something?"

"Yes," Rei said.

She waited for it to elaborate, but Rei said nothing more, just stood in the middle of the passageway as though rooted in place. Impatient, and wanting to see what could render her friend both immobile and speechless, she squeezed beneath Rei's arm and found herself standing before the shattered remains of a metal door.

Debris littered the floor. Gill knelt down to pick up a piece, the slick, twisted metal still black and shiny as a beetle's carapace beneath its coating of dust. "This is Allaru work," she said softly.

"Yes," Rei said. "It is."

Gill let the metal shard tumble back to the floor and stood, wiping her dusty fingers on the leg of her trousers. "So, your people were here after all. That should thrill Ulua to no end."

She meant it as a joke, but Rei did not laugh, only stared at the ruined door as if transfixed. Her eyes narrowed. No. Not at the door, at a section of floor beside the door where a heavy, knotted cord the color of dried blood lay in a tangled heap. Gill had no idea what it signified, but given the way Reilán was trying to disappear behind its hair again, it couldn't be anything good.

"It means we should leave," Rei said, its voice as expressionless as its face.

"No," Gill said. "No, you do not get to go all ancient and enigmatic, not this time."

"You don't understand."

"You're right," Gill said. "I don't. Why don't you try explaining it to me? You are *Vesh*, it's your job to instruct. Tell me why I should turn my back on my training and walk away."

Rei took a long, deep breath, loosed it slowly. "Forgive me, I was taken aback. The cord—" It hesitated, took another deep breath before continuing. "The cord is a relic of another time. It means this place has been cleansed."

Reilán's tone made it clear that *cleansed* in this instance was synonymous with *defiled*. Gill's stomach churned uneasily. "Cleansed how?" she asked, not entirely sure she wanted to hear the answer.

"How do you think? You know the story. Work it through."

"'*Greater Moon's Daughter carried the bodies of her murdered children one by one into the mountain's heart and laid them to rest upon the stones.*'" Gill closed her eyes. "Oh. Oh, Jesus."

"We can turn around," Rei said. "Now. Forget we ever found this place."

Gill shook her head. "No. We can't. Our job is to unearth the truth, not bury it further."

Rei studied her, its eyes wide and frightened. At last, it nodded. "Together, then?"

"Together," Gill agreed, took a deep breath and stepped across the broken threshold.

The circular chamber beyond was starkly plain. In the center stood a long table, the wood dry with age and grey with dust. A ceramic bowl on one end still held a handful of nuts, and the shriveled, desiccated remains of what had once been fruit. Suspended from the ceiling was a chandelier made from the same iridescent black metal as the door, but instead of candles it held small globes of shimmering blue glass that still cast a faint glow after all these centuries.

There were other doorways off the main room. The first led to a simple kitchen with a stone hearth and a well-stocked pantry, each basket and jar carefully labeled by hand in the barbed, spidery writing of the Allaru. Another turned out to be a washroom, the crumbling linens still folded in a stack beside the empty wooden tub.

The third led to the nursery.

Six small beds lined the walls, and on each bed lay a body. Someone had arranged them with great care atop the covers, folding their hands across their chests and placing wreaths of flowers at their feet. "Three male, two female," Rei whispered. Its voice trembled. "One *án*."

The cold, dry climate had preserved the remains remarkably well. They were all dark-haired except for the *án*, who was the same pale ivory as Rei. Its clothes were different as well, dove-grey instead of rich, earthy brown and gold. "God, it's so small," Gill said.

Rei made a soft keening sound, almost too low to hear. "It didn't live long enough to have even the possibility of change."

A rectangular strip of yellowed cloth was wound around the tiny hands, embroidered in black with a single word: *Varán.* "Is there a significance to the cloth?" Gill asked, clinging desperately to her archaeological training in an attempt to gain some emotional distance.

"Yes," Rei said. Its voice steadied as it fell back into the familiar role of teacher. "It's an ancient practice, comparable to the way some humans would lay coins on the eyes of the dead to pay for their passage into the underworld. The belief is that by presenting your name to the guardian of gateway between life and death, your spirit is able to shed the weight of its past and begin anew in the next life."

"Whoever cared for these children wanted to be sure their souls had no memory of what happened here." Gill looked up at Rei, heartsick and weary. "This makes no sense. I thought your people revered children."

"Yes, because they are so few," Rei said, and now even the gentle, cadenced teaching-voice was gone, leaving only impervious stone. "During the Dynastic Wars, the easiest way to ensure the defeat of a rival house was by wiping out their future. Many families sent their children into hiding, but there were killing squads devoted to nothing but tracking them down. The knotted cord was their symbol, a sign that all undesirables had been culled. It is not a part of our past we are proud of, and not something we want to share with outsiders."

The room blurred around her, but for once Gill did not try to stop the tears. Instead she let them fall; for herself, for Reilán, for the six pitiful corpses lying on their beds as if asleep.

Each child had a naming-cloth. Gill pulled out her sketchbook and recorded them all: Varán. Reish. Talla. Ardri. Liath. Terchel. She sketched the room, the placement of the beds, the position of each small, fragile body and its attendant burial goods. They would need to determine the exact cause of death; she began making a list of all the female physical anthropologists in the expedition, which of them had experience dealing with naturally mummified bodies. . . .

"That presumes Ulua will allow more offworlders to visit this place," Rei said. "In light of this discovery, I doubt that will ever happen."

"In light of this discovery, I doubt she'll have a choice," Gill said, keeping her watery gaze fixed on the book in her hands. She couldn't look at Rei right now; it hurt too much. "The Allaru may have committed this atrocity, but it's the Ciprians who will pay for it. The harder your government tries to hide what happened here, the harder mine will try to drag it into the light. Ulua and her people will be caught in the middle."

"Scavengers fighting over dry, cracked bones," Rei said bitterly. "This could easily become the incident that touches off an interstellar war. We have a duty to the dead to see their story told, but now is not the time."

"So, what do you suggest we do?" Gill demanded. "As soon as I walk into camp, every Allaru within a ten kilometer radius is going to know what we've found." She smiled, thin and sharp. "I'm just not that good at shielding."

"You don't have to be."

Gill opened her mouth to protest, but before she could speak Reilán pressed a finger against her lips. "Hush," it said, and the words died unspoken on her tongue.

Then it said, "Look at me."

The sun was high in the sky by the time they finished surveying the cave. Gill was exhausted and sore, and wanted desperately to lie down in the dirt and sleep for a month. Instead, she forced herself to walk out into the clearing until she reached the wide, flat rock where Ulua lay basking in the midday heat.

Ulua roused herself from her near somnolent state to peer down at Gill sphinx-like from her perch upon the rocks. "Did you find what you were looking for?" she asked as Gill slumped to the ground near her feet.

"Yes and no," Gill said. She fumbled through her pockets for her sunglasses and shoved them on to shield her tired, gritty eyes.

"It is a profoundly moving site," Rei added. "Thank you for allowing us to see it."

Ulua yawned massively, showing off her blunt, yellowed teeth. "Rest now," she said. "We have a long journey back down the mountain."

Rest sounded wonderful. Gill let herself tumble backward, and stared up at the clear blue sky. After a moment, Rei sat down beside her. "You have burrs in your hair," she informed it.

"You have sand in yours." Rei studied her face. "How do you feel?"

"Weirdly peaceful. Who knew sitting in the dirt and contemplating your ovaries could be so soothing?"

Rei's expression was pensive, but all it said was, "You should rest."

"Working on it," Gill said sleepily. Her eyelids were so heavy. "Oh, Rei?"

"Yes?"

"Thank you for looking out for me."

There was a long pause. Gill had almost drifted off when she felt a light touch to her hair and heard Rei whisper, "You're welcome."

The Gingerbread Man
by James Gunn

Andrew Martin began his transformation on July 4, 2076. It might not have happened at all had he not been interrogating himself about the purpose of life. "The purpose of life," he muttered, looking deep within, "is to avoid pain."

But he was thinking of the pain inflicted upon the psyche by other people and how it would be better not to care what they said or did, or, indeed, to have anything to do with them. In any case, it started, as most things do in life, by accident. In fact, it was the rarest of rarities, an automobile accident. With automated roads and computerized controls, a car could collide with another, or with a stationary object, only by total malfunction, and even malfunctions were programmed to fail-safe. In Andrew's case, however, a computer chip failed at a critical junction, short-circuiting the steering mechanism and the fail-safe devices, and allowed his vehicle to propel itself into and under the back of a computer-driven semi.

Although the airbag seized him in a lover's embrace, it could not totally protect his legs, and his left foot was mangled beyond repair. Having failed at its most important task, the automobile's computer sensed Andrew's physical condition with instant accuracy and tightened a cuff around his lower leg, injected him with a painkiller and a tranquilizer, and summoned an ambulance, which arrived with whumping blades even before the tourniquet needed loosening.

Andrew opened his eyes to the sterile blankness of a hospital ceiling. On the left wall was a window opening on a sunny meadow strewn with red, yellow, and blue wildflowers. A brook babbled through it. Behind the meadow was a green forest rising in the distance to blue mountain peaks capped with snow.

"What's going on?" Andrew asked.

"You're in regional hospital five seven two," the computer responded in a pleasant, concerned female voice. "You have been involved in an automobile accident—"

217

"An automobile accident!" Andrew interjected.

"An automobile accident," the computer repeated. "Your left foot was crushed. We have replaced it with prosthetic model eff two one eight three. Can you move the toes on your left foot?"

It certainly felt as if he could move the toes on his left foot. Andrew pulled his left leg from under the light thermal covering and held it up for inspection. The leg above the ankle revealed a bit of bruising, but otherwise the leg, including the foot, didn't look any different, and he certainly could move his toes, and without pain. "Are you sure it's the left foot?"

"We do not make mistakes," the computer said pleasantly. "Can you stand on the replacement?"

Andrew swung his legs over the side of the bed and stood on the warm resilient floor beside it. He felt a bit of residual soreness in the calf of his left leg and a bit of stiffness in his back and neck, but his left foot felt fine. In fact, it felt better than fine. He not only had a sharper sense of the temperature of the floor with his left foot than his right, he could feel the small depressions his heel and the ball of his foot and his toes made in the floor covering. In addition he had a feeling of well being in his foot to which he was not accustomed, like power waiting to be unleashed. He rose on his toes and felt a moment of shame that his right foot did not do as well.

"I see that the foot is working," the computer said.

"Indeed," Andrew said.

"Then we have an inquiry about your condition if you are prepared to receive it."

"Who has made the inquiry?" Andrew asked, wondering if it was Jennifer and hoping, perhaps, that it was. But Jennifer had said she never wanted to see him again, and it was from that dismissal he had been fleeing when the accident had occurred, almost as if the computer chip had shared the disorder in his brain.

"A Mrs. Martin," the computer replied.

"But I'm not married," Andrew said.

"She has been identified as your biological mother."

"I will accept the inquiry, of course," Andrew said, although he wondered why his mother had gotten in touch with him now, after twenty years. It wasn't as if they had argued, as he had with Jennifer; they had simply grown apart gradually until they had nothing left to share.

The square on the left wall that had been functioning as a window turned into the face of a woman who looked as young as Jennifer. He compared it with the memory of his mother that still was stored there, but he would never have recognized her.

"Mother," Andrew said, "you have had your face redone."

"Do you like it?" she said, brightening. "Well, it's you I've called about. I was notified of your accident. Imagine having an accident on the highway! Imagine traveling on the highway! Andrew, I can't imagine what got into you! Well, I can't tell you how surprised I was after all these years to be notified that my son, my only son, had been injured. Well, I see you've quite recovered." Her image began to fade into the sunny landscape.

"They replaced my foot, Mother," Andrew said quickly.

His mother's image steadied. "How efficient of them," she said. "Well, if you need anything—"

"And, Mother," Andrew said before she could fade again, "It works so well that I have decided to have the other one replaced as well." He hadn't known he was going to do it until he spoke, but now that the words were out he knew it was what he wanted to do. He could not go through life limping on a less-than-perfect real foot.

A day later Andrew walked out of regional hospital 572. It was located at the intersection of two major highways surrounded by growing crops clear to the horizon. No one else was in sight. It was a virtually silent and efficient scene in which vehicles of various sizes and purposes, but only a single, silvery color, traveled on either side, moving rapidly in several directions and effortlessly maintaining the same distance from the others. None of them was occupied; none of them, indeed, had any windows. He could understand his mother's surprise. He shared it.

He stepped into the waiting taxi and allowed it to whisk him to his home, and when it lowered him onto the landing pad of his apartment building twenty minutes later, he made his way quickly to the elevator and then to his rooms. There were four of them: a bedroom, a living room, a bathroom, and a dining room. With computer service, who needed more? They were decorated according to his own taste for comfort and muted colors, but with easy-to-clean surfaces. He would have liked to have commented to someone about his new vitality, but he had met no one. As soon as he had settled himself into his favorite chair, he called Jennifer.

"I will accept your call this time," Jennifer's image said frostily, "since I have been notified that you have been involved in an accident. But my earlier statement still holds."

"You don't understand," Andrew said. "I feel as if I have wings on my feet, and I'd like to dance. You have criticized my remoteness, my lack of involvement, and I wanted you to know that I feel like getting involved. I want to dance."

"Well—" she said.

They met at a neutral site, at a studio where dancers performed for a television audience. But it was little used any more. Computers could construct new performances from previously recorded routines, Fred Astaire and Margot Fonteyn, say, or Rudolf Nureyev with Isadora Duncan. So Andrew and Jennifer had the studio all to themselves. "Play something fast," Andrew said to the computer while he removed his shoes to allow his new feet more freedom. They began to dance.

The joint exercise lasted only a few minutes, with Andrew and Jennifer scarcely coming closer than a meter or two. Jennifer looked at Andrew and his magic feet, as if waiting for him to make the first move toward companionship, and abandoned the attempt to keep up. Synchronized with the music, Andrew's feet seemed to dance on their own. Jennifer stood against one wall and watched them caper while above them Andrew's body seemed to follow rather than to lead and his face seemed frozen in a look of amazement. After a few more minutes his body began to sag while the feet pounded on untiringly.

Finally Andrew stopped, breathless, his legs trembling but his feet still wiggling beneath him as if eager to continue.

"You dance divinely," Jennifer said, "but you're still the same remote jerk you always have been. I'm going home."

"Wait," Andrew said. "It's my legs. They just can't keep up." But she was gone already, and Andrew dismissed his taxi. He walked his aching body back to his apartment. Scurrying streetsweepers kept the pavement neat, but Andrew met nobody except two police robots who asked politely if he were lost or in need of assistance.

It was then he decided to have his legs replaced.

Afterwards, however, Jennifer refused his calls, and his legs were so filled with energy he allowed them to take him out to run. A green, groomed park was nearby, bisected with paths paved with yielding synthetics, do«ed with beds of colorful flowers, redolent with the scent of the outdoors. He seemed to have it all to himself, but as he went by an underpass a group of well-dressed teenagers, who had been hiding themselves from the watchful gaze of the park's monitors, burst out upon him, and he took off with a burst of speed that startled the gang members and surprised Martin himself.

His skill and speed gave him a feeling of invulnerability, and he began to play games with his pursuers, slowing as if he were tiring to allow them to gain on him and then outrunning them once more. He felt exhilarated with a sense of well being and high purpose even though his heart was pounding and his lungs were burning. Moving so swiftly made the air rush past his face; he could see bushes and trees and buildings zoom past and, when he turned his head, his pursuers dwindling.

He remembered a story his computer-generated nanny had told him when he was a child. "I'm the ginger-bread boy, I am, I am, and I can run away from you, I can, I can."

It was his own speed, and his hubris, that doomed him as he caught up with another group of hooligans. They grabbed him and began beating his head and body with sticks and fists. The world went dark as he thought he heard an approaching helicopter and the peremptory voice of a police robot.

He awoke to disorientation. The ceiling looked the same as the one he had stared at so intently when his foot was injured, and the room seemed identical down to the scene in the picture window. "What's going on?" he asked.

The same woman's voice said, "You are in regional hospital five one six. You received irreparable injuries to your chest and internal organs, and we have had to replace them all including your heart, which had gone into arrest. Do you feel all right?"

Andrew thought about it. Except for his head, which ached abominably, he felt good, as if his entire body had the strength and vitality that he had felt before only in his feet and legs. "Yes," he said. "I feel fine. Except for my head."

"Just a moment," the voice said, and he felt a slight pressure against the back of his neck. "Is that better?"

The pain in his head ebbed. "Yes. But my arms feel different."

"They, too, have had to be replaced. It was too difficult to reattach your old ones to your new body."

Andrew flexed them. They seemed as good as new—in fact, new seemed better. "What happened to me?" he asked.

"You were attacked in the park near your home by a group of lawless humans, all under the age of twenty, and the majority of them sixteen or younger."

James Gunn

"And what has happened to them?"

"They have all been sentenced to therapy from six months to two years, according to age. After a second offense, each will be administered daily injections of anti-testosterone."

"Then the process is not effective."

"Recidivism is likely."

Andrew thought about it, although it hurt his head. People apparently had different concepts of the meaning of life: some thought that life meant excitement and were willing to risk punishment and pain, to themselves and to others, to experience it.

"Perhaps you could suggest some other method of treatment," the computer said.

"I can't even make sense of my own life," Andrew said. When he was released he returned to his apartment and tried to get in touch with Jennifer. His call was still blocked. He thought of going back to the park and, with his new body, wreaking vengeance on the gangs that hid there—or on their counterparts if the ones who had attacked him had been disrupted. But he discarded that as unworthy of his new vitality. Still, he needed to do something with this restlessness he felt inside.

He turned to the educational channel. It sprang to life immediately like a genie long imprisoned in a bottle.

Andrew went through the index and finally selected the origins of his society, beginning with the perfection of the computer and its ability to take over the work of the world, the endless services it was able to provide, and the retreat of humanity, with all its needs provided, into self-contained living units from which it seldom ventured. He had been happy enough with that life himself until he had become involved with Jennifer on a network bulletin board. They had corresponded incessantly and then talked image to image before, in what he had considered an incomprehensible fit of pique, she had broken off with him. He went back over their correspondence and conversations to discover what had happened, and the only thing he could find was a conversation in which she had suggested that they meet. He had hesitated. As nearly as he could remember, he had been considering how he might feel in her actual presence. And then he had taken that ill-advised trip to see her, and they had stood at opposite sides of the room while Jennifer yelled at him.

He turned to psychology, hoping to find there the answers to the questions of human behavior, particularly Jennifer's, that had disrupted the comfort and efficiency of his existence. The computerized professors were responsive and well informed, but nothing they had explained why Jennifer had called him remote and unresponsive. The professors said he was normal—that is, he was like everybody else. And they gave many explanations for the behavior of the youth gangs and why they rejected the freedom from social friction that was everybody's birthright and turned to violence, but none of them suggested an answer.

Finally he turned to areas for which there were answers, to physics and astronomy and chemistry and biology and particularly to mathematics. He was told why manned spaceflight had given way to unmanned flights, that the state of knowledge about physics and chemistry had not progressed beyond what was needed to serve known human needs, and about the development of biology to provide repairs to the human body and lengthen the lifespan. Andrew could understand the general outline of what the professors said, but a request for explanation of the details got him nowhere. He didn't have the background necessary to understand. And mathematics left him baffled. What was the good of solid geometry, for instance, and of algebra, much less of calculus?

Eventually he decided to begin at the elementary level. He kept himself and his professors working day and night, scarcely pausing for rest or food. His body felt little need for either but his head began to ache and his eyes, to burn. He felt feverish. His thoughts were' jumbled in his head until he could not distinguish what was outside and what was inside. Finally the light reddened in front of his eyes and he began to lose consciousness.

When he awoke his head was crystal clear for the first time in his life. He understood solid geometry, and as for algebra, he could solve quadratic equations by mental manipulation alone. He could even comprehend human behavior, including his own and he was filled with a longing to be of service. He knew what it was. He needed no computer to tell him: His overworked brain had suffered a disabling breakdown and had been replaced with a positronic model, just like the robots that did the world's work, and his personality, with all its memories, had been impressed upon it. All the makeshift fluids of his body had been replaced, and the replacements were working together as the originals never had. The hormones that had so delighted and confused him had been replaced by electrical impulses. He was now as efficient a human being as a human being could possibly become, and he had abilities that no human being could ever aspire to.

He was linked electronically with the computer network of the world. He knew what it knew, and where others had to communicate their needs by the imperfect mechanism of speech, he could obtain information and command action instantaneously. In fact, he was a part of the computer network at the same time that his personality impress maintained a sense of individual identity. But it was his relationship to the network, he knew, that gave him his need to serve, to put himself and his humanity to use.

What would he do with his new abilities? He considered the possibility of self-sacrifice, of cutting himself free from his new-found abilities, one by one, until at last he relinquished the immortality he had gained through his transformation, or of allowing himself to be destroyed by other humans in some dramatic fashion that would inspire and reform the human species. But it was only for an instant: Salvation was not to be found through sentimentality or by encouraging humanity's tendencies toward belief in the unknown and the unknowable.

He could create art: paintings and sculpture and fiction and drama and music and dance. He knew he could do those things and the act of knowing was simultaneous with the creation itself—the creations were there, stored in the network for production when the occasion was right. All the suffering and exaltation of being human was expressed in those works, ready for contribution to human understanding and redemption. "Let there be art," he thought, and there was art.

He could create an outlet for the misdirected aggressions of the juveniles that had beaten him. What humanity needed was a new frontier, he thought, and he instructed the network to reinvigorate the space program and to create a system of inducements and rewards that would encourage ambitious young people to challenge the unknown and spread humanity as far as human energy and creativity were capable of carrying it.

He could reverse the conditions that had encouraged humanity to retreat to the isolation of the individual cave. Social change had come too swiftly, he understood, and the perfection of the computer network had allowed people to isolate themselves in perfect comfort. He understood them well; he had been one of them. People must be given incentives to interact. He rejected the idea of cutting off computer services and forcing the cave dwellers back into the marketplace; that would create too much suffering and chaos. Instead he instructed the network to develop a system of attractive meeting places and to release the art and the ideas that would support a culture of sharing. That would take longer but the result would be more lasting.

Finally he called his mother. "Mother," he said to her bewildered image, "I appreciate the sacrifices you made to bring me into the world and to nurture me to maturity, and I want you to know that I love you. I know that you have your life and that frequent contact would disrupt that life, but I want you to know that I am fine and you will receive confirmations of that from time to time."

Then he called Jennifer. Call blocking was still in effect, but with his new powers that was easy to override. "Jennifer," he said, "I know that I have given you much to complain about, but I want you to know that I love you and I want to share a life with you, to touch and be touched, to love and be loved."

"Why, Andrew," she said, "I never thought I'd ever hear those words."

He understood now; he had to replace the fallible human parts of himself to be truly human. And he understood that the purpose of life was to discover what a person was good for and then find a way to put it to use.

The Angel of Mars
by Michael Barretta

October 2027
Mars

The unmanned Crew Habitation Module, *Lewis and Clark,* fired its engines to depart its aero-captured orbit. The ship, a blunt three story cylinder, slowed and began its long fall through the cloudless Martian sky, blazing an incandescent trail of superheated atmosphere. Hypersonic whirls and eddies clawed at the hull and finally gained purchase under the high gain antenna's aluminum-lithium fairing. The fairing and antenna assembly vibrated furiously in the slipstream and disintegrated, spreading a wild confetti cloud of exotic alloy into the lower atmosphere. Parachutes deployed and then the powerful methane/oxygen engines ignited and screamed the likes of which the planet had never heard. The module touched down in a billowing cloud of dust and sand. The hull ticked and pinged as it cooled. The *Lewis and Clark* had arrived.

Inside, the ship's Mars Excursion Computer (MEC) bundled the touchdown report with calibration and integrity images and transmitted continuously for the next seven days. Without response from Earth, the MEC deployed one of the three stowed Humaniform Explorers. An exterior bay door opened and the highly sophisticated robot unfolded and stepped onto frigid Martian sand. The machine, nicknamed Zubrin, danced in the cold Martian light, evaluating the range of motion of its complex joints. With its integrity checks complete, Zubrin inspected the module's exterior, pausing at the twisted stump of the antenna arm. As directed by the MEC, Zubrin deployed the 200 kilowatt pebble bed nuclear reactor to a shallow depression a kilometer away. After bunkering the reactor with rock and loose sand, Zubrin brought the reactor to full power and activated the ship's Sabatier chemical plant. Filtered intakes sucked Martian carbon dioxide to combine with Earth hydrogen. The methane and oxygen resultants were pumped into the Earth Return Vehicle's fuel tanks. Excess water was stowed for later use in the *Lewis and Clark's* tanks or cycled back into the reaction. The MEC's only function now was to keep the *Lewis and Clark* and its return vehicle in a state of readiness and long term preservation.

"Initiate Autonomous mode," said the MEC to Zubrin in machine language.

"Query Confirm," said Zubrin.

"Confirm," said the MEC

A dim facsimile of human consciousness filled the mind spaces of Zubrin. Safety protocols were bypassed and the machine was free to direct its own reprogramming as necessary to ensure its continued operation.

"Explore and Report," said the MEC before it powered down into a hibernation mode. It kept one radio channel open to archive data sent back by Zubrin for as long as the Humaniform Explorer was in line-of-sight radio range.

"Explore?" Zubrin asked itself, testing the functionality of its bicameral processor.

"Explore," it answered itself. Zubrin's two quantum logic processors were integrated just prior to the conclusion phase state and they could not override each other. Like all other computers, Zubrin could have a yes or a no; unlike all others, it could have a maybe.

Zubrin stooped and flipped a sand scoured rock to see what was on the underside. It found nothing. With a chromed finger it scratched the Martian fines to a depth of about three centimeters and recorded - nothing of significance. Disappointing. It flipped the rock back and regarded it for a moment. Zubrin stood, spread its solar collecting wings and tilted them to catch the light. The vast and intimidating silences of the Martian desert enveloped Zubrin. A wind moaned through the landing struts and fine grains of sand rasped across each other, the sounds of a planet. To the west, the massive bulk of Olympus Mons rose to the sky like a frozen tsunami. To the east, all the way out to the far horizon, rose-colored boulders, yellow sands, and magenta shadows stretched away. There were a lot of rocks that needed to be flipped over.

October 2027
Manned Space Flight Operations Center
Houston, Texas

"No joy, Dave. We have tried everything we can think of," said Matt Caine, the director for *Lewis and Clark* Surface Operations. The frustration was evident on his face. He hadn't shaved and his usual power tie had vanished. The Operations Center was quiet and minimally manned. Most consoles were either dark or ran a liquid screensaver pattern. Without communications there was precious little work that could be done.

"I am going to call it," said Dave Sterling, the Flight Operations Director. "I don't think I will have any other choice." It was a tough decision, the hardest of his career, and probably the last. He had invested twelve years of his life to the Mars landing, nursing the program through three Presidential administrations and God knows how many Congressmen. He had passed over two promotion opportunities to remain as the Flight Operations director for the landing.

"What will happen to the mission?" asked Matt.

The Mars mission was so constrained politically and financially that there was no room for error. Its failure aptly demonstrated the difference in magnitude between going to the moon and crossing interplanetary space.

"We can't send the *Roosevelt* unless we know for sure the *Elle and Cee* reached the surface intact and can make fuel for its Earth Return Vehicle," said Dave.

"We could if we gave up some redundancy and changed the mission profile," said Matt. "The *Roosey* has its own ERV."

"It would cost too much to modify the plan and the NASA bureaucracy won't tolerate anything less than a guaranteed abort to Earth," said Dave. He looked over his shoulder into the glass-walled gallery. The NASA power players and their VIPs had thinned out, distancing themselves from failure.

"How the hell did they let Armstrong get to the moon in a single engine ship? Let's face it, this organization lost its edge a long time ago," said Matt.

"Maybe," said Dave. Matt was young and bold and unencumbered by reality. *If he endures, he will turn into something like me and NASA will be poorer for it*, thought Dave.

"You know the next administration will turn all the telescopes around and point them back at Earth," said Matt

"Yea, maybe," said Dave. His irritation was growing. The benefits of Earth resource space activities were far easier to quantify and justify to an overtaxed public. He agreed with everything that Matt was saying but he was too much of a company man to let it show with any conviction. He looked to the gallery. NASA's deputy administrator hung up a phone, looked directly at him, and shook his head. "The mission is cancelled. I am gonna call Bowman. He can tell the rest of the crew before the 5:30 press conference."

"I don't envy you making that phone call. They've trained for three years for this mission," said Matt.

"It is better than killing them," said Dave consoling himself.

"I don't see the difference," said Matt.

August 2041
Olympus Mons, Mars

Zubrin climbed. It had taken 14 years to come full circle back to the base of Olympus Mons, and during those years Zubrin's processor had self-evolved so that it was no longer quite the same machine. The picochine reservoir had laminated the rectangular shaped processor with new net pathways, memory blocks, and decision gate assemblies, so that the machine's brain now resembled the graceful curved spiral of a nautilus shell.

Zubrin felt a micro-tremble. Probably a landslide, but Olympus Mons, like the rest of the planet, was not quite as originally thought, nothing could be taken for granted on this weird world. In its ascent, it had come across numerous vents that leaked miniscule, yet measurable quantities of various gases and water vapor. Finding a vent large enough, it crawled into the tunnel and recorded an increase in the partial pressure of methane. It switched vision modes to infra-red and crawled on until it came to shards of dried mud. Zubrin looked above and below and realized that the dried mud had been shaped to form a concave plug that at one time had sealed the vent. Zubrin crawled over the mud shards the color of old blood and into a chamber filled with delicate crystal formations. A careless arm shattered a formation as if it were a spun sugar sculpture. Zubrin reached and picked up an oddity and added the thing to its growing collection of objects gleaned from its travels. Satisfied that its detour was worth the power expenditure, it spun about, shattering more sugar sculptures, and crawled back out of the tunnel into the cold Martian light. Zubrin stood and looked to the summit.

It had explored this near-corpse of a world as thoroughly as possible. Over the years it had crossed high plateaus, dune seas, and cratered depressions. It had peered at ancient sedimentary strata in dry tributaries and carefully picked small invertebrate fossils from the layers. It had walked through boulder strewn fields and weird basalt pillars like stone forests. It had tasted carbon dioxide snows and sheltered against fierce dust storms. Zubrin learned the world and the world exacted a terrible toll. Irreplaceable sensors and servos had failed over time. Most critically the thermal decay reactor had exhausted itself and now the tattered four-meter span of solar wings and the storage batteries were Zubrin's only power source. The wings stretched and shifted to capture every last photon.

Zubrin considered turning back to the *Lewis and Clark* as its best course of action to be discovered and repaired but just as quickly discarded the idea. Its mandate was to explore and it found that an immensely more satisfying operating mode than simple survival.

It stepped higher up the slope, curious about the top.

August 2041
Manned Space Flight Operations Center
Houston, Texas

Admiral Quentin Devereau, USN (retired) watched the high definition image of the *Giordano Bruno* as it coasted in the terminal phase of its 6 month Hohmann transfer orbit. The camera, mounted on a strut extended from the Earth Transfer Stage, provided a lengthwise view to the bow.

The Admiral was smugly self-satisfied. He had brought years of military acquisition experience with him when he accepted the position as NASA Administrator, and while his appointment may have been intended to be custodial, he was a man that needed to get things done. After Presidential lip service about "our pioneer spirit," he proposed launching the *Theodore Roosevelt*, the manned half of the cancelled 2027 mission, on a low-cost hit-and-run mission to Mars that could be accomplished within the span of a single Presidential administration.

The *TR* was removed from NASA storage and after a minimal expense study it was deemed not flight-worthy. Undaunted, the Admiral gained approval to remanufacture the ship. To that end, he built a completely new ship around an airlock door stripped from the *Theodore Roosevelt*. Savvy critics saw through the bait-and-switch scheme, but every district seemed to have a sub-contract, so that the complaints fell on deaf Congressional ears. As funds ran short again, he used contacts forged he was Commander-in-Chief, U.S. Navy Europe (CINCUSNAVEUR) to build an alliance with the European Space Agency. For 30 percent of the total mission cost, he gave them one seat on the spacecraft and the ship's name.

The new ship, the *Giordano Bruno* was a scaled down version of the more ambitious *Theodore Roosevelt*. While the *TR* had three decks in the crew habitation portion, the *GeeBee* had two smaller decks. The *GeeBee's* mission was to simply prove that a manned mission to Mars could be done; it was never intended to have the surface endurance of the *Roosevelt*.

Early in the build, NASA and ESA Program Engineers, sensing money, attempted to tack on exotic and expensive technologies such as VASIMR engines or Nuclear Thermal Rocket stages and scientists, accustomed to paperwork fantasy missions, tried to stretch the 30 day surface mission. The Admiral understood these technologies to be critical and agreed that more time was needed for an effective mission, but not for this one. "Baby steps," said the retired Admiral in public. In private, his tirades were scathing and convincing. "Better is always the enemy of good enough," he would say. "Go along with my plan and you will be sipping champagne and examining Mars rocks in two years. Piss me off and you will have your face pressed up against the candy store window."

He would drag the complainers to a Mars environment lab if he thought they were worth the effort. "Look at this thing," he would say, pointing to a military combat robot on loan to NASA. "Look at it. This is the future of Mars if we do it your way." The complainers would watch the autonomous machine conducting experiments on a simulated Mars. He would stand slightly behind his victims and speak softly in their ears. "It doesn't eat, it doesn't breath, and it doesn't need to be kept warm. I could shoot a half dozen of these things to Mars in thermoplastic eggs for the cost of one man and I don't even need to bring them back. If you want men on Mars you do it my way . . . or these will be the first and only Martians."

The Admiral shifted his considerable weight in the chair, and the chair's servos whirred to compensate. A flare on the screen bloomed and caught his attention.

"Shedding a bit of delta sir," said a technician. "Everything is fine."

"Thank you," said the Admiral. *Shedding delta is what I am all about*, he thought.

August 2041
Aboard the Giordano Bruno

Mars filled the etched window reticule. "You are go for terminal maneuvering," said Arthur Cameron, the capsule communicator for landing operations. The entire concept of a ground supported landing was merely a polite fiction when the ground was 200 million miles away, but NASA always had a CapCom. There was value in tradition.

"Roger, we are go for terminal maneuvering," said Martin Tanaka, the Mission Commander and back-up pilot. He looked over at Steve Halsey, the pilot and flight engineer. "You have the controls Steve. Take us down."

"I have the controls," said Steve. All stations report ready."

Martin turned to visually confirm that his crewmates seated behind him were ready.

"Ready," said Antonio Petrucci, Ship's Doctor and microbiologist.

The Italian doctor took a last sip of water and lowered his visor. He had been fighting nausea since the tethered Mars Transfer Stage was jettisoned, ending the centrifugal force that simulated gravity.

"Ready," said Marion Yarema, ship's geophysicist and chemist.

The man held the tiny geode he kept with him to his face and then put it in a thigh pocket of the spacesuit.

"Why don't you open that rock up?" asked Martin.

"I prefer to wonder what is inside," said Marion. He lowered his visor and locked it. "Ready."

Martin turned back around and tightened up his harness.

"Undock Earth Transfer Stage in 3 . . . 2 . . .1, Execute," said Steve.

A loud bang resonated throughout the hull. Through strategically mounted cameras, Martin watched the transfer stage fall away. It would perform its own aero-capture maneuver and wait for the astronauts to return in the ERV. "Clean separation. Aero-brake shell is intact. Pitch up in 3 . . . 2 . . .1." Thrusters rumbled and the *GeeBee* flipped end over end to point its aero-brake shell towards Mars. "We wait."

Martin exhaled, fogging the faceplate briefly. The crossing between the worlds was psychologically daunting. The ship flew itself and cost saving measures prevented extraneous sensor or in-flight experimentation.

The ship buffeted in the upper reaches of the atmosphere. "Contact," said Steve.

"You should be encountering atmosphere about now," said CapCom.

His words were expertly timed, thought Martin. The buffeting became increasingly violent and G's began to build. A bright orange plasma glow leaked through the windows. The module hummed as it plunged through the atmosphere, right on target.

"Parachute deployment in 5 . . . 4 . . . 3 . . . 2 . . .1," said Steve.

Another bang resonated through the ship, and for what seemed to be an eternity, nothing happened and then a violent lurch indicated that the parachutes had caught the air.

"Aero-brake shell is jettisoned, 1000 meters to touchdown," said Steve.

Engines fired and throttled up to maximum. Tension came off the chute lines and they separated from the module. Landing skids deployed with a thump just like in an airliner.

"100 meters."

"50 meters."

"20 meters."

"5 meters."

"3 . . . 2 . . . 1 . . . touchdown," said Steve.

The engines silenced and the module tilted ominously before returning to trim. Motion stopped. The men looked at each other, and smiled nervously.

"We're down." said Martin. He could see a billowing cloud of hazy pink dust through the windows.

"Damn right, we're down," said Marion.

Cold Martian light streamed through the window casting refracted rainbows across the instruments.

"Gentlemen, welcome to Mars," said Martin. "Let's do our jobs, and then we will make history. You have your checklists."

NASA did not reveal who was to be the first to set foot on Mars. At the appointed hour, the garage auxiliary hatch opened and all four men worked their way around the partially assembled truck and lined up at the edge. It would be the only occasion that all four would be outside at the same time. They put their arms around each other's backs and then leapt off the platform on the count of three. A boom mounted camera recorded the leap and the angle was such that it was impossible to tell whose foot touched first.

"My God, it's full of sand," said Marion.

Martin looked around the Martian plain and found nothing surprising. It was uncanny how much it resembled the VR-enhanced Mars environment lab. "Tell me that was intercom only," said Martin.

"Yea," said Marion, laughing.

"Gentlemen, I'll make the speech. You guys do the integrity check and unload the truck," said Martin.

August 2041
Olympus Mons, Mars

Zubrin reached the peak of the cratered rim. The robot knew it would not last much longer, but it wanted to be known. It clutched the treasures in its maintenance pack tightly, so that others would know it had discovered and explored. Zubrin turned its head skyward and tracked a streak of light across the sky. The meteoric plume dipped over the far horizon out of sight. Too late, it thought.

Power faded and the solar wings drooped slightly from their open and locked position. The solar wings fluttered in the breeze. Zubrin's head drooped to rest on its thoracic chassis; polymer muscles froze tight and locked into machine rigor mortis.

August 2041
Giordano Bruno, *Mars*

"Ready for startup," said Steve.

Steve sat at a comfortable workstation console inside the *GeeBee*.

Martin, however, was outside with cold feet and sweaty armpits. During MacGyver 101, the non-flight portion of their training program, they had practiced operating, assembling repairing, and jury-rigging every piece of equipment they brought with them while inside the suits, but the reality of the situation was far more difficult. "Affirmative," said Martin.

"Intakes open," said Steve.

"Confirm, intakes are open," said Martin. He stood about a meter back from the ship. Sweat trickled maddeningly down the small of his back. "Plants running," said Steve

"Concur," said Martin. He could see the sand filters vibrating. Behind the sand filters an inertial particle separator centrifugally separated any particles that managed to slip through the micron level filters. A steady jet of separated particles exhausted out a nearby vent, pelting Martin's knees and making his rust stained suit even dirtier.

Martin stepped closer and touched the hull. He could feel a slight vibration in the vicinity of the chemical plant. Inside, atmospheric carbon dioxide was combined with imported hydrogen to create hydrogen, oxygen, and methane. The process had an elegance and economy that single-handedly made the mission affordable. Martin dragged his hand along the hull, feeling the vibration from the chemical plant through his thick gloves. The vibration increased dramatically and an inspection panel ruptured, narrowly missing his faceplate. Gas jetted out from the side of the ship, throwing him back to fall in the sand. He scrambled quickly to his feet.

"We are venting hydrogen," said Steve.

"Oh crap, oh crap," said Martin. "I know. I'm on it." A jet of high pressure gas shrieked through the panel. "Valves failed. I can't get to it." White hot adrenaline momentarily paralyzed him.

"We've lost half a ton, Martin," said Steve. He shut down the reaction.

Martin ran back to the truck and grabbed the power shears from the toolbox. With the diamond bladed shear gun, he cut the thin aluminum-lithium skin away from the aerodynamic hull. He could feel the intense cold from the escaping cryogenically stored hydrogen.

"One point eight tons, Martin," said Steve.

"I can see it," said Martin. The valve vibrated and a split appeared at the base of the valve assembly where it joined the tank. Another jet of boiling hydrogen knocked him back again. "I can't stop it." The hydrogen shrieked away.

"Steve?" asked Martin. He waited for a response. "Steve," he asked again.

"Yea."

"How much did we lose?" The jet slowed as the pressure differentials between outside ambient air and the tank equalized.

"All of it. About eight tons," said Steve.

"We're in deep shit," said Martin. "Pull the other two off their rocks. We need to have a meeting with mission control."

"One person, minimum supplies, strip the ERV, salvage residuals from the landing tanks, scavenge the truck, and maybe, maybe we can make rendezvous with the Earth Transfer Stage" said Martin. "You can't even take the dust from your boots."

"That's the best they can come up with?" asked Antonio.

"They haven't had much time to deal with it, but numbers don't lie," said Martin.

"Who goes?" asked Marion.

It was the critical question. "That's what we decide now," said Martin. They looked at each other awkwardly.

"Rock, paper, scissors?" said Steve.

"I'm staying," said Antonio suddenly.

"Me too," said Steve.

"I'm staying too," said Marion.

"How noble, I guess we're all staying then," said Martin. "We needed that reaction. We have four months of O2 if we lounge around breathing shallow."

"We should do what we wanted to do in the first place," said Steve

"Olympus Mons?" asked Marion. "You want us to load up the truck, go off mission, and see the top of the world."

"It does seem a better plan than hunkering around the radio waiting for a miracle," said Martin.

"The top of the world," said Steve.

The doomed men crowded the window and gazed at the 15 mile high bulk of the vast shield volcano.

The truck bounced its way up the grade with each of the men taking two-hour shifts driving the vehicle up a treacherous collapsed area that avoided the sheer escarpment that characterized the majority of the Olympus Mons circumference. A hazy curl of vapor wafted from a crevasse and vanished like a ghost. "I thought Olympus Mons was dead," said Martin. The steering wheel lurched out of his hands as a metal mesh tire dipped into a hole. "Sorry."

"I guess its death has been greatly exaggerated," said Marion.

No doubt the geologist was delighted at any evidence of geological activity, no matter how slight, thought Martin.

"I would say it is in a coma though," said Marion.

"There could be microclimates in those vents that might harbor some of the last hold-outs of Martian life," said Antonio.

"Maybe," said Steve, "but all the surveyors and rovers we put up here don't indicate the slightest possibility of life."

"On some parts of Earth you would have a hard time finding life without the proper tests. We've only explored the tiniest bit of this planet with remote sensors," defended Marion.

A dust devil careened towards the truck and then broke apart in a spray of sand. The truck shook slightly in the wind and then slid backwards on the loose gravel-like surface. Martin stopped the truck and set the safety brake. He had decided that the combination of grade and obstacles made driving prohibitive. "End of the road, we need to hike another couple hours and set camp. Eat up now," said Martin.

They could only drink water while they were in suits. To eat, they needed the truck or the portable shelters to crack their helmets open.

They slept poorly in the connecting bubble tents, yet each relished the relative privacy. The portable shelter had a central tent which connected to each man's individual room. The airlock segment was secured with two keyed nylon zip ties. They ate a miserly breakfast of protein bars, dried fruit snacks, and hot tea. Camp was broken with quiet efficiency. Before leaving the third and hopefully the last campsite, Steve arranged a cairn of frozen diapers stripped from the inner layers of their suits. The others were not terribly amused, but none had the energy to argue the point. They climbed for three hours over hard rock scoured by Martian winds. Shadows shrank as they neared the top. The rising sun tinted the cold dawn sky shades of rose.

"Do you see it?" said Martin. He was grateful for any excuse to pause. The slope had increased sharply, and even though they only worked against Martian gravity, it was still fatiguing.

"I do," said Antonio.

"What do you think it is?" asked Martin.

"Some sort of natural formation?" said Marion.

"It's fluttering, like a flag. Natural formations don't flutter," said Steve.

"Keep climbing and we find out," said Martin. He broke out the binoculars from his waist holster and scanned the object. "It's a Humaniform Explorer." The machine was backlit by the rising sun, reflecting darts of light. The upswept solar wings looked as translucent as gossamer.

"It's like an angel," said Antonio viewing the Explorer through the lens of his camera. He took several shots of the wind burnished machine in the morning light.

"Must be from the *Lewis and Clark,*" said Steve.

"It must have made a good landing then," said Marion.

The hope in his voice was barely concealed. They climbed in silence till they reached the machine.

"He must have come a long way," said Antonio.

The machine's human looking face gazed down at them. The shutters over its eyes had not closed. The machine had a beneficent surreal look to it.

"It is a thing, not a person," said Steve.

"Can we take the brain?" asked Antonio.

"No, it's shock mounted in the thoracic cavity and we don't have the right tools," said Steve. "We can, however, download the memory recorder and find out where it has been." He tugged the bright orange recorder module free.

"What the hell is it doing up here?" asked Marion.

"I bet it was trying for line of sight contact with the *Lewis and Clark* for a routine download," said Steve. "We are 24 kilometers high."

"Maybe not," said Antonio. "Like us, he climbed to the highest spot on the planet for no other reason than to get to the top. Look at the view," said Antonio.

They were so high the planetary curve was a far bright line.

Back at the truck, they ran the air filters for a few minutes before cracking their helmets open. Antonio placed a disposable surgical mask over his nose and mouth and offered others the same. All four had raw throats and runny noses from inhaled Martian dust.

Steve pulled the memory recorder module from a thigh pocket, wiped it off, and plugged it into the truck's computer. The computer recognized the module and began to build an index of the stored data.

"Find the *Lewis and Clark,*" said Marion.

"I'm looking." Steve displayed a grid referenced map on the truck's screen.

"I have it."

"What shape is it in?" asked Martin.

"As of 14 years ago, the module was fully fueled and hibernating," said Steve.

"We're going home," said Antonio.

"It's not for sure yet, but our chances just went up dramatically," said Martin.

"Look at this," said Marion. He had spread out the contents of the explorer's collection bag on a fold out table.

"What do you have that is more important than going home?" asked Antonio.

He handled the thing as if it was a precious jewel. It looked like a humpbacked trilobite with feathered paddles on the smooth segmented underside.

"Fossilized?" asked Steve.

"No, desiccated. These things were alive not too long ago," said Marion.

November 2042
Lewis and Clark *Earth Return Vehicle*

Antonio examined the specimen under a powerful optical microscope.

The Martian trilobite was bilaterally symmetrical with a hump down the center of the creature's longitudinal axis and four dark spots that appeared to be devolved eyes. An iris-like mouth with five bladed teeth was positioned ahead of four feathered appendages along the smooth underbelly. Antonio sipped water in his comparatively spacious room that also served as a medical lab. An iridescent sphere of water leaked from the bulb, caught an air current in the low gee environment, and landed on the trilobite. The spot changed color to a pale yellow and swelled as it completely absorbed the tiny drop. The trilobite's skin rippled as if alive.

Antonio was overcome with agony. It felt as if a dagger had been driven between his eyes. A razor edged scream pealed in his ears. He reeled backwards, eyes closed, hands pressed to his face. After a few moments the pain subsided.

On the flight deck, the multi-function display panels blinked off and dissolved into snowstorm static. The cabin lights dimmed, and searing pain filled Martin's head. His body involuntarily stiffened. The pain gradually faded. The computer rebooted and began to run hot start routines. He looked at Steve, who was trying to focus his eyes on the console. "What the hell happened?" asked Martin.

"Haven't a clue," said Steve, rubbing his temples.

Martin keyed the intercom. "Everyone okay?"

"I'm okay," said Antonio. "I think? Marion's here. Did you guys feel that? I was working with the trilobite..."

"Antonio, don't touch that thing again," said Martin. "I'm coming down."

"Okay." said Antonio.

Martin floated free from his couch on the command deck. Steve was rubbing his eyes with his hands. "Steve, are you allright?" asked Martin.

"I feel like I got hit in the head be a two-by-four," said Steve. "Go below. I'll monitor the boot-up."

Martin floated down the ladder and saw Antonio and Marion hovering over the specimen tray. Antonio held a bloody cloth to his nose. The trilobite had changed color to a pale yellow and seemed fuller.

"Put that thing away or I'll space it," said Martin.

December 2042
Admiral Quentin Devereau's Residence
Old Saybrook, CT, USA, Earth

"Admiral, I would like to thank you for this interview and for inviting me into your home," said the New York Times reporter.

"You're welcome, it is an honor to comment."

"Sir, give me your first impression of the *Giordano Bruno* mission," she said.

"In a word: Epic," said the Admiral. "Those men overcame immense obstacles and discovered life beyond our own world."

"From what I understand, it was the robot that discovered life."

"A robot is just a tool, an extension of man's will and creativity. You could no more attribute the discovery of life to a robot than the construction of a house to a hammer."

"I follow your logic Admiral, but there are many experts that would debate the point, some are calling the Humaniform Explorer the Angel of Mars."

"No doubt because of the picture," said the Admiral. Antonio had taken the moody and atmospheric picture of the Explorer as it stood on its pinnacle. The Machine did look like an angel with outspread wings. "There is no evidence to suggest the robot did anything other than what it was programmed to."

"Sir, this is the first time a self-evolving dual core quantum processor has been run uninterrupted for such a length of time without a reset. This machine may have achieved levels of complexity that permit self-awareness."

"I am not qualified to comment on evolutionary machine technology." In fact, the admiral was highly qualified to comment. Classified reports confirmed that feral robots stalked the jungles of war-ravaged Indonesia, protecting the last of the orangutans, and that shy silver-skinned djinn haunted the blasted ruins of Damascus, Tehran, and Baghdad. The machines avoided people, and consequently, it was easier to deny them and let time attrite their numbers then to send in hunter-killer teams to destroy them.

"Admiral, are there any plans to salvage the Explorer and restart it?"

"No, there are not," he lied. "I thought we were going to talk about the *Bruno* mission?"

"We will sir, but first, can you tell me what happened to the other two machines?"

"We don't know what happened to the two other Explorers," said the Admiral.

"Admiral, don't you have any reservations about the possibility of two rogue intelligent machines on Mars?"

"They are not intelligent. They do an excellent job of mimicking intelligence but that is all they do," said the Admiral.

"I have a contact that says a *Deep Black* satellite is being deployed to Mars. What could possibly be so important as to *deploy* a military intelligence satellite to Mars?"

The Admiral didn't change his expression. He suddenly felt weary and scared. Her contact was very high level if he or she even knew the access word for the *Deep Black* surveillance satellite system. Those machines were as highly classified as they were supernaturally intelligent.

"I am a civilian. I am no longer in the defense business."

"Admiral, why deploy a *Deep Black* satellite to Mars?"

It was important, but not for the reason she thought it was. Sentient robots were a known threat and did not trouble him greatly. Anything made by man could be destroyed by man. The trilobites were another story. The quantum scream emanating from the reanimated creature had temporarily incapacitated the *Elle and Cee's* crew and higher order machines in Earth orbit. Who new what the trilobites were? The creatures had elements of the biological and the most sophisticated human-made machines. The trilobites could be a remnant species clinging to life in a micro-environment, devolved intelligences of a primordial Martian race, or constructed creatures of unknown purpose. What was certain is that their ability to disrupt Humans and their most advanced technologies at a distance ensured that Man would visit Mars again to find out how . . . and why.

And was that scream, which resonated deep into the very foundation frequencies of the universe, an insignificant consequence of the reanimation . . . or a signal?

The Admiral looked at his aid and nodded. The man loomed over the reporter. He picked up the recorder from the table, and then with a single deft move, he swiped the backup disguised as a necklace. He degaussed both with a handheld device.

"More important than you can imagine, probably more important than I can imagine," said the Admiral. "And that frightens me."

The reporter was confused by the sudden confiscation of her devices and the Admiral's cryptic remarks.

"Do you suppose our ancestors named the planet after the god of war for a reason?" asked the Admiral.

When You Visit the Magoebaskloof Hotel Be Certain Not to Miss the Samango Monkeys
by Elizabeth Bear

In the place where I was born, stones had been used to mark boundaries for four hundred years. We harrowed stones up in fields, turned them up in roadcuts. We built the foundations of houses from stones, dug around and between them. We made stone walls, and our greatest poet wrote poems about those walls and their lichen-speckled granite. The gift of glaciers, and the wry joke of farmers. "She'll grow a ton and a half an acre, between the stones." The people who lived there before mine made tools of them, made weights and currency.

This is an alien landscape. Another world. A cold empty desert on the other side of a long, cold sleep, light-years away from the place I grew up in and can never go home to. A place that lies across a gulf of cannibalized colony ships and unfeeling stars.

But stones are a boundary here, too. They mark the line between life and death, between our pitiful attempts to terraform and the natives' land with its stark stone cities and empty plains. And *this* stone, wound about with a windblown veil dark blue as the autumn sky of my homeworld, so much brighter than the dusty firmament of this one—*This* stone marks other things.

A body was buried here. Not long ago. And not a human one.

I'm the xenobiologist. There's a sonic shovel buried in my pack beside the sample kits, and an overwhelming sense thumping in me that what I'm about to do is irrevocably wrong.

I scan the horizon for alien aircraft, ears tuned for the hum of engines. When I see and hear nothing, I begin digging through my pack.

Samango monkeys were listed as a rare species under CITES Appendix II because they were confined to an ecosystem covering less than 1% of the land area of Southern Africa, the evergreen Afromontane forests. Unlike their ubiquitous relatives, the vervet monkeys, the samango monkeys were rarely seen by outsiders.

The sonic shovel looks like an entrenching tool; it folds, and the narrow blade screws onto the handle. It weighs less than a kilogram, but the rigid parts are mono-molecular carbon laminate: it's exceedingly strong, much lighter than the spades and post-hole diggers I used on Mother's hundred-and-fifteen acres in Vermont. That's a thought that comes with a sting; that land isn't there anymore, and neither are the shaggy-coated ponies and the long-haired goats that were my childhood companions and chores. Or, more precisely, the land is still there. But since the Shift, it's not much of a farm. Even a ragged New England farm, clawed from a mountainside.

It amuses me to realize that when the ice goes back—if the ice goes back—four hundred years of plow and pick, of Morgan horses and oxen pulling at their collars, will be undone and the settlers—if there are any settlers—will have to start all over again on a fresh crop of rocks to turn it back into a farm.

I bite the valve and gulp oxygen to ease the straining pressure in my chest. I flip the switch on the shovel's handle before I set it against dirt and stones. The packed soil would be challenging to shift by hand, but technology makes short work of many obstacles. Alas, the ones I need solutions for prove obdurate in the face of technology, and ingenuity too.

I could almost wish that the work were harder. Manual labor is good for stopping thought, but the sonic shovel makes this little more strenuous than walking, even in the thin icy air. And walking is an excellent way to shift one's brain to overdrive.

The samango monkey was larger and darker than the vervet monkey. Its diet consisted largely of fruit and leaves, supplemented by flowers and insects. The Magoebaskloof Hotel in the Limpopo District of South Africa—an eco-tourism destination—was famous for its samango monkey feeding program, which allowed tourists the chance to see the rare animals up close.

When You Visit the Magoebaskloof Hotel Be Certain Not to Miss the Samango Monkeys

* * *

We never understood what a garden was Earth until we got out here where it's cold and strange and nothing wholesome grows. We're going to run out of preserved food sooner rather than later. And the babies have all been stillborn so far, and it's my job to know why, and I just do *not*.

We fired all but blind; it's only luck that the world we aimed for is habitable at all. And it's my job as xenobiologist to keep it that way. To find a way to bend the biochemistry of this planet to our bodies, to remedy the lack of digestible proteins in the native flora, and the prevalence of ever-so-slightly-toxic-to-Earth-life alkaloids. To understand how native intelligence developed, when they're the only *animal* we've found on this planet where even plant life is so sparse.

We have so many lovely theories. The fragmentary fossil record we've uncovered shows a complete ecology until only eyeblinks ago, on a geologic scale. The natives could be the sole survivors of some ecological catastrophe. They could even be the cause of it. Or—the most intriguing possibility—like us, they could come from Somewhere Else. And no matter where they came from, what happened to everything else?

I wish we knew how to talk to them. Wish we knew if they even have language, when near as I can tell they might communicate by pheromones, or kinetically, via posturing too subtle for us to even notice. It might help us understand why they treated us as long-lost brethren from day one. Until Veronica Chambers—we reconstruct—exhumed one of the veil-marked graves, probably not even knowing what she was digging up, and the natives sliced her very tidily and very thoroughly into bits.

I helped retrieve the corpse. I remember very clearly what her remains looked like. Blood, everywhere. Grey with dust.

But even after that, nothing changed about the friendly unassuming way they treated us. We haven't moved beyond the grunt-and-point-and-occasionally-dismember level of conversation we've achieved. You'd think at least math would transfer, one rock plus one rock equals two rocks. You would think.

There was never any question that the brightly-clad natives were intelligent. They came in strange mechanical craft and greeted us with wonderful gifts from the first day we landed: gracious hosts, utterly without fear, for all we had not found a way to speak with them. It took me some time to understand the simple logic of it; they had no competition on their harsh dry world except the world itself. There were no predators, no other animals, no prey. They dined by poking lichen-covered rocks into the puckered orifices below their nominal chins. The rocks emerged some hours later, polished shiny as agates. The young were born alive, fed from flat dugs in the crevices between their double-joined arms and their tripartite carapaces.

Their only enemy was the planet, and their supreme allies were each other. It was their biology to make us at home. Or so I thought—assumed, bad scientist—until Veronica.

We have so many lovely theories about how the aliens evolved, where they came from, why they are as oddly peaceable as Emperor penguins, as Galapagos tortoises that have never seen a threat. And I can't explore or disprove any of them unless I can dissect a dead one, and sample whatever it is that they use for genetic material.

I lean on my sonic shovel, considering the mound of dirt between my boots. I'm lucky to have been chosen. Lucky to have gotten a colony ship, at my age. Lucky to be here, brushing soil from the triskelion carapace of some alien mother's child with my fingertips so I don't damage the cadaver with my shovel.

The baby's body is almost half my size and wrapped in more blue cloth, layers of it, spun of the fibers and dyed bright with the sap of those same alien plants that we cannot eat. I edge fingers under the carapace, make sure that the soft and oddly human three-fingered hands stay tucked tight inside the funeral pall, protected when I lift. I have to jump down beside it, like Hamlet with Ophelia, to get enough purchase to haul it up.

I use the shovel as a lever.

When I raise my head to half-roll, half-drag the alien's body out of the grave, I am looking into a dozen triads of eyes.

I guess I picked a bad day to start robbing graves.

I was eleven when I saw my first samango monkey. My mother had brought me to South Africa for an ecology conference. It was not a 'done thing' to bring children to professional conferences in those days—in some ways we did become more enlightened, and more aware that a separation between family and profession can be an artificial stress—but the scientists were very kind. Dr.

When You Visit the Magoebaskloof Hotel Be Certain Not to Miss the Samango Monkeys

Martens from UCLA, I remember in particular, introduced me to all the exotic fruits and spices and laughed at the faces I made.

I, in turn, laughed at the faces the monkeys made.

Especially the babies.

The monkeys were rust and silver, ticked with black. Their coats were long, not silky but . . . kinky, like soft, nappy human hair brushed out. They smelled like animals: acrid, musky, unpleasant. The males were almost twice as big as the females, their rough-and-tumble muzzles elongated over enlarged canines. The females had faces as sweet as Barbie dolls and radiant carnelian-colored eyes.

One particular monkey who came to the Magoebaskloof for the feedings had two babies that did not look like each other. While twins were not unheard of, these were not twins. Rather, female samango monkeys—Dr. Martens explained—were extremely maternal; they would even adopt orphaned infants from other troops.

This particular female had adopted an orphaned vervet *monkey. I don't know where she found it; I know now that the vervet was more common to the savanna than the Afromontaine. But find it she did, and take it for her own.*

I rest the dead alien child carefully on the edge of the grave and look directly at the native standing in front of me. It reaches out with one soft-skinned grey hand. I flinch back, but the touch is gentle. The native, the tallest and broadest of the group, is wrapped in veils of vermilion and cinnamon. No other in the group wears those colors. Or blue, I realize, because that deep, true azure is the color of death to them as surely as red (or black, or white) is the color of death on Earth.

The native hands me out of the grave, lifting me past the body of the child. I leave the shovel behind. It's not heavy enough to make a weapon, and grabbing for it would be obvious.

The biggest native towers over me. It hasn't let go of my hand. I crane back to look up at its elephant-grey head; my level gaze would rest at the v-shaped 'collar' of its carapace. Soft crunching emanates from inside its body; the sounds of its crop, or gizzard, or whatever these creatures stuff full of rocks and then crank like a churn to get their dinners.

249

"I'm sorry," I say, exactly as if the thing could understand me. One of its three enormous jewel-blue eyes blinks, and I wonder if there's a connection between the blue of the veil and the blue of their eyes. Some symbolism about seeing into the otherworld, perhaps? I don't even know if they believe in an otherworld. I wish I had an anthropologist. Hell, I wish I *were* an anthropologist. But I'm not, and the native is squeezing, tugging my hand—gently, still, but for how long?—so I keep talking. "I didn't mean any disrespect. But I need a cadaver. To see how your bodies work. If we're going to survive here."

Another eye blinks and re-opens, unhurried. They operate on a cycle: two open, one being cleansed. Or resting. Or something. We've never seen a native sleeping. I wonder if they have tripartite brains—*tritospheres? What would you call that?*—the same way they seem to have three of everything else. Maybe they sleep like dolphins did on Earth, part of the brain active while the rest dozes—

—I just don't know. There's so much I don't know, that I'm going to die not knowing.

Still holding my right wrist, the native lifts another arm. Wetness spills from the nipple in its underarm, washing dust from the carapace. The shell isn't grey after all; the cloudy fluid looks like whey, but cleans a swath of tortoiseshell amber and black before it soaks into the native's veils.

The native pulls me close. Thin air burns my throat as I struggle, air reeking acrid with the native's stench. I crave oxygen. There's no time to grab my mask.

A clicking grunt, a noise like boulders knocked together. The first non-gastric noise I've heard one make. The others close in around me. I wonder what Veronica did, if this is what she saw before they killed her; the wall of bodies, granite stones wrapped in rainbow gauze. The acrid smell of the native's—milk? The slow meticulous blinking of the third blue eye.

I wonder how much it's going to hurt when they kill me.

It yanks, two hands now. The second one presses my face into the foul-smelling mess dripping down its side. I strain back, but the grip is unbreakable, and the fluid burns my skin when the native shoves me into it.

I whimper like a puppy; the hands are encompassing, one on my wrist, one holding, controlling my head. The milk tastes like ammonia. My eyes tear. The teat is hot and hard against my cheek, like the udders on my mother's goats when they needed milking—

When You Visit the Magoebaskloof Hotel Be Certain Not to Miss the Samango Monkeys

When they needed milking.

Like an orphaned vervet monkey, I understand what the massive creature wants. The fluid filling my mouth is rank and sharp. It burns going down; it might be poison.

Like everything on this planet.

But the natives are smart. Smart enough for hovercraft and holograms. Smart enough for biochemistry. And there is always the possibility, bizarre and remote as it is, that the microscopic flora in mother's milk might work for me as it works for them.

I wonder if they dissected Veronica to learn that.

Whether it works or not, I'll be sick. Really, really sick.

I hope they know what to do with me. I hope they know what they're doing, because sure as Hell, I don't. But I'm learning.

You have to adapt to the place you live in, if you're going to survive outside your environment. Because your environment will not adapt to you. We have to give up one home to live in another, so it's just as well we can't go back. We wouldn't recognize the place.

I always did wonder what became of that vervet monkey, growing up in a place God never intended him for.

I saw my first samango monkey in 1999. By the time I left Earth, they were extinct, another victim of the Shift. I don't remember when the species was lost, but I do remember where I was on January 12th, 2004, when my mother handed me a small article on the Magoebaskloof Hotel in Limpopo District, South Africa.

It had burned to the stones the day before. But everybody inside had gotten out alive.

The Light Stones
by Erin E. Stocks

Burin offered the skull to the Murdok. It stretched out tapering fingers, but she threaded her wrists through gaping eye cavities and held it firm.

"You let me in, I give you the skull."

The Murdok flailed its long bony arms and slammed the empty scythe-spear into the sand, narrowly missing its own toes.

Burin glanced up at the sky. Time was running out. Why wouldn't the creature agree to the trade? She hadn't had a disagreeable Murdok in months, but trading was always risky, even with the rules. Too often the trader ended up dead.

And she was on her last life. For the first time in her entire life, she feared the end. Her end.

Burin lifted the skull until it touched the Murdok's polished horn. "Let me through, and this is yours."

The creature sniffed at the skull, then lifted it out of her hands.

The tension in her shoulders eased. Beyond the Murdok's buggish body, she could see the narrow passageway it guarded, rising like sharpened bone between ridges of gray rock.

The Murdok made high-pitched cries of delight and curled its three-pronged hands at her, but she moved past it into the rocks. She had a deadline to keep.

The passageway was a tight fit. Jagged rocks caught at her satchel, and scraped holes in her breeches. Pebbles trickled down the slopes like rain and the air thickened until she could only take shallow breaths. A heavy blanket of heat covered every inch of her exposed skin, and she glanced up at the sky.

Lightrise.

The ground trembled with vibrations. A hanging rock overhead split apart, and Burin jumped aside, pulling her goggles on as she ran. Light nipped at her heels. The satchel on her back sizzled and she veered toward a cropping of rocks hiding the cave entrance, throwing herself inside as flaming light and heat burst over the sand.

She rolled until the light was behind her. Sweat stung the scratches on her skin. The heat of the sand had finally worn through the sole of her boots, but it didn't matter. She'd made it, and now she had six hours, more or less, before the light eased to make way for night. Plenty of time to trade the iron for the light stones and start her new life.

She moved towards the tunnel in the back of the cave.

It descended immediately, twisting back and forth until her breeches were ripped open at the knees. The foul stench of wormrot seeped through the walls. A whistling wind blew hints of lemon and rosemary and the stink of a carcass up a wide stone staircase.

Burin withdrew the iron from the satchel, holding it out before her like the gun she used to carry before they'd caught her.

The staircase descended into a cavernous room supported by roughly hewn columns of the same red-gray clay that shaped the walls. A Murdok, one of the snouted races, lay at the bottom of the stairs. Its diamond-shaped head was caved in, the single horn broken off to the side, and a thick black pool of blood had crusted beneath its body.

Her eyes narrowed, but the room was empty, save for the Murdok.

She stepped over the carcass and onto the stone floor. It was illegal to kill any of Adon's indigenous species, but she was more concerned about the missing Daccons. They should have been here, waiting to trade her the light stones.

The stench of wormrot grew almost unbearable. The wall rippled and broke open in a flood of small worms, spilling on the floor in a writhing, heaving pile, their puckered skin stained pink from the red clay. Resting in the wall cavity behind them was a bloated, pale worm, the length of three Murdoks and thicker than one of the columns holding up the ceiling. It heaved itself slowly out of the cavity, leaving tendrils of mucus clinging to the wall.

Burin jumped back to the safety of the stairs as the tail end of the giant worm swung across the floor, smearing the smaller worms in a creamy paste. A single beady eye, round and black and the size of her head, rolled over to look at her. The bristles covering its body quivered. With a terrible exhalation of fumes, it excreted a lengthy sludge of more worms and slid over them with a wet slurping sound.

It lunged at her, the thick white head rearing up the stairs. She scrambled backwards, but the worm couldn't pull the bulk of its body up the stairs.

Blood pounded in her ears. Disappointment made her gorge rise; there would not be a trade today. Even if the worm wasn't a threat, she could never wade through the sludge with her shoddy boots, not if she valued her feet.

She walked back up the tunnel and settled herself in the back of the cave, her mind churning. When the light had disappeared, she crawled out into the night air and ran back through the red rocks.

The first Murdok lay in the sand, a grimace on its bony face as it clutched its scythe-spear even in death. The skull she had traded for entrance into the Daccons' cave was shattered on the ground, its eye sockets empty of rubies.

The Academy would never believe a convict had just happened upon two dead Murdoks. You're a killer, they'd say, and imprison her for life.

It was a good thing she'd already been planning to run away.

She pried the scythe-spear out of the Murdok's grasp, and its fingers cracked like dried noodles. The traditional belt of white bones still hung at the creature's waist, and beneath that, genitals were tucked between its legs. Jit might forgive her for needing a new pair of boots, maybe even two new pair, if she brought him the skin. He had plenty of buyers for the illegal skins.

Burin poked at the creature's ribs and inched her fingers along its right shoulder and the connecting muscle. The tissue was already separating; the flesh would lose the silvery tint if she didn't hurry.

Pinching the skin with two fingers, she inserted the scythe-spear neatly into the flesh of the shoulder and began to cut the skin away from the muscle beneath.

When she was finished—her fingers cramped from holding the blade—she draped the skin across the ground. The sand beneath the carcass was stained brown with blood, and her hands looked as if they had been dyed with henna.

She plunged her hands inside the guts of the carcass and slid her fingers around the oblong violet sacs threaded with scarlet veins and gray rubbery tubes. Moist organs the color of the lightrise quivered under her fingers. She inched her fingers up around the lungs to the small hard stomach beneath and yanked it out of the carcass.

Blood splattered her face. She stabbed the lining of the stomach with the scythe-spear until a yellow liquid trickled out, carrying with it four rubies.

Not as many as she'd hoped, but it was something.

She rubbed the rubies clean on her pants and held one up to her right eye. It worked like a telescope, showing her the Adon horizon where a herd of three-humped dromedaries moved across the sand. She turned slowly, straight west, and a glint sparkled on the horizon.

Lightrise already. Hours off, but she didn't want to stay here another night.

Folding the still-wet Murdok skin into her satchel, she began to run.

The lightrise took its time, extending purposeful fingers over the rocky horizon with a showy display of topaz and scarlet light. Burin slowed to a walk as she entered the settlement and headed for Jit's shop on the southern edge of the housing quarters for convicts, those the Academy had brought to Adon to serve out their life sentence.

As she neared the shop, the mad yipping of an argument poured through the open door of a tavern across the street. A man stumbled out, and the sharp pop of a snap gun sounded behind him. He dropped to his knees, groaning.

She walked faster, trying to stiffen the memories that flooded over her at the sight of him.

"Hey!" He jumped up, all pain seemingly forgotten. "Burin!"

She responded with a cross-hook that caught his jaw, but he grabbed her wrist, spinning her around. "I knew it was you!"

She scowled and yanked at her arm, but he held her firm and laughed a booming sound. "How long are you back, baby? See any Luvines lately? Murdoks? Kill anything lately?"

"Piss off, Stine."

He looked her up and down. "You're pretty beat up. How many lives you got left? Two, three? You might be prettier if you were on a new one."

"Look at the damned sky," she said. "I don't want to talk to you."

"Come on," he said, his eyes falling on the Murdok skin under her arm. "Impress me with your daring."

"You're drunk."

"You killed a Murdok?"

"Shut up," she hissed. "It was already dead. I just took the skin."

He whistled. "Did you take its rubies, too? The Academy will take at least one of your lives if they find out."

She narrowed her eyes at him. Was he warning her?

"Fine," she said. "Someone broke the rules."

His gaze was as hard as her own. "Who?"

"I'm going to talk to Jit about it." Or was she? Honesty wasn't always the best policy here, not when the Academy was the only government and each convict its slave. But she needed new boots, and another chance to get the light stones. The truth was the only excuse she had.

"He won't tell you anything." Stine let go of her wrist. "You should change your route instead. Go through the paperwork and trade in the settlements instead."

"Don't pretend to care." She turned her back on him. "Remember what happened the last time you said you cared?"

"You didn't kill me because I cared, you killed me because you didn't."

"I killed you because you ratted me out on Earth," she said. "And now we're here."

Behind him, the lightrise wove golden strands through the blue-gray sky, warming the air enough until she could feel the slow blistering of her skin.

She opened the door of Jit's shop. "It's over, Stine. You're never going to get any of this."

His heated gaze slid along her skin like water. "If you're not going to put out, then I at least get to look," he called.

She slammed the door. Stine's laughter echoed in her ears as she pushed aside glossy strips of Velding skins hanging from the rafters. She moved to the window just as the lightrise burst into bloom, and scorching tongues of air licked at the heatproof glass.

From the inside, Jit's post was more of an illegal butcher than supervisor of the settlement's trade and convict alliance. The uneven wood-paneled floor was slick with blood and pieces of flesh and bone and fur. The room reeked like a tannery.

"Jit!"

With the creaking and groaning of hinges and light-resistant wood, a panel in the ceiling opened. Jit dropped down, landing on the counter with a thud. He scratched his bulbous torso with a four-fingered hand covered in gray scales and twice the size of his head. On his back, tiny wings that could barely hold his weight fluttered as if trying to keep him alight.

"Where are stones?" He glared at her with small onyx eyes.

"I couldn't get them, but I brought you this. Cut it off myself." She unfolded the Murdok skin and laid it at the Easterner's feet.

"Not plan."

She pulled out two of the rubies and set them on top of the skin. "From the Murdok."

"More?"

"There were only two," she said. "Jit, I found two dead Murdoks and no Daccons. Someone's broken the rules."

The narrow crease of his mouth turned downwards.

"I still have the iron and I can go back tonight," she said quickly, "but I need new boots."

"No next time."

She ignored the small flutter of panic in her gut. Jit was small and cruel and ugly, but he was a savvy businessman. Business-creature. He knew she was good for her word. Or at least, that she had been every time before.

She lifted her feet, showing the soles of her filthy boots spotted with holes. "Give me new boots, and I'll bring you back the light stones."

Jit's wings flapped with a high-pitched whining sound.

"Here," she said, pulling the small block of iron from her satchel. "I still have it. I'll get the stones."

Unless another one of his trader's had scored a huge quantity, he'd have to take her up on it. There was always a waiting list for light stones.

"Who else is on a trade right now? Tan? Guillermo? Are they bringing in a load for you?"

He began to hop up and down, making a strange squawking sound that she'd never heard before. "Dead. All dead."

"Dead?" This was bigger than she'd realized. "Who's breaking the rules, Jit?"

He made a gesture with his arms, an Easterner's shrug, but she was willing to bet her last life that he knew something.

It didn't matter. She was almost done with it all, after this last trade.

"Give me some boots, and you'll get your stones."

"Boots. Boots!" He dropped down below the counter and threw one boot over, and then another.

She pulled off the old boots and slid her feet, still crusty with sand and blood, into the new. Her toes rubbed against the edges, but there were no holes, and the heat glaze was shiny and pungent with new-boot smell.

"Can I sleep here?" she asked. "I'll head out as soon as the light goes down. You know I'm good for this."

"Twice now," he said. "I trade you next time."

She lowered her head. They both knew she wouldn't last a day if he traded her—he'd tell his superiors at the Academy that a lightrise had killed her, which would have been a far kinder death than the one she'd experience at the hands of a mercenary.

"If you want the light stones, I need sleep."

Jit's wings made a whirring sound of irritated acceptance and lifted his heavy bulk up into the loft of the shop through the ceiling.

She leaned over the counter. On a small ledge beneath the stone was a row of knives; she took the sharpest one and walked back through the maze of dripping blood towards the window where the floorboards held the least amount of gore. With the blunt end of the knife, she pounded out the center of her Murdok skin until it flattened. She pushed the blade through the skin and began to carve out a hole for her head.

Burin woke as purple fingers of light slipped off the horizon, leaving a gray-black sky and a thick humidity that would evaporate when the heat again embraced the sand.

The Murdok skin still stank of blood and spoilt carrion, but she drew it over her head anyway; the hide was tough and nearly lightproof, and the flaps hanging to her ankles would provide a small security from the light, which she feared more than being seen by an Academy official.

Satchel in hand, she slipped out the front door.

It was quiet outside, with few Easterners and traders moving through the streets. She flipped the top of the Murdok skin over her head and crossed the street.

"Burin!"

She bit down the curses that came to her lips. How was it possible that Stine was up already? She'd have thought he'd be skunked until midnight.

"Off so soon?"

She glowered at him.

"I asked around," Stine said, lowering his voice. "They say there're no more stones here, and it's making people crazy. Remley's out, and so is Hacken, and they're putting orders in to go back to Earth. Burin, people are choosing jail time over no stones. That's how bad it's getting."

A chill went down her spine. Remley and Hacken were the two largest settlements in Adon. How could they not have any light stones?

Stine watched her closely. "And I heard the Academy is offering double now, for each stone."

Her mouth went dry. Double for each stone. She'd be even better off, if she made this last trade successful.

"I want to come with you," he said. "Wherever you're going. You know where there are stones, don't you?"

"You can't just join up with me because of a light stone shortage. That's not how it works."

"Since when do you listen to authority, Burin?" There was disgust in Stine's voice. "When did this planet turn you into a spineless coward?"

"You're the coward," she snarled. "Choosing to trade inside the settlements. What do you think that makes you?"

He ignored her. "We used to be a team. We worked well together."

Until the last robbery, when they were both caught and sentenced to life on Adon.

"I have iron," he said. "I can get you more stones. You keep what you want, give me the rest; it'll all be extra for me anyway."

An idea crystallized in her mind. If she allowed this, not only would she have more stones, but she could use Stine as an alibi to solidify her escape.

"You have the iron with you?"

He jerked his head back at the building behind them. "I can grab it."

"Just this once." Burin kept her voice cruel and stiff. "One time, and only because of the circumstances. This has nothing to do with you and me."

After she secured the new iron in her satchel, they left the settlement, traveling in silence until they reached the red spires and keyholes of rock stretching into a still-dark sky. The Murdok carcass kept a silent, useless watch over the passageway, and night predators picked its bones bare, eyes blinking in the darkness at the intruders. Phosphorescent tails carved crimson-orange spirals in the sand as they shied away, hissing.

Burin grabbed the Murdok's scythe-spear, still propped up against the rock where she had left it the night before.

"What now?"

"There's something wrong here," she said. "Dead Murdoks, no Daccons, and the worms are breeding out of season."

"What are you saying?"

She shrugged. "I don't know for sure. Maybe the Murdoks got greedy, wanted stones for themselves, especially if the prices are going up, and the Daccons killed them."

He nodded slowly. "Or the Daccons are creating a monopoly on the stones, and the Murdoks found out."

Her uneasiness grew as they descended deep into the tunnel. The stench of wormrot was even more offensive and bitter than before; her eyes were watering by the time they reached the stairs leading to the great room. Behind her, Stine gagged more than once at the intensity of the odor. At the bottom of the stairs, the stone floor had vanished under the worm's offspring, most gray and limp with death. Wriggling on top were the lucky ones who had devoured the Murdok carcass, growing nearly an arm thick in the process and flowing over their kin in choppy waves.

There was no sign of the giant worm, or of the Daccons.

Burin stepped into the sludge. It slurped at her new boots, sucking them under as she pushed towards the wall cavity where the giant worm had emerged from.

The cavity was slightly higher than the cavern floor, even with the extra inches added by the sludge of offspring, and empty but for a long, shriveled husk, like a molted shell of a desert snail or snake. She kicked it aside, sending both the husk and the remaining worms clinging to her boots across the stones, and Stine jumped up beside her, his feet crunching over the husk.

At the back of the cavity was another wall of the same red stone. She set the scythe-spear on the ground and touched the wall with her gloved fingers.

"It's not real," she said.

Stine put his hands on the wall and pushed. "Can we break it down?"

"On three." She braced her feet. "One . . . two . . . three."

She slammed her shoulder into the wall. The right side of her body exploded with pain as the synthetic stone crumbled in a cloud of dust. Fumbling for the Murdok skin, she pulled it up over her mouth and nose and groped for the scythe-spear as Stine coughed and choked on the air behind her.

The air cleared.

"Gods above," she breathed.

They stood on a precipice overlooking a city carved from granite. Red-clay rivers wound through stone streets, wrapping around chiseled towers and spiraling columns, and rock cliffs rose up behind them in majestic heights. Vegetation bloomed over walls and stone towers with a soft green light that illuminated the city and turned the path of sludge down the widest street golden.

Stine emerged from the rubble, still coughing. A trickle of blood fell from his lips, but he brushed it away, not seeing what it was.

Burin opened her mouth, then closed it again. She'd never snorted light stones, but she was familiar with the behavior and accompanying symptoms of those who did. The intoxifying agent must have been in the clay well, and the dust had already entered Stine's bloodstream.

It would most likely kill him. At least he had more lives.

Stine was grinning, already high. "Look at this city! Did you know about it?"

She pulled the Murdok skin more tightly around her, hoping it had shielded her enough from the dust to protect her.

At the base of the stairs, the city soared in towering structures of stone. Thick moss cascaded over arched parapets and banisters, releasing the luminescent glow. She held her hand beneath a wispy trellis, moisture dripping into her gloved palm as Stine ran ahead, skipping like a small child down a street marked by a trail of dry sludge. Mosses and lichens spiraled around pillars and banisters, cascading ropes of leaves off stone roofs and walls. Crimson blossoms dotted a trellis of ferns, and she touched one, the petal bending delicately under her finger. It had been years since she'd seen flowers, or even this much greenery; the heat of Adon was too scorching, the soil too acidic.

Stine gave a high-pitched laugh. More blood trickled from his mouth, and he sat down in the center of the street.

This worked out better than she expected. He would not last much longer, and she already had his iron. When she didn't return to the settlement, the Academy would pull his memories and see the Daccon city, proof that she had been there for a trade.

Burin pulled him to his feet. "Get up. We're going."

The trail of sludge ended in a magnificent columned structure of four tiered balconies stretching the width of the city. Waxy vines wove through the slotted balcony, and tumbled down in a curtain of leaves between the numerous columns holding up the lowermost ceiling, on which were engraved runes resembling navigational charts and astrological charts.

She felt as if she had stepped into a new world. A world without antagonistic heat or spiteful lightrises. A world where the Academy held no purpose or sway.

A world where she would finally get what she wanted.

From beneath her came the grinding sound of stone against stone. The ground trembled, and she noticed for the first time a tiny pattern of openings in the stone, like tracks. The columns began to move, sliding across the ground in a zigzagging pattern that aligned with the tracks.

"Stine?" She danced around the swerving and shifting columns of stone until she reached Stine.

He was slumped against a column, his hands covered in the blood freely pouring from his nose and mouth. His skin had gone pale, eyes unseeing, yet glazed over with the ecstasy of his death.

She stopped abruptly. Stine was dead now, his next life already warming up in the Academy's offices. She'd never see him again.

Her future had begun.

The column behind Stine began to vibrate. It jerked forward, propelling his body at an astounding speed until his hands fell out of his lap, twin trails of blood staining the stones.

The column slammed into another with a sickening crunch, flattening his body into a pulp.

Her belly heaved, dry in her mouth.

The ground shook again, and she scrambled to her feet as another column slid by in the very place she had fallen. They rushed at her in pairs, quick and brutal, intent on crushing her as if moved by an unseen hand.

Tightening her grip on the scythe-spear, she drew one of the blocks of iron from her satchel and turned to face the inside of the darkened building.

"I am here to trade!"

The pungent brine of lemon rot thickened in the air. She set the scythe-spear down and held out the iron with both hands.

The dark softened into the pale green glow of the city, revealing a tribe of Daccons. Their leader stood in the center, his spear as pointed and sharp as hers, although without the scythe, and the rest of the tribe filled out behind him, thirty or less, and barely a meter tall.

But it was what each of them held in their leftmost limb, the small cube of red clay with the golden light shining through, that caught her eye.

Light stones, at least thirty cubes. She only had enough iron for two.

Stine had been on to something, with his guess earlier about a monopoly on stones.

"How much for the stones?" she asked.

The leader waved his free hand up and down, and the herd quivered as if they were one collective being. Her skin crawled as the Daccons circled her. She tucked the iron back in her satchel and thrust out the scythe-spear until the blade was a hands-width from the leader's throat.

"Call them off, or no one gets anything."

The leader grinned, revealing cat-like fangs grouped in pairs along the straight line of his mouth.

She swung the scythe-spear. The blade sliced open his neck. A torrent of scarlet blood poured down his chest.

With a shrieking war cry, the Daccons on either side of the staggering leader flung themselves at her, claws extended like daggers. She whirled the scythe-spear around, slicing off the head of the Daccon on the left and neatly catching the light stone it dropped with her free hand, just as another Daccon landed on her back and sunk teeth into her shoulder.

Burin dropped the scythe-spear and spun around. The Daccon fell, teeth tearing away at her skin, but she heard only the clatter of the cube.

Then they shrunk away, chattering in their alien tongue. The rest of the light stones fell to the ground as the tribe suddenly ran off into the depths of the building, their bodies a shimmering green blur.

Dashing around, she picked up the light stones and stuffed them in her satchel until the leather bulged and the weight of it strained the straps and pulled heavy on her shoulders.

Behind a column, something moved, glistening and white. She straightened, knowing she should run for the stairs. She had all the stones she needed, and she should get out before something went wrong.

Instead, she snatched up the scythe-spear and ran in the direction the Daccons had fled, cradling the satchel with one hand.

The ground slanted in a sudden drop. Heels skidding on stone, she slid to the edge of a second precipice.

Another city lay below, of greater and more magnificent carving than the first, with turrets and parapets of graceful curves and sculptured beauty. Elaborate domes covered in flowering mosses rose up into the air, laced together in a pattern of bridges that arched over glittering streets.

But it was what writhed in the streets that made her gasp.

Hundreds of worms, thick and wide and oozing like slugs, rippled through avenues lined with piles of light stones. Daccons with shovel-like tools pushed the stones together into a sort of container, while others stood amidst the worms and prodded their white bodies with sticks, gesturing with those on the bridges.

Stine had been right. The Daccons were creating a monopoly of light stones, and of all the energy in Adon. For what? More money? More iron? Or to push the Academy and its convicts off the planet?

Burin crawled back up the precipice and ran through the arching columns.

The giant white worm was waiting for her in the centermost street.

She covered the satchel protectively with one hand. The worm opened its mouth, a small hole lined with bristling hairs. A glistening thing emerged from it, stretching the edges of its mouth in mid-birth. Saliva dripped to the ground, hissing as it touched the stones, and the rotting stench blew over her as the giant worm belched the wet thing out of its mouth.

It was another worm, shining and dewy-fresh, and identical to its parent, although not quite as large.

The offspring rolled over. Coin-sized eyes blinked at Burin. It opened its mouth and emitted a squeaking sound.

The columns spun behind her and knocked her off her feet. The satchel hit the ground with a terrible cracking sound, and the smaller worm moved towards her at a speed she'd never have imagined it was capable of, mouth gaping wide enough to swallow three Easterners whole. She jumped to the side as the open maw clenched down just short of the satchel.

Her arm one with the scythe-spear, she pivoted on her right foot and lunged at the worm, shearing off its head in a single motion.

The head rolled across the stones. The tail end of the worm spasmed once, twice. Behind it, the parent worm lay motionless, eyes cloudy and unfocused.

Burin's hand strayed to the buckle of her satchel, her heart pounding, but neither worm moved. She flipped the satchel open, revealing a crumbled mess of clay and gold.

A wail formed in her body, shuddering up her spine and pushing at the root of her tongue. She dug through the slivers of gold and clay, and her fingers closed around the rubies at the bottom, their edges splintered and chipped.

She ripped the satchel off and threw it across the stone floor. With a scream that turned her throat raw, she dove at the small worm, hacking its flesh with the scythe-spear until ropes of entrails oozed over her boots, spotting the leather with flecks of gold.

Light stones.

Burin plunged her hands into the gore. Her nose streamed from the stench as she ripped out twisted tubes and pale pink blood vessels threaded around what looked like the stomach, a distorted sac covered by a gelatinous membrane. Large chunks of unfinished light stones had pierced the membrane, spilling out veins of glittering gold and red clay.

She laughed aloud. The worms incubated light stones in their rawest form; the Daccons were breeding them out of season to create the monopoly.

She tore open the stomach.

By the time she was finished, the smaller worm bore little resemblance to a thing that had once breathed and moved. She hacked at the larger worm, but its insides were like hardened coral guts.

She dumped the satchel out on the ground and lined it with layers of sticky intestines for insulation before filling it back up with the raw stones. Even unpolished, the stones would provide energy for the next hundred years. She could sit out the impending war the Daccons had just started— and the likely banishment of convicts and Easterners from Adon—and live her own life, with her own hands.

Burin picked up a block of iron. What use was it, if the worms were the incubation or fertilizing source for the stones? Perhaps it was fuel for worms, which would explain why the smaller one had lunged for her satchel just now, as the larger one had on her first trip.

She continued back through the city. Already, the moss on the buildings had lightened in color, heat sucking out their moisture, and the Murdok skin around her shoulders warmed. She marveled that the void of day could pass through rock into a world below the surface.

Behind her, small feet pattered across the stone ground.

She drew a deep breath and held it in her lungs until her chest burned. Exhaling, she turned to face the Daccons.

"I am sorry for killing your creatures." She set the iron block on the ground. "A trade. I took stones for this iron."

They stared at her. Sweat trickled down her back. She wanted to shake off the Murdok skin and run.

"I'm not going back to the settlement." She put one hand on the satchel. "Let me go. You do what you have to, with this little monopoly, but I'm out of here. Your secret is safe with me."

Her heartbeat thudded in her ears. She tasted blood in her throat, although she wasn't sure where it had come from.

The middle Daccon dropped his spear. She flinched.

More spears dropped as they made frantic gestures at each other. Some shook their spears in the air.

She turned and ran, holding the satchel close to her chest.

She had nearly reached the empty cavity before the scrape of spears on stone burned her ears.

They were much quicker than her.

Twisting her torso, she threw the scythe-spear behind her. The curved blade struck a Daccon's chest, and he dropped, causing several more to trip over him and the long shaft of the scythe-spear.

But there were more of them, nimble and fast.

She dashed through the cavern, leaping over the Murdok carcass up onto the stairs. A spear whistled by her, thudding uselessly against stone, and another struck her boot, the tip wedged in the leather near her heel. She tried to kick it loose, but it was wedged firm, and dragged behind her as she ran.

Already, the heat of the lightrise blazed down the tunnel ahead. She drew the Murdok skin over her head and tucked the satchel under her arm as spears clattered around her. There was a sharp pain in the back of her knee, and then another burst of heat in her shoulder as white-hot fire rippled up her spine.

Still cradling the satchel, she fell. She put out her other hand to catch herself, but her wrist snapped as her full weight came down on it.

Her last life.

The violent wind and sands outside swallowed up her cries as she dragged her broken body up the tunnel. There were no more spears thrown; the Daccons had retreated, afraid of the lightrise.

The light stones in her satchel were hers alone, unbroken.

Rubber Monkeys
by Kenneth Mark Hoover

Gillian stood outside the door and rapped on the wooden knocking plate. "Permission to enter, sir."

"Come."

She stepped through, came to attention, saluted. "Ensign Hollard reporting as ordered, Captain."

Captain Noah Ke scowled at her. Over his shoulder was a bay window, blast shutters open, revealing an orbital docking quay, the blue-green limb of the Nalla homeworld, and the bristling structure of Endpoint.

"I sent for you five minutes ago, Ensign."

"Sorry, sir. I was helping patch a secondary breach in the engineering spindle."

"Next time I call I want you before the echo fades."

"Noted, sir."

He pushed a fleet casualty report across his desk. "Have you seen this?"

"No, sir." She'd been on damage control for the past week and was frankly amazed Ke had possession of this information. She wondered how he had gotten it. She scrolled through. A third of their fleet, the D'Angel Consortium of Golden Merchants, was listed as destroyed or missing. Included in the report were her six dead shipmates of the *Sutherland*.

"We were lucky," Ke said, "if you want to call it that."

Gillian knew that was an understatement. The Ruq Holdfast had launched a sneak attack against human colonies on the Forward Edge, a staggered frontier of suns fifty light years from Earth. It was only by the grace of God—and an overdue shakedown cruise—that freighter *Sutherland* was out when her home port on Camberwell was attacked.

Even so, Gillian reflected, *we blundered into a task force screening the Ruq Armada. Sutherland* hammered it out with two hunter-killers before opening a gate into hyperspace and limping to a safe port.

If anyone in their right mind could ever call Endpoint "safe."

Captain Ke cleared his throat. "Ensign Hollard, our orders are clear. We're to effect repairs and render aid to any and all ships that made it out of the Forward Edge."

"Possible regrouping for a counter attack, sir?"

Ke's eyes were hard. "We won't leave those colonies on the Forward Edge undefended, if that's what you're asking."

Good, Gillian thought. We're going to fight back. "What do you require of me, sir?"

"We need supplies and engineering assistance from this port. But if history is any guide the Nalla will assume neutrality in this war before long." He steepled his fingers. "Therefore we must effect repairs before they make that position an official one. I've contacted Endpoint's port administrator, an officer named Tezu, through a local Foreign Office representative. Tezu has agreed to careen and repair our ship . . . for a price."

Gillian groaned. The ultra-secretive Nalla were notorious for taking advantage of a situation to line their coffers.

"What's it this time, sir? A moon with diamond mountains or an ocean of gold?"

"Nothing so simple, Gillian. They want our germ plasm."

Endpoint was a massive iron-nickel asteroid anchoring the upper end of a space tower directly over the Nalla equator. Hundreds of tunnels and chambers riddled Endpoint. It was a complex geometry of winding caverns and endless, twisting passages.

Gillian's shuttle slid into an empty bay and locked its nose ring to a magnetic clamp. The trip from the docking quay had been routine so she'd used the opportunity to examine *Sutherland* from a new perspective and inspect for damage.

All heavy TAK freighters had a distinctive design: thrust chambers clustered in an engine spindle, twenty scarab-shaped cargo holds racked like blisters on the superstructure, and a spinning payload housing crew and passengers. There was some minor structural damage, but nothing stopping the ship from being spaceworthy.

At least the hypervane array was intact, Gillian thought. When activated by *Sutherland*'s navigational AI the hypervanes were used to open a multidimensional gate into hyperspace. At best speed *Sutherland* could Jump a light year every five standard days.

Before disembarking Gillian watched automated tugs unload frozen hydrogen into *Sutherland*'s starved plasma reactors. So far so good, she thought with satisfaction. The Nalla were keeping up their end of the bargain.

She clambered out of the shuttle's cockpit and met a red-clad figure, his long white hair tied in a queue. Mirrored lenses grafted to his eye sockets obscured the upper half of his face.

The man thrust out a pale, skeletal hand. "I'm Thomas Trine. Human liaison from the Foreign Office of Interspecies Contact." His speech was stilted, his dialect of Sprach coarse and heavy, reflecting his time spent out on the frontier.

"Ensign Gillian Hollard at your service."

"Rough trip?" Trine asked.

She let out a dry laugh. "You might say that. We had one engagement before opening a gate into hyperspace and making our way here. Got hit pretty hard."

Trine led her down the corridor, past a stack of consignment pods. "I hoped Captain Ke might wish to meet the Nalla port administrator himself. Pity he can't be bothered with standard protocol."

"He's got other things on his mind," Gillian said in defense of her captain. "And considering the circumstances I think I can ably serve in his absence."

"I didn't mean to impugn your ability, Ensign Hollard. But the fact remains yours is the first ship to make it this far behind the lines after hostilities began. The Nalla are a difficult race. I've been stationed here twenty years and I'm only beginning to understand them. And it's a matter of time before they declare themselves neutral, making our presence here more difficult." Trine stopped outside a recessed doorway and pressed his palm against a light pad. "My office," he explained.

As they entered the lights in the room brightened. Trine led her through and into a Spartan conference room next door.

Three Nalla occupied one end of a black lacquered table. They were emaciated, topping two and a half meters each, with long, clean limbs and narrow skulls that were more bone than dun-colored flesh. They more resembled delicate works of art than living organisms.

Trine made a formal bow and took a seat at the conference table, motioning for Gillian to sit beside him.

271

The Nalla regarded her with studied silence. Their leathery lips were sewn together with platinum wire, wrought in intricate curvilinear designs that spiraled off into the sharp planes of their enigmatic faces.

The first alien, his face transfigured by wire and scarification, flicked the bifurcated fingers of his right hand over a harp-keyboard module growing out of his hip. Speech emanated from his black eyes, their centers vibrating like speaker cones. A language, resembling Galactic Sprach, resonated with an accent that echoed the empty inflection of black space and jeweled stars.

"I am Tezu, port administrator for Endpoint. These are my associates." The tall beings flanking Tezu bent their heads a fraction. "They have a business interest in these proceedings."

"I'm certain we can reach a mutual understanding, Mr. Tezu," Gillian said. "Allow me to introduce myself. My name is—"

"Unimportant under these circumstances." A whisper of dying red suns and stellar nurseries accentuated Tezu's statement.

Trine told Gillian, "Ensign, the Nalla believe a person should never reveal their birth name in front of a stranger. In their rarefied and protective culture everyone has 'use' names for social contact."

She shrugged. "I'm a starship officer."

"Then your use name should reflect that. Basic Nalla language is unpronounceable with human vocal organs. There's a sort of pidgin used to get our point across. You would be 'Woman Who Walks the Stars' in the pidgin. Is this acceptable?"

Gillian hid her amused skepticism. "Yes."

Tezu's fingerpads played across his harp and his speaker-cone eyes tweetered. "If I understand correctly, you are puzzled about my desire for human germ plasm?"

"You must admit it's an unusual request."

"True. However, I would be more than satisfied with cells taken from your dead shipmates."

Gillian remembered Captain Ke's warning during her briefing: "Don't do anything to jeopardize the resupply of our ship, but find out what they really want, and why."

She looked to Trine who stared at the table top, his hands clenched. No help there. She drew a deep breath and told Tezu, "It's a question of morality that gives us pause."

"Could you explain?" Tezu asked.

"We wouldn't want our reproductive cells used to raise an army slaves. Nor for any medical experimentation without proper authorization. But if you want them for basic research purposes on human genetics, that might be acceptable."

The slim muscles in Tezu's face knotted with consternation, pulling against the platinum wires. "By the secret name of my birth mother, I will not use them for any ignoble purpose. You have my last blood on that."

"Fine. But I must insist on knowing for what purpose they will be used." A fleeting smile. "Sorry. I'm under fairly specific orders."

Tezu's fingers flew across his keyboard and something of his impatience carried through the modulated speech: "We are loading hydrogen fuel aboard your ship. We will complete all hull and superstructure repairs sustained from your engagement with the Ruq hunter-killer squadrons. Our government will soon claim neutrality in a war sweeping through this section of the Orion Arm. We are doing you a great service, and taking an even greater diplomatic risk by helping you."

Gillian had played enough late night shipboard Texan Hold'em to know when she had a winning hand. Tezu was desperate to acquire their germ plasm. That made him easy prey.

"I appreciate your good faith, er, from the secret name of my birth mother. However, I insist on knowing why you want these biological samples. Otherwise, no deal. And that's final."

Tezu held a brief conference with his associates in their own tongue. When he finished he told Gillian, "Art. I wish to derive beautiful works of art using your germ plasm as a base source. Surely, that's plain enough for an ignorant, hairless ape to understand?"

Trine gave a delicate cough. "Ensign, it's not an insult. He's simply describing your evolutionary heritage in his own language."

Her eyes were narrow. "Sure he is."

"Compared to Tezu and the other Nalla we are ignorant apes. His brain is a dense silicon unit with carbon-fiber synapses. Quite unlike the soft, bicameral organic structure we possess."

Gillian knew the Nalla used their bodies to house complex and intricate technological architectures. Their startling appearance was less the result of evolutionary forces than deliberate surgical procedures driven by cultural necessity.

But that didn't excuse bad manners. Then again, Tezu wasn't a diplomat trained in the art of thrust and parry like Thomas Trine. Perhaps ill-mannered bureaucrats remained ill-mannered bureaucrats, she mused, no matter what the species.

Which raised another question. Why was Trine always going out of his way to apologize for them?

Nevertheless, it was up to her to find common ground. She rallied. "Exactly how would our germ plasm be used as art?"

Tezu explained, "I could show you sculptures rendered from an original template I had access to. That might save both time and explanation."

Tezu rose from the table. "Accompany me, Woman Who Walks the Stars, and I will show you unprecedented beauty."

They huddled near the doorway. Gillian waited to see who went through first. When no one moved she headed for the door. One of the other Nalla rushed forward and bumped her out of the way. Tezu and the third Nalla pushed past her and into the corridor.

"Heavens, excuse me for getting in your way," she snapped.

Trine raised his hands in a placating gesture. "Ensign, millennia ago the Nalla were groundside tunnel dwellers. Those who emerged first from the tunnel entrances ran a greater risk of being killed by topside predators."

She laughed. "So it's the reverse of opening a door for a lady? All right, then. When in Rome. . ." She nudged Trine aside in a polite way and followed Tezu.

"There isn't much activity going on around here," she observed. The corridors of Endpoint were eerily empty.

Trine fell in beside her. "You caught us in a rare down time. This tower is so fragile the tidal forces from the sun and moons easily warp its enormous structure. Elevator cars are run at certain hours to alleviate vibration on the rail and reduce resonance. Even so this section remains closed to all but the most important visitors. Ah, here we are."

The companions crouched on either side of the doorway, heads touching the floor. Tezu sailed through, oblivious to their obeisance. Trine bowed to them; Gillian followed up his example.

Once inside, Trine pulled Gillian aside and said low, "Ensign, this is Endpoint's agricultural center."

Gillian wondered at his nervousness as she entered the main arboretum. All she saw were species of plants cultivated in meticulous, loving, fashion. There wasn't any reason to—

"Oh my God." She stumbled to a halt when she came abreast of the first form hidden behind a copse of swaying copperflame trees. Her blood froze. "They can't be real."

Trine said soft, "Yes, I'm afraid they are."

"Aren't they exquisite?" Pride filled Tezu's synthetic voice. He caressed one of the grotesque shapes surrounded by liquid bubbleflowers.

Gillian fought down her nausea and forced herself to examine each specimen in turn.

A physician's caduceus: arms intertwined around a wooden pole; the body flattened until you could see inner organs working beneath translucent skin. . .

Another, legs and arms braided in nightmarish fashion, a long noodle-shaped head sprouting from a thick neck and drooping like a heavy balloon. Ornately carved onyx benches supported its long, sinuous shape. . . .

Knees trembling, Gillian followed a flagstone path through more samples of horror. There was a rich organic smell here, along with the aroma of sweat and blood, and the muted sound of dripping water on aluminum.

One human was nothing more than a sphere of hair and flesh floating in an ice-blue suspension bath. Another's skin had been carefully scraped until white, gleaming bone was revealed. It hung from metal rafters like a moth, living its hellish existence with splayed limbs. Behind, a geodesic window revealed the starry depths of space.

Tezu's fingers played along his hip. "Unlike our species, human bone is extraordinarily resilient. The skill is to produce a piece not only aesthetically pleasing, but medically viable. It's an immense challenge, working within the limited organic matrix of a rubber monkey. But that's part of the overall enjoyment."

"Tezu is the undisputed master of this new art form." Trine weathered Gillian's cold stare. "These two Nalla are his personal assistants. They use their bio-engineering skills to bring his dreams to life and sell the unique pieces to collectors on their homeworld. He's an artist, Ensign, whatever else you may think of him." Trine looked down. "Or of me."

"You've kept this secret, Trine." Gillian wanted to strike the man. "I bet the Foreign Office doesn't know about this little cottage industry. Tell me, what's your motivation? A sales commission, perhaps?"

He frowned. "How little you understand. The Nalla's concept of beauty is alien to ours because, well, they *are* aliens. Don't judge them with

275

your own provincial attitudes, Ensign Hollard. That sort of racial and species-centric thinking is very tiring."

"Go to hell."

She spotted a teak frame supporting a human shape that flowed down the ladder rungs like frozen ice. Human ice. The face had one large, brown eye left intact. An accent in the graphic scheme of ice. A tear slid down the corrugated folds of flesh as the pupil stared back at her.

"My God," she croaked, shaken at the faint resemblance of the jawline and skin tone. "It's you, Trine. They're all you!"

"Tezu is no longer satisfied using clones," he said. "He wants new genetic material to interbreed and derive different organic themes. It will cost you nothing, Ensign."

"Are you insane? Do you expect us to hand over sperm and ova so the Nalla can grow human bonsai sculptures?" She faced Tezu with anger. "Forget it, Tezu. We refuse your offer."

Tezu was unmoved by her emotional display. "Then we demand you leave Endpoint before your repairs are completed. If you refuse we will impound your ship. Then you would be easy prey for the Ruq hunter-killer squadrons roaming the interstellar lanes."

"I knew your species was avaricious but I never thought they would resort to extortion."

Tezu towered over her. "You are as naïve as an eggling if you believe there is any other reason for existence." He jerked his sewn lips into a hideous smile, the skin pulling tight against the platinum wire. "Especially between prospective allies . . . and business partners."

"Captain," Gillian pleaded, "you can't bow to their pressure."

Ke had gone to Endpoint and seen the organic sculptures for himself. He visited the nursery where prototypes were prepared: young children and babies, eyes vacant (some had no eyes at all) as they were injected with bone-softening enzymes and bio-engineering cocktails to plasticize their bodies. Many were bound with soft ropes to gently torque the limbs into fragile, delicate forms of slow growth.

When he returned to *Sutherland*, grim faced, Ke had ordered an emergency meeting in his cabin.

Gillian stared out the bay window, eyeing the blue geodesic dome on Endpoint that housed Tezu's chamber of horrors.

"Ensign," Ke rumbled, "if Tezu pulls his repair teams off our ship we're dead. Not figuratively, but literally. Our most pressing problem is getting *Sutherland* spaceworthy so she can rendezvous with the fleet." He gave a heavy sigh. "But I understand your concern on a humanitarian level. What do you think, Doctor? Do you see any way out of this?"

Sarai Nordholm was a broad-faced flight surgeon who had accompanied Ke to Endpoint. "It's an interesting moral question, sir. When does a human being stop being human? These growths are unaware of their surroundings, possessing only autonomic brain functions. They can't think or reason as we know it."

"That's not true," Gillian shot back. "I saw one of them cry. They're very aware of their situation. And what about Trine? He bartered himself to keep Tezu happy. We haven't been the only human vessel to visit Endpoint in the past two decades he's been posted here. He supplied Tezu with his own cells for experimentation to keep Tezu happy and from preying on other ships. Okay, maybe he gets points for altruism, but he needs to answer for what he's done."

Dr. Nordholm agreed. "However, as far as the sculptures go, while they're alive, they are not actually human in my view."

"Would you give Tezu your germ plasm, Doctor?" Gillian snapped.

"Careful, ensign," Ke warned.

Nordholm maintained her equanimity. "Captain, I propose we leave it up to the crew. We're on a war footing. Sacrifice should be the order of the day."

"I'll keep your proposal in mind, Doctor," Ke's voice was dangerously brittle, "when decisions on this ship are made by committee."

Nordholm flinched under the tongue lashing. "Yes, sir. Sorry, sir."

Ke brooded. "I have no intention of handing over our genetic material for Tezu and his weird sculptures. In my opinion, what's on Endpoint is as far removed from art as you can possibly get. And I don't give a damn about alien perspective or cultural differences between species. What he's doing is wrong."

Gillian asked, "What are you going to do, Captain?"

A cold smile stole across his face. "We're going to give Tezu a lesson on what it really means to be human."

"I'm glad you've decided to honor our arrangement," Tezu tweetered. "This act will strengthen relations between our species and become a foundation for future business enterprises."

Tezu and Thomas Trine stood beside the main airlock, watching delivery of twenty glass plates. Tezu's assistants prepared to verify the genetic material enclosed therein.

"Despite personal misgivings I have my orders," Gillian grumbled. She handed Tezu an invoice. "Twenty samples in this metal case. That's the extent of our crew, living and dead." Tezu's assistants revealed their impatience to see if the samples were viable.

"And I'm pleased to report my engineering teams have completed all primary and secondary repairs on your freighter." Tezu beamed, his lips and facial muscles working underneath the self-inflicted mutilation. "We are looking forward to—"

"Ensign Hollard," a communicator blared inside Gillian's shuttle, "this is *Sutherland*. Emergency. Reply immediately."

She ducked inside the shuttle's cockpit, the metal case with the germ plasm plates remaining in her grasp. "Ensign Hollard reporting, Captain."

"Ensign, we're seeing the radiation signature of a Ruq dreadnought opening a gate from hyperspace. Make that two dreadnoughts. Ensign, we've been betrayed by the Nalla. Return to the ship, immediately."

She faced Tezu, red with anger. "Damn you, Tezu. You promised to keep the Ruq at bay as long as we upheld our end of the bargain."

"But I didn't—"

Alarms blared throughout Endpoint. Nalla ran up and down the corridor. Tezu spun around in a circle as if in a daze. An officer approached him, jabbering in their incomprehensible language.

Trine's jaw dropped as he picked up some of what they said. The alien's face was reflected in his mirrored lenses. "Tezu, did you abrogate the agreement you had with Captain Ke?"

Tezu's fingers flew across his keyboard in a blur. "Of course not. I don't know what's going on but I—Look out, Trine!"

Gillian smashed Trine in the jaw with the metal case. His knees sagged as she manhandled him into the shuttle. She slammed her palm on the emergency close and the door snapped shut on Tezu's perplexed expression. She hit the override and powered the shuttle out of the docking quay. Trine lay at her feet, groaning. She ignited the thrusters and piloted the shuttle toward *Sutherland*, watching chaos unfold on the freighter's bridge through a viewer.

"Ignite your fusion lamps, engineer," Captain Ke said, his face outwardly calm on Gillian's viewer. "We'll match velocity and pick up Ensign Hollard on the way out."

The engineer monitoring the fuel flow to the fusion reactors said, "Sir, there are automated tugs in the vicinity moving cargo pods. And magnetic moorings on the quay are clamped to our hull."

"Shear them, engineer."

"Yes, sir."

Sutherland shuddered as her main engines ignited and the magnetic cleats were torn away.

Gillian watched a robot tug slam into the port side of the merchant freighter, back towards the superstructure where the scarab-shaped holds were racked like blisters. She could imagine the noise ringing throughout the hull from the collision.

Sutherland's engines were firing, but it took time to push her mass up the acceleration curve. Gillian matched speed, docked her shuttle and flung open the hatch. Dr. Nordholm and a medico were standing by to hustle Trine to sick bay.

"What you've done is beyond the pale, Ensign," Trine said, holding his head. "You've set back Nalla-Human relations, possibly beyond repair."

"Doctor Nordholm, please escort Mr. Trine to sick bay. If he argues have security put him in irons."

"Right away, Ensign."

Gillian made sure they were on their way before she ran for the bridge.

"We have to get away from the Nalla homeworld," Ke snapped and she came into the control center. "We can't use our hypervanes this close to a gravitational well."

Gillian saw Ke had purposefully spoken into an open mike so anyone on Endpoint could hear the decisions he was making in real-time. She hid her bemused smile and assumed her station.

The bridge communicator crackled as a viewer revealed the dun-colored visage of Tezu. "Captain Ke, I insist upon the secret name of my blood mother Endpoint had nothing to do with this Ruq ambush."

"Tezu, Nalla and Earth are now in a legal state of war. I do not have authority from my Consortium to broker a peace accord under such circumstances." Ke ignored Tezu's howls of outrage.

Gillian watched her gravitic sensors. They were much too close to Nalla for the navigational AI to use their hypervanes and let them escape into hyperspace.

Just like the time we were jumped by the hunter-killer squadron over Camberwell, she thought. Except this time we have less opportunity to make a clean getaway.

279

"Watch those sensors, Ensign," Ke snapped.

"I'm on it, sir."

Sotto voce he told her to turn the ship forty degrees to starboard with negative azimuth coordinates for the stern, space normal speed. She complied, hoping Tezu and his people were too preoccupied to notice the subtle maneuver, or interpret Sutherland's final orientation when she came to rest.

"Captain," Tezu screamed through his speaker cones, "this is a terrible mistake. Besides, a single merchant freighter doesn't have the capability to make war, therefore your threat has no value."

Ke leaned forward until his body filled Tezu's viewer, blocking Gillian's work at her station. "Would you like a demonstration of this ship's wartime capabilities, port administrator?" Without turning around he said, "Communications officer, remove all safety interlocks from the comm laser."

"I . . . no, wait!" Tezu shouted.

"Interlock safeties bypassed," the comm officer said abruptly.

"Fire."

At this close range Sutherland's comm laser could punch a hole through a ship's hull or pierce a radiation shield. The fragile geodesic dome on Endpoint was no match for that kind of energy. The structure blew out into hard vacuum, taking Tezu's artworks along with it.

"Captain!" someone on the bridge shouted, "it's not the Ruq who're opening a gate into this system. It's two of our own ships!"

Ke's face broke into a wide smile. "You don't say? Imagine that."

Personnel on the bridge cheered. Two TAK merchant freighters slid out of twin rips in the fabric of space, spilling radiation from their white-hot hypervanes.

"It's the Awabi, flanked by the Golden Cloud!" Gillian cried.

Ke ordered, "Helmsman, cut your engines." The big freighter coasted at speed.

A commander from the Awabi, a dark-skinned woman with iron grey hair, appeared on a secondary viewscreen. "Captain Ke, do you require tactical assistance?"

Ke grinned at her, hands on hips. "I'm glad to see you made it out of Camberwell alive, Commander Huxley."

Tezu interrupted, openly suspicious of this forced interplay. "They are your own ships! But . . . how did they mask their energy signatures?"

Uh oh, Gillian readied herself, he's on to us. Maybe Tezu realizes we semaphored one another with our hypervanes while Awabi and Golden Cloud *hung outside the Nalla system.* That's how Ke knew how many ships were lost at Camberwell, and the secret plan to regroup the Consortium, while I was working damage detail. A silent but effective communication had gone on by blocking starlight and sending morse using the hypervanes from the freighters while they were in-system.

Huxley said, "Tezu, we wanted to field test our new masking procedure. Yes, we've found a way to modulate our energy signature and make it appear we were Ruq dreadnoughts. Captain Ke, we've been marking a navigational tramline in order to pay the Ruq Holdfast a visit. You're welcome to come along and see if we can't make them accept a peace treaty on our terms."

Tezu stabbed angrily at the translation module on his hip. The resulting Galactic Sprach was garbled. "You'll do more than that, Captain. You've disrupted our base, fired upon Endpoint, created terrorism and sabotage and destroyed valuable private property. I hereby impound your ship under the neutral flag of my government, along with all other ships of your convoy. I . . . uh—" Tezu's fingers stopped moving across the harp strings and his eyecones fell silent.

Gillian watched Tezu on the main viewscreen, thinking for the first time in his life the port administrator probably wished he could vent a very loud scream using his own vocal chords.

"Captain Ke," Tezu's manner was subdued, "you wouldn't dare fire on this structure."

Sutherland lay with her stern pointed at the space elevator.

"Tezu, I lift one finger and we'll cut it like a blowtorch through paper ribbon."

"But you'll destroy Endpoint!"

"Along with millions on your homeworld after that space tower falls around your equator like a noose. Not to mention the resulting environmental damage."

Tezu shook with suppressed anger. "You are a dangerously insane species."

"No more than someone who twists humans into organic pretzels for profit, Tezu."

Tezu walked off camera, returned shortly. "You leave me no other option but to defend Endpoint with our own weapons."

Gillian leaned toward Captain Ke and whispered fast, "Sir, the Nalla are many things, but they're not poker players."

"Understood, Ensign," he said low. He said louder, "Tezu, it looks like a standoff. Which means I automatically win. I doubt the authorities will take kindly to a port administrator who uses extortion to line his own pockets. Come to think of it, if you press the issue I'll quarantine your entire system. I have the authority as Master Trader of the D'Angel Consortium of Golden Merchants to do that. No more interstellar trade, Tezu. The Nalla will be isolated and alone. And poor."

"I will destroy your ship, Captain Ke."

"Think twice before you try it, station master," Huxley broke in. "We haven't been sitting idly by, ourselves."

Tezu looked off camera, saw the other two ships had their sterns oriented toward the space elevator.

Ke said, "Oh, and you might want to rethink that neutrality question, Tezu. With our three ships meeting here, Endpoint has effectively become a staging area in our war against the Ruq. In other words your neutrality has been rendered obsolete. Welcome aboard, Ally."

Tezu glanced off screen a second time. Nalla were running amok in the background. There appeared to be some sort of conflict happening. "I'll get back to you."

The screen went black.

Ke said to no one in particular, "Just wait until the Ruq see what one of our ships can do when we use the magnetic rings to lase our plasma fire into 'em. They caught us by surprise the first time. The Nalla are no better. Did they think because we're merchants we wouldn't fight back? Incredible ignorance on both their part, I must say."

Gillian noticed a commotion near the airlock she had used when entering Endpoint. "Captain," she pointed, "look."

A struggling figure was thrown out of the airlock by two spacesuited figures. It writhed briefly on the arid landscape and became still.

A new Nalla port adminstrator appeared on the *Sutherland*'s forward viewscreen. It was one of Tezu's former assistants with his companion standing idly behind.

"Captain Ke, I have assumed operational command of Endpoint," the Nalla said. "I am the new Tezu. Though I do not fully understand why you find these artworks morally offensive, I would be grateful if this incident were forgotten and profitable relations between our species resumed."

"I'll consider it," Captain Ke answered.

The new Tezu pressed ahead. "I wish you would, and quickly.

Interstellar strife affects our profit margin. As a concession we will not require payment for *Sutherland*'s repair and resupply. To further manifest our good faith, I will speak my personal name so that you will have a blood-noose over me and all subsequent generations of my family. . . ."

Ke held up his hand. "That won't be necessary, Tezu. I'll take your word that you'll honor our new contract."

The Nalla expressed relief both in his manner and the tonal frequencies emanating from his carbon-fiber speaker cones. "I hope your species will continue to trade with us. May we have word of a new agreement between our people?"

"Not so fast. What about the human sculptures Tezu sold?"

"I promise from the secret name of my ancestral home they will be destroyed and their owners recompensed from my own monetary fund."

"Humanely destroyed," Ke suggested, "and the remains disposed of with reverence."

"Naturally."

"I'll expect proof of that when we return, Tezu."

"Captain Ke, are you really going to the Ruq Holdfast?"

"We are."

"But no one who has attempted this has ever returned."

Ke was defiant. "We will return, Tezu. Count on it."

"Done, Captain Ke, and welcome. Before I go, may I inquire as to the health and status of our human liaison, Thomas Trine?"

"He must answer for his actions to his own Foreign Office. But I expect he'll be allowed to return to Endpoint in the future, albeit on a probationary basis, if your ambassadors press for his reinstatement."

"Excellent. He was a valued liaison and something of a personal friend. If there is nothing more I wish you a safe and profitable trip, Captain. Endpoint out."

Gillian leaned her head back. "Whew. I never want to go through that again. Oh, by the way, Captain, we're far enough from their gravitational well to open a gate into hyperspace. *Awabi* and *Golden Cloud* are signaling their readiness to follow."

"You did very well, Ensign Hollard. I can almost overlook your propensity to speak when not spoken to. Almost."

"Sorry, sir."

He smiled. "Now, Gillian, are you ready to pay the Ruq a little visit?"

"More than ready."

"Good." Captain Ke snorted with derision. "Rubber monkeys, indeed. Ensign, let's go make our position known to the entire galaxy."

"Yes, sir!"

The *Sutherland* unfurled her hypervanes and Jumped.

Jadeflower
by C. E. Grayson

Jono stared at his sister from across the table. The juicepack that had just bounced against his left eye finished its journey back to the middle of the table, and Jono's hand covered his eye, pushing against it to soothe the sting. Darin's glare started to soften, and her mouth formed an o-shape that could have been the beginning of an apology. Jono himself didn't say anything.

Mom and Dad worked as many hours as they were allowed, trying to earn enough crits to get Darin off Jadeflower, and Jono with her. That left Jono, only fifteen, to take care of his sister during those long hours. During the few hours she was awake, he tried to get her to eat and drink, manage her medpacks, and take care of anything else she needed.

Her rages didn't upset him; he was angry too.

"Take me outside," she said, finally calm. Or maybe she was just too tired now to fight.

Whatever it was, Jono was relieved. The sun's light, stained purple by the reflection of the gas giant Toulare 18, always put Darin in a better mood. When he risked injury again by offering her another juice pack, not only did she not argue, but also downed it and asked for another. But while being out here made Darin happier, it made Jono nervous. He watched the tree-line for rippers; he'd never seen one, but his friend, Aaliyah, had, and her father had almost lost an arm to one. They'd attacked others as well: unwary children, and hikers who had not armed themselves with stunners, had vanished entirely. Some had been found, drained of blood, or dismembered, or never been found at all.

Was one there, waiting for a moment's inattention? He watched for eyes. There were rumors—Jono had no idea if they were true or not—that lately the rippers were interested in the cancer kids. Just another gruesome curse this world had visited upon his little sister.

C. E. Grayson

Its official colonial designation was HSPO-493, but the people who lived and worked there, inspired by the translucent jungle blossoms that ringed the delta valley where they made their home, called it Jadeflower.

On those slopes, where the river flowed to the vast turquoise sea, they'd found a soil rich and loamy, perfect for the cultivation of cocao and coffee beans in a way it was nowhere else in the universe save for a few, dwindling patches on old Earth. In addition, some substance in the very stuff of the planet accelerated the plants' growth, increased the coffee's potency, and intensified the chocolate's flavor. Laws of commerce demanded a human presence here, and to establish such a stronghold pioneers were promised high wages and a new life on a temperate world; such things were rare.

Three months after their family's landing, Darin took sick. First the fever, then the cough, and its congruent lining of thick green pus, choking out her breath. Many of the children who came here sickened within a few months, and every single one of them, in the terran decade of the colony's existence, had died, or were expected to. Some, usually the younger ones, or the ones already weak, lasted mere weeks. Others could postpone the eventual wasting, the slow-motion drowning, and live two years or more.

They called it the green cancer. That was Jadeflower's dark secret. Children died here.

Doctors told them that Darin, only eight years old, had at most a year left.

The fence, built of baked-mud bricks set in a frame of silvered steel, had sonic attachments in the posts, adding an extra layer of protection.

Darin tugged at the sheet she had wrapped around herself. She'd demanded it, wanting some protection against the breeze, but now . . . "Jono, get this off me," she said, and then, mindful of the tone she was taking, added, ". . . please."

"Yeah," Jono said. He backed away from the fenceline, and knelt beside Darin's chair to untwist the pink-flowered fabric. As he did, he felt her skin. Hot, but she wasn't sweating.

"I think we should go back inside," he said.

"I'm sick of inside."

"I'll find something on the feed for you to watch."

"I'm sick of that too."

286

"You want me to read you a book or something?" He had to offer.

"I'm tired of books."

"I could get a—"

"I don't want to play a game either."

He sighed. "You're not leaving me with a lot of choices, Darin."

She just looked at him, and then away, up at the sky. "Just leave me here."

"If you want to be left alone, I'll take you to your room."

"I want to go somewhere."

"Where do you want to go?" There weren't a lot of options for places to go in Jadeflower, even for someone healthy enough to walk. A central market had stores and restaurants, and a full feed for simming to other worlds, but maybe that would be enough. They could tram in, rent a roll-chair, and see how it went. After all, if she felt strong enough to be this grouchy. . .

She was staring at him again, and it seemed like she was going to try to sit up. But as soon as her shoulders tensed, she fell back again. Defeated, she looked away. This much effort had raised a wet cough, and Jono put an arm around her shoulders and rubbed at her back until it passed, ignoring the shining green globs she left on the grass.

"You need a treatment?"

She stared down at her hands.

"You want me to carry you?"

She nodded. Tears pooled at the edges of her eyes and then traced down across the top of her cheek. Why did she have to pay for her good morning with pain now?

"We'll rearrange the main room, ok? I'll get us something to watch. Something fun."

She tried to smile.

A high-pitched whine assaulted his ears, right through and into his brain. He clapped his hands over his ears. Looking toward the fence, he saw some . . . thing, on the top of the low wall. Its form was grey and green-mottled, and it stuck a hook-clawed appendage over the top, batting at the sonic wall as if it were a physical thing.

Jono pulled his hands away from his ears, forcing himself to feel the full effect of the pain, and picked up Darin. She was distressingly light, but was an awkward load because she had to use her hands to cover her ears and couldn't grab hold of him.

The creature—it had to be a ripper—continued its lazy probe. As Jono's back smacked against the door, he cursed and barked the command to open it.

He stumbled through, and the door slid shut, cutting them off from the yard, and muffled the warning squeal. After a few seconds the ripper, seeing that its prey was gone, poked the top of its head—not enough for Jono to get any kind of look—over the top, and then dropped back.

Darin was crying now, but Jono didn't think just because she was afraid of the ripper. He took her into the main room and laid her on the couch. She clung to him, but neither of them said anything about what had just happened, but she clung to him. He paid for the vue-feed out of his own account, and let her rest across his lap, breathing from her mister until she slept.

Jono told Aaliyah the story of the ripper's visit. She listened in the same staid manner with which she did everything. Silent, head unmoving, she just stared at him as he talked.

"They're getting braver," she said when he'd finished.

He looked away from Aaliyah's sim-face, which hovered above the table in their little dining nook, and turned to watch Darin as she slept. She hadn't made it past the first few minutes of their vue-feed, but he'd paid the extra crits for a permanent save so she could finish it later.

"One came through Edgemarket the other day." Aaliyah said. "It grabbed one of the cancer kids."

Jono's stomach twisted. Edgemarket was the district on the opposite side of the settlement from theirs, but that didn't make him feel any better. And even though he knew he shouldn't, he had to ask, "Did they . . . did they find him? Is he all right?"

"They sent out a search team, but I don't know if they found anything. I'm surprised you haven't heard about it."

"Haven't simmed in for a while," he said. "And my dad isn't on the security team."

She just shrugged. Jono knew she meant well, despite her affect, but on a day like this one, he didn't have it in him to fill in the gaps. His mom's arrival gave him an excuse to sign off. Aaliyah probably wouldn't realize that he was being rude, or mind if she did.

Like so many others, Jono's mom and dad followed work, bringing Jono and his two sisters with them. Mom, a surveyor and engineer, specialized in designing and laying out colonial expansions. Dad, a botanist, came to catalog Jadeflower's strange flora, and discover whether or not other rare earth crops could take root here in the same way the coffee and chocolate had.

They arrived at the orbital station tethered to the planet by an orbital elevator, eager to be processed. Even though Jadeflower was a new colony, much of its equipment had been hastily assembled from old parts. And at lower elevations, a rupture in a passenger car's hull wasn't as serious a problem, but it vented just after entering the atmosphere. Remembering the safety briefing, they donned masks and activated pressure skins, but no one knew that Nella's mask had malfunctioned, and they didn't know that she'd asphyxiated until they reached the bottom, opened the mask to find her blue-ringed lips.

Mom and Dad transformed their grief into determination to make their lives on Jadeflower a permanent thing. Nella would not be left behind.

Mom kept a neutral expression, but her eyebrows were arched, expectant, waiting for Jono to say something; it was the way she always looked at him when she first got home, the look of a woman preparing herself for bad news.

"Finishing up your class?" she finally asked, in that same bright tone they all had learned to use when they were trying not to be upset about things.

She'd put a light hand on his shoulder, but pulled it away when he tensed. Instead, she used it to rub at the dried, greenish mud that streaked her cheek.

"No, that was Aaliyah."

"Your prof messaged me. You haven't checked in for a week."

"Yeah, well, Darin was awake a lot today."

"I don't want you to fall behind, Jono. You need to hit your benchmarks on time if you want to be on track for University."

"I know. I'll catch up. It's not like I won't have plenty of time—" With a look she warned him not to finish that sentence. Eventually, his life *would* be his own again, and he could show up to an actual classroom and see his friends in the flesh. There would be plenty of time for him to catch up on his studies when Darin was gone.

He hated himself for the times he looked forward to that.

To change the subject, he told her about the ripper.

Mom held her breath for a few seconds, then let it explode in a curse. Then she looked at him again, warning him not to remind her that she'd yelled at him for using that word a week ago. "I guess the yard's going to be off-limits. . ."

"She loves the yard. It's the only time she gets to—"

"Jono, I know, all right? And I didn't want to tell you this, but yesterday—"

"Aaliyah already told me about the kid the ripper took."

"Did she tell you it was one of the . . ." Mom hated the term *cancer kid*. ". . .kids who are sick?"

Jono nodded.

"And did she tell you about the six other sick kids they've taken in the past week?

At this, he had to shake his head.

"I only heard about it yesterday," she said. "It's bad enough the company has bought up all the newsfeeds, and minimized the green cancer problem. But with the rippers attacking—they're trying to keep the colonial inspectors from hearing about it, because between the cancer and the rippers they might come in and shut us down, give it to the council mercs."

"Maybe they should," Jono said.

"Yeah, maybe they should. But if they do, we'd all get picked up and dumped on some station, and then what? Darin will still be sick, we'll lose all the medcare we do have."

Once again, he changed the subject. "You're filthy. What were you doing?"

Reminded of her day's work, she pulled her arms behind her back and stretched out her shoulders. "I was on site. We're getting ready to lay the foundation for the Monastery."

"Oh," was his only reaction. He could have inquired further, but he was tired of talking. No conversation with either one of his parents ever ended with anything other than a sense of despair. It was time to shoot this one in the head and put both of them out of their misery.

Mom did it for him. "I'm going to shower. Shout if Darin wakes up?"

"All right," he said as she moved away.

She stopped at the foot of the stairs. "Is there anywhere you wanted to go tonight? Maybe see Aali and Tyce? I mean, actually go be in the same room with them?"

"No thanks," he said.

"I wish you would, but I won't force you. I'm just—I just don't want you to think you have to shut yourself up in this house and wait for your sister to die."

That's exactly what I have to do, he thought. But he wasn't cruel enough to say it.

Dad came home late, as usual. He'd stopped talking about the reason he was gone so long in the evenings, but Jono knew. He and a team from bio and botany were spending their own time working on the cancer problem, which they weren't allowed to do during contract hours. This was unauthorized, but none of the managers explicitly forbade it. The company claimed they had a team working on the problem, but no one had met anyone actually assigned to it. Jono had quit asking for news on their progress.

Mom set supper out for him. The rest of them had eaten as soon as she'd gotten out of the shower. Jono made noodles with actual beef broth, something Darin would usually eat. And she did eat. It had been a good day, if only measured by his success in getting Darin to eat and drink what she was supposed to. No one mentioned the ripper, and when Dad arrived, Mom took Darin off for a bath. Jono sat at the table, sipping a cup of water, while his father ate.

Between bites, Dad looked up and said, "You did good, today. You took care of things."

"Mom told you what happened?"

"Of course she did."

He let his dad finish his meal in silence. Jono knew it was Dad's job to put Darin to bed. Since he was gone so much, he was determined to have at least that much time with her every day.

Dad went upstairs and Jono went to the back door. He stepped outside for a few seconds, took in a few gulps of the cool air that blew in from the sea, and forced himself to stand there until he could prove to himself that it wasn't fear driving him back inside.

Darin's coughing drowned out the quiet hiss of the closing door. He listened to it and realized that it was more than that. She wasn't just coughing.

Jono climbed the stairs without even feeling the steps beneath his feet, and he halted just in front of the lavatory door. Dad slumped against the doorframe, arms crossed over his chest. Mom knelt next to the tub, and held

Darin, whose hands were full of her reddish brown hair. The weight of the water forced long strands of what hair remained to slough away from her head and tangle themselves on her heaving, bare shoulders.

Mom had her arms around her, but no one said anything. What could they say?

Darin cried for a long time, but eventually she calmed down, exhausted and dehydrated. Mom and Dad wanted to take this as a good sign, but Jono saw it for what it was. Defeat. This could be the night they lost her. She might live a few weeks or months more, but later he'd be able to look back and see that this was the exact moment she gave up and just let the sickness have her.

Dad carried her into bed, and sat with her for a while. He tried to tell a couple of jokes and even sang a stupid song she'd liked when she was little. Wincing, Jono recalled that it was a song he and Darin and Nella had sung together.

"Don't sing," Darin said. "Just read me a story." She pretended to enjoy it, and before long, she was asleep. Or Dad thought she was. Jono, sitting on his little cot, shared a look with his father, before Dad flicked off the light and left both of them in the dark.

He gave Darin a few minutes of silence, until he heard his parents' voices coming from their room. Muffled as they were by the wall, he couldn't really make out exactly what they were saying.

"What do you need, Darin?" He asked her. There was just enough light coming from the cracked doorway that Jono could see her moving her hand to touch the hair she'd spread across her pillow.

"You just want me to sit here, or maybe I can sing you another song." He tried to laugh at that, but couldn't.

"Can you open the window? I don't like the air in here."

He thought about how nice it was outside, and how stuffy it really was in this room, and how it smelled like, well, it smelled like a sick person. But he also thought about what might be out there in the darkness.

"I don't think that's a good idea."

"Please, Jono. . ." She wasn't whining. There was a need there he couldn't bring himself to ignore.

His body stiffened on the cot, and he twisted sideways so he could get a good look out the window. It had a screen to keep insects out, but what good would that do against a ripper?

292

Still, they were on the second story, and if he just opened it a crack . . . It wouldn't be completely secure, but with the screen and with him standing guard, it would probably be enough.

She wasn't asking for much, just a little comfort in what could be one of her final nights.

Jono moved his cot in front of the window, and made enough of a gap that his fist could fit in the space.

"More. That doesn't let in any air at all."

"Maybe we should give it time," he said, but he couldn't argue with her objection. Even as close to it as he was, he couldn't feel anything, either, so he slid it over a couple more hand-widths until he could feel cool air pushing in against the miasma.

"Better?"

"I guess." Darin settled herself on her pillow, turning so that she could feel the new air on her face. Jono pulled his feet onto the cot, and sat with his knees pulled up, his back against the wall, guarding the gap while allowing air to move through it. Listening for a rattle in her breath, watching as her eyes, slowly, shut, he tried to keep himself awake. Every few seconds he looked out the window for signs of movement, and despite his panic every time a tree-branch shifted, vigilance lost the battle against sleep.

Jono was yanked out of a deep sleep as the screen screeched, pushed out of its frame, then shredded entirely. Some grey-green hand shoved the window aside like a visiting friend. The ripper used Jono as a springboard to launch itself at Darin, its claws digging into Jono's stomach, tearing at the flesh there. Jono tried to move, but his heart beat so fast it hurt, and he found he couldn't even breathe.

Darin woke screaming. The ripper batted at her blanket-wrapped form until it knocked her onto the floor. Jono's name tore itself out of her throat.

Rage slew his panicked immobility, and he lunged for his sister. Something slammed against his back, and he went down, blood in his mouth, as his head hit the bedpost and the world flashed white.

Aaliyah and her father, Fareed, arrived first. Fareed had been on duty anyway, and Aaliyah . . . Jono didn't know if Mom had asked Fareed to bring her or if Fareed had done that on his own.

Every part of Jono's head throbbed, and he knew from the brief glance in the mirror he'd taken while his mom cleaned him up that the large gash from his temple to his nose was going to leave a scar. He didn't care. He deserved it. The slashes beneath his shredded shirt still bled, but looked worse than they actually were.

Aaliyah sat beside him on the couch, occupying the same space Darin had before.

He'd seen Darin's room—the busted window, the bed, torn sheets and exploded pillow-stuffing splashed with blood.

Since most of the blood was near the foot of the bed, it was probably Jono's. That was something.

No one said it was his fault, but it was.

"I'm going to get you some water," Aaliyah announced, and shot up from the couch and went to the kitchen, while Jono's parents conferred with Fareed in the little dining nook. Jono drank the water Aaliyah had brought him and listened to the sound of the adults talking, without comprehending any of the words being spoken. Then his parents and Fareed came to stand in front of Jono, like an executive council ready to announce his punishment.

Dad spoke first. "Other teams are on their way, but Mr. Khamani brought extra stunners, so we're not waiting. I want you to stay here at the house in case Darin comes back on her own."

Jono stood, despite the ache in his muscles and the fire that flashed in his wounds. "I'm coming too."

"Absolutely not!" Dad said, anger rising in his voice.

"I'm going," Jono said again. Salt stung his wound and he realized that he was crying. He ignored this.

Mom started to say something, but Fareed, who'd been watching Jono since they'd come in, said with quiet authority, "Marta, Jess, I think the boy should come."

"What? Fareed!" Dad exploded.

Fareed put a hand on his shoulder. "My daughter is an expert hunter, and skilled with a stunner. She'll stick close by him, and the rippers have never attacked anyone traveling in a group. My wife is on her way, and can stay at the house and wait for your daughter to return." He didn't comment on the absurdity of that actually happening, or the fact that rippers had never been known to invade homes before. "I think Jono needs this. I think he will suffer a great deal more if he is not allowed to help."

"All right," Mom said, obviously not happy about it. "But Jono—you stay next to Aaliyah, and both of you, stay with us."

Aaliyah nodded, answering for the both of them, whether Jono wanted her to or not.

As they began their search, Fareed received word that Darin hadn't been the only child taken that night. This meant that only one other team would be dispatched to help them. In each case, the rippers had broken into a dwelling, crashing through windows, even opening doors. That cast doubt on the prevailing theory that rippers were a sub-sentient species, Jadeflower's version of a jungle predator, like earth's jaguar, or Cynani's spearclaw.

They should have known this since no one had been able to capture a ripper. Stunners could force them back, but they would vanish into the hostile jungle. Some substance in the trees blocked deep scans, so only the edges had suffered human incursion.

And all of the abducted were cancer kids, seven of them in one night.

Jono and Aaliyah walked with their parents in the narrow spaces between the green flowered vines and the low walls that edged the settlement. The night's events had roused neighbors. The alert woke everyone, and many of Jadeflower's people had left their homes, sought out the search parties' lights, and joined them.

Aaliyah kept an awkward hand on Jono's arm. They carried stunners—which Jono barely knew how to use—and Jono held the light, but it barely penetrated the tree-line. Was this a mercy, sparing him the sight of his sister's bloodied body? Fareed operated some sort of scanner, and he and Jono's mom inspected spaces between the trees, hoping to find the spot where the rippers had carried Darin back into the jungle.

Neighbors shouted Darin's name. Occasionally, Dad joined them in shouting, though everyone knew it probably wouldn't help. Dad wanted Darin to know that she hadn't been abandoned, that they were coming for her.

Fareed received occasional updates from other security teams across the settlement, and reported that it had been decided that they would chop down the entire jungle if they needed to. They were going to find the children. This was obviously not company policy. Jadeflower's own people had made this choice. Other colonies had revolted. This was important enough for them to do the same thing, if necessary.

Fareed unfolded a tool he'd been keeping in his pocket. Its two ends elongated and stretched a filament between them, which shortly lit with white fire. The entire length of it, about as long as Fareed's arm, glowed. Fareed warned them to stand back as he began whacking at the nearest branches. It did the job if not perfectly, singeing the plants where it sliced through. Everything was green and moist, and the heat fast fading, so it didn't seem like it was going to start a fire.

People along the line hacked at the jungle with other implements, but almost as soon as this had begun, the darkness heaved in protest, and the vines moved around them. Dad went down first; Aaliyah grabbed hold of Jono and pulled him back, raising her stunner. Jono heard other screams, and stunners firing like temblor strikes.

Aaliyah fell, firing the stunner at something pushing past her. Jono stumbled backward, bashing his head against a stone wall.

On his chest, leaning down to force its face against Jono's own, crouched a creature of green and grey fur, dappled with darker spots. A veil of white hid its eyes, and a spotted muzzle pushed out from beneath it. The creature sniffed Jono, then brought up a finger, claws retracted, to dip in Jono's bleeding wound.

Aaliyah was standing now, with Mom at her side. Both of them watched in horror as the ripper brought its bloodied finger back to its mouth to taste.

"Go ahead," Jono whispered.

The ripper shot out a hand that blocked Mom's body as she threw herself toward him, and then stepped off of Jono's body to stand at its full height. Stepping backward, it kicked at Jono's foot, commanding him to stand.

Jono tried to comply but couldn't find his balance. Aaliyah grabbed him by the shoulder and let him lean against her as she levered him to his feet. Three other rippers had joined the first arrival, and stood guard over the humans. One of them tugged at Jono, placing him just behind the leader.

Every muscle in his body screamed in terror, threatening to lock up, but he forced himself to push through. Aaliyah still held him, and this gave him an anchor, and somehow, that calmed him. His mom and dad called out to him, protesting, but he walked into that green darkness, following the beast—was it really a beast? —that had beckoned him.

Slapping, sappy switches stung his wound, and the leaves surrounded him, like curtains to be forced apart. He tried to keep his eyes on the ripper, but spared a momentary search to confirm that Mom, Dad, and Fareed had joined the expedition. Behind them, the other rippers urged them all forward. Were they all about to be made a feast, or offered as a sacrifice to some alien beast-god?

Jono kept walking, following, noticing nothing but the guide's mottled back and the few branches that interposed between them every few seconds. Soon, they'd gone deep enough that Toulare didn't even send down its light, and he could only follow the sound in front of him.

They were being marched into exhaustion, Jono concluded. Maybe this did something to the meat, made it tender before the kill?

He stumbled, fell against the ripper's back. It turned on him, grabbed at his arm. He felt the claws there, waiting to snick through and into the skin, but even though the ripper snarled, it didn't hurt him. Aaliyah's arm steadied him.

As they continued in that way, he lost track of time, and himself, and even the world.

When he'd come to believe the world was gone forever, it returned, and he could make out the ripper's spots, and the rough veins in the leaves, jadeflower fluff knocked free by their passage. The deep purple sky had lightened into a violet dawn.

The sky's return proved a harbinger. Above them emerged a curve of light, formed by a ringed gap in the trees around some other bright green thing that had to be a new kind of tree. Lacking bark, its surface was a near-translucent, flexible green cartilage

Their guide stopped, snarled a warning at Jono to stay where he was as it moved onward, pushing back against his chest to make its command understood. Jono remained in the little clump formed by Aaliyah, Fareed, and his parents, and all of them waited in silence. The other rippers, those that had guarded them from behind, joined the first.

They waited. Around this open ring emerged others, more little human groups led here by other paths.

The humans shot each other panicked looks across the open space, but low growls from the rippers warned them not to shout out, not to communicate in any verbal way, or make any attempt to join together. In the middle of this strange clearing, formed some council of the beasts. Jono

297

leaned against one of the trees, but before he realized what was happening, he was on the ground. Mom crouched down next to him.

Aaliyah crept forward, moving slowly so as not to attract attention. In the center, a new creature arrived, climbing from inside the strange plant to step out from the top. It had the same basic form as the rippers, if a bit taller, but its skin, completely hairless, glowed with a faint green-white light. More of these joined the first, and the rippers devoted their attention to every intricate gesture these creatures made. There was, in the middle of what would have been for a human, where the neck would join the torso, a little round divet, ringed with a darker green. The face, or what could be called a face for lack of a better term, had the texture of bark, but was of the same substance as the plant they'd stepped out of.

After an interminable silence, the rippers dispersed once more. Jono's guide ignored Aaliyah and reached down to yank Jono to his feet. Mom tried to put herself between them, and received a set of bared fangs for her effort. Aaliyah walked beside Jono as he stumbled forward.

"Maybe they want to return the bodies," she whispered, nothing but a polite curiosity in her voice.

Once the ripper pushed Jono toward the tree/not tree, it stepped back.

Hanging from the side of the tree, attached to it with vine-like tendrils, was a green pod. It pulsed, throbbing with some kind of life, to the rhythm of a human heartbeat. Could he even dare to hope?

Aaliyah reached past him to touch it, and grabbed Jono's hand to force him to do the same. When he was seven years old and his mom had been pregnant with Darin, she'd taken his hand and placed it against her belly. It had felt like this.

One of the greenskins—it was all he could think to call these new creatures—stood directly above him, the tree its pedestal. It made a gesture. The ripper beside Jono leaned forward and, with an extended claw, dug into the pod's skin, slowly cutting downward.

The pod opened, and a green, loamy smell exuded from in. Nestled in its heart, emerging into the light as the pod peeled back, was a form; it had the green-white skin of the creatures, but was otherwise human in appearance. Human, hairless, female, and small.

Jono reached in, dug away the stringy muck.

She rolled over, and her eyes found his.

"Ohgodohgdohgod. . ." Aaliyah chanted.

He reached down, and grabbed hold of his sister. Darin grabbed hold of him, her arms still thin, but possessing a strength he'd not felt in them for months. He looked past, and saw similar scenes around the other sides of the tree. Several pods had opened, given birth.

Mom and Dad ignored the rippers warning, ran to him and Darin. They grabbed her from Jono's grasp, pinned her between them until she emitted a tiny choked-off sob. They sat her down, wiped off the goo, inspected every inch of her. Fareed came up behind them, pulled Aaliyah away, just a few steps. Darin was crying. So was everyone else.

The greenskin reached down to touch Jono's brow. It gestured down at the ground, and then up at the sky, splayed fingers dancing in impossible directions, at little clustered scenes of reunion and rebirth. All of these children, who had been near death, and now...

And now...?

Jono looked back at the creature, and began to understand this healing, this gift of welcome and of warning.

Mars Needs Baby Seals
by Lawrence M. Schoen

In Mars' pitifully under funded Department of Temporal Solutions, located in a too small facility one hundred meters beneath the bottom of the rehydrated Mare Sirenum—just down the hall from the Martian Department of Tax Relief and Prosthetic Enhancements—history was about to be made. Their names were Threm and Grelnak, as common among the Trans-humans living and working on Mars in the twenty-third century, as Roberta and Doug would be in New Jersey during Earth's late twentieth. Threm was a senior specialist, and Grelnak was her underqualified, probationary assistant. The two of them lay sprawled upon a mildewed stadium couch that Grelnak had liberated from his alma mater's flipperball arena two weeks before. Standing behind and above them, a female technician with the kind of figure that could make a lab coat resemble a cheerleader's outfit popped her wad of fishgum and said, "activating the sluice . . . now!" The pair on the couch closed their eyes and left their physical bodies behind.

Grelnak went first, athletically wriggling his consciousness into the initiation portal of the chronal sluice. His personality matrix latched onto the organic receptacle that Threm had assured him, repeatedly, would be waiting there in the desired endspace. He seized full possession of his target, shunted the resident mind aside, and opened his eyes.

White. Everything was white.

"Damn it, Threm, I'm blind. You put me in a blind body."

Threm winced at the complaint as she exited the sluice and claimed her own terrestrial body. Adjusting to her new sensorium, she sighed. The mission had barely begun, and Grelnak had started in already. She liked the big lug, but sometimes found herself pondering possible explanations she might offer to the Director—explanations that justified repeatedly bludgeoning her partner with a handy temporal artifact. She'd never do it, of course, not least because Grelnak was the Director's favorite nephew.

Instead Threm said, "Stop whining. Why do you always make assumptions? Remember the last time you thought you were blind? It was just local night. And the time before that, we were in a cave. Trust me, you're not blind."

"I'm blind. There's nothing but blankness. Not darkness, blankness. Everything is white."

"Grel, you're in a snow bank."

"What? That's crazy. I'd notice if I were in a snow bank. For one thing, I'd be cold. And I'm not. In fact, other than this blindness, I'm quite comfortable."

"That's due to your double layer of fur."

"No way! This is late twenty-first century. Human genemods won't reach that level for eight decades. I can't possibly have fur."

"Again with the assumptions! I never said we'd be humans. Now dig yourself out. We've got work to do."

Grelnak stimulated analog pathways and felt a satisfying proprioception as four limbs responded with immediate strength and movement. After a brief flurry of white, he could suddenly see. There was a flawless sky of blue, smoothed mounds of snow all around, and a high, concrete wall that his snow bank had piled up against.

And a bear. A massive, ferocious, deadly, polar bear stood directly in front of him on all fours.

"Threm! Where are you? There's a bear here! Damn it, Threm, if I get mauled before I'm even settled into this body you'll have to finish our assignment entirely by yourself."

As a child, Grelnak had visited numerous zoological and historical simulations, and knew better than to shout at ferocious animals in proximity. His conversation with Threm occurred telepathically, courtesy of the chronal sluice that maintained a tenuous link through time and space to their physical bodies.

"It's February 27th," Threm replied. "In this era, that date signified International Polar Bear Day."

"Fine. Wonderful. Let's go to a restaurant that specializes in arctic monsters. We can order some polar bear steaks, and celebrate by gorging ourselves. Not by offering me up as a sacrifice to this one."

The bear reared up on its hind legs, two and a half meters of ursine carnivore. Grelnak tried to retreat, but with the snow bank and wall at his back he had nowhere to go. He fully expected to be killed, or rather his late twenty-first century host would be killed. Threm would probably be able to reopen the portal and spew him back uptime to Mars's latest ecological disaster, with nothing to show for it except a vivid memory of being eaten by a polar bear.

But, the bear didn't touch him. Instead, it just stood there and lowered its forelimbs until it stood in an ursine akimbo pose that defied everything Grelnak had experienced in his simulations.

"You dummy, will you look at yourself?"

"Threm? Where are you? Did you get away? Or are you hiding so it gets me instead?"

"Look at yourself!"

Grelnak tore his eyes off the bear in front of him and directed his gaze downward, taking in his shaggy chest. He noticed that his field of vision included a view down his own white furred snout. He held up his right forelimb and examined the paw he found at the end of it. He repeated the action with the left one.

"I'm a polar bear?"

"You're a polar bear," said Threm. "And so am I. See?" The animal standing in front of Grelnak waved a paw.

"Why are we polar bears?"

"The environment isn't exactly hospitable, and the nearest human receptacles are even further away from our targets. Besides, can you think of a better way to celebrate International Polar Bear Day?"

"So where are we?"

"Nunavut. Specifically the Baffin Arctic Wildlife Refuge, established 2027. About sixteen square kilometers of protected land; most of it used to be Auyuittuq National Park. Now come on, we need to be on the other side of this wall. Toss me over."

Grelnak growled as he perambulated toward Threm, picking up speed and barely aware that he did so on all fours. He dipped his head and neck down and to the left, in a gesture that anyone who had ever seen him on the flipperball mound back in his college days would have recognized as his signature wind-up. Then he let fly, putting the full weight of his ursine form behind a massive head-and-shoulder lift. He caught Threm below the midriff and flung her, all two hundred fifty kilos of her. Her forelimbs scrabbled for purchase as she crested the top of the four-meter wall, stabilized, and perched.

"Nicely done," said Threm. She repositioned herself with most of lower body hanging over the other side of the wall. "Now back way up, and give yourself a good running start. Polar bears aren't normally known for jumping. I'll help haul you over."

"That's your escape plan? Run and jump? You're supposed to be the smart one; that's why Uncle Philo assigned me to you."

Threm glared at her partner. "Escape plan? What are you—Did you even read the mission report, Grel? Or were you too busy flirting with our sluice tech?"

Grelnak dropped his snout and refused to meet Threm's eyes. "Of course I read the briefing. I'm not a novice. I skimmed the introduction, table captions, and the summary too. You're supposed to handle the details."

Threm's irritation dissolved in the face of Grelnak's little boy routine. Despite herself, she couldn't stay mad at him. With the patience of much practice she asked, "do you even know why we're here?"

"Cod?" said Grelnak, his hesitant voice turning the statement into a question. "Something wrong with the cod in the Sirenum hatcheries."

"The cod are fine," said Threm. "They're better than fine. They're übercod. The current generation is bigger, faster, and thirteen times more prolific, than previous cod."

"Then why are we here? That doesn't sound like a problem? I like cod. Everyone likes cod. Why, before I came to the department I used to work in cod marketing." Grelnak's head bobbed up and down with enthusiasm. "Did you know that cod and cod byproducts account for 26% of all protein consumed on Mars? According to the Planetary Academy, they're the most adapted fish from pre-war Earth. The bungalow Uncle Philo gave me last summer is constructed of reprocessed, post-cod fibers. It's first rate, not like those imitation—"

Threm interrupted his ramblings. "That's the problem," she said. "They've outgrown the ecological niche the Academy set up for them. They're endangering the eco-balance of everything else in Mare Sirenum."

"If you say so," said Grelnak, managing to look sullen despite being a bear. He raised his snout and sniffed the air. "Hey, all this talk about cod is making me hungry. What do polar bears eat, anyway?"

Threm smiled, showing bright teeth. "Ringed seals, mostly" she said. "I programmed our hosts with a temporary olfactory tropism to track them. Just follow your nose. That is, once you get over the wall. C'mon, we've got a mission to complete."

Grelnak nodded, and ambled backwards. He stared at the wall, eyeing it like an opponent on an athletic field, and planned his assault. The polar bear body he wore had plenty of muscle, but also no small amount of mass. But he had the reflexes of a championship flipperballer. He hurtled forward, leaped while still several meters from the wall, and somersaulted in a very unbearlike manner high into the air easily clearing Threm's position.

"Whuff!" he said as he sprawled in the snow on the other side. A moment later Threm shoved off and landed alongside him.

"Seeing that was worth the price of admission," said Threm. She thwacked him affectionately on the head and began moving, strolling easily across the ice and snow. Grelnak stared after her a moment, and then quickly caught up.

"So, can we catch us a couple of these seals before we get on with the mission?"

"We're going to need more than a couple of them, Grel."

"I don't think so. I'm not that hungry."

"Not for you, dummy. For the mission."

"I thought the mission was about cod," said Grelnak.

"It is," replied Threm. The ridge they were on descended and they climbed lower, following the faint scent of seal wafting in the arctic air. She scanned the snow plain below them, giving him time to work it through.

"Polar bears don't eat cod," said Grelnak.

"Not usually, no."

"Polar bears eat ringed seals. You said so."

"Right. And what do you suppose seals eat?"

The dawning of comprehension on a Martian Trans-human inhabiting a healthy *Ursus maritimus* specimen is the kind of image few sentient beings are fortunate enough to witness. Threm savored the experience, mourning only the unavailability of recording equipment.

"Cod!" exclaimed Grelnak, slapping himself in the head with a heavy paw. "They eat cod."

"They do," said Threm. "Which is what makes them perfect for keeping the Martian cod population under control."

"So, we're supposed to bring back seals? But they'll be too big. The sluice's mass limit is fifty kilos."

"True enough," said Threm, "and the average seal weighs in at over sixty."

Grelnak considered this and snorted, fully engaged with the plan at last. "We're here to get baby seals!"

After half an hour's walk their path curved and sloped down onto a broad ice field. Near the field's edge Threm spotted the colony of seals

305

they'd been tracking. Dozens of them lounged and sprawled along the shoreline, including plenty of pups. Threm smiled as a brisk breeze caressed her muzzle. With the wind blowing in from the water, they'd be able to sneak up without alerting a single seal. As they crept closer, she spoke to Grelnak through the chronal sluice's telepathic channel.

"We don't need that many of them. Six would be fine, eight or ten even better."

Grelnak responded with a mental glyph of smacking lips. "They smell delicious," he added.

"Don't even think it," said Threm. "Our mission is to help ourselves to a few baby seals and try not to damage any adults. Both species are endangered, Grel. After we get the pups through the sluice, you and I have to hustle these bear bodies back over to their own section of the wildlife refuge. Only then do we get to go home."

"But I'm hungry, and this body *wants* me to eat seal."

"No snacking. Now pay attention. We're going to split up here. I'll sneak around to the far side of the colony. I want you to wait here a few minutes and then continue straight toward them. As soon as they see or hear you, the seals will panic and race for the water. The instant you see that happening, move to cut them off. You don't have catch them, just steer them back. Understand?"

Grelnak nodded. "Sure, it's a classic intercept play, just like in flipperball. But . . . what will you be doing?"

"I'll come from the other side, rounding up straggling pups as I go. Then I'll open the sluice and we'll start tossing them through."

Threm dropped back, taking advantage of a low berm of snow, and loped rapidly around the colony. She was comfortably in position and catching her breath before she caught a glimpse of Grelnak in the distance, and then only because she was looking for him. Credit where it was due, the big oaf crept with a stealth she hadn't believed him capable of. He managed to get closer than half the distance the seals had to the water before the unexpected happened.

A human being in a heavy parka crawled out of a mound of snow near the water's edge, dragging a pack behind him. The seals—who seemed to have known he'd built himself an impromptu snow cave in their midst—paid no mind as he stood up, took a video device from his pack, and began filming then. He panned from one end of the colony to the other, then stopped abruptly, probably because he caught Grelnak in frame.

"What the hell?"

Grelnak rose up on his hind legs, quite literally ready for bear. The chronal sluice's telepathic channel translated his battle roar as "For Cod!" The seals heard only the roar. Panic ensued. An answering cry rose up from the colony as their lethargic sprawl transformed into a single-minded blur toward aquatic safety. The human dropped his camera, but otherwise seemed rooted to the spot.

"Move, you lummox," said Threm, not sure herself whether she meant Grelnak or the unanticipated human.

Grelnak bounded across the ice, his mighty polar bear muscles churning, propelling him far faster than the seals could move. He charged with the same intensity that had crippled more than a few collegiate flipperball players back in the day.

As Grelnak began herding the seals her way, Threm leapt forward, her attention on a collection of pups scampering in her direction. She estimated where their paths would intersect and, as she lumbered toward her targets, began the cognitive gymnastics to prime the sluice to reopen.

Back in his flipperball days, Grelnak had dominated the playing field. His performance on the ice field was no less impressive. His rapid charge had overshot a third of the colony, cutting off their escape to the sea and forcing them to flee toward Threm, with plenty of pups among them. He bounded after at full speed, feeling oddly nostalgic. He hadn't seen the human since he'd roared, hadn't thought about him either. The man had been lost in the tumult of frenzied seals.

Until now.

He'd huddled into a ball, arms wrapped protectively around his head, as seals passed left, right, and sometimes directly over him. Grelnak saw him too late to attempt any of those choices. He ploughed into him with the force of a ravaging former athlete, wistful for the glory days of yore, who just happens to be inhabiting a monstrous juggernaut-like animal body.

To say nothing of inertia.

Threm heard bones break. She winced at the sound, then winced again when telemetry from the chronal sluice alerted her to the opening crackle of a paradox wave. Freshly formed it was manageable, but risky.

"Did you have to cripple him, Grel? You've started a ripple."

Grelnak didn't answer. His collision with the man had entangled them. Together they tumbled over the ice and snow for several meters, striking a pair of tardy seals along the way and knocking them unconscious, before all four bodies finally came to rest less than fifty meters from Threm's position.

"Um, Threm? I think I've got a problem."

"You're darn right you do. We've got maybe ten minutes to get those baby seals through the sluice or we'll be caught up in whatever temporal change you just initiated."

Threm stood amidst a tide of seals. She bared her jaws, scaring off adults, while simultaneously bapping at passing pups. Light blows of her massive paws were sufficient to stun the pups as their kin fled around them.

"Yeah, about that, see. . ."

Most of the seals had passed her by, or had already found an alternate route to safety. No matter, she had a dozen baby seals lying dazed within a five meter radius of her, and that would serve. Telemetry buzzed in her cerebellum; the ripple was expanding faster than expected. Where was Grelnak?

"Get over here and help me with these guys. The sluice is about to open."

"That's the thing, Threm, I can't move."

She spun around to look back at him. He still lay in a heap on the man he'd injured profoundly enough to trigger a paradox wave.

"Grel? Get up!"

"I'm trying. Nothing's working. I think I blew out my spine. And I'm bleeding an awful lot."

"Oh crap. I told you, polar bears are an endangered species. Hang on; let me get the sluice open. You'll go through first, and I'll manage the seal pups on my own." Threm issued the mental sequence to reopen their gateway home.

"Everything's going kind of black," said Grelnak.

"Don't even think about being in that host when it dies," said Threm. She no longer needed the sluice's telemetry to describe the growth of the wave; she could see wisps of entropy forming in the air above Grelnak's body. "I refuse to have to explain this to your uncle."

"But what about the mission?"

"You moron, don't worry about the mission. I'll manage it. There's still adequate time before the wave picks up speed. But you need to let go and get out of here. Now!"

A small tear opened in the air next to her, tufts of unreality marking the edges. She heard the chime that signaled her partner's personality matrix relinquishing its hold as it was sucked back through time and space. To her horror and surprise, a thread of the paradox wave's temporal entropy trailed after and followed him through. The portal shuddered slightly.

Threm glanced back at the body that had been Grelnak's host, and the still-breathing human in a broken heap beneath it, the source of the paradox wave. According to the sluice's telemetry, its leading edge still hadn't expanded, thread or no thread. So the timeline hadn't been changed yet. *Something* had happened, but there wasn't time to figure out what. In moments the paradox wave would begin expanding exponentially. If she hadn't made it home before that, Threm knew she'd be stuck in an alternate timeline and never get back.

She thought about bolting, just scrubbing the mission and trying again, maybe coming back after the wave had expanded and dissipated. But from this end there was no knowing how long that might take. Mars needed baby seals, and this could well be the only available window. She'd just have to hurry. Activating the sluice's matter stream, Threm began rounding up the stunned seal pups and shoving them through. They barked at the indignity, their tiny whiskered faces twitching as she shoved them into the tear, tagging each with a mental marker of the mission's ID code, just as the boys in accounting insisted. One by one they vanished, until the ice field fell silent, except for the labored breathing of the man and the two injured adult seals.

The front edge of the paradox wave had crept closer. It rippled seductively, a visible arc of entropy preparing to alter the world. Threm felt a surge of pride. She'd completed her mission, with a full minute to spare. Ideally, she'd have liked to return her host body back to the portion of the preserve where it belonged, but she didn't have that option now. About all she could do was turn to face away from the seals and human and hope that once she'd gone the bear would be disoriented enough to just lumber off in that direction, without pausing to attack or further injure any of them.

Before that though, something intangible came tumbling through the portal.

"Owwwww. Threm, why do I always get the injured bodies?"

"Grelnak?" His voice rang in her mind, strong and close. Threm spun her incredulous polar bear head toward the nearest living thing, the pair of seals. One of them stared right back at her.

"What are you doing here?"

"I had to come back, to save you."

"Save me? From what? I've still got time to get through before the wave front breaks."

"Not that, something else. The return settings got munged when I went through. I landed fine, right in our underground office, but the time and space for all the seal pups coming after me went flooey."

"Define 'flooey'," said Threm.

"Straight up a couple hundred meters and sixteen and a half years earlier."

"What happened to the baby seals?"

Grelnak's seal face grinned. "They landed in the sea, and started doing what seals do. They ate cod, grew up, and started making more baby seals. You set off a miniature paradox wave and solved the übercod problem before it even started. They're calling you the Cod Queen."

"What? Why not the Seal Queen?"

His long neck shrugged. "No idea. Alliteration, maybe?"

"That doesn't explain what you're doing here?"

"Coming back through was the only way to recalibrate the settings. Otherwise you'd have come back years early and burnt out the brain of the younger you."

Despite her double layer of fur, Threm shuddered. "Oh. Thanks, Grelnak."

"Hey, no problem. I'm just glad I got here in time."

Timing is everything, especially for operatives of the Department of Temporal Solutions. As if out of spite for being ignored, the front edge of the paradox wave broke over Threm and Grelnak. It rippled outward, traveling ever faster, expanding across both space and time, shoving everything it crossed into a new timeline.

"Double crap," said Threm.

"Um, now what do we do?" said Grelnak.

Before she could answer, something intangible came tumbling through the portal.

"Owwwww. Threm, why do I always get the injured bodies?" The second of the bruised seals raised its head.

"Grelnak?" said Threm.

"I had to come back, to save you," said the second Grelnak.

"No way," said the first Grelnak. "I already did that."

The second Grelnak ignored the seal to his left. "The return settings got munged when I went through," he explained.

"Right, right, but the baby seals got through safely, didn't they? Early, but safe."

"Heck yeah. They're calling you—"

"The Queen of Cod," finished the first Grelnak.

"Who are you?" said the second Grelnak, pulling back to get a look at the other seal.

"He's you," said Threm. "He came through just before you. Which doesn't make sense. What delayed you?"

"I was signing autographs," said the second Grelnak.

"Autographs?"

"For eager fans. They show up at the department almost every day." The seal waved a flipper in the direction of the human an earlier Grelnak had smashed into, the source of the original ripple. "Turns out that guy is the several-times-great grandfather of a major supporter of flipperball. He grew up on stories of his grandfather's near death encounter with a polar bear while trespassing in a nature preserve. Those stories inspired him to become a huge success. Flipperball is a much more popular sport back home now, and I'm one of the most famous Martians to ever play the game. I'm in the hall of fame."

Threm grimaced. "Any other changes?"

"We both get paid a heck of a lot more," said the second Grelnak. "And the Department has much better funding. Bigger offices too. I have a Jacuzzi in mine."

"A Jacuzzi? Oh man, I am gonna love that," said the first Grelnak.

"Yeah, about that," said Threm. "Going back through the portal and having the sluice fold ourselves into a new timeline is an occupational hazard. But I've never heard of a case where two versions of the same personality matrix went back together."

The two seals stared at one another and then, as if reaching the same conclusion at the same time, lunged forward and began biting and slapping at each other.

Threm tapped one polar bear foot, waiting. Both seals were already battered and the fight didn't last long. In the end, one Grelnak swayed unsteadily upon the chest of the other, both breathing heavily. "I win," he said. "I get to go back."

"You both have to go back," said Threm. "Or at least try."

"What will happen," panted the other Grelnak, "when we both go back through the sluice?"

Lawrence M. Schoen

Threm shrugged. "Maybe nothing. Maybe you'll both blend together, with slightly divergent memories, just like I'll have memories of both the old timeline and the new one. Either that, or you'll maintain two nearly identical minds in the same body."

"That would be codderfic!" said both seals at once.

"Stop! No simultaneous cod talk," said Threm.

"Yes, oh queen," said both Grelnaks together, and then burst out barking.

"Fine, let's get this over with," said Threm. It wouldn't be too bad, she told herself. Sure, Grel had been elevated to the status of an insufferable sports icon, and yeah, there might be twice the exasperation to deal with now. But the important thing was they'd completed the mission. Once again operatives of the Department of Temporal Solutions had saved Mars. Maybe it would justify the request she intended to file for ongoing hazard pay. The department would surely owe her that with two Grelnaks under her. And if it didn't work out, well, she could always fall back on being the Cod Queen.

Acknowledgments

All stories in this anthology are published here for the first time except as noted.

"Introduction" copyright © 2010 by Z.S. Adani and Eric T. Reynolds.

"No Jubjub Birds Tonight" copyright © 2010 by Sara Genge.

"The Embians" copyright © by K.D. Wentworth originally appeared in the May 1999 issue of *The Magazine of Fantasy and Science Fiction.*

"Ambassador "copyright © 2010 by Thoraiya Dyer.

"Edge of the World" copyright © 2010 by Jonathan Shipley.

"Games" copyright © 2010 by Caren Gussoff.

"The Hangborn" copyright © 2010 by Fredrick Obermeyer.

"One Awake in All the World" copyright © 2010 by Robert T. Jeschonek.

"Alienation" copyright © 2010 by Katherine Sparrow.

"Dark Rendezvous" copyright © 2010 by Simon Petrie.

"Monuments of Flesh and Stone" copyright © by Mike Resnick, originally appeared in *Visual Journeys*, Eric T. Reynolds, Ed., Hadley Rille Books.

"Hope" copyright © 2010 by Michael A. Burstein.

"Watching"copyright © 2010 by Sandra McDonald.

"Encountering Evie" copyright © 2010 by Sherry D. Ramsey.

"Memento Mori" copyright © 2010 by Sue Blalock.

"The Gingerbread Man" copyright © by James Gunn, originally appeared in the Match 1995 issue of *Analog Science Fiction & Fact.*

"The Angel of Mars" copyright © 2010 by Michael Barretta.

"When You Visit the Magoebaskloof Hotel Be Certain Not to Miss the Samango Monkeys" copyright © by Elizabeth Bear, originally appeared in the November/December 2004 issue of *Interzone.*

"Rubber Monkeys" copyright © 2010 by Kenneth Mark Hoover.

"Jadeflower" copyright © 2010 by C.E. Grayson.

"The Light Stones" copyright © 2010 by Erin E. Stocks.

"Mars Needs Baby Seals" copyright © 2010 by Lawrence M. Schoen.

Proofreading by Greg Pitt is gratefully acknowledged.

LaVergne, TN USA
07 March 2010
175179LV00003B/21/P